Her Sudden Groom

ROSE GORDON

D1263542

HER SUDDEN GROOM

© 2011 C. Rose Gordon
Front cover image © 2011 LFD Designs
Back cover design © Liberty Digital Graphics Designs

Published by Parchment & Plume, LLC
www.parchmentandplume.com

Other Titles Available

SCANDALOUS SISTERS SERIES
(Now Available)
Intentions of the Earl (Book 1)
Liberty for Paul (Book 2)
To Win His Wayward Wife (Book 3)

GROOM SERIES
(Now Available)
Her Sudden Groom (Book 1)
Her Reluctant Groom (Book 2)
Her Secondhand Groom (Book 3)
Her Imperfect Groom (Book 4)

BANKS BROTHERS BRIDES SERIES
His Contract Bride
His Yankee Bride
His Jilted Bride
His Brother's Bride

OFFICER SERIES (AMERICAN SET)
The Officer and the Bostoner
The Officer and the Southerner
The Officer and the Traveler

For Grand Paw 1938-2011
Definitely the most unique individual I've ever met. One who could always be counted on for an outrageous story guaranteed to leave you doubled over in laughter and who often coined the most bizarre, yet fitting, words for all sorts of unusual situations.

And for my husband. One of the few who can put up with my scientific tendencies and doesn't complain about my rocket talk or temperature conversions—especially during our first (and only) game of croquet!

Chapter 1

Watson Estate
April 1814

Alex Banks sat paralyzed as the cold fingers of death closed around his neck, choking the life right out of him. Gasping for breath, he reached one tanned hand up and slipped two fingers under the cravat-turned-noose that hung around his neck, then jerked, loosening its suffocating hold. Who knew that little scrap of fabric he normally wore only to appease the females in his life could transform into such a deadly weapon?

Well, it hadn't really, but it might as well have become a hangman's noose for all it mattered to Alex. He'd just been given a death sentence, as far as he was concerned.

"Are you certain?" he rasped when he'd loosened the garment enough to catch his breath.

"Quite certain," his father told him apologetically.

Alex took his spectacles off and rubbed his eyes, pressing them so hard bright shapes burst in front of him.

Edward Banks, Baron Watson, put his glass of water on the nightstand beside him. Readjusting himself in his bed, he blinked then reached for the stack of papers on the bed next to him. "Here." He handed the papers to Alex.

Alex jerked the papers from his father's limp grasp with far more effort than necessary. "Sorry," he murmured as he thumbed through the life-altering—nay, life-shattering—documents.

Leafing through the papers, his panic didn't ease like he'd hoped; instead it escalated with each page he scanned. There *had* to be a way out of this mess. He exhaled a deep, shaky breath and patted the ends of the papers against the tabletop to straighten them back into a neat, even stack.

Placing the papers on his father's bedside table, he slouched in his chair and ran a hand through his unkempt hair, giving it a hard, painful tug to make sure he wasn't in a nightmare. No such luck. The nightmare was a reality, and he was only at the start of it. He glanced to his father, who was having yet another nasty sounding coughing fit.

"There might be a loophole," Father said when he was done hacking. His voice was weak and uneven.

Alex's ears perked up, and he impaled his father with his eyes, waiting for him to divulge *anything* that would allow him to escape the equivalent of an innocent's lifetime sentence in the Tower of London.

Father patted his aching chest and tried his best to swallow a gulp of water before looking at Alex. "You could marry another."

Alex looked at his father, dumbfounded. He could have sworn he'd just read a betrothal agreement that linked his name to Lady Olivia Sinclair. How could he possibly marry another without: one, creating a scandal; two, being termed a cad; or three, being called out by her brother?

Father coughed again. "You only scanned the agreement. You missed the contingency part."

"Thank goodness," Alex muttered. "What page is that on?" He thumbed back through the papers.

"It's on the final page," Father said with a harsh cough. "This whole fiasco is all contingent on your being single on the date of your thirtieth birthday."

Alex frowned. "Why?" He moved his eyes slowly over each word on the last page, making sure not to miss a single word.

His father at least had the good manners to look somewhat guilty. As guilty as one can possibly feign when one is on one's sickbed, that is. "Well, you see, son." He flickered a glance at the wall just past Alex's left shoulder before meeting Alex's eyes again. "Joseph, the former Lord Sinclair, and I were good friends. We went to Eton and Cambridge together and remained close ever since. We thought it would be ideal to have our children marry."

"Without their consent," Alex muttered, irritation bubbling inside him.

His father frowned. "Marriages oftentimes are arranged. Mine was."

"I know." Alex had always had sympathy for the plights of his mother and father. Neither of them had even had a chance to find a spouse of their choosing. Apparently, he was about to endure the same fate. How fortunate for them, his parents had received a much better bargain than he was destined to have.

"Anyway," Father said, breaking into Alex's thoughts, "when Lady Olivia was born, I joined Sinclair at his house to celebrate, and in a drunken state, we marveled at the irony that she was born on the same day as you. Well, eight years later, of course."

"Of course." Alex vaguely remembered the night of his eighth birthday. That was the night he'd snuck out to see his first mare and witnessed his father coming home foxed, singing the Hallelujah Chorus, and claiming to have some excellent news.

Hell's afire. The "excellent news" Father was exclaiming about had been this confounded betrothal contract, binding him to Lady Olivia for life. *Lady Olivia.* Nobody could be a worse match for him than Lady Olivia. He swallowed hard, trying to return the bile rising in his throat back to his stomach.

Father coughed. "Sinclair and I thought it would be a brilliant arrangement. My son. His daughter. *Our* grandchildren. However, none of us knew just how shrewish Lady Olivia would grow up to become."

A shudder wracked father and son simultaneously. "No one could have known," Alex grumbled. Looks were one thing; personality was another. Alex considered himself mature enough to see past her always-tangled, fire-orange hair, rotund figure, horrid teeth, and absurd fashion choices. Her physical appearance, however, paled in comparison to her personality, which was enough to test the patience of a martyred saint. She was whiny, clingy, hateful, and suffered more ailments than he was aware even existed. Everything she did was completely self-serving in one manner or another. If anybody believed otherwise, they were a fool.

Clearing his throat, Father said, "That's of no account now, son. Either you'll have to marry her, or go ask her brother if he'll honor the last page of the agreement."

Alex's eyes flew to his father. "Why wouldn't he?" It was right here, combined with all those other suicide-inducing papers. There was no reason for him not to.

"Because that was an addendum added some eight years later. It was the only page not originally part of the agreement, and it isn't signed by a third party," Father explained after a brutal coughing fit. "The originals—" he grabbed the stack of papers and pointed to the bottom of each page as he flipped through— "were all signed by Sinclair, me, and Richard Barnes. Barnes is a mutual friend who was there celebrating with us, and who happens to be a solicitor. As you can see, the last page has only my and Sinclair's signatures on it."

"If he signed it, it's legal," Alex argued flippantly.

"Not exactly," his father rasped. "It could be contested, and it might not stand. Now that Joseph is dead and Marcus has taken his place, it would be my word, which won't mean anything in a few weeks, I'd wager, versus a court."

Alex gulped. He hated to think that in a matter of weeks, or even days, his father might be gone. Six months ago, Father had become ill, and since then his health had been declining rapidly. After several fruitless attempts to cure him, the physician concluded his condition was internal and medicine wasn't going to help. Father took the news in stride and continued to read, talk about science, go down to dinner, and even ride his horse. It wasn't until the past week he'd taken to spending most of the day in his bed, too frail and exhausted to do much more than read and go down for dinner. Watching Father's illness progress in the past months had been terribly painful for Alex. "All right," Alex said softly. "I'll see what can be done for it now."

Father pulled the covers up to his chin. "Son, I'm sorry I made that agreement. But if you can get Marcus to honor the contingency, you're halfway there."

"Yes, then I just have to find a lady to agree to marry me in a month's time."

"Considering that you'll have to marry Lady Olivia if you don't, I think you'll find a way." His father flashed him his best attempt at a smile.

"That's all the motivation one needs," Alex said, twisting his lips. He removed his spectacles and rubbed his nose. "Why was I never told of this before?" His voice was flat and dry, almost disinterested, belying the nervous excitement coursing through him.

Father shrugged. "I always assumed you'd find a bride on your own, thus voiding the agreement per the conditions on the last page. With that assumption, I didn't tell you when you were younger because I didn't want to heap this upon your head then. As you both got older, I saw what kind of a girl Lady Olivia had become, and I assumed her father would let you out of the agreement altogether. However, since he passed away last year, I'm not sure you can count on that possibility. Her period of mourning ended less than two weeks ago and I received a letter from the solicitor yesterday. That makes me think the agreement has not been forgotten."

Alex sighed. He couldn't fault his father for not telling him this. The poor man must have been living in a delusion thinking Alex would somehow find a young lady who would actually want to marry him. When in reality, some would think marrying Lady Olivia was the only fathomable solution to marriage for a gentleman who had somehow acquired the nickname Arid Alex.

Smoothing the covers and rearranging the pillows, Alex did what he could to make his frail father comfortable before leaving his sickroom.

Dorset it was, then. He needed to go see Marcus post haste.

Chapter 2

Caroline Sinclair stared at her cousin Olivia in pure bewilderment. "Pardon?"

Olivia rolled her eyes and breathed an exaggerated sigh. "Caroline, have you considered investing in an ear horn?" She kicked her slippers off and propped her feet up on Caroline's lap. "Could you pull those stockings off for me?" she fairly shouted.

Caroline looked at her quizzically. "Why?" She curled her fingers into the fabric of her skirt and commanded herself to breathe through her mouth if possible. She'd spent enough years in her cousin's company to know that breathing through one's nose once Olivia had taken off her slippers was a guaranteed way to make one's last meal reappear.

"I can't reach them." Olivia wiggled the toes on her bunion-covered feet.

"Then perhaps you should decrease your body's density," Caroline muttered to herself. She used her thumb and forefinger to grab the top of Olivia's stocking and pulled until five unclipped and slightly yellow toenails were exposed. Closing her eyes to the view in front of her, Caroline flung the stocking as far across the room as she could before doing the same with the other stocking. "All right, now what was it you were saying?"

"Hmm?" Olivia reclined on an overstuffed pillow. "Rub those, would you?"

"Not on your life," Caroline retorted beneath her breath. She cleared her throat. "I can't," she lied. "I seemed to have hurt my hand yesterday."

Olivia frowned.

"I was outside collecting—"

Olivia groaned. "Say no more. I don't want to hear another word of it. You're as much of a dullard as Arid Alex Banks. It's unfortunate enough I'll have to listen to him drone on and on about his scientific nonsense for the rest of my life. At least I'll still outrank you and be able to tell you to stuff it."

Stung, Caroline swallowed an unladylike retort and nodded. Olivia had always belittled anything Caroline found interesting. If they weren't cousins and Lord Sinclair wasn't her guardian until her twenty-first birthday, Caroline would have distanced herself from Olivia and her rude manners years ago. Unfortunately, she still had another six months to endure Olivia's ill-treatment.

"So then you're going to marry him?" Caroline asked to be polite.

"Yes." Olivia curled her lip and sniffed as if marrying Alex Banks would be the worst fate on the planet. "Not that I want to. I'd rather marry just about anyone else."

To Caroline's way of thinking, Olivia was the more fortunate of the two. Not that she knew Mr. Banks well. In fact, she'd only met him once or twice. But having known Olivia all her life, it wasn't hard to distinguish who'd been dealt the losing hand.

"I swear, Caroline, if you would do something about that hearing problem of yours, I wouldn't have to repeat myself on this matter. In less than thirty days, I shall be Mrs. Alex Banks, and shortly after that, I shall be a baroness." Her tone was full of excitement, a stark contrast to the pout contorting her face.

Caroline tried not to show her disgust at Olivia's tactlessness. Olivia should be happy some gentleman was going to marry her despite the title he would one day possess, or that he'd been nicknamed Arid Alex due to his slightly unusual personality. But what got Caroline's hackles up more than that was Olivia's excitement over the prospect that the current baron might die soon. Actually, it did more than get her hackles up. It made another round of nausea pass through her—one which outdid the wave she'd experienced earlier.

"You should be a bit more compassionate," Caroline said firmly and a tad sharply. She may not be particularly fond of Olivia, and she really didn't like it when Olivia got into one of her "moods," but Caroline wasn't going to sit idly by while Olivia planned her future father-in-law's funeral in her head. If risking a black mood and a possible week of attending Olivia's sickbed was the result of speaking her mind, so be it.

Olivia sniffed. "*You* should be more compassionate. I'm the daughter of an earl. I should be marrying an earl or higher, not a baron." She crossed her arms and sneered. "He won't even be a baron when we marry. He'll only be a mere mister for who knows how long. Well, unless his father dies even sooner." A small smile tugged on her lips.

"You're heartless," Caroline said without thinking.

Olivia shrugged. "No. I'm practical. I always have been. I never wanted to marry for love, and I shan't. Nor do I have any delusion that he has any such feelings for me."

"That's not what I meant," Caroline said tersely. "I was talking about the blackhearted way you're speaking of his father as if his death means nothing to you besides gaining a title."

"Doesn't it?"

"Yes. It does mean something. It's going to mean a lot to Alex when his father dies, and as his wife, you're going to be the one he turns to for comfort."

Olivia shuddered. "He can turn elsewhere for any comfort he requires. Besides the consummation of our marriage, I have no intention of acting as an outlet for his 'needs'."

Caroline tucked a long tendril of her dark brown hair behind her ear. "You do know it will be your duty to give him an heir."

Closing her eyes, Olivia said, "Then he had better hope he gets it right on the first try."

Caroline nearly laughed at the absurdity of Olivia's proclamation. "He has no control over that."

"And how would you know?"

"I just do," Caroline said evasively. "Some couples conceive right away, and some don't."

"If he wants an heir, he had better hope I conceive right away. I have no interest in the activity, and I'm only enduring it with him once."

"Or what?"

"Either he'll have no heir or a cuckoo," she said evenly, inspecting her nails.

"What?"

"You know, a child that he technically is not the father of."

8

"I know what a cuckoo is," Caroline said, closing her eyes and willing herself not to pull her hair—or Olivia's—out in frustration. "But you just said you have no interest in the activity. Why would you want to do it with someone else?"

"I said with him. I might enjoy the activity with someone else."

Caroline shook her head. Poor Mr. Banks. "You might enjoy it with him." Knowing Olivia had no desire to be faithful, let alone a desire to give the gentleman in question a chance before declaring she'd need to seek comfort elsewhere, was disheartening.

Olivia snorted. "I won't."

"How do you know?" she countered. "Just because he wears spectacles, talks continuously about science, wears his clothes slightly askew, and has been publicly dubbed Arid Alex, doesn't mean there's not something you might find enjoyable about him."

"There's not," Olivia assured her. "Anyway, I can just imagine how awful our first—and only—time will be. 'Now, hold very still, I'm going to insert my penis,'" she said, imitating a man's voice.

Caroline's eyes went wide. *She* knew the mechanics of procreation because she liked to be outside and from time to time she'd helped with the animals. But how Olivia had learned such a thing was a mystery she didn't wish to uncover. "He won't say that."

Olivia rolled her eyes. "It doesn't really matter."

Caroline shook her head. It was probably best not to mention that in England, the law was on the husband's side with regard to bedroom affairs. It really wasn't her business what did or didn't take place in any bedchamber apart from her own.

She had no idea how Olivia had snared an unsuspecting Mr. Banks into agreeing to marry her, but she had, and the poor gentleman was surely going to suffer for it.

Actually, how had they become betrothed? Caroline was just about to ask when a commotion sounded down the hall.

"I wonder who that could be." Olivia mused in a voice that was so sugary sweet Caroline had to take a second glance.

Resisting a groan, Caroline shut her eyes and counted to ten. Olivia only spoke in this tone and adopted that ridiculous smile when she was about to play nice for company.

"Could you gather my stockings, dear?" Olivia asked, trying to sit up straight on the settee.

Caroline was tempted to pretend she couldn't remember where she'd tossed them and let whoever was here see Olivia in all her indescribable glory. But then pity for their caller overtook her and Caroline couldn't bring herself to subject anybody to such a fate. "Just a moment," she murmured, walking across the room to pick up the stinky stockings. Pinching them between her thumb and forefinger, she brought them to Olivia, and tossed them on the settee next to her. "Here you go. I'll be right back."

"Where do you think you're going?" Olivia asked with a growl. "I need help with my slippers."

Ignoring Olivia's pout, Caroline stepped away before Olivia could clutch onto her skirt and keep her at her side. "I need to go get Marcus."

"Why?" Olivia demanded, still pouting.

"I glimpsed out the window that our guest is a gentleman. I need to ask Marcus to act as a chaperone."

Olivia pursed her lips then gave a single nod.

Caroline left the room and darted down the hall in the direction of Marcus' study. Ever since Lady Sinclair died five years ago, Marcus had been forced to act as their impromptu chaperone whenever necessary. Which wasn't very often. Between Olivia's beastly attitude and Caroline's being a poor relation with no society polish, gentleman callers had been rare at best between the two of them.

Before he died last year, Olivia's father had successfully pressured his widowed sister-in-law into acting as Olivia's chaperone for things like house parties and whatnot. But that hadn't happened very often, either, and never was Caroline included.

Now that Marcus, Olivia's brother, had inherited, there still wasn't anyone to act as a proper chaperone. Marcus had written to all of their female relatives asking them to come stay at Ridge Water, but they'd all found some reason or another to refuse. It didn't take a great mind to know why. Olivia's demeanor was truly *that* awful. As it was, if Caroline and Olivia were to go anywhere, a maid went with them, and on the rare occasion a gentleman came to call, Marcus would join them in the drawing room and brood in the corner.

Caroline brought her knuckles to the door, gave three quick knocks, and then waited for Marcus to bid her to enter.

"Marcus?" She opened the door to the darkened study and peeked in.

"Caroline," he said flatly.

Caroline's eyes adjusted to the darkness, and she searched the room for Marcus. As usual, he was sitting behind his dimly lit desk. "We have a visitor," she said with a swallow.

Marcus sighed. He scrubbed his fingers over his heavily scarred face, the outline of his action filtering through the few rays of sunshine streaming in from the break in the curtains behind him. "Who is he?" His voice was tight and held a slight edge.

"I don't know."

"Could you go find out, please?"

Caroline nodded. As she left the room she chastised herself for not discovering the identity of the gentleman before going to get Marcus.

It wasn't that Marcus was a snob—quite the opposite, actually. But only his family got to see what a sweet, caring person he really was. To the rest of the world, he was either a self-important snob or a laughingstock. It just depended on who one asked, really.

He'd had an accident twelve years ago, and since then he'd become a recluse who only went into Society when absolutely necessary.

"Chapman," Caroline called to the butler. "Who is our guest, and where have you put him?"

Chapman didn't even blink at her directness. He'd been working with this family so long he'd long ago stopped questioning their quirks or rudeness. "Mr. Alex Banks. I put him in the library. I thought he'd be more comfortable there."

Caroline nodded. She didn't know much about Mr. Banks, but from what she did know, Chapman was absolutely right. He would definitely be more comfortable in the library. There, or in the conservatory. Or the fields. Or by the pond collecting specimens. Or...or... There were so many places he'd rather be than in a drawing room. And to be honest, she quite agreed. She'd rather be any of those other places than in the drawing room, too.

"All right. And Lady Olivia, is she in there, too?"

Chapman's eyes widened. "Gracious, no. I wouldn't subject anyone to her without at least one other person in the room to act as a bulwark."

"Very good," she assured Chapman before turning to go get Marcus.

"Who is it?" Marcus asked without ceremony as she opened the door.

"Alex Banks. Chapman put him in the library. Your sister is still in the drawing room, trying to reattach her slippers if I had to guess." She waited at the door as Marcus limped over to her side.

Marcus grumbled something she couldn't understand, then raised his voice. "Probably for the best she's occupied at the moment. I have a feeling her presence would be unwanted in my meeting with Alex."

Caroline knit her brows. If Olivia and Mr. Banks were engaged, why would her presence be unwanted? Oh well, not for her to worry about.

Outside the library, Caroline stood with Marcus for a minute. Was her presence unwanted as well, or should she offer to act as hostess for the men?

As if sensing her discomfort, Marcus said, "You might as well come in with me, Caroline. No sense in subjecting you to Olivia's company any more than you already have been."

"All right." Caroline smiled slightly. Marcus was a good cousin. He and his sister were complete opposites in so many ways that she'd actually caught herself questioning Olivia's parentage on more than one occasion. However, when Marcus made a comment about Olivia's unpleasant personality, it wasn't to be cruel, but because he was always forthright and painfully blunt. She supposed that was the product of growing up in this family. That, or he'd become that way as a result of his accident. Either way, he meant no real harm in his words.

Marcus opened the door and let Caroline walk into the room in front of him. Caroline's eyes immediately flew to Mr. Banks sitting by the fire, an open book on his lap.

"Alex." Marcus took a seat in a chair that he'd strategically placed in the shadowed corner for times like this.

"Good to see you, old fellow," Mr. Banks said uneasily. "I...uh...I." He swallowed hard and cleared his throat.

"May I introduce you to Miss Caroline Sinclair?" Marcus interjected, stretching his legs out and crossing his ankles. "She's my cousin."

Mr. Banks' bespectacled, brown eyes swung around to land on Caroline. He nodded and blinked a few times. "Nice to meet you," he murmured, not bothering to stand up.

Caroline would have taken offense to his lack of greeting—especially since they'd actually been introduced before, which apparently he'd forgotten—if she hadn't detected his unease. Although, she wasn't sure if his unease was because she was in the room or because of his meeting with Marcus, in general.

"It's nice to see you again, too." Caroline took a seat across from him.

Mr. Banks blinked owlishly at her. "Right. The *Society of Biological Matters*," he muttered, twisting his lips.

Ah, so he did remember her. Good. Though she might feel bad for him for being permanently attached to Olivia for the rest of his natural life, she'd still not forgiven, nor forgotten, the way he'd had her tossed out of the *Society of Biological Matters* for no real reason four years ago. "Yes, I believe we met there." She glanced at Marcus to see if he'd get the conversation going.

Mr. Banks cleared his throat again. "Marcus, I know we're not really chums these days, but I've a favor to ask you."

The room grew so quiet after his words that Caroline was almost certain a piece of lint would have been heard, had it fallen to the floor.

"What kind of favor?" Marcus drawled after watching Mr. Banks shift in his chair for a few moments.

Mr. Banks nodded once, then dug into his breast pocket and pulled out a bundle of neatly folded papers. "I'm sure you know what I'm holding. But—" he shuffled through the papers until he found the one that he wanted— "I'm not sure if you've seen this one." He stood and walked a piece of paper over to Marcus.

Marcus grabbed the paper and scanned it while Mr. Banks returned to his seat.

A minute later, Marcus broke the silence with a chuckle. "Is this what you want, Alex?" He held the paper in the air.

"Yes, please," Mr. Banks said with a gulp. "I know there's no third party signature, but you cannot dispute that your father and mine signed it."

"I can see that." Marcus tapped the piece of paper against his leg. "All right. I'll acknowledge the addendum, if you wish."

"Thank you." Mr. Banks jumped up and rushed over to shake Marcus' hand.

Caroline watched them, completely bewildered. They'd both ignored her presence entirely.

Mr. Banks took back the paper from Marcus' hand and turned to walk from the room without so much as a fare-thee-well to either of them.

"Oh, by the bye, Alex," Marcus called as Mr. Banks reached the door.

Mr. Banks spun around. "Yes?"

"I just thought I'd let you know, I wouldn't have held you to any of that asinine agreement if you'd only asked."

Mr. Banks groaned and shook his head. "Is it too late now?" His brown eyes were full of hope.

Marcus chuckled. "I am Afraid so. You said you'd like to honor the addendum, so that's what we'll stick to."

Nodding curtly, Mr. Banks muttered, "Thank you, again."

"Just think of it as an experiment," Marcus suggested with a smile.

"An experiment? I love experiments," Caroline chirped excitedly before she could think to stop herself.

Marcus eyed their guest shrewdly. "Say, Alex, why don't you include Caroline in your endeavor?"

Caroline practically leapt off the settee. "I'd love to help with your experiment. First, we shall need to write down your question or goal," she said to no one in particular, running across the room to grab a piece of parchment and a quill. A groan floated to her ears about the time she reached the secretary. She wasn't sure who the creator of such an irritating response was and chose to ignore it.

"I'm not sure that's a good idea," Mr. Banks protested. Unfortunately for him, his words went virtually unheard as Marcus brooded in the corner, whistling a merry little tune and Caroline scribbled down the scientific process on a piece of parchment.

"All right, Mr. Banks." Caroline looked up from her paper with a bright smile. "What's the point of this experiment?"

He coughed and his face flushed a bright red.

"Why don't you stay for dinner?" Marcus invited jovially. "That way you and Caroline can have more time together."

Chapter 3

Alex could no more say no to Marcus' invitation than he could break contact with Miss Caroline Sinclair's sparkling, deep blue eyes.

"All right," he said against his better judgment.

"Excellent." Marcus reached into his pocket and removed his watch. "Dinner will be served in about an hour and a half. Shall I leave you two alone to discuss this matter?"

Alex stared at him. Did the man actually intend to leave Alex and Miss Sinclair alone without a chaperone?

Marcus limped across the room and stopped, turned his head, and winked at Alex. "I'm not worried about leaving her alone with you. I know you won't do anything with my cousin you wouldn't do with your own."

Care to place a wager on that? Currently the thoughts he was entertaining of him alone with Miss Sinclair were *not* very cousinly. "Right," Alex said hoarsely, trying to push inappropriate thoughts of Miss Sinclair from his mind. "We'll only speak about science, nothing else."

Marcus gave him a curious look, then shook his head and departed.

Alex had no idea what Marcus was about, nor did he care to know. He'd just been granted a reprieve from being forced to marry Lady Olivia. If her brother wanted him to entertain the beautiful Miss Sinclair with talk of science in return, he wasn't going to argue.

Taking a seat by the small secretary Miss Sinclair occupied, Alex tried to focus on making up an experiment. He'd understood Marcus' brilliant suggestion to approach finding a wife like running an experiment, but he couldn't tell Miss Sinclair that was Marcus' meaning. He may not know a lot about females, but he knew enough to know it would be best not to mention something like this to her.

"Your experiment, Mr. Banks?" Miss Sinclair prompted, tapping the end of her quill against her pink lips.

"Call me Alex," he murmured, stalling for time.

"And you may call me Caroline. Now that we have that settled, you can tell me about your experiment, Alex."

"I'm trying to recruit people to the *Society of Biological Matters*," he blurted before thinking.

"Might I suggest you open membership up to both sexes?"

Alex closed his eyes and tried to keep from scowling. "I'm sorry about that," he said. He drummed his fingers on the arms of the chair for a moment, an idea forming. His fingers stilled with one final thwack. "All right then, Caroline, you are officially a member-contingent."

She gasped. "Excuse me?"

Alex didn't know whether her response was due to being offended she was a member-contingent or due to actually being considered for membership. He chose to believe the latter. "Absolutely," he said with a smile.

She cleared her throat and bored holes into him with her eyes, crossing her arms over her chest. "And why am I being considered a member-contingent?"

His smile slipped. "Well, because I don't know what you do or don't know about biological matters." He idly scratched his chin.

"I know quite a lot, thank you," she said stiffly.

Alex didn't know what that really meant. His younger sister had attended the best girls' school in London and knew not a hint about science. "All right." He nodded in contemplation. He walked across the library to where the science texts were kept and plucked down a few, then strode back over to her. "Here, study these and you'll be allowed full membership."

"Excuse me?" she repeated, her voice a bit firmer this time.

Alex put the stack of heavy books down on the edge of the secretary. "All the gentlemen there like to discuss relevant topics in biology, specifically those which appear in a circular titled *Prominent and Avant-Garde Horticulture,* which long ago was informally nicknamed, by my own father, no less, *Popular Plants.*

The most notable articles from that circular we discuss are written by a fellow named E. S. Wilson. Also, the other gentlemen all have had some sort of study in biology before. It would be best if you knew the basics. Then you can understand the articles we read and contribute to the discussions."

She pushed the stack of books off the edge of the secretary, missing his toes by mere inches. "I don't think so."

"I'm sorry, but that's the way it is," he said softly. "Everyone must have some basic knowledge of the subject." As her eyes continued to spear him, he smiled. "Don't worry, your examination won't be too hard."

"You're insufferable," she muttered. "This is the reason your membership is down. You're so selective about who you allow to join." She shook her head. "If it's not because they're a lady, then it's because they've not had proper schooling. Heaven forbid if they're a lady who's not had proper schooling. Then, Mr. Alex Banks, president-extraordinaire, gives them a giant stack of books to read, followed by an examination before they're allowed to join. Good gracious."

When put that way, he'd never been made to feel so ungentlemanly. "Forgive me. I didn't mean to offend you. I was just trying to make sure you'd be able to contribute without embarrassing yourself by asking elementary questions."

"No need to worry," she said, waving a hand. "I know as much about biology as any of the gentlemen there."

"All right," he said hoarsely. "You may join."

"Free of a contingency?"

"Of course. Although, I'd strongly suggest—Stop rolling your eyes, this is serious. You should probably start reading up on E. S. Wilson and his past articles. They're all the rage in the world of biology just now."

"All right, I'll read them," she agreed. "Now let's start thinking of how we're going to increase the membership. One new member is not enough."

Suppressing a groan, Alex plopped down in a nearby chair. Caroline might enjoy coming up with ways to gain new members into the *Society*, but he didn't have time to worry about that. He needed to worry about finding a suitable bride, and soon.

Alex leaned his head back and closed his eyes, hoping it would help him think better to block out the lovely sight of Caroline.

After twenty minutes, he opened his eyes and glanced at her. She'd been writing nonstop since he'd sat down. "What are you writing?" he asked, resisting the urge to tease her about how the three sheets she'd scribbled across looked like the beginnings of a novel.

Her eyes looked up and held his gaze while the fingers of her left hand rubbed her right wrist. "Lists," she said as if it explained everything.

"Lists?"

"Yes." She picked up her papers and fanned them in front of him. "See, on this page I wrote our goal: increase membership of the *Society of Biological Matters*. But then on these, I've been coming up with ways to do that. Research, if you will."

He blinked. She was taking this far too seriously. "Very well," he croaked, ducking his head so she couldn't see him smile at the absurdity of it all. Here he was trying to plan how to get a wife in the next few weeks, and she was dutifully jotting down all sorts of nonsense ways to increase membership into a society that didn't lack members. Oh, the irony.

"Are you going to help me?" she prodded.

"How?" They were at cross purposes, and he'd rather brood about how to charm a young lady to be his wife rather than how to charm members.

She stared at him and twisted her lips in a way that shot straight to his groin, making him need to look away from her yet again. "I'm not going to do all of this for you," she said, bringing his attention back to her.

"Right-o." An idea came to him. "May I have a quill and paper, too?"

A smile that could light up the room took her lips. "Of course." She reached over and grabbed a few sheets of parchment and a quill, then set them down and moved her chair to the left. "Actually, why don't you sit by me? We've only one pot of ink."

He strolled over to where she was sitting and sat in a chair positioned so close to her that every time she moved, her arm brushed his. Though the gesture wasn't overly erotic, it certainly caught his attention and made his skin prickle with awareness.

Dipping his quill in the ink, he positioned it over his paper and froze. His plan was to write down a list of possible brides. He couldn't do that sitting so close to her. If she looked over and saw his list, she'd ask why he was writing down only female members of the *ton*. Well, that was one reason he couldn't make his list, and the other—probably the bigger problem—was he hadn't a clue who to write down.

"Awfully busy over there, Alex," she said after a few minutes. Her tone was light and he thought he glimpsed a little smile curving her lips.

"Sorry," he muttered, frowning down at his paper. It was still blank except for an ink spot the size of a half-penny that had formed where his quill had been poised to write for the past ten minutes. "I can't think of what to write."

"You're the one who asked for the paper. What had you thought to write?" She put her quill down and turned to look at him.

"Names," he said evasively.

"Excellent idea! I've been thinking of *ways* to get members. I completely forgot *who*, specifically, we should be pursuing."

"I don't know, either," he admitted.

"Clearly." She tapped her finger on her lower lip in the most seductive way. "What about your friend, the Earl of Townson?"

Alex snorted. "I assure you, he's not interested."

"You never know until you ask." She picked up her quill again and continued writing.

He shook his head. He didn't have to ask—he already knew. Andrew, Lord Townson had as much interest in biology as Alex did in knitting, none. Actually, that wasn't true. Andrew had an interest in biology. The procreation sort, that is. Andrew married Brooke, Alex's cousin, only two years ago and they were already nearing the arrival of their second child. Hell's afire, at the rate those two were going, they would fill up Rockhurst in no time. Perhaps he did need to speak to Andrew. His friend might benefit from a candid discussion about how to control breeding.

Alex dashed Andrew's name on the paper. Not only would

seeing his name on the parchment remind him to speak to his friend, it would also appease Caroline to see at least one name on the list.

"Thank goodness," she mumbled. "You finally put a name down. Who is it?"

"Andrew." He rested the quill on the edge of the ink pot.

"Who?"

"Andrew Black, Lord Townson." He tipped one shoulder up in a lopsided shrug. "I took your suggestion. You never know what results you'll get until you speak to someone."

"Good. Now, come up with some other names."

He leaned back in his chair. "I can't."

"And why not?"

"Everyone I know who is interested has already joined," he said simply.

"Not everyone," she muttered.

He sighed. "I said I was sorry about that."

"It's fine." She flashed him a queer look. "Let's speak of it no more."

"Agreed."

He took a deep breath and nearly snapped his quill in half. Her hair smelled of lavender. He'd always claimed that scent could be a man's undoing. And on her, he had no doubt it was truly possible. He inhaled again, letting the sweet aroma fill his nose. Perhaps his wife would smell good... He nearly snorted. He had only a month to find a wife. He didn't have time to be too particular about what she smelled like. As long as she didn't stink, she'd smell good enough for his purpose. Right now he just needed to think of one to pursue.

"Which ladies are you thinking of?" Caroline asked a few minutes later.

He froze. Did she know he was thinking of suitable brides? "Pardon?"

"Females who would like to join," she explained. "Like me, surely there are others of the fairer sex who have been denied entry and would be delighted to join."

She was onto something. "Good point. Do you know any ladies interested in science?"

"How should I know? You're the one who denied them membership," she said with a shrug. "Who are they?"

Tightening his hands into fists so tightly his knuckles turned white, he said, "It was only you and your cousin I denied membership. No one else. Ever."

"I see," she said slowly. "I suppose I would have been allowed to join had Olivia not wanted to as well?"

"Probably." He shot a rueful grin in her direction. "Guilty by association, I'm afraid."

She rolled her eyes and muttered something under her breath he couldn't make out. "All right. Enough said. What about Lady Almay and her daughter, Lady Lucinda? I've read they both enjoy visiting people's gardens at parties and balls and such."

"Yes, yes." He grabbed his quill and jotted down their names. Lady Almay and Lady Lucinda did both enjoy exploring everyone's gardens. For different reasons of course. Lady Almay enjoyed the greenery and Lady Lucinda enjoyed the gentlemen in the gardens.

He tapped his quill on the paper again, letting his thoughts wander. If Lady Almay did have a true biological and scientific interest like he believed, and Lady Lucinda a minor one, then wouldn't that also mean the younger sister might as well? Not that it really mattered at this point. He had to find someone — anyone — to marry, and if she liked science, it was only a boon. But it would help tremendously if she either liked science or had grown up hearing people talk of it. At least that way she'd know what to expect in a marriage with him. That's what made Lady Lucinda and her sister so perfect — they'd both probably grown up hearing their mother discuss science.

He frowned down at the pen as he went to write Lady Lucinda's sister's name. What was her name? He was fairly certain it started with a C. But that was all he could remember. Was it Catherine? Caitlin? Christine? No, none of those seemed right. He looked at Caroline and shook his head. No, Lady Almay's daughter wasn't named Caroline, but she — the Caroline sitting next to him — would probably know. Dare he ask? No, better not. He wasn't entirely certain of the age of Catherine, or Caitlin, or Christine, or whatever her name was, anyway. He suspected she'd be coming out this year, but he wasn't positive and didn't want to field questions from a curious Caroline.

Instead, he grabbed the quill and wrote a giant C then a few scribbles, followed by a T and a few more scribbles. That was close enough. He'd know who he was talking about.

He closed his eyes and listened to the clock on the wall ticking off the seconds mixed with the rhythmic scratches of Caroline's quill. It was enough to put someone to sleep. So tranquil and quiet, with only a hint of soft noise. He rubbed his eyes. He needed to be thinking of possible brides, not the relaxing sounds of the room.

Closing his eyes tighter, he tried to dredge up pictures of last year's left over debutantes. But not one image came to his mind. Instead, he could only picture Caroline. And not just because she was sitting next to him just now. He remembered the blue dress she'd worn the first time they'd met when she attended that *Society* meeting some four years ago and how it had matched her beautiful blue eyes perfectly.

Now that he thought about it, not a thing about her had changed. From the raven hair pinned in an elaborate coif that showcased its length and beautiful curls, to her alabaster skin that covered her dainty facial features, she was exactly as he remembered. When he'd first met her, he'd struggled, much like he did now, to stay attentive to his task. Her mere presence was far too distracting.

"You could ask Olivia," Caroline said, shocking him to the core and putting an abrupt end to his pleasant thoughts. There was absolutely no way he was going to ask Lady Olivia to marry him.

"I don't think so," he said smoothly, trying to blink the image of Lady Olivia out of his mind.

"Probably just as well. She might drive all the members to leave. Then you'll be worse off than you are now."

"Exactly so," he agreed, relaxing. She'd been talking about for membership into the *Society*, not for marriage. He needed to relax or he was going to give himself away. Furthermore, even for membership there was no way Lady Olivia's name was ever going to join the roster.

Caroline laughed lightly, drawing his attention back to her. She was a pretty young lady, he had to admit. Why Marcus had left them alone together was beyond his comprehension. "I've written a treatise and you've written four words," she said with a slight shake of her head.

"Sorry, I'm not quite finished." He hoped they could leave it at that.

"It's fine. Hmm, what about your cousins?"

He almost choked at her suggestion. His three cousins, Brooke, Madison, and Liberty hadn't a speck of interest, neither did their husbands. "Not interested, I'm afraid."

"Write them down," she said, tapping his paper with the end of her quill. "You're assuming they're not interested. You must ask to know for sure."

No, he was fairly certain those six were not interested in marriage to him. But to appease her once again, he wrote their names down.

"That's a start." She tucked a long, curly tendril of dark hair behind her right ear. "You've got nine names. However, you *think* six will not join. Which means you need to come up with more names."

He wanted to groan. Of course he needed to come up with more names. Out of the nine he'd listed only two could be considered potential brides. And that potential hung by a thread. He'd never been good with the fairer sex. Never. They were either put off by his scientific interest, cowed by his intelligence, or were dismissive of him in general before even meeting him. On the few occasions he'd *tried* to become acquainted with a young lady, it had never ended well. For some reason he couldn't explain or fathom, he was awful with unspoken responses. He had no idea how to read facial expressions or interpret "unspoken or implied messages" as his mother referred to it. Quite simply, if a person didn't come out and say it, he had no idea what they wanted.

With gentlemen he could use the *old friend routine*. He'd call them old fellow or chum, or try to talk to them using ridiculous words or phrases. It had always worked for him at school and in Society. It made him more acceptable, it seemed. But he couldn't talk that way to females. He couldn't call them old fellow, or chums. Nor could he use simple language with them. It just didn't work that way.

"It's almost time for dinner," Caroline told him. "Stay after and we'll work on this some more."

He was about to tell her he couldn't when a light knocking sound came from the door. "Dinner's almost ready," Marcus boomed.

"Thank you, Marcus," Caroline said breathlessly as she picked up the stack of heavy tomes she'd knocked to the floor. "We'll be out in a minute. I've finished, but Alex hasn't."

"What?" Marcus roared. He opened the door a crack. "Caroline, out. Alex, don't even think about leaving. I need to speak to you. I'll be coming in that room in two minutes."

Alex and Caroline exchanged looks. Alex had shared a room with Marcus at Eton for almost five years. During those five years, he'd never once heard Marcus raise his voice. Something was off.

Caroline put the books down and quietly left.

Exactly one hundred twenty seconds after his declaration, Marcus reentered the room. "I did *not* give you permission to seduce her," he hissed.

Alex crossed his arms. "I didn't."

Marcus clenched his jaw. "Then what *did* you do?"

"We worked on science. See?" He went over and grabbed the stack of papers Caroline had abandoned in her hurry to depart the room.

Marcus blinked, then groaned and tossed the papers on the settee. "So you did," he said dully, scrubbing his face with his hands. "Why?"

Now Alex blinked at him. "Because you suggested to her I could use her help with an experiment. Which, by the way, was more difficult to work on with her in the room."

Leaning against the back of a chair for support, Marcus stared at him. "Do not tell me you told her."

"I didn't. I told her I needed to increase membership of the *Society of Biological Matters*."

Marcus shook his head. "Of the two of you, I don't know who is the more obtuse."

"Her," Alex said automatically. "She actually believed it and worked on ways to recruit people. I, on the other hand, came up with a list of names of possible brides." He gave his list to Marcus.

"No, Alex." Marcus scanned the parchment. "I think 'Most Obtuse Man Who Ever Lived' is the title you came into the moment you entered into the world."

"What's that to mean?" Alex tugged on his annoying cravat.

Marcus shrugged. "You're far more obtuse than she is. Why are half these names of men?"

"Just look past those," Alex said testily. "Oh, and my cousins, too. I had to put them on the list because Caroline thought I was compiling a list of possible *Society* members."

"I hope that's why Lady Almay's name also made the list," Marcus mused.

With a sigh, Alex ran his hand through his hair and gave it a tug before letting go. "It is," he bit off. "But her two daughters are possibilities."

"Lady Lucinda and Lady Ca—C something?" A smile tugged on Marcus' scarred lips.

"Yes. Lady Almay's other daughter."

"Ah," Marcus said, nodding in understanding. "I believe her name is Christina, but a recluse like me might be wrong."

Alex grinned. Now he knew her name.

"Alex," Marcus started again, "the reason I believe you to be the more obtuse of the two of you—and of everyone in England at that—is because you sat in this room for more than an hour and only came up with two names." He limped over to the secretary, grabbed Caroline's abandoned quill, and wrote something on Alex's paper. "As for me, it took less than ten seconds to come up with the perfect person. Someone you didn't even have on your list." He handed the paper back to Alex and walked from the room.

Not wanting to appear too impatient, Alex waited until he was sure Marcus was down the hall before looking at the list. After he read it, he blinked and read over the paper again.

~~Andrew~~
~~Lady Almay~~
~~Lady Lucinda Almay~~
~~Lady Cmmmtmmm Almay~~
~~Brooke~~
~~Benjamin~~
~~Madison~~

HER SUDDEN GROOM

~~Paul~~
~~Liberty~~
Caroline Sinclair

Chapter 4

Caroline nearly flew up the stairs. She had no idea why Marcus was so upset. She'd have to puzzle it out later. For now, she needed to contend with Olivia, who was caterwauling so loud Caroline could hear her from where she stood at the bottom of the stairs.

"What's happening in here?" Caroline demanded as she swung open the heavy oak door to Olivia's room.

"*She* is useless," Olivia screamed, pointing at Nettie, her maid.

Pity for Nettie quickly built in Caroline's heart. "What's wrong?" she asked of no one in particular.

"She has absolutely no fashion sense. And she won't do as I've instructed, besides," Olivia said, raising her chin a notch.

Caroline looked over to Nettie. The maid was white as chalk. Next to her sat Emma Green, a longtime family friend. Emma, who had golden blonde hair and green eyes, was nonchalantly scratching her nose, a signal they'd made up to tell the other one when Olivia was lying.

"What did you ask of her?" Caroline asked cautiously, casting an apologetic look at Nettie.

Olivia pointed to an array of feathers lying on her vanity table. "She will not put them in my hair," she said with a pout.

Caroline's eyes went back to Nettie, who was slowly nodding. Swallowing, Caroline didn't know who to ask what.

Emma cleared her throat. "The problem seems to be Olivia has asked Nettie to put *all* the feathers in her hair."

"And what is wrong with that?" Olivia demanded, stomping her foot and glaring at Emma.

Emma bit her lip and turned her head. Poor girl probably didn't want to tell the truth, which was putting seven feathers in one's hair at one time was a bit much. Three or perhaps four that

28

were coordinated with each other and the colors of her gown would look nice. However, Olivia had laid out every color of the rainbow (in order naturally) and expected Nettie to put them all in her hair for her.

"Perhaps a compromise," Caroline suggested, knowing full well she'd be ignored.

"A *compromise!*" Olivia's shout instantly disproved Caroline's "being ignored" thought. "I am Lady Olivia Sinclair, daughter to the fifteenth Earl of Sinclair, sister to the sixteenth. She—" she pointed a fat finger toward Nettie— "is a lowly servant. Therefore, I get to tell her what to do and when to do it. Now put those blasted feathers in my hair. Now!"

Nettie moved to walk across the room, and Caroline touched her arm to stay her. "She will not. She is also my lady's maid, and I require her services just now. You've monopolized her time enough today. It's my turn. Come, Nettie."

"Oh, no you don't," Olivia snapped, stomping her foot with so much force the floorboard groaned. "We may share a lady's maid. We may even share a last name. However, you do not outrank me, *Caroline*. I am *Lady* Olivia. If it were not for my family, you would be sleeping in a brothel tonight."

Caroline's heart raced. Every time she got on Olivia's bad side, Olivia insisted on reminding her of her past.

"No need to be nasty," Emma said, taking her place at Caroline's side. "Yes, it was the generosity of your father that allowed Caroline to stay. But he also gave her his name. Which, though she doesn't share the same courtesy title as you, in the eyes the law, she's the daughter of an earl, making her your equal."

"But *you're* not," Olivia returned with a sneer.

"That's enough." Caroline walked over and looped her arm through Emma's. Emma may not be offended by Olivia's remark, but if they stayed in the room much longer, Olivia would find something offensive to say. That was a fact that could be counted on, just as sure as the sun rose each day. "Let's go," she said to both Emma and Nettie.

"But who will do my hair?" Olivia whined, latching onto Nettie's arm.

"You will," Caroline answered, jerking the fabric of Nettie's dress from Olivia's fingers. "I need her assistance."

Olivia's lower lip shot out and her eyebrows snapped down. "That's not *fair!*" She punctuated her last word by stomping her stocking-clad foot on the hard floor yet again, cracking the floorboard this time. "You don't have a betrothed to impress like I do."

Caroline forced herself to hold her tongue and keep walking, not giving in to the temptation to turn around to say something unkind.

"You may go, Nettie," Caroline murmured as soon as they were safely away from Olivia's room.

"Thank you." Nettie scurried off.

"How do you tolerate her?" Emma asked as they walked down the hall to the staircase.

Caroline shrugged. "I've lived with her nearly fourteen years. I've gotten used to her, I guess," she lied. Nobody with their brain still fully intact could become accustomed to such behavior, but when a person has no other choice they learn to make do.

Caroline nearly asked Emma the same question before snapping her mouth shut. Emma's personal life wasn't her business. Emma was six-and-twenty, never married, and hated going to London for the Season. Caroline suspected that was because Emma's sister, Louise, was there, and so was Louise's depraved husband.

Twelve years ago, Louise had been betrothed to Marcus. Shortly following his accident, Louise broke the contract and married a gentleman slicker than mud. This gentleman was a duke and had more money than the bank of England. But more than wealth and privilege, he detested Emma. Probably because Emma had tried to discourage Louise from jilting Marcus for him. That, or because Emma had refused his amorous advances. Caroline didn't know which tale was the truth, nor did she feel it was her place to ask. All she cared about was that Emma continued to be a friend and practically an older sister to Caroline these past almost fourteen years.

Caroline would be lying if she didn't admit she'd always wondered why Emma continued to come around, though. It seemed odd that she would, considering what her sister had done to

Marcus. However, Emma had no one else besides Louise, and dealing with Olivia's black moods and the contempt Marcus held for her sister was probably a small price to pay for not being lonely.

For a time Caroline entertained the idea that perhaps Emma had romantic designs on Marcus, but she found no proof to back that up. And like all good scientists, Caroline refused to believe anything that lacked the proof to back up the theory. Therefore, she'd concluded Emma was lonely and enjoyed Caroline's company.

The door to the drawing room door was open a crack. Together Caroline and Emma went in, and Caroline's manners instantly flew out the window as soon as her eyes landed on Alex.

The gentleman sitting (yes, *sitting*) in the chair by the fire was the Alex Banks she'd met in London at the *Society of Biological Matters* four years ago. His cravat was askew. He had ink stains on his sleeves and fingers. His brown, slightly longer than fashionable hair was pulled in every which direction. His spectacles were pushed to the top of his nose but were slightly tilted to the right. Most would think he looked unfit to be out of his private bedchamber. But to her, he looked positively handsome—in a disheveled sort of way.

"Have you been working on the experiment?" she asked bluntly, taking a seat on the settee across from him.

His eyes went wide for a second. "Yes." His voice held a slight edge.

"Good. I'd hate to do all the work." Caroline made herself more comfortable.

Alex glanced to Marcus who was sitting in the far corner in such a way the dim light only shone on half his face. "You won't. I promise." One side of his lips tipped up.

Emma came and sat next to Caroline, reminding her she'd forgotten to do the introductions. "Alex, may I introduce you to Emma Green? She's a close friend of mine. Emma, this is Mr. Alex Banks, Olivia's intended."

A strangled, choking noise came from Alex's throat, giving her the strangest impulse to go smack him on the back. It wouldn't be appropriate for her to touch him, though, so she looked to Marcus for intervention. Marcus, however, wouldn't meet her eyes. His face was slightly pink and his scarred lips appeared to be having trouble staying clamped closed. By Caroline's guess, she'd say, he was trying to hold his composure. She frowned. What was wrong with him? Not Alex, but Marcus. Why did he find it so amusing his guest was choking to death? Good gracious. It was official, Marcus was cracked.

"Perhaps you should help him," Emma murmured to Caroline.

Meeting Emma's green eyes, Caroline saw something she'd never seen before and couldn't place. She tore her gaze away and padded over to Alex's side. "Are you all right?" She bit her lip and debated if she would be of more help to him by patting his back or yanking his cravat completely off.

"I'm all right," he wheezed, holding up a hand. "Just a slight coughing fit."

"Are you sure?"

"Yes. Quite."

Caroline resumed her seat next to Emma. "I thought he was going to die there for a minute," she mumbled.

"Wouldn't you want to if you were Olivia's intended?" Emma asked. "I know I would."

A tiny fit of insuppressible giggles overtook Caroline and Emma grinned.

"Ladies," Marcus warned.

"Sorry," they murmured in unison.

Caroline composed herself the best she could, which was one extremely difficult task.

She looked back to Marcus, who was slouched in his chair with his leg propped out. He'd been dealt a tough hand. At seventeen, he'd endured a disfiguring accident which had changed his entire life. His left leg had been broken so badly it had never healed properly, causing him to limp. His once handsome face was now covered in scars, the left side slightly worse than the right. She'd never actually been told what happened to cause his injuries, nor did she know the extent of them. The scars on his face and neck disappeared under his cravat. She'd often wondered if they existed under his clothes because his hands were also scarred, but once again it wasn't her place to ask.

Following his accident and broken betrothal, he'd become a recluse due to the jests and snide remarks that surrounded his accident and the ghastly aftereffects. And now he had to act as guardian to two young girls, one of whom was extremely difficult to get along with. But that was where Marcus was different. Better even. He and Olivia had never been particularly close, but he'd always done his best where she was concerned.

When they'd lost their mother a few years earlier, Marcus had endured Olivia's obnoxious caterwauling with nary an unkind word. He'd let her cry on his shoulder and had wiped away more tears than any person should be exposed to. Then last year, Uncle Joseph, the former Lord Sinclair, died and Olivia had turned into a Bedlamite once again. The screaming. The crying. The fits of anger. The sheer madness of it all was more than Caroline could handle. But not Marcus. As the dutiful older brother he was, he'd once again tolerated all of it.

He'd once told Caroline he may not understand Olivia, but she was his sister and that created a bond that couldn't be broken no matter what Olivia did. Not to say he didn't get annoyed with her. He did. Quite often actually. On more than one occasion, Caroline had seen Marcus blister Olivia's ears for being selfish or cruel. He'd also meted out punishments for her. Unfortunately, nothing seemed to take hold with her, and her nasty personality didn't change.

"Is she ever coming?" Marcus said abruptly, jarring Caroline from her musings.

"She was undecided about her wardrobe last I saw her," Caroline told him.

Beside her, Emma shook her head and bent down to fix her slipper. "What is this experiment you're working on, Mr. Banks?"

"It's not an experiment really," he said. "Caroline has agreed to help me work on increasing the membership of an organization I'm president of."

Emma nodded. "Oh, that's nice. I think I hear Olivia."

"Good." Marcus shifted his weight in his chair.

Olivia made her grand limping and groaning entrance a moment later, rendering everyone speechless. "Good evening," she whispered hoarsely.

Caroline stared at her cousin unblinkingly. She'd put on a gown that could only be likened to the color of a lime's peel. On top of her head, she'd attached all seven of those feathers she'd had set out on her vanity. She'd used something to color her lips and cheeks an unusual shade of red that clashed with her red hair. Around her neck, she wore at least a dozen necklaces, some pearls, some just a simple gold chain, and others were strings of gaudy diamonds or emeralds.

Caroline swallowed. It would be rude not to pay Olivia some sort of compliment on her attire for the evening, she just needed to find something to compliment first. Caroline let her gaze slip lower, praying she'd find something she could compliment. A large opal butterfly brooch caught her attention. That's what she'd compliment. She cleared her throat and paused. Was it just her, or was that brooch too heavy for that dress. She blinked. No. It wasn't just her. If the fact she was able to glimpse the top half of Olivia's left areola meant anything, then that brooch was indeed too heavy for that dress. Pity. That would have been the perfect thing to compliment. Of course she couldn't now, because then everyone's eyes would take in Olivia's ample bosom, areola and all.

She tore her eyes away and swallowed uncomfortably. It would probably be best to just glance at the slippers on Olivia's feet, which were probably Caroline's anyway, and say they looked nice. Dropping her gaze to the floor, Caroline gasped. "What happened?" She stared at her cousin's foot, dumbfounded. Olivia's foot was wrapped with enough strips of linen to make a bed sheet.

Olivia raised her foot. "I seem to have broken the ball of my foot," she said with a pout.

"I bet it was all that stomping she did upstairs," Emma whispered.

Caroline nodded. She couldn't do anything else. She couldn't form a single coherent response to Emma, nor could she pull her eyes away from the giant, over-exaggerated bandage on Olivia's foot. She was in awe. Was Olivia *looking* for sympathy? If she was, she wasn't getting it from Caroline.

Caroline stiffly turned back toward Alex. She just *had* to see the look on his face.

***

It had been nearly two years since Alex had last seen Lady Olivia, and there was no doubt about it, people change. She'd changed. She must have gained at least three stone since he'd last seen her. Her dress's fabric was a color he'd never seen on a person before, and adorning her hair he'd swear were feathers the color of the rainbow. He blinked. Surely he'd been wrong. Red, orange, yellow, green, blue, indigo, and violet. No, he'd not been mistaken. Clear as day, the rainbow sat right upon the top of her head.

His mouth was hanging open and he couldn't do a damn thing about it. She must have seen it too, because she hobbled over to him, moving in a way that made her left breast pop out of her bodice. She giggled and quickly tucked her nipple back in, then continued hobbling toward him, the feathers on her head bobbing wildly with each step.

She placed her fingers on the underside of his unhinged jaw and with more force than necessary, pushed it shut, creating a loud noise as his teeth painfully snapped together. "I know I'm stunning. No need to catch a fly admiring me though." She shifted in a way that made her other breast make an unwanted appearance.

As soon as she released his jaw it fell open again.

She smiled and batted her eyelashes at him as she pulled her bodice back up.

He tried not to grimace as he willed his mind to forget the image that the impromptu visit from her breasts had left in his mind. But his efforts were futile.

"Olivia," Marcus snapped. "Make sure you keep those things in your gown for the rest of the evening, please. Nobody in this room wishes to see them again."

Lady Olivia licked her lips and winked at Alex. "I'll try."

"You had better do more than try," Marcus said, stealing the words straight from Alex's mind. "If you need more fabric for your dress, perhaps you can borrow some from your foot."

Caroline and Miss Green snickered, drawing Alex's attention. How was it possible Caroline and Lady Olivia were related? He shook off the thought. That didn't matter one iota. What did matter was he would do absolutely *anything* to marry Caroline instead of Lady Olivia.

"I can't," Lady Olivia whined, catching Alex's attention once again.

"Right." Marcus nodded. "Because you broke the ball of your foot."

"Do you doubt me, Marcus?"

"Yes."

Alex sat still. Very, very still. If he recalled correctly, Lady Olivia had a terribly foul temper. He was afraid he was about to witness it firsthand.

Marcus sighed. "Olivia, I've never heard of such a thing before. Do you require me to send for the physician? Mayhap he can just saw off your foot so this won't happen again."

"No!" She turned and batted her eyelashes in Alex's direction for a few seconds. "What I meant to say is, no. I'll just prop it up for a few days in my room, and Caroline can wait on me."

Alex could have sworn he heard some teeth grinding but couldn't tell if the sound was coming from Caroline or Marcus.

"That will not be happening," Marcus said tightly. "She's not your maid."

"Perhaps a visit to Bath, then," Lady Olivia suggested.

"Very well. A trip to Bath it is," her brother agreed. "But for now, a trip to the dining room."

Alex took to his feet, ready to be done with this blasted meal. He'd much rather eat next to Caroline, but since he was legally betrothed to Lady Olivia, he'd likely be subjected to sitting next to her for the next hour. He blew out a breath and carelessly righted his left cuff.

"Oh, Olivia." Marcus' words halted her pathetic limp mid-step. "Why don't I escort you down to dinner?"

"Why?" Lady Olivia's shrill voice made Alex wince.

"I think our gait is better suited."

Alex smiled at his friend's jest. At least Marcus was able to make light of his injuries and their lasting results. Alex didn't know if his own attitude would be the same.

"But I'd prefer to sit with Alex." She resumed her limp.

"Caroline will be eating with Alex," Marcus said firmly. "They have some science experiment to work on together."

Lady Olivia screwed up her face in a most unflattering way. "Must the two of you spoil a good meal in that manner?"

"Afraid so," Alex answered, feeling not a pang of regret at his words.

"Fine," she said, sneering. "You two are the dullest dullards I've ever met. Enjoy your boring science talk."

Caroline cracked a smile. "We will."

Alex offered Caroline his arm and glanced at Miss Green. She lacked an escort. He looked back to Caroline. She was staring at him most oddly. He had no idea what she was trying to convey and still didn't know if he should offer to escort Miss Green or not.

Alex remained still, debating what to do about Miss Green when Marcus' smooth voice cut in. "Emma, if you don't mind walking with a couple of cripples, I'd be honored to escort you to dinner."

Relieved the problem had rectified itself, Alex led Caroline out the door and down the hall, all the while scheming in his mind how he'd go about winning her over.

Chapter 5

In his estimation, Alex had two weeks to woo Caroline enough to accept his proposal. That wasn't very long at all. It had been long enough for his friend, Andrew. But Andrew was Andrew and Alex was Alex. In short, they were complete opposites in nearly every way.

Alex chuckled. Two years ago when he'd last seen Lady Olivia, Andrew had told him she'd actually proposed to him. Too bad his friend refused her offer due to his feelings for Brooke. That would have eliminated the situation Alex was currently in quite nicely. He looked over at Caroline. She didn't seem a bad sort at all. He even rather liked her. She'd certainly gotten his attention when she'd dropped that stack of books on the floor. He just didn't know if he could charm her into marriage in such a short time.

Andrew was coming to Watson Estate tomorrow to look at Alex's stallions. Perhaps he would swallow his pride and ask for some ideas on how to win a wife in such a short time. That seemed a good idea, actually. Andrew had done most of his wooing of Brooke at Watson Estate during a house party his mother had hosted. The pair had visited the conservatory only three days before they'd gotten married. If showing Caroline the conservatory translated into a hasty marriage, he'd give her a tour tonight.

"Alex," Caroline whispered, tugging on his sleeve.

"Yes?"

"We've passed the dining room." She glanced at him briefly then to the wall he'd almost walked them into.

"Right you are," he agreed, steering her back around. "I just thought we'd walk around a bit, in order to give the others some time to catch up." He hated lying, but what else could he say? *Sorry, Caroline, I was too busy thinking of how to get you to marry me so I don't have to marry your horrid cousin, and I forgot to turn into the dining room?* That statement wouldn't be met with much excitement, he was certain of it.

Walking into the dining room, Alex blinked. He'd become accustomed to small tables that were big enough only for the number of people eating. Inside this room was a table that was no less than twenty-four feet long. There were enough chairs to seat at least twenty guests. Yet, there were only five place settings out, and they were placed in such a way there was no confusion as to where each of them was expected to sit. At one end of the table, there were three settings. One on the end and one on either side. Clear on the other end of the table were two other place settings set out. Side by side.

He glanced at Caroline, and she shrugged.

A moment later, Marcus and his pair of females came in. "I thought the two of you could sit down there so not to bore Olivia with your talk."

Alex was almost moved to kiss the man's feet in thanksgiving. Almost. He didn't give a hang about boring Lady Olivia with details of science. He was more relieved he wouldn't be tortured with whatever tales she wanted to impart on him. Andrew had once commented having Lady Olivia as a mealtime companion was enough to drive a man to suicide, or at least give him nightmares. Luckily he'd never had the experience himself; however, he didn't doubt his friend's words.

"I've been thinking," Caroline said, setting her goblet down, "perhaps you should solicit members to the *Society* at some of your other organizations."

"Good idea," he said, quickly dismissing her suggestion. Not that it wasn't a good one. It was. He just didn't care about that just now.

She put her fork down and turned her beautiful blue eyes to him. "Why is it I get the impression you're not taking this seriously?"

"I am," he lied again. "I just don't think of it as a priority just now."

"And what would be a priority to you?"

"Above increasing membership to the *Society of Biological Matters*?"

"Yes." She picked her fork up and delicately poked one of her turnips.

"The trees in my orangery," he said honestly. "Say, do you like orangeries?"

She shrugged. "I've only been in one once when I was visiting a friend of Marcus'. But it's been a long time."

"I'll have to show you mine," he said with a wide grin.

"Really?" There was no mistaking the excitement in her voice.

"Really." Alex took a swallow of his drink. "I wanted to grow orange and citrus trees a few years ago, so I talked my father into splitting the conservatory in two and letting me grow citrus trees on one side."

"Fascinating."

His fork stopped halfway to his mouth. Was she being sarcastic? It was hard to tell. He put his fork down and stared blankly at his plate. Before Caroline and Miss Green joined Marcus and him in the drawing room to wait for dinner, Marcus had offered this advice: talk to her about science, but not too much. Alex frowned. Why did Marcus have to be so cryptic?

Testing Marcus' brilliant advice just now, he turned to Caroline. "What are your interests?"

She smiled at him. "You don't have to make small talk, Alex. I've heard from *many* sources you don't like to talk about anything except science."

Alex threw a scowl down at two of the three people at the end of the table. He'd bet Marcus and Lady Olivia were the ones who'd told her that. "I'm perfectly capable of talking of something besides science," he declared, hoping he wouldn't prove himself to be a liar.

"All right." Caroline put her cup down. "What are your other interests?"

He blinked at her as he searched his mind. "History, pistols, and swords," he said at last.

"Pistols and swords?"

"Yes, pistols and swords," he confirmed with a scowl. After letting his mouth get away from him two years ago and challenging someone to a duel, only to have it promptly pointed out to the room that he'd die the next day due to his inability to successfully navigate either weapon, he'd made an attempt to fence while in London and spent at least three hours each week shooting at targets. That was all the time he could spare for such frivolous pursuits. But it was enough to claim them as interests. "Now that you've heard mine, you can tell me what you're interested in."

She bit her lip. "Promise not to laugh?"

"No," he replied honestly. "But I'll try."

She rolled her eyes and shook her head at him. "I don't know if I can tell you, then."

"Yes, you can. Just spit it out."

"I like games," she blurted, exhaling a deep breath.

"Games?" Why was that odd? A lot of people liked games. He wasn't necessarily one of them, but he was acquainted with enough other people who liked them.

She nodded enthusiastically. "I don't think you understand. I *love* games."

"What kind of games?"

"All games," she answered, fingering the corners of her napkin. "Parlor games, board games, lawn games, even nursery games."

He stared at her. "You'd love my Aunt Carolina. She loves parlor games."

"She does?" Her eyes grew wide.

"More than anything. I think charades is her absolute favorite."

"I love charades," she chirped. "Do you?"

"Not particularly." He snorted. "Actually, I dislike the game so much that only last year I was able to get myself and several other family members exempt from playing it when I suggested we go off to my father's study to talk about science. Unfortunately, that didn't work out like I'd planned. Instead of discussing the fascinating facts I'd found about a couple of hedgehogs I'd been observing down by the pasture, they all wanted to talk about Paul and Liberty's explosive marriage. Andrew claimed it still followed the guidelines, since we were discussing combustible elements: Paul and Liberty." He scowled as she broke into peals of giggles. "What could you possibly find humorous about that?" he asked in mock agitation. From an outsider's perspective it probably was humorous.

"It's true," she said between bursts of giggles.

"What?"

"That you cannot have a conversation without speaking of science," she answered when she'd gathered her composure.

Hell's afire, she was right. He'd proved himself a liar in less than two minutes. "Sorry," he murmured.

"It's quite all right. Shall we talk about the experiment now?" She pushed her plate away.

"No. Why don't you tell me what your favorite game is instead?" He flashed her what he hoped to be an encouraging grin.

"Lawn chess."

"We've a set at Watson Estate."

Her eyes grew huge again. "Truly?"

He nodded. "Would you like to come and play?"

She twisted her lips. "I probably shouldn't. With you being Olivia's betrothed, it wouldn't be right."

He tried not to scowl. He was not betrothed to Lady Olivia. All right, he was, but that wasn't going to stick. He was going to marry Caroline, not Olivia. He couldn't tell Caroline that though. If he did, he'd have to explain about his father's mistake during a drunken stupor. That would not look very good to a potential bride. Nor would the idea of asking her to help jilt her cousin only because he didn't want to marry her. Best to just keep quiet for now.

"Sure it would. Tomorrow your cousin is going to Bath. Just come to Watson Estate while she's there."

"I can't," she protested. "I've no chaperone."

"That's not a problem," he said dismissively. "My mother can act as your chaperone."

"Don't you think you should ask her first?" Caroline's lips twitched. "She may not wish to spend her day chaperoning a stranger, you know."

"She'll do it," he said offhandedly. Mother would chaperone the devil himself if it meant her son wouldn't have to marry Lady Olivia. He had no idea why, nor did he care her reasons, but his mother detested Lady Olivia in the worst way.

"Are you certain?"

He cleared his throat. "Quite."

She clapped her hands together. "All right, you've convinced me. I'll come."

"I had no idea I had such powerful influence," he said dryly.

"Well, you do. But we'll have to talk of the experiment." She leaned back to let a footman refill her glass. "Olivia will know where I'm going, and steam will spiral out of her ears if she thinks I'm going to see you for any reason other than science."

"Fine," he grumbled. They'd talk about her experiment for the two minutes it took him to set up the chess board, but not a minute more. He had better things to do. One such thing being to woo her.

"Are you two done?" Marcus asked, pushing to his feet.

"Just finished," Caroline answered.

Alex glanced out the window at the end of the hall as the group left the dining room. "I'd better be off. It's nearly dark." He turned and said his goodbyes to Caroline, reminding her of their agreement for her to come play lawn chess tomorrow.

***

Early the next morning, only twenty minutes past the hour that marked morning to be precise, Alex's eyes sprang open as his body shot up from his bed. He ran his hand over his perspiring face and shoved his fingers through his hair. Scooting to the edge of his bed, he put his feet on the floor to remind himself he'd only had a nightmare.

He put his hands on his back just above his waist and arched backward to stretch, his fingers touching the scars in remembrance of a lost innocence. He shook his head and brought his hands to his knees. As much as he wished for it, nobody could rewrite history, even if it would be to the benefit of a scared little girl.

Nothing for it now. He shot to his feet and lit a candle before throwing on his dressing robe. Nightmares didn't happen to him often, but when they did it was hard to get back to sleep. There was only one thing to do now: take a trip to the library to read up on one of his real experiments.

Grabbing his candelabra, he left the room and headed to the library, mentally making a note to talk to Marcus privately in the next day or two. There was something about that awful night he needed to know.

Chapter 6

Caroline barely slept in anticipation of her afternoon with Alex. She squeezed her eyes shut tight. She should *not* be looking forward to such a thing. He was her cousin's betrothed, for goodness' sake. She had no business going to his house to play chess, let alone being so excited about it.

Due in part to her deceased mother, Caroline's love for lawn chess was so great she couldn't have declined a game with Lucifer. She remembered being a little girl and her mother would take her to Ridge Water to play. Of course she'd been too young to know how to play by the rules, but she loved to watch people push their pieces around, nonetheless. Her mother was always happiest when they were playing lawn chess or looking out at the stars with a telescope.

Caroline smiled. She'd loved her mother more than anyone in the world. She'd been such a happy person, even if the world seemed determined to kill her joy, usually in the form of her own husband. Caroline's father was the vilest creature Caroline had ever met, and the less she thought of him, the better.

She sailed down the stairs and went to the front door. She'd told Marcus she intended to go to Alex's today. He hadn't asked any questions except to confirm Alex's mother would act as her chaperone. Other than confirming that, he didn't seem to care what they'd be doing while she was there. His dismissive attitude surprised her a bit. He didn't normally care about details on the whole, but she thought he might be interested since this time it involved a gentleman. Apparently not.

The carriage ride to Bath was extremely uncomfortable. Olivia complained of her foot the entire time, except when she complained about marrying a dullard like Arid Alex, that is. Olivia knew full well where Caroline was going, and surprisingly didn't seem to care. In fact, Olivia told Caroline it was excellent the two of them had similar tastes—it would benefit her after they were married. She'd worked it out in her head. Caroline could stay at Watson Estate and act as Olivia's companion since she'd never find a gentleman willing to marry her. Then, when Olivia could take Arid Alex's incessant science chatter no longer, she'd send Caroline in to listen to his nonsense.

Caroline frowned. He really wasn't so bad to talk to. Sure, he was known for talking about all subjects relating to science, but she'd learned in their short time together there was a lot more to him than that. And she couldn't help herself for wanting to discover more, even if nothing could ever happen between them. He was Olivia's intended, she firmly reminded herself once again.

She looked down at the papers in her lap. She'd brought her notes with her today so they could discuss their experiment about gaining membership to the *Society*. She reread the first page. She'd come up with some really good ideas. Too bad he didn't seem as interested in working on this as she was. Well, like the ever dutiful scientist she was, she would insist that they discuss their experiment today. She would *not* let him get away with dumping the whole thing on her.

As the carriage rolled up the drive at Watson Estate, Caroline's excitement rose. Today had the workings to be one of the best days of her life. Not only would she get to play lawn chess, she would also get to play it with Alex, and for some reason that made her much more excited than she thought possible.

The carriage came to a stop, and from the window she could see Alex and another, larger gentleman talking. She blinked. Forget larger, he was massive. Almost like a giant marble statue. Yes, a marble statue with coal black hair. She'd heard enough gossip from Olivia's lips to guess this had to be Lord Townson, Alex's closest friend.

The carriage door swung open, startling Caroline.

"Coming down?" Alex asked, reaching a hand up to her.

Caroline came to the door and took his hand. "Thank you," she murmured after she'd descended. She looked at Alex and silently asked him with her eyes to introduce her to his friend. Not that she had a hankering to meet nobility. Quite the opposite. She'd

only even seen possibly half a dozen titled gentlemen in her life—
and her uncle, Marcus, and Marcus' friend, Lord Drakely, made up
half of those. The reason she wanted to be introduced to Lord
Townson was to help ease the tension that had fallen over the trio
as they stood there together.

"Allow me to introduce myself, seeing as Alex here is too
enamored by you to make introductions," Lord Townson said with
a grin. "My name is Andrew Black, Earl of Townson." He did a
quick, low bow and came back up to meet her eyes.

"Caroline Sinclair," she said, doing the sloppiest curtsy she'd
ever attempted. She didn't do it intentionally; she'd just never
actually done one before anyone of importance before. It was quite
nerve-racking.

Lord Townson didn't seem to mind though. "Nice to meet you,
Miss Sinclair."

"It's nice to meet you, too, my lord," she greeted with a smile.
"I'd prefer it if you'd call me Caroline."

"Caroline it is," the earl said.

"Andrew came by this morning to look at my new
thoroughbred. He was just about to leave," Alex informed her.

"While he was here, did you talk to him about Biological
Matters?"

Lord Townson gave her a queer look and a choking sound
came from Alex's throat. "Yes, he talked to me," Andrew said
tightly. "And I'd suggest he not do so again."

Caroline's eyes widened. She had no idea he'd be so opposed
to joining the *Society of Biological Matters*. Mayhap Alex was
right when he told her he wouldn't be interested.

Alex crossed his arms defensively. "That's not—"

"No more, Alex," Lord Townson said in a warning tone. "I
think I'm old enough to make those decisions for myself." He
turned to Caroline and his tone softened considerably. "It was a
pleasure to meet you, Caroline. I sincerely hope to see more of you
in the future." He turned back to Alex and gave him a look she
couldn't see.

Alex smiled and nodded at his friend. "Give my best to
Brooke."

"I will," Lord Townson said, mounting his horse.

"That was most peculiar," Caroline mumbled as he rode off.

Alex smiled at her. "He's a good sort. I know you think he's angry with me, but he's not. He's a good man."

"If you say so." Caroline turned to walk toward the house. "I brought my notes with me today. Perhaps after chess we could discuss your experiment."

His head snapped in her direction, his eyes wide and intent, almost like he was guilty of something. "Oh, right," he said with a slight shake of his head. "We'll see."

She was about to say something in response when a lady with Alex's same dark brown hair and matching eyes came walking down the front steps toward them, the skirts of her red day dress swishing back and forth as she walked.

"Mother," Alex said as the older lady approached. "This is Miss Caroline Sinclair. She prefers to be called Caroline. Caroline, this is my mother, Regina Banks, Lady Watson."

"It's nice to meet you," Caroline said, attempting another ill-executed curtsy.

Grabbing Caroline's elbow to help her back to proper standing position, the baroness flashed her a smile. "There is no need to curtsy, dear. I shan't be returning one."

Caroline stared at her. Had she just been insulted?

The baroness laughed. "I can't. This dress does not allow me to do so without falling on my derriere. Anyway, we're a *very* relaxed family around here. Such formalities aren't necessary." She turned to her son and wagged her finger playfully. "As host, you should have told her that, Alex."

"My apologies, Caroline," he said, turning to Caroline. "It was remiss of me not to mention it before. However, after the curtsy I witnessed you giving Andrew, I couldn't help but want to see it again." He winked at her. "But Mother is right. We're not formal here. In fact, you can take off your slippers and spend the afternoon in your stockings, if you'd prefer."

She stared at him. He had to be jesting with her. Just to test him, she said, "You'd like that, wouldn't you? A gentleman can never resist a chance to peek at a lady's undergarments."

He blinked and his mother laughed. "She's teasing you, Alex," his mother said with a wide smile that looked like a mirror image of Alex's grin. "Caroline, I do like you. Shall we go have some luncheon?"

Caroline nodded her agreement and Alex came to stand next to her, his hand on her shoulder. Adding the slightest amount of pressure to her shoulder with his hand, Alex walked forward, leading Caroline to do the same. They'd walked up two of the front stairs when suddenly Alex's hand moved to the small of her back and he stopped walking. Confused, she glanced at him. He was looking over his shoulder. Twisting her head around further, her eyes fell on his mother standing with her hands behind her back, staring intently at the sky. Caroline smiled to herself. Alex's mother had moved his hand!

Her eyes caught Alex's as he was turning his head back straight. The tips of his ears were slightly pink, as were his cheeks. She would have laughed if she didn't think it would have embarrassed him further.

"Shall we?" he asked hoarsely.

"I'll be right behind you," Lady Watson said suddenly. "I need to go check on something."

Alex nodded and led Caroline to the room—or perhaps closet—they would eat in. The room was tiny, only about eighteen feet long and twelve feet wide. Half of Marcus' table wouldn't fit in this room. She stared at the little table that couldn't possibly hold more than six diners. On the table sat several covered dishes with the appropriate serving pieces resting next to them.

Alex walked to one of the chairs and pulled it out for her. After she sat and Alex pushed her in to her satisfaction, he went around the table and pulled out a chair she assumed was for his mother. Then he came back to her side of the table and sat next to her.

She looked at him quizzically. Wasn't he going to wait for his mother to sit down?

As if reading her thoughts, he said, "She prefers to scoot her own chair in. She says others push her too far forward." He shrugged as if he didn't really care one way or the other.

A minute later Lady Watson came into the room, a wide smile on her face. "No need to get up," she said, taking her seat.

"We weren't," Alex said cheekily.

"Yes, I know." Lady Watson smiled at Caroline. "Alex means well, but sometimes he pushes me so far forward I eat three bites and hit the table."

"Think of it as a way to keep fit," Alex teased.

"I *fit* just fine in my current gowns, dear boy," she returned with a mischievous smile.

Alex shook his head and grabbed a serving fork. "Would you like some roasted chicken?"

Caroline blinked at him. He was serving them lunch? Where were the footmen? A delicate cough brought her eyes up to meet the warm, brown eyes of Lady Watson. "As I said before, we're terribly informal here. We enjoy luncheons by ourselves. No servants or distractions."

Caroline was taken aback. She'd always been served by servants while eating at Ridge Water, no matter what the meal or how many were present. The only time she hadn't been served a meal was when she was a little girl up in the nursery at her house in London. But that was when her mother was still alive. Her mother would come up at every meal and eat with Caroline and Nurse. She'd even carry the trays up and down the stairs, claiming no servant was needed because meals were meant to be spent with those who were most important, and to her that was Caroline and Nurse.

"Yes, please," she said when she realized Alex was still waiting on her answer, holding the serving fork just above the chicken.

He put a sizable piece on her plate before doing the same for his mother then serving himself.

"Tell me, dear," Lady Watson said to Caroline, grabbing a piece of bread off the plate Alex was holding out to her, "I know the current Lord Sinclair is actually your cousin. My husband was very good friends with his father, Joseph, but I'm not very familiar with his brothers or their families, I fear. Which of Joseph's brothers was your father?"

"None," Caroline said quietly, dropping her gaze to her plate.

"Oh," Lady Watson said a minute later. "You're Sophie's daughter, then."

Caroline gulped and forced herself to nod as her world

crumbled around her ears. The inside of her hands grew so clammy she nearly dropped her fork. If Alex's mother knew who her mother was, this was going to be a very uncomfortable afternoon. Though she'd loved her mother dearly, the *ton* had not. Nasty rumors had always swirled around her mother's name. Caroline was too young to know the truth back then, but what her aunt and Olivia told her was enough.

"I attended a girls' school with her," Lady Watson added. "Only for a short while. About two months or so."

Caroline nodded numbly. Any mention of her mother at a girls' school usually led to the revelation of her downfall.

"We shared a room," Lady Watson continued, seemingly oblivious to Caroline's discomfort. She laughed. "Care to hear something humorous?"

"Always," Alex muttered with a game smile. The way his tone belied his answer and his facial expression made Caroline smile despite the discomfort of the room.

Alex's mother shook her head. "Alex, I have no idea what I'm going to do with you. I hope you find a lady who can make you socially acceptable."

"I do, too," he said, his tone gravely serious as an unspoken message passed between mother and son. "Do tell whatever you'd planned to before pointing out the flaw in my personality."

Shaking her head again, Lady Watson smiled warmly. "Sophie and I once had a discussion during bedtime of what we'd name our children. Her first choice for a boy's name was Alexander, and my first choice for a girl's name was Caroline."

"It seems you both got what the other wanted," Caroline commented with a hint of a smile.

"I suppose so," Lady Watson agreed. "Even when I did finally have a daughter, I didn't get to use the name Caroline."

"You have a daughter?" Caroline asked, shocked. No one ever told her Alex had any siblings, least of all Alex.

The baroness cocked her head and looked at her queerly. "Yes, her name is Edwina, named for my husband Edward and myself. She's only sixteen. She's at Sloan's School for Young Ladies. That's where your mother and I attended."

"Oh," Caroline said dully. "Does she come to Watson Estate

often?"

Alex snorted. "No. Unlike the rest of the family, Weenie prefers the city."

"Weenie?" Caroline squeaked.

"That's what we all call Edwina," Alex explained.

Caroline knew her eyes were bulging. She just couldn't help it.

"It's just a nickname we use to shorten her name." Alex shrugged. "Well, that's not exactly true. That's just what we say. The real story to how she got the nickname in the first place—"

"Alexander Christopher Banks," his mother broke in sharply. "That will be enough."

He shrugged again and a slow, teasing grin took his lips. "Why? It's a rather amusing story. Don't you agree?"

Ignoring him, Alex's mother turned to Caroline. "Believe me, if it were not done affectionately, I would not allow my boys to call her that."

"Boys?" Caroline echoed. He had brothers, too?

The baroness gave an exaggerated sigh and groan all rolled into one. "Really, Alex, did you not tell her *anything* about our family?"

"No," he said, not a hint of emotion in his voice.

"I have four children, Caroline." Lady Watson ran her fingers up and down the stem of her glass. "Alex is my oldest at nine-and-twenty, then he has two brothers, Elijah and Henry. They're both two-and-twenty, twins of course. Then there's Edwina."

"Where are your other sons?" Caroline asked. Why had she never heard of their existence before?

"In America," the baroness said sadly, developing a sudden interest in the portrait landscape on the far end of the room.

Alex leaned down by Caroline's ear. "My Uncle John went to America as part of his Grand Tour and didn't come back for more than twenty-five years."

"Why not?" Caroline asked, curious as to why someone would prefer America to England.

"He fell in love." Alex brushed a hank of Caroline's dark hair away from her eyes. "That's where he met the charade-loving Carolina. She was an American. He decided to stay. Mother's afraid Elijah and Henry will do the same."

"How long have they been gone?"

"Six months," he said. "Before that, they traveled the continent for a while and even made their way all the way to India. Since they're twins, they've always liked doing things together."

"Are you close to them?"

"Yes and no. We have a lot of things in common, but I'm not a twin. It's difficult to explain. See, I'll always be their brother and share a close bond because of that, but I'll never be as close to either of them as they are to each other. Does that make sense?"

"Yes."

"Do you have any siblings, Caroline?" Lady Watson asked, a wobbly smile returning to her lips and the tears gone from her eyes.

"No." Caroline didn't meet the baroness' eyes. "Not unless you want to count Marcus and Olivia. But they're not really my siblings." Was it just her, or did Lady Watson's teeth clamp together at the mention of Olivia's name? She blinked away the thought.

"I'm sorry to hear that," Lady Watson said, reaching across and placing her hand on top of Caroline's.

"Thank you," she said softly, meeting her eyes again.

"Alex, dear, could you do me a favor before your game?"

"Of course, Mother."

"Could you make sure they've put a lounge chair outside for me?"

He stood up. "Of course, I'll be right back."

After Alex had departed, Lady Watson touched Caroline's hand again. Caroline looked up and met her eyes. "Caroline, I want to apologize to you. I hope I haven't made you uncomfortable today. I didn't realize who your mother was, and when I did, I should have left it alone."

"It's all right," she said quickly, swallowing convulsively.

"As I said, I knew her," the baroness continued, "not well, of course. But well enough to be able to distinguish what's true and what's not. I've never thought less of her, nor do I think any less of you, either."

Caroline stared at her, confused.

Lady Watson sighed. "Caroline, I don't know what will or won't happen between you and my son, but I want you to know that you're welcome in my home anytime you wish to come."

Caroline blinked back the tears that pricked the back of her eyes. Marcus had always been accepting of her. Her uncle had, too. But not Olivia, nor her aunt. To have a stranger who seemed to know everything about her mother's past accept her was astonishing. "Thank you," she croaked.

"There's nothing to thank me for." She gave Caroline's hand a quick squeeze. "Let's go play chess."

Caroline stood up and walked with the baroness to the door. "I hope he's not too good."

"You'll just have to see for yourself." She lightly tugged on Caroline's sleeve. "Let's go this way. It's closer to where we want to be."

Caroline nodded and followed the baroness down the hall to where a servant was waiting to open the side door for them. Stepping outside, Caroline was pleased to find she wasn't blinded by sunshine like she'd expected. Right above the door they'd exited was a private balcony with several hanging flower baskets acting as an excellent screen from the sun. Close to the door was the lounge chair Alex's mother had requested. About fifteen feet away was a little stone table with thirty two smaller stones lined up in four neat rows on top with a chair on either side of the table.

Caroline blinked at the little table and a giggle escaped her lips.

"Did I miss something?" Alex asked, walking up beside her.

"No," she said quickly, staring at the chess table in disbelief.

The baroness, smart lady that she was, stepped up. "It's not what you expected, is it?"

Alex looked at them, confusion marring his handsome face. "What do you mean?"

"Caroline was expecting lawn chess," Lady Watson explained.

He gestured to the table. "This is lawn chess."

"No, this is lawn chess," his mother argued. "She was expecting *lawn chess*."

"And what, pray tell, is *lawn chess*?"

"This is fine," Caroline put in quickly. "Let's play."

"No." Alex shook his head. "I want to know what *lawn chess* is."

His mother sighed. "Do you remember when you were fifteen and we took you to the Tollison house party?"

He nodded.

"Remember that giant, wooden platform they had in their backyard that was painted black and white and all you boys moved around those giant chunks of carved wood that were so big it took two of you to move them?"

Alex's jaw dropped. "You were talking about *that*?"

Caroline bit her lip and nodded sheepishly. "Yes."

He turned back to his mother. "And you knew she was expecting that?"

His mother repeated Caroline's gesture. "I had a slight inclination. Years ago, your father and I used to go play *lawn chess* over at Lord Sinclair's. They had a set and we'd all play together."

Caroline swallowed. They *had* a set was right. After her mother died, Uncle Joseph got rid of it before her father could voice any claim to it.

"Caroline, let me tell you a secret I've learned from being married to Alex's father for more than thirty years. Like Edward, Alex will give you anything you ask for. But you need to be specific. Don't be afraid to ask for what you want. He'll give it to you or get it for you."

Caroline nodded as she absorbed what Lady Watson told her. She smiled. From what she could tell, the baroness' observation seemed undeniably accurate.

"Not to fear though. This can still be salvaged," Lady Watson chirped.

"We'll just play regular chess." Caroline moved closer to the chess table.

"Nonsense. You were expecting to play an outdoor game that is more physical than sitting in a chair, and you shall have it. I asked a footman to set something else up."

Alex groaned.

A twinkle shone in Lady Watson's eye. "On the other side of the house I directed a pall mall course be set up."

"What's that?" Caroline asked, intrigued.

Alex groaned again. "Nothing."

"I think you'll like it, Caroline," Lady Watson assured her.

"Judging by how displeased your son seems to be, I think you're right." Caroline grinned at Alex.

"Now, Alex, Caroline is your guest, you need to be a gracious host and play whatever she wishes," his mother said, her shoulders shaking with mirth.

"Yes, she is," he acknowledged with a single, slow nod. His face was nearly expressionless. "If you wish to play pall mall, so be it. But you may not like it. It's difficult, so playing it the first time may not be much fun."

She looked curiously at him. He really didn't want to play this game. "You never know, I might be a natural," she ventured.

He snorted.

That strengthened her waning resolve. "I think I'd like to play," she told him primly.

"Very well."

He offered her his arm, and they had almost walked around to the other side of the house when suddenly his mother's airy voice floated through the air. "Oh, Alex, remember your manners and let Caroline choose her color first. And if she wants the pink one, be a gentleman and let her borrow it."

Chapter 7

Alex hated pall mall. As far as he was concerned, it was the worst game ever invented. Tapping a wooden ball through a series of iron hoops in the least amount of strokes was nothing short of misery for someone who liked logic.

In an effort to stem such vile thoughts, he glanced over to Caroline. She was beautiful with her mahogany hair, light skin, and dainty features perched there on his arm. She'd make the perfect wife for him. He only needed to charm her into thinking the same. Earlier, when Andrew had been over to see his horses, Alex had asked with all the subtlety of an elephant how he'd gained a wife in such a short time. Andrew's response had been as helpful as a horseshoe for a dog. He'd said, "Take her to the orangery and let instinct take over."

Alex scoffed. *That* was immensely helpful. Perhaps for a natural born rake it would have been excellent advice. But a natural born rake wouldn't need to ask for advice. Nor would a natural born rake find himself only weeks away from being forced to marry a dragon. And if he had, he'd have found a suitable bride an hour after being told the consequences of making it to his thirtieth year unwed. He scowled and pushed the thought from his mind. There was no need to even think of such things; he was going to marry Caroline.

"Here we are," Alex said to Caroline as they came upon a wooden rack next to the house.

On the rack there were six mallets, all different colors. Below the mallets, in a trough-like tray, sat six balls, each the color of its corresponding mallet.

"What was it your mother said about the pink one?" she asked, reaching out and wrapping her fingers around the handle of the pink mallet.

Instinctively, his hand flew to hers and covered it. The feel of her warm hand under his sent a jolt of desire from his fingers and palm straight to his groin. With a silent curse, he forced himself to let go of her hand. "Go ahead," he said irritably. Nearly everyone else he knew had heard the story. Why not her, too?

She snatched the pink mallet from the rack and turned it over in her hands. She blinked up at him, her lips twitching. "Why is your name carved into the handle?" The way she was staring at him made his insides uneasy.

He ran his hand through his hair. "It's a long story."

She fingered the four letters permanently engraved into the handle of the pink mallet. "I've got all day."

Sighing, he met her gaze straight on. "As you can guess by my mother's laughter and my earlier groans, this is not a game I enjoy. To say I loathe this game would not be an untrue statement. The reason I do not enjoy this game is partially due to the lack of thinking that goes into playing it. The other reason is, uh, to be honest, I don't stand a chance at winning."

"You mean you only like to play games you're sure you can win?" she interrupted. Her lips stretched into the biggest smile he'd ever seen.

"Doesn't everyone?" he countered, returning her grin.

"I suppose so," she agreed. "But that does not tell me how your name found a permanent home on the handle of the pink mallet."

His face grew warm—hot even. "The rules of the game say you have to hit the ball with the mallet and send it through all the hoops in the least amount of strokes. While the rest of my family can pass through all ten of the iron hoops with scores between forty and fifty strokes each, I usually average about a hundred." Heedless to his face burning in a way that might suggest it was being licked by flames, he stared at Caroline. She clapped a petite hand over her mouth, failing miserably to keep her laughter silent. He shrugged. In for a penny, in for a pound. "As it is, due to my lack of talent at the game, one of my brothers—I've still not determined which—decided because I play like a member of the fairer sex, I should have to play with a mallet painted a color suited for a lady. Since Weenie had a fondness for the red one, that only left the pink one available for them to carve my name into."

Caroline was no longer able to stifle her laughter with her hand and peals of that happy noise filled the air.

He shook his head. "And yes, everyone has insisted I play with it every time Mother drags us out here to play. And yes, I've been asked by many guests who've come to house parties as to how my name ended up etched into that mallet."

"Oh, Alex," she gasped between bursts of laughter. "I'm sorry to laugh at you. It's just hard to picture all that. Well, not really since you're such a nice man. I'd already realized you'd do anything for those you loved. Even play with a pink mallet if they insisted on it. It's just a humorous story, that's all."

And just then, in the span of one second, all the embarrassment surrounding that ridiculous pink mallet and all the emasculating innuendo that went along with it dissolved. She was right. He'd only played with that ridiculous thing to humor his family. They would have never carved his name into it just to be cruel. But only his family knew that. Everyone else who'd seen the mallet had openly questioned his masculinity, but not Caroline. No, she'd seen what the others couldn't. And for some reason, knowing she could see that unsettled him.

"All right," he said raggedly. "Are we going to play or admire the game pieces?"

"Let's play." She put the pink mallet back on the rack. "I know you said you always play with the pink one, but if you could pick a color, which would it be?"

"Green," he said without delay, reaching out to snatch the green mallet from the rack.

"How shocking," she muttered as he picked up the green ball. "I'll take blue."

He handed her the blue mallet. Then with the end of his green mallet, he rolled the blue ball off the rack for her. "All right, now as I said, the object is to hit your ball through all the iron hoops with the least amount of strokes."

"That's it?"

He scoffed. "It's not as easy as it sounds."

"All right. Who goes first?"

"You can." He looked around to locate the first hoop. When he found it, he pointed to a patch of grass near a giant tree. "Let's go over there. That's where we'll start."

"Brilliant. Perhaps while we play we can discuss your experiment. I don't think this game takes as much thinking as chess does," she said.

He groaned. "Caroline, let's not."

"Why not?" She abruptly stopped her steps.

"I thought we would just have a good time together," he said hastily.

"And not speak of science at all?" Her eyes were huge.

He chuckled. "I'm going to make an honest attempt at trying to make it through an hour without doing so, yes."

"Good gracious, people really can change," she muttered. "All right, fine. But after we're done with this game, we're talking about that experiment."

His jaw clenched. He hated it when she brought up his made-up experiment almost as much as he hated playing pall mall. Every time she referred to his experiment, panic seized him. What if she put the pieces together? What if he accidentally slipped up and said something he shouldn't? He couldn't let her continue to talk about his experiment. "Fine. After the game we'll talk about our campaign."

"Campaign?" she repeated. "I thought it was an experiment."

"It's not. You should know that," he replied.

She shrugged. "I know. But Marcus told you to think of it as an experiment. And I must say, I rather like thinking of it that way, too."

"Well, think of it however you wish, but it's not an experiment. It's a campaign, and I'd prefer if you called it that."

She turned to look at him and he glanced away. He was such a cad. Not only was he treating his courtship with her as an experiment, but now he was taking her fun away because he was afraid of accidentally exposing himself.

"Fine. A campaign it is," she said dully.

"Thank you. I promise before you go home this afternoon we'll spend at least half an hour speaking of nothing but that."

"I'm going to hold you to it," she said.

"I bet you will."

They walked over to the grass he'd pointed to and she carelessly dropped her ball to the ground. Standing next to her ball, she swung the mallet back so far she almost knocked herself in the head with the heavy chunk of wood on the end. Then she brought it forward with a swing that would have been more appropriate for a links course. The mallet hit the underside of the ball and sent it straight up into the air.

Caroline shrieked and brought her arms up to cover her face as the ball flew back down to earth only ten inches from where it was originally placed.

"Congratulations, Caroline," Alex said smartly. "You're ten inches closer to the hoop!"

She made a face at him and he chuckled.

Alex dropped his ball to the ground in the same place she'd started and brought his mallet back only about ten inches or so. Lightly swinging the mallet forward, he tapped the ball and sent it rolling straight ahead. His ball rolled smack into hers, but because it hadn't been a hard hit, his ball stopped and rolled back about two inches.

"Oh congratulations, Alex," Caroline said sarcastically. "Your ball is a whole eight inches closer to the hoop."

"It would have gone further had yours not been in the way," he returned with a teasing grin.

"Excuses, excuses." She walked up to their balls with him. "Who goes now?"

"You do," he said. "We always go in the same order, even if there's a gap."

"Oh." She blinked at the balls that were no more than two inches apart.

He bit back a smile. The head of the mallet was about four inches long, the only way she'd be able to hit that ball was if she either hit it to the side, knocking it off course, or turned her mallet to the side and hit it with the side of the mallet, which would probably only make it roll a half inch away. "Your turn," he prompted.

She sighed and leaned down to pick up her ball.

"Don't," he commanded more harshly than he meant, stepping backward. "It's against the rules to move your ball." Not to mention that when she'd leaned down, her shoulder had unintentionally, but still seductively, brushed the fall of his pants.

"What should I do?"

"Put your stick between the two balls and give it a flick with your wrist," he suggested, feeling grateful nobody else was here to hear him say those words. There were too many ways that sentence could be misconstrued.

She angled her mallet sideways between their balls and hit hers just far enough to get it out of the direct path of his.

"Good work," he said approvingly as he strode up to his ball. He swung and hit it, sending it about eighteen inches in front of him.

"Nice shot," she said with a look on her face he couldn't interpret.

"Thank you," he said tentatively. "It's your turn."

She walked up to her ball and got in position to club it again. "What are you doing?" she squealed as his hands descended on her.

"Helping you," he murmured in her ear. Covering her hands with his, he stood as close to her as he dared.

"Where did your mother go?"

He froze. "She probably went to check on my father. She'll be back shortly. Don't worry, I won't do anything I oughtn't."

"I know," she said with a swallow.

"Now, the problem is you're trying to hit it for all it's worth. That won't work with pall mall. It's more about tapping the ball. Just bring it back this far—" he pulled their arms back together until the mallet was only about a foot from the ball— "then, smoothly bring the mallet forward. All right, let's try it for real this time."

She nodded and let him help her move her arms back, then swung forward. The ball rolled about three feet. "Did you see that, Alex?" she squealed, his arms still wrapped around her.

"Yes. I might wear spectacles, but I *can* see," he teased, fruitlessly willing himself to let go of her.

"Your turn." She twisted in his arms, presumably to get free.

He let her go. "Right," he clipped. He walked to his ball and knocked it a good twelve inches.

Paying him and his poor playing no mind, Caroline took her turn and without his help, hit her blue ball so well he had to take a second glance to make sure it had in fact gone through the hoop. Hell's afire, she truly was a natural.

In less than twenty minutes, Alex crossed through the first hoop and Caroline's ball sailed through the fifth. They'd gotten in a habit of yelling to the other when they'd finished with their turn so the other could go. More than once, Alex had contemplated picking up his ball and throwing it further ahead when she wasn't looking. But he'd never cheated at a game before and he wasn't going to start with pall mall!

Alex stood with his mallet poised behind his ball, waiting for Caroline to scream it was his turn. Instead, her words came out sounding a bit different. Usually she said, "Your turn." But this time she said, "Wait a second, Alex. I'm going to help you."

His lips twisted into a snarl. There was only one thing worse than cheating: getting help. He swallowed and swung his mallet back. He didn't care if he hit the ball in a way that would send it backward. He just wanted to hurry and hit it before she got here to "help" him. Staring down at the ball, he brought his mallet forward to hit his ball when suddenly a purple slipper came into view and settled on his ball.

"What are you doing?" she demanded, hands on her hips.

"Taking my turn. Now, if you'd remove your dainty slipper, I'll get on with it."

"Not so fast." She grabbed him by the lapels. "I said I was going to help you. Didn't you hear me?"

"Yes. But I don't want your help, so I ignored you."

She rolled her eyes. "Too bad. Now stand still." She came around to stand behind him, wrapped her arms around him, and put her hands on his.

Never in his life had he been torn between feeling two vastly different emotions. On one hand, he was rather embarrassed she was helping him. On the other, lust and desire coursed through him at an astonishing rate as her soft breasts rested against his back. "Perhaps we should back up," he rasped. With how responsive his body was to hers, when they swung that mallet, her hands were going to feel something else that was long and hard if she didn't allow him some space.

"Nonsense," she said, pressing closer to him. "The problem is you're stiff."

Yes, I know. But how did you? "Excuse me?" he asked raggedly.

She brought her hands to his shoulders and kneaded his muscles. "You're body is too tense. Relax."

He wanted to groan in vexation. As long as she stood pressed up against him like this, his body would not relax.

He let her help him swing, and the ball went about as far as it had when he'd done it alone.

She shook her head. "You're too rigid, Alex. If you'd soften up and relax, your game would improve."

"I'll keep that in mind," he said dryly. "Now go take your turn."

She scurried away, and he checked his pocket watch. He didn't know when Marcus was expecting her back, but in twenty minutes Mother would want to take early afternoon tea. If Caroline was still here, she'd likely be asked to join them in visiting Father after tea.

He quickly played out the rest of the game, taking notice that when he loosened his shoulders as Caroline suggested, he hit the ball further. Amazing.

"I win! I win!" Caroline screamed, running toward him. "At least I think I did."

"Did your ball just go through the last hoop?"

She nodded with so much vigor several tendrils of her beautiful hair shook free from her pins.

"Then you won," he confirmed, grinning. "Shall we put this away, or are you going to make me play out the rest?"

She waved her hand dismissively. "I wouldn't wish to torture either of us that way."

He chuckled. "Thank you. Did you happen to bring your mallet and ball with you, or did you abandon them in your joy?"

"Well, I started to..." She blushed. "But, I may have dropped them somewhere between there and here..."

Alex shook his head ruefully. "Shall we go look for the missing pieces?"

"Indeed."

They found the ball and mallet, and like he suspected, they were not together. "Let's go put these back. A footman will get the rest." He tucked both the balls in his coat pocket. Using his right hand to hold the handles of both mallets, he offered her his left.

"Thank you for playing even though you don't like it," she said as they approached the wooden rack that held the mallets and balls.

"You're welcome. It was more fun than usual."

"Is that so?" his mother asked from behind them.

He turned to face her. "Do not entertain any ideas that I'm agreeing to play that wretched game more than the once a year you already require."

Her lips curled up. "What if Caroline asked you to play?"

He glanced at Caroline. "I'll play twice a year if she asks."

"Good to know," Mother said, smoothing her skirts. "Need I ask who won?"

"I did!" Caroline's face was still glowing from her victory.

The corners of Mother's eyes crinkled. "Can't say I'm surprised." She glanced at the watch pinned on her bodice. "Sorry to leave the two of you so long. I hadn't realized forty-five minutes had passed. I genuinely thought you two would still be playing."

"Caroline took mercy on me. After she won, she let me stop."

"Oh." Mother drew the word out for a good five seconds. "Hmm, let's see you two played roughly forty minutes. You got to what, the third hoop, Alex?"

He scowled and crossed his arms. "Something like that."

"That's not true," Caroline protested in his defense. "He was almost done with the fifth. Although, it probably would have only been the third had I not helped him."

Mother looked at Caroline with wide eyes. "He allowed you to help him?"

"Not exactly," she said. "I undeniably forced myself on him."

"Indeed?" Mother glanced at him in a way that made his face burn.

"Yes. The trick is to relax the shoulders," Caroline said easily as if she were completely unaware of the unintended double meaning of her earlier words.

"You should keep that in mind for future game play, Alex."

Mother flashed him a laughing smile before turning her gaze to Caroline. "Caroline, dear, would you like to stay for tea?"

"Can you give us just a moment, Mother?" Alex said quickly, taking hold of Caroline's elbow.

Mother nodded. "I'll wait by the door."

"Caroline, you don't have to stay," he said earnestly.

She blinked. "All right. I suppose I should be going home."

"What I mean is, you can stay if you wish."

Her brows furrowed. "What's gotten into you?"

He released a breath. "Caroline, if you stay for tea, my mother is going to invite you to come meet my father."

"Oh."

Rubbing his jaw, he blew out another deep breath. "I don't know what you've heard, but he's not well. It's not something you can catch from him, mind you. But it's not something the doctor seems to be able to cure, either."

She stared at him with those big blue eyes of hers. "Is he really that ill?"

"Yes," he said hoarsely. "He is. If you're not comfortable meeting him, don't be afraid to say so."

"What do you want, Alex?"

His heart stopped beating momentarily. What *did* he want? Under normal conditions, he'd not be in control of whether she met Father or not. Father had the type of personality that some might find offensive, but he never let that stop him from letting his presence be known—especially around his own house. Now things were different. Father's illness had made him merely a shell of the man he'd once been. No longer as tall, strong, or imposing. No, now he was weak and vulnerable.

Allowing Caroline to meet him was meaningful. More so than Alex originally thought. He looked at her thoughtfully. He may not know her well, but he trusted her. If she was to be his wife one day soon, she'd need to meet his father anyway. But more than that, Father would like her, and she'd probably like him if she could get past his crude remarks.

"Are you going to be comfortable—"

She placed a finger on his lips to silence him. "I asked what you want, Alex. Don't answer my question with one of your own."

He grabbed her wrist and pulled her finger away from his lips. "I want you to be comfortable," he said, still holding her wrist.

"That's not what I asked." She didn't fight his hold of her wrist.

He sighed. "Caroline—"

She put all the fingers from her other hand on his lips to stop him. "Alex, I asked what you want. Don't make me ask again."

He wrapped his fingers around the wrist of her hand which now rested against his lips. "I want you to stay," he whispered against her fingers. Then, before she could move her hand away, he tightened his grasp on her wrist and pressed a lingering kiss on her gloved fingertips that made her eyes widen and her pretty, pink lips part as a blush colored her cheeks a fetching shade of pink.

Chapter 8

Tea with the baroness went by in a blur. A nervous blur, but a blur all the same. Now it was time to meet the baron.

Uncle Joseph used to speak of Lord Watson, his closest friend, quite often. He'd always remarked upon how sharp the baron was. Much like Alex, the baron was vastly interested in all subjects pertaining to science and had spent most of his youth doing all sorts of unusual experiments.

As excited as she was to meet such a great mind, she was also nervous. Meeting him under different circumstances might make it easier. But to meet him standing next to his son, who happened to be betrothed to her cousin, was a bit unusual. She glanced at Alex, and for the first time in her life she was envious of Olivia. Olivia was extremely fortunate and didn't even know it. Nor did she care. To Olivia, marriage to Alex was just a means to an end. She'd gain a title from the marriage (at some point) and he'd gain a headache. But that was Olivia's fate, not hers, she reminded herself once again as they left the drawing room and moved down the hall to where the baron was resting.

The baroness knocked on the door and showed them in. "Edward, we've a guest to see you."

"Good. I need some fresh company," he said, pushing himself to sit up against his pillows.

Caroline followed Alex's lead and after murmuring a greeting to his father, she joined Alex by the wall. She'd never really been in a sickroom before. Not counting Olivia's, that is. Her mother had died suddenly with no lingering illness, pain, or suffering. Her aunt and uncle had also passed quickly. This was the first time she'd actually seen someone who had to truly be suffering, and a strange feeling of pain settled in her chest. She glanced at Alex and lowered her lashes. She didn't know which of the two men she had greater sorrow for. The baron, who suffered from such horrible illness that was hurting him so, or Alex, who the illness seemed to be hurting just as much, just in a different way.

"Miss Caroline Sinclair," the baron mused, bringing her from her thoughts.

"My lord?"

"Allow me to apologize on my son's behalf," he said, picking up a glass of water off his nightstand. He took a drink and placed it back down. "You might think I'll apologize he misled you about the Banks family owning a lawn chess set, but I won't. No, my dear girl, I wholeheartedly apologize for your having to play pall mall with him."

She took an instant liking to him and his undeniably false apology. "Truly, he wasn't so bad," she defended playfully.

The baron's greying eyebrows shot nearly to his hairline and his eyes bulged. "Gel, you must know that mistruths around here are highly frowned upon. In this household we're only allowed one falsehood per year. I'm afraid you've just used yours, and now you must be completely honest around here until this day next year."

She grinned and put her hands on her hips. "Why, Lord Watson, we've just met and already you're calling me a liar." She clucked her tongue. "I'll have you know, your son is quite talented at pall mall."

He snorted. "All right, Regina, order gruel for her dinner."

"Right away, my lord," his wife said, winking at Caroline.

"Gruel?"

"It's what they always used as punishment when we were naughty," Alex explained. "Trust me, it's bad. I'm sure you've had it at some point. But the gruel that Cook makes is the worst I've ever tasted, and that includes all the gruel I ate during my years at Eton."

Caroline wrinkled her nose. "But I haven't been naughty," she protested. "I told the truth. He's a good player."

Alex's father blinked at her. "Pray explain."

"The reason he couldn't play well at first was because he was stiff. Really, *really* stiff," she explained.

Alex coughed and his cheeks flushed a light red. Lady Watson tapped her husband on the shoulder and shook her head ever-so-slightly, confusing Caroline.

Her husband waved her off. "I imagine it's hard for a gentleman to play when he's in such a state," he mused, grinning like an idiot.

"Exactly. Once he relaxed and his body became less rigid, it was easier for him to swing his mallet."

"Is that so?" The baron appeared to be choking on his laughter.

Alex sounded like he was choking to death right next to her, but the cause of his choking didn't appear to be from laughter. "Are you all right?" she asked, truly concerned.

"Just stop talking," he said with a harsh cough.

She frowned at him.

"Tell me something, gel," Lord Watson said, gaining her attention.

"Stop, Edward," his wife said in a warning tone, shaking her head a little. "She's not used to you and your humor. Don't embarrass her."

"I'm not," Lord Watson told his wife. "I don't know what you and Alex think we're talking about, but Caroline and I are just having a friendly discussion about Alex's stiffness during game play."

"Exactly," Caroline agreed.

Alex groaned.

Caroline looked at Alex. What was wrong with him? Was he embarrassed she'd told his parents she'd had to help him swing? Surely not. He played pall mall with a pink mallet to appease his family, for goodness' sake. Accepting help was no comparison to that.

"What's wrong?" Caroline whispered to him again.

Alex shook his head. "I'll explain another time. Just stop talking."

"Why?" she demanded with a frown.

"Yes, Alex, why?" his father asked, putting the folded up handkerchief he'd just coughed into back on the nightstand.

Alex looked sharply at his father. "Don't. Caroline was good enough to come see you. Please keep that in that disturbed mind of yours."

"Right you are, son," the baron agreed, pursing his lips. "I apologize if I've embarrassed you," he grumbled in Caroline's direction.

"No apology needed." Really what would he need to apologize for? Alex and his mother were acting most bizarre.

"I didn't think so." Lord Watson shot his wife and son a smug look. "Joseph once told me you had quite a fascination with science, Caroline. Do you still?"

"Yes, my lord," she said, relaxing a bit now that the tension seemed to have left the room. "In fact, I've just become the newest member of the *Society of Biological Matters*."

"Is that so?" Lord Watson nodded approvingly. "I'm glad to hear that. There's always been a lack of ladies on the membership roster."

"That might have something to do with their being denied membership," Caroline said as nicely as she could. She'd never fully accepted being denied membership due to her sex.

"Pardon me?" the baron asked, not unkindly.

Caroline bit her lip. "Please forget I said anything." She should have kept her mouth closed about this.

The baron looked at Alex, who was shifting his weight from foot to foot. "Do you know what she's talking about, son?"

"I might." Alex cleared his throat. "Caroline here is helping me campaign to increase the membership in general. Our main focus will be on recruiting ladies."

"While I'm glad to hear that as well, I'd like to know who was ever denied membership and when."

Alex sighed. "Caroline was. Three, no, four years ago."

"Why?" his father demanded, his sharp eyes darting back and forth between Alex and Caroline.

"On the basis of my sex," Caroline answered quietly. "But it is of no consequence now. Alex has recently granted me membership. All has been forgiven."

Lord Watson crossed his thin arms. "While it's nice you've forgiven the dimwit who denied you membership, I have not. Your uncle was one of my closest friends. He often bragged to me about how smart his niece was and even told me that if she were allowed to attend Eton and Cambridge she might unseat either Alex or me from the awards we'd earned." He shook his head. "He was very adamant about it. Did he know you were turned out?"

"I don't know," she murmured. To be honest she didn't care about that just now. She was positively thrilled Uncle Joseph had thought her to be intelligent. What's more, he'd bragged about it! Generally speaking, academics were not usually encouraged for young ladies, especially those which required use of one's brain beyond knowing which colors coordinated well with one another.

The baron made a harrumphing sound. "I may be an old man now, but I have every intention of letting the rapscallion who was the president at the time know how I feel about him denying you for such a senseless reason. Grab me my quill and paper, Regina."

"What's he doing?" Caroline whispered to Alex.

"Don't worry about it." He placed one searing hand on the small of her back and the other on her forearm then pointed her in the direction of a settee positioned by the window across the room. "Let's have a seat." He applied pressure with his fingers and she shivered at the tingly sensations he was unknowingly sending through her body at this simple, yet possessive gesture.

Caroline picked up a stray gold colored pillow from the settee and moved it out of the way before sitting down gingerly and arranging her skirts in a way that kept them nice, but still gave Alex room to sit next to her. Then with all the grace of an elephant on ice skates, Alex plopped down next to her and rested his arm along the back of the settee.

"Does he know it was you?"

"No," Alex whispered. "Don't worry though. I'll tell him when the time's right."

She glanced over to Alex's father. He was scribbling just as fast as his shaky hand could move across the paper. In a chair next to him, his wife sat, trying to read the letter over his shoulder.

Caroline sighed. "I didn't mean to cause any trouble."

"You didn't. He thinks you've been greatly wronged—which you have—and it makes him feel better about everything if he does this."

Caroline stared down at her cuticles and listened as Lord Watson's quill scratched across the paper. "Perhaps I shouldn't have stayed," she mumbled.

"Nonsense." Alex put his hand on her shoulder and pulled her closer to him. "This is just how my father is. Whether you had stayed or not, he would have still made the same jokes about my lack of being able to play pall mall, and he still would have been upset had he found out about your being denied membership."

"But he never would have found out," she pointed out.

Alex poked his lower lip out in the most overdone, mock frown imaginable and raised one shoulder. "It doesn't matter. I'm glad he did, actually. It makes him feel important to be defending you. You should take it as a compliment."

"I'm flattered," she said dryly.

Chuckling, Alex used his fingertips to massage her shoulder.

"All right," Lord Watson said tersely after he was done. "I'm going to read this out loud. Tell me what you think." He handed the quill back to Lady Watson and she quietly put it away. "'Dear,'" he looked up at Alex, "Who is the imbecile I'm writing to anyway?"

Alex waved his hand dismissively. "Just read the letter to us, then I'll tell you how to address it."

"Fine. My hand is paining me anyway. All right. Here goes. 'Dear Mr. Imbecile.'" His eyes shot up to Alex. "Perhaps I should leave it like that. What do you think?"

"If you wish," Alex said, scratching under his chin with the index finger of his free hand. "Would you just read that thing, already?"

The baron twisted his lips in the worst mock sneer Caroline had ever seen. "'Dear Mr. Imbecile, It has recently been brought to my attention you denied a young lady membership into the *Society of Biological Matters* based on her lack of a male appendage. While it grieves me that it took me so long to learn of this travesty, I wish to bring it to your attention that had I been president of the *Society* at the time, I would have denied your application due to your lack of a brain. This young lady has more intelligence in her little finger than you do in your whole body. I think you realized she was of higher intelligence than you and dismissed her because of it, which is a cowardly thing to do, making you not worthy of said male appendage which she lacked. Due to your cowardliness and despicable past behavior, I request you withdraw your membership post haste. The *Society* was created to allow a place where people could come to discuss matters of biology, not inflate a self-important idiot's brain-box by denying membership to those of a higher function. Yours, Edward Banks, Baron Watson'."

Hand clamped tightly over her mouth so not to give into the urge to laugh, Caroline peeked over at Alex. He had a thin smile on his lips, as did his mother.

"You don't need to send that," Caroline forced herself to say, fanning her flaming face and trying diligently to keep her lips closed and her laughter contained.

"Nonsense." The baron took the quill and ink from his wife's hands. "I'm sending it today. Alex can post it just as soon as I write this pompous coward's name down. Now what is his name?" He turned his pale blue eyes to Alex.

"It's rather difficult to spell. Perhaps I should spell it aloud for you so there's not a mistake."

The baron sent his son an annoyed look. "Well, get on with it," he said tightly. "I want this franked and sent with today's post."

Alex nodded. He then spelled out every letter of his full name, pausing for nearly ten seconds between each letter and space.

"Was that it?" the baron asked agitatedly. "I thought I was going to pass away several times when you kept pausing. Really, son, the man's name doesn't sound so difficult. Long, perhaps, but I didn't find anything unusual. Except the 'X'. But that's not so unusual, even your name has an 'X' in it." He frowned and his eyes shot to his paper. His lips moved as he read the words he'd just written. His eyes snapped back to Alex. "It was you?"

"That's right, Father, I'm the self-important, cowardly imbecile who rejected Caroline due to her sex."

Caroline's heart squeezed. She wanted to reach over to touch him in some way to help reassure him. But she couldn't be so affectionate with a gentleman she hardly knew. It wasn't done. Instead, she kept her hands in her lap and flashed him a weak smile.

"Why would you do that?" Alex's father snapped.

Alex ground his teeth. "I'm not at liberty to say."

"Why the blazes not?" Lord Watson demanded hotly. His face grew dark red and he had to reach for his handkerchief again to cover his mouth and nose while he hacked.

Alex waited for his father's coughing to subside before he

answered. "I was asked not to," he said simply.

"By whom?" Lord Watson took the words straight from Caroline's mouth. Who could possibly have wanted her to not be allowed to join?

Alex shook his head. "I really don't wish to discuss this. I've apologized to Caroline already and I'll do so again, but I don't want to make this worse."

"Make it worse?" his father echoed. "How could you possibly do that?"

"Trust me, I could."

"I don't believe it." The older man crossed his arms. "Did her uncle know about this?"

Alex looked at Caroline for an extended second and squeezed her shoulder, an apology for something she didn't understand in his eyes. "Yes, he knew. He's the one who asked me to have Caroline and Lady Olivia turned out."

"Excuse me?" Caroline and the baron said in harmony.

Alex sighed. "A few years ago Lord Sinclair caught me outside my tailor's in London and asked me to have Caroline and Lady Olivia banned from attending the meetings. I explained I couldn't do that. I told him the *Society* was open to all patrons and I didn't have the authority to turn them out for any reason. I told him he'd have to forbid them from going if he didn't want them to attend. He was relentless about it though, claiming I would be doing a favor for my father's closest friend. He pursued me every afternoon for a week before I finally agreed."

"And you used the excuse of their sex for what reason?" Lady Watson asked quietly, surprising them all. With the exception of getting a quill and paper for her husband, she'd practically faded into the wallpaper for the past ten minutes.

Alex met her gaze and swallowed hard. "Lord Sinclair asked me to reject them without them knowing he was the one who requested it. I had no doubt in my mind Lady Olivia didn't have the intelligence to stay and would have rejected her on the basis of not having enough knowledge on the subject, but the problem was Caroline. To be honest, I didn't know what Caroline did or didn't know about biology, and it would have seemed suspicious if I had to deny them for different reasons."

"So you picked their sex," Alex's mother said tartly.

"Well, yes." He crossed his arms. "It was the only thing they both shared that nobody else did. At the time we had no other ladies in attendance. Besides, many organizations are only open to gentlemen. I didn't see a problem with it." He locked gazes with Caroline. "As I said, I'm very sorry. I would never have done that if I hadn't been pressed."

Bile burned the back of her throat. How could Uncle Joseph have done this to her? He may not have spoiled her the way he had Olivia, but he'd never intentionally been cruel. Or so she'd thought. She nodded numbly to let Alex know she had at least heard his words.

"I just don't believe it," the baron said, sighing. "Did he say why?"

"No." Alex solemnly shook his head. "I asked, but he wouldn't say."

Lord Watson shook his head. "It just doesn't make sense that he'd brag about her to me one minute, then do something like this." He ran his hands through his unkempt hair the same way Alex always did. "And he never gave any indication as to why?"

"No, he didn't." Alex shifted in his seat. "I have my suspicions, but he never said, so I don't know for sure."

"Well, since the man isn't here for us to ask, your suspicions are as good as we've got. Spit it out, boy," his father urged.

Caroline's ears perked up. She was just as interested in hearing this as Alex's father seemed to be.

Alex's body stiffened next to her and his breathing grew labored. "I don't know for sure," he began slowly, "but I think it had something to do with Rupert Griffin joining the *Society* at the meeting prior."

His words made a wave of nausea pass through her like she'd never experienced before. It had been years since she'd heard the name of the horrifically vile man who dared call himself her father. She'd thought he'd been dead all this time. Apparently not. Apparently he was alive and well, and she'd even been in the same room with him only four short years ago when she'd attended her first, and only, meeting for the *Society of Biological Matters*.

Suddenly gratitude for Uncle Joseph washed over her. He'd

had the foresight to have her thrown out of the *Society* in a way that not only didn't expose him as the force behind it, but also didn't expose her to the knowledge of her father's presence still on this earth. She hadn't been this thankful for him since he and a stranger had rescued her in the dead of night from Rupert's evil clutches.

Silence filled the room, and Caroline stared at her white knuckles.

"You're likely right, Alex," Lord Watson acknowledged at last, his voice so quiet there was no doubt in her mind the baron knew just who Rupert Griffin was to her.

"I should probably be going now," Caroline whispered, still not daring to look up from her lap.

Alex shifted and pulled out his pocket watch. "You're right."

Caroline used the arm of the settee for support as she tried to stand on her shaky legs.

"Are you all right?" Alex asked, steadying her as he stood up next to her.

"Yes," she said weakly, trying to hold onto every shred of dignity she had left. She looked at him, and where she expected to see disgust or disapproval, concern and tenderness were present instead. Her breath caught. Either he didn't know, or he didn't seem to care. She swallowed and chanced a glance at his parents. Then just as quickly, she jerked her gaze away.

"Caroline," Alex's father said a moment later.

She moved her eyes in his direction, but was not able to meet his. "My lord?"

"Don't 'my lord' me, I don't like it," he said, his lips twisting in distaste. "I wanted to ask a favor of you, if I might."

She nodded. "Of course, anything."

He scratched his jaw. "Well, you see, one of my greatest friends may have done something some might consider ungentlemanly. I'd hate for such a thing to be known about him. And I'd like to know his secret is safe with you." He paused, not long enough for her to reply, but long enough for her to see the earnest look in his eyes. "In return for your silence on this matter, I'll give you the assurance that any secret I may ever happen to learn about you will never pass my lips."

Tears welled up in her eyes as she comprehended his meaning. He knew. He knew everything there was to know about her past and he wasn't judging her for it. Whether he'd been so cryptic about telling her this for the sake of her pride or because there was a chance Alex didn't know, she wasn't sure. She honestly didn't care. All she cared was that her secrets were safe with the baron. "Your friend's secret is safe with me," she said weakly.

Lord Watson nodded and winked at her. "Very good. What about my son's? He acted far more ungentlemanly, I must say. I'd say you could spread that rumor about him, but I'm afraid it might tarnish my good name, too."

Despite herself, a hint of a smile crossed lips. "I'll keep his secret, too, I suppose. I'd hate ungentlemanly behavior to be associated with the Banks name."

"Phew, I'm relieved," the baron said, wiping the back of his hand across his forehead. "Now I won't have to live out my last days in the shame of my son's transgressions."

Alex scoffed. "I never caused you the level of embarrassment most sons have."

"You're right," his father conceded thoughtfully. "You've been an excellent son. Would you mind coming back to talk to me a minute after you see the beautiful Caroline to her carriage?"

"Yes, Father. Wait here a moment, Caroline, I'll be right back. I need to go order your carriage and send for your maid or we'll have to wait a few minutes downstairs." He quickly slipped out the door, leaving her alone with his parents.

Alex's mother walked over to her to say goodbye. Caroline met her steady gaze and saw the same thing in her eyes she'd seen in Lord Watson's: compassion. They didn't pity her, nor did they hold her in contempt.

A few silent minutes passed before Alex came back and walked her down the stairs. "Are you sure you're all right?" he asked, stopping outside the front door and turning to face her.

"Yes," she said, not meeting his eyes.

He sighed. "I didn't want you to know any of that. Your uncle didn't do it to hurt you. There's more to it, something you don't know." His eyes moved up and down her face. "Caroline, please don't hold a grudge against either of us about this."

"I'm not," she said truthfully. She was thankful to each of them for their roles in protecting her from Rupert.

"Are you sure?"

"Yes."

"Good." He escorted her to her carriage and stopped her before she could step on the first stair. "Do you think it might be all right if I came by to see you tomorrow?"

"Why?" she blurted, blinking. He was Olivia's intended, he should be calling on her, not Caroline.

"We ran out of time to talk of the campaign like I promised. And seeing as how my past is riddled with ungentlemanly behavior, I need to mend my ways, starting with keeping my promises." He tucked a tendril of her hair behind her ear.

"I suppose that's acceptable," she said with a rueful shake of her head. Alex Banks, or Arid Alex as the rest of England referred to him due to his unfailing gentlemanly behavior, was the furthest thing from ungentlemanly.

"Excellent," he said, helping her ascend the steps to the carriage. When she reached the top, he didn't release her hand immediately. Instead, he stood at the bottom of the steps and pressed a searing kiss to the top of her knuckles. "Until tomorrow."

***

Alex whistled as he walked back to his father's room. His courtship with Caroline was off to an excellent start. She didn't seem too terribly put off by his father, which, he must admit, was a good sign.

"I've returned."

"I see that," Father said before choking down another one of Cook's nasty tonics.

Alex plopped down longways on the settee he'd earlier sat on with Caroline. He propped up his feet on the end and gritted his teeth in anticipation while he waited for his father to speak about the unspeakable topic Alex knew he was about to be forced to discuss.

"Is she the one, son?"

"The one?" Alex echoed in shock. He hadn't expected to come back in here to talk about Caroline.

His father threw the covers off his thin legs. "You know, the one you want to marry instead of Lady Olivia."

"That's my hope."

"Mine as well." Father reached down to adjust his stocking. "She seems a good match for you."

"Doesn't she?" he agreed, crossing his ankles and carelessly knocking the sides of his boots together. "We practically enjoy all the same things. Except lawn games. I still detest those. But she likes to study science. That's far more important."

Father shook his head. "Son, I know you like science—and hell, so do I—but after I married your mother, I learned there's a lot more to life than case studies and experiments."

Alex blinked at him. He knew there was more to life; he just wasn't interested in discovering it.

Scrubbing his face, Father said, "I think you'll find there's more to enjoy in life if you stop thinking with that overworked brain of yours all the time."

"And what should I think with?" Alex asked, grinning. He threaded his fingers together behind his head, then leaned his head back and closed his eyes.

"Learn to rely on feelings and emotions a bit more," his father said, a slight edge to his voice.

Alex frowned. "So you're saying I should let my heart lead me?" That was no better than Andrew's stupid suggestion of taking Caroline to the orangery and letting his instincts take over.

"Yes," his father agreed. "Think more with your heart. And with an organ that resides about eighteen inches lower."

Alex's eyes snapped open and his jaw dropped. "I can't believe it," he said after he'd recovered from his slight shock.

"Believe it, my boy. I am actually encouraging you to think with the head that possesses no brain. Not a lot, mind you. Just every once in a while. You'll be surprised at how much it will enrich your life."

Alex nodded mutely. This was the most bizarre conversation they'd ever had. This even outdid the awkwardness from the time four years ago when he'd been eating in the breakfast room, and without even a word of greeting, Father had walked in and asked Alex if he was still a virgin. "I'll not do anything to bring shame to Caroline," he said defensively.

"Good. I didn't ask you to. Her uncle was my friend, after all. I think he—and she—deserves far more respect than that. What I'm trying to say is you think too much. You analyze everything to the point that you overlook, and sometimes ruin, so many things. If you'd allow something else to enter the equation, you might find you like what you see."

"And you think I'm going to accomplish that by thinking with my genitals more often?"

"Absolutely," Father agreed heartily. "But not too much. Thinking too much with a man's John Thomas can only lead him into trouble."

"Yes, that I can imagine," Alex murmured, closing his eyes again.

"You don't believe me," Father said, his voice quiet. "Look at me, boy."

Alex respectfully opened his eyes and sat right on the settee. He may be nearly thirty and his father nearly to his grave, but they both knew to whom respect was still due. "I believe you."

"No, you don't. I can see it by the look on your face." Father crossed his arms. "Look at your friend Andrew. Do you think it was his brain that got Brooke to be his countess? No, it was the randy urges associated with his St. Peter. Which is also why those two seem to be so happy together—"

"And why she's breeding all the time," Alex mumbled under his breath.

"That, too," Father agreed, winking at Alex when his eyes went wide. "I heard you. Just because I'm dying doesn't mean I'm in need of an ear horn."

Alex sighed. "You forget. Those two are the exception, not the rule."

"That may be true, but they're not the only ones." Father picked up a glass of water and took a large swallow. "Love before, or after, marriage is rare, I grant you. But it can happen. However, mutual respect and companionship are more likely to happen, which can be enough."

"What can be enough?" Uncle John asked, peeking his head in the bedroom door.

"Mutual respect and companionship within a marriage,"

Father quickly informed him.

His uncle blinked at both of them. "Why are the two of you discussing marriage? You're not thinking of letting Edwina marry so soon, are you?"

"No, not Edwina. Alex is getting married within the month," Father said proudly.

Uncle John turned to Alex. "Congratulations, Alex. I must have missed the announcement."

"That's because there wasn't one," Alex bit off, shoving one of his mother's throw pillows behind his back for comfort.

"Oh," his uncle said, sitting in a chair across the room. "And who is the bride?"

"Miss Caroline Sinclair," Alex said quickly before his father could even *suggest* Lady Olivia.

"He hopes," Father said without a hint of humor in his voice.

"He hopes?" Uncle John's curious gaze darted back and forth between the two.

Father shrugged, making the sleeve of his nightshirt slip to the edge of his bony shoulder. "He hopes she'll agree to marry him."

"But you just said he's getting married within the month," Uncle John countered.

"He is," Father agreed. "Either to Caroline or Lady Olivia."

Uncle John made a choking noise and his eyes nearly popped out of his head. "What have you done?" he asked with all the authority of a man who'd been a minister to troubled souls for slightly less than thirty years.

"*I* didn't do anything. He did," Alex accused sourly, jabbing a finger in his father's direction.

"What my son means to say is, at one point in time I might have agreed to a betrothal between Alex and Lady Olivia," Father said innocently.

"*You what?*" Uncle John's face turned so pale Alex thought his uncle might faint.

"I have no need to defend myself to you, little brother. The facts are I made the agreement, and Alex has until his thirtieth birthday to either find another bride or marry Lady Olivia."

"And you waited this long?" Uncle John asked, turning his piercing blue eyes back on Alex.

"Not intentionally, I assure you," Alex said irritably. "I didn't even know of this confounded agreement until a couple of days ago."

"For goodness' sake, Edward, why did you wait so long to tell him?" Uncle John burst out. "He's not Andrew. He cannot meet and marry a young lady in less than a fortnight." His uncle leaned his head forward and tapped his fingers against his temples.

"Oh, hush up, John," Father told his brother. "He may not be as slimy as two of your three sons-in-law, but he isn't incapable of finding a bride, either."

"Well, that's good news," his uncle said a bit sarcastically. He looked at Alex and swallowed. "I'm going to say something that had better never leave this room. Understand?"

"Of course," Alex agreed.

"I'd rather go on a platform before all of England proclaiming my love and admiration for both Andrew and Benjamin than be any kind of relation to Lady Olivia."

Alex bit the inside of his cheek so he wouldn't ruin his uncle's glory by pointing out that even if Alex married Caroline, they'd all still be *some* relation to Lady Olivia. Instead, he nodded.

"Do *whatever* it takes not to marry that wretched young lady," Uncle John continued. "Lie, cheat, steal, beg, or barter if you must. Just do whatever it takes so I do not have to share a last name with that awful creature." He shuddered. "As much as it irritates me to suggest this, ask Andrew for advice. He seemed to have no difficulty meeting, ruining, and marrying my daughter in hardly any time at all."

Alex dropped his gaze to the floor. He didn't exactly wish to admit he'd already done that and had been given terrible advice.

"That's what I suggested," Father piped in.

"No, it's not," Alex said, shaking his head. "You said nothing about asking Andrew about his strategy. You told me to stop thinking with my brain and make my decisions with my—" He broke off abruptly when he remembered there was a minister in the room.

"Tallywag," Father supplied for him, garnering a snicker from his brother.

"You think *that's* funny?" Alex asked his protestant minister uncle.

Uncle John shrugged. "I'm used to it. I grew up with him. He may be six years my senior, but I was not immune from hearing his tasteless remarks. You know he only says half the things he says and does half the things he does for a reaction. And, my dear nephew, he seems to have gotten the reaction he desired from you."

Alex shook his head. His entire family was insane, there was nothing else for it. "You're not used to it," Alex said suddenly. "Just last year, he shocked you when he asked Paul a rather personal question about his relationship with your youngest daughter."

His uncle snorted. "It wasn't the words that shocked me. I was merely surprised he'd been so bold as to ask the poor man such a question in front of a room full of people."

Father and Alex both shook their heads. "Say what you wish, brother, you were not merely surprised. You looked furious. Which, don't get me wrong, I do understand. I would be rather uncomfortable in your position, too. But someone had to ask the man, he wasn't offering up any useful information."

Raising his hands, Uncle John said, "All right, I admit I was shocked. But not nearly as shocked as Paul." He smiled. "My discomfort was a small price to pay for the look on that man's face. He and I had previously had several awkward conversations privately, but none quite like that."

"While I'm glad I could be of help to you in making your son-in-law squirm," Father drawled, shifting back against his pillows. "This talk of making others uncomfortable does nothing in helping Alex in his quest of a bride."

Alex tensed. Did even his own father think him incapable of anything but studying? Everyone else did. He just hoped at least one person could see him as more than that. He stood. "While I've enjoyed listening to your invaluable advice about letting my privates lead my decisions, I must be going."

Father sighed. "That's not what I said. I hope you don't leave this room only remembering that. I said to rely on your feelings and think with other parts of your body." He made a sound of aggravation and ran his hand through his hair, pulling it before letting it go. "Alex, ladies are told they're not supposed to enjoy certain attentions from a man. But they do. Or they can, if it's done right." He took another swig of water. "What I'm trying to tell you is I think you'll have better success if you quit being so damned logical all the time."

"He has a point," Uncle John said quietly, steepling his hands in front of him. "As much as I don't like to think about my children in such a manner, all three of my daughters seem very happy with their husbands. I'd be blind if I didn't see the affection passed between them and their husbands."

"Yes, you would have to be blind," Father retorted with a snort. "For pity's sake, John, in less than two years you've managed to marry off all three of your daughters, gain two grandchildren, and you have two more on the way."

His brother smiled brightly. "You're right. I'll admit, I think you're right about where their happiness stems from. *And* I'm big enough to admit that even if I didn't approve of two of my three daughters' husbands at first, I am very pleased with how everything turned out."

"See?" Father said smugly. "I was right."

"Well, none of this will even matter if Caroline doesn't wish to marry me. I'll not force my attentions on her," Alex repeated firmly. "We'll not be forced to marry due to a scandal." His statement struck a nerve with his uncle, Alex just didn't care. He had no wish to bring shame to Caroline. It wasn't her fault his father had stupidly made a betrothal agreement; therefore, he couldn't see any reason to expose her to public censure.

"That's fine," Father said testily. "I'm just giving you a bit of advice I'd wished my father had given me. My marriage was arranged for me. However, I was fortunate to be paired with your mother. You're not going to be so fortunate with Lady Olivia." The sour look on his face that accompanied his words made a wicked idea form in Alex's brain.

"You never know, we just might suit," he drawled with a shrug.

Father's eyes narrowed. "You wouldn't."

He leaned against the doorjamb. "I just might have to. It was a binding contract you signed, wasn't it?"

"That was a foolish mistake on my part. But it can be rectified if you marry another. You still have nearly a month."

Alex shoved his hand in his pocket and ran his thumb around the edge of his pocket watch. "Yes, but you seem doubtful in my ability to find another bride. Perhaps I should just resign myself to the idea of making Olivia my bride, and one day Baroness Watson. If I post the banns today, we could have the wedding on my birthday."

"Son, stop talking," Father croaked. "You have no idea what marriage to that harpy would be like."

Alex bit back a smile at the twin expressions of what he interpreted to be horror that had come over the other men's faces. Schooling his features to look impassive, he said, "Aren't all females the same in the dark?"

A gagging, choking, strangled sound emerged from father's throat. "Hell, no. And how can you even think of bedding her?"

He couldn't, but he wasn't about to admit to them that in the event he was forced to marry her, he'd not even come close to consummating the marriage. Elijah could inherit Alex's title upon his death for all Alex cared. "Don't I owe it to the barony to secure an heir?" he drawled, willing his stomach to calm down.

"Elijah or Elijah's son can inherit," Father said tightly. "I want to sleep soundly in my grave, not spin in circles at the gut wrenching possibility of any spawn of Lady Olivia getting my title."

"Who knows, Edward, he might only have girls. I did," Uncle John said, rubbing his forearm like he was suffering a chill.

"That's possible," Father said excitedly. "Perhaps you should just assume Lady Olivia is unable to give you a son and stay away from her bedchamber."

"I'm not a monk. I'm not about to make a vow of eternal celibacy. And you never know, the nights might get cold, and I might get lonely," Alex replied as smoothly as he could while trying not to choke on his own tongue.

Father crossed his arms. "There are precautions a man can take."

"But why would I do that?"

"So she doesn't conceive," Father said as if he were talking to a simpleton.

Alex made his eyes go wide. "But I might want children, you know? And what of you? You seem awfully jealous of Uncle John and the fact he's been made a grandfather nearly four times over. Wouldn't you love a little plump, flame-haired, freckle-faced urchin to dandle on your knee while he—or she—caterwauls and screams at you to tell another story?"

"Oh, Alex, please stop. That mental image is going to give me nightmares," Father said, pushing on his eyes with the tips of his fingers.

Uncle John laughed. "At least my grandchildren are attractive. Their fathers may be scoundrels, but at least they're handsome scoundrels."

Father laid his head down on his pillow and sighed. "It really doesn't matter. We all know I won't be around to see any of my grandchildren, no matter who the parents."

A hush fell on the room as everyone contemplated the reality of his words. It was true he wouldn't be around to meet any of his grandchildren. But he would likely be around to see who Alex married. At the least, he could go to his grave in peace, knowing his title would be passed to a decent sort, preferably the son Alex created with Caroline.

Alex moved to the door. "Rest well, Father. I've not given up hope on Caroline."

Chapter 9

Caroline slipped out the servants' door and walked down the path that led down to the storage shed where her telescope was presently stored. After the uncomfortable end to yesterday's visit at Alex's, she honestly didn't expect him to call on her today. She assumed he only asked to be polite. She stopped walking. When had she ever been told of Alex Banks saying something only to be polite? Never. He was polite of course, and always a perfect gentleman, but she'd never heard rumors of him only saying something out of politeness and not following through. She glanced at the house before shrugging and continuing her walk to the shed. If he really was coming, he could speak to Marcus while he waited for her to come back. Right now she had no desire to go back in that house.

Olivia had been on a tirade ever since she'd gotten in the carriage in Bath. She'd ranted on and on about how it was all Caroline's fault her foot was broken and how the bath had done nothing to heal it. Caroline let her words fly in one ear then immediately tumble out the other as she stared out the window and prayed they'd get home soon.

This morning, Olivia wanted to whine and complain about her blasted wedding to Arid Alex again, and Caroline could take it no more. She no longer was only irritated when Olivia spoke about him and marriage to him that way; she'd also discovered she had a slight pain in her chest as well. A slight pain she had no business feeling. Alex was Olivia's intended, not hers. She shouldn't be entertaining any thoughts about him unless directly related to their experiment—pardon, campaign—or the fact he was about to be her cousin's husband. Anything else was not for her to think of.

A strong gust of wind caught Caroline's skirts and she nearly tripped. Righting herself, she swallowed an unladylike phrase she'd like to direct at Olivia. If it weren't for Olivia, her telescope wouldn't be stored in the shed. And if her telescope wasn't in the shed, she wouldn't presently be outside being blown about. But her telescope was in the shed, which was actually the safest place for it as far as Caroline was concerned.

A few years ago Uncle Joseph had allowed her to set it up in the drawing room. The location was perfect for Caroline to stargaze from the warmth of the house. The location also seemed to be an ideal place for Olivia to use the telescope to hang flower pots, dirty stockings, drying laundry, or anything else she could find around the house to drape over it. Caroline repeatedly asked her not to, and as usual, her request was ignored. She would have moved the telescope to her room and been done with it, but the only window in her room had a giant tree just outside it. Marcus had offered to have a building erected for it. She'd refused, of course. It was one thing to rely on him and his family for her basic needs. She couldn't possibly accept something so extravagant from him. Therefore, she'd resigned herself to allowing it to be stored in the shed.

"Wait," a man's voice called from behind her, halting her steps and speeding up the pace of her heart.

"Alex! What are you doing here?"

He smiled at her. "I asked if it was all right to come by. You said I could. So here I am."

She blushed. He'd really come! "Yes, I remember the conversation."

"Good. What are you doing out here?"

She shot a quick glance at the storage shed and bit her lip. "Getting my telescope," she said at last, hoping he'd not object to her getting it out by herself.

"Why? It's not quite noon." He leaned with his shoulder against the side of the building.

"I know. It's for tonight. If my math is correct, there's to be a lunar eclipse tonight." She shook off the dirt that had blown onto her green skirt.

He nodded. "Your math is correct. But you don't need a telescope to see the eclipse, you know." His mouth was bent in a smile that took the starch right out of her knees.

"I know that," she said defensively. "I just wanted to look at the constellations and planets while I waited for it."

"I can understand that," he said, looking around. "Where is it?"

"What?"

"Your scope."

She pointed one finger to the shed. "In there."

He blinked at her. "You store it in the shed?"

"No. Yes." She cleared her throat. "It's safer than in the house."

"I can understand why," he muttered, moving his hands to the lock. "Where's the key?"

"I have it. What are you doing?"

He held his hand out with his palm up. "I'm going to get it out for you."

"I'll get it," she said quickly, tightening her grip around the key. There was no way she was going to allow him in that disastrous shed.

He frowned. "I've a lot of ungentlemanly behavior to make up for as far as you're concerned. Let me demonstrate my good manners by getting your scope."

"No." Caroline shook her head wildly. That shed was offensive, to say the least. Olivia didn't believe in throwing *anything* away. Ever. That shed was full of all sorts of odd and ends from Olivia's past. Most of which amounted to broken or stray pieces of outdoor games, torn paint canvases, ripped or broken furniture, outgrown clothes, and anything else Olivia couldn't bear to part with for some sentimental purpose or another.

"Why not?" he asked, crossing his arms and blocking the door.

"Alex, please, if there was ever a time not to ask questions, this might be it."

He didn't budge.

She sighed. "That shed has a lot of personal things of Olivia's, and she'd be unhappy if she knew you'd been in there."

He looked like he didn't believe her at first. "Very well. But as soon as you get your scope out of there, I'm going to carry it for you. No arguments."

"Agreed."

Alex moved out of her way and she unlocked the door, simultaneously sending up a prayer pleading that everything would not fall out as soon as she opened the door. Slowly, she cracked the door just far enough to be able to go slip in and said a prayer of thanksgiving when nothing fell out.

Pushing her way inside, she paused a minute and let her eyes adjust to the dimly lit little room. Three of the walls were solid brick and mortar, but the far wall had a window that was about two feet tall and ran the length of the wall.

"This is a mess," she muttered, squinting at the giant pile of junk that was heaped in the little space.

She did a quick scan of the shed to find her telescope and sighed. Of course her telescope was over in the back corner. Where else had she expected it to be? The front? No. That would be too convenient and heaven forbid Olivia allow Caroline to get to her telescope without having to work for it. She bit her lip. Perhaps she should just go fetch a footman to dig it out for her. She shook her head. She was already here. Besides, if she left the shed now, Alex would insist *he'd* get it for her, and the last thing she wanted was for him to see the inside of this shed.

"Need any help?" Alex called impatiently from outside.

"No," she said, stepping over a broken easel. "I've got it."

She lifted her leg as high as she could so as not to knock over a stack of moldy, leather-bound tomes. Sadly, her hard work was for naught and the heavy fabric of her skirts sent them tumbling as she lowered her foot back to the rubbish pile on the other side of the stack. "Good gracious," she said between clenched teeth as she tried to yank her skirt out from under the books that had just fallen on it.

"Caroline, are you sure you don't wish for any help? I couldn't care less about seeing your cousin's tokens of her girlhood," Alex said loudly.

"I'm almost done, I promise," she lied, wishing it was the truth. She turned her attention back to her skirt which was now trapped under what used to be a not-so-tidy stack of ruined books. She needed to get free. Clutching a fistful of her skirt, she jerked a little harder than necessary—partly because of haste, partly from pure irritation. The jerk did not free her skirt; instead, she lost her balance and gave a high pitched yelp as she collapsed on top of the junk.

"I heard that," Alex said tightly, opening the door. "Hell's afire, Caroline. You could have been seriously hurt digging around in this rubbish." He walked over to where she was lying and picked her up with more care than she imaged him capable of. He set her down on a somewhat flat area and kept his arm wrapped around her for support. "Where's the scope."

She inclined her chin a notch to stave off her extreme embarrassment. "In the corner."

His eyes went to the corner. "I see it. You wait outside and I'll get it."

"No. I'll help," she protested.

"No, you'll wait outside. Now."

She sighed. "Fine. But please leave the drape on it until you get it outside. I don't want it to get scratched."

He nodded.

Caroline stood outside the shed and waited, trying not to smile or grimace as she listened to Alex mumbling phrases she couldn't quite make out, but somehow knew they were inappropriate nonetheless. Two minutes later, he emerged holding her telescope over his head, one hand on the tube of the telescope and the other supporting it at the base where it attached to the tripod.

"Thank you," she said, blushing. She wasn't an extremely neat person, but she'd be deathly embarrassed if he thought she kept her things that way.

"No problem," he said, setting her telescope down with care. "Have you ever heard the term blivet?"

Caroline stood frozen and stared at him. She knew what a *blight* was. She gave her head a little shake. That's probably what he said. "I believe so, yes."

He cocked one eyebrow at her. "Is that so? My father used to use that term, I always assumed he'd made it up," he informed her quietly, untying the ties at the bottom of the drape. "When I was a boy, my father would come into my room and look around at all my specimens and instruments and say, 'Boy, this room is a blivet.' I just thought he was saying my room was a mess. Then, when I was about fifteen, my father came to visit me at Eton during the middle of the term. He walked into the room Marcus and I were sharing, let out a low whistle and said, 'Boys, this room is a blivet and a half.' Marcus looked bewildered and I was about to explain to him Father thought our room was a mess, but just as I got my mouth open, my father shook his head and said, 'Marcus, a blivet is when a man has a box or a bag that is designed to hold five pounds worth of stuff and he tries to shove ten pounds worth of stuff into it instead. And you boys are trying to shove fifteen pounds into this five pound room.'"

Caroline smiled. "I can only imagine what you two boys had in that room."

He shook his head. "I bet you can't."

"You're probably right," she agreed, watching as he untied the last tie. "So are you trying to say that shed is a blivet, Mr. Banks?"

"No," he said earnestly. "Nor is it a blivet and a half. It's two."

She burst into laughter. "I tried to spare you."

"I know. But it didn't matter in the end. I still had to come in to rescue you." He smiled at her in a way that made her heart double its pace. "Now, are you going to uncover this thing or what?"

She proudly walked up to her telescope, grabbed the top of the drape, and pulled it off, letting the cloth fall to the ground beside them.

"I know Marcus was never interested in astronomy," Alex commented, running his fingers along the side of the scope tube that was facing him. "Every once in a while he'd come ask me to show him a constellation or planet. Knowing that, and assuming he did not suddenly develop an astronomical interest since school, it begs the question of how Ridge Water ended up with a telescope that lives in a shed."

"It belonged to my mother," Caroline said proudly, beaming at him. "She used to like to stargaze. She even took me with her sometimes. When she died, my uncle bought the telescope from my father and kept it here for me to use." She shrugged. There was no sense in telling any more of the story. He could think what he wished.

"Well, it's a nice scope." He bent to peer through the eyepiece. Nodding, Caroline didn't bother to wait to hear his expert opinion on the magnification of the eyepiece. She went straight to the end so she could clean the lens of any smudges that might block her view when she tried to see the stars tonight. She pulled the hem of her sleeve down with her fingers and gasped. The blood rushed from her face and her heart hammered out of control, and all she could do was helplessly stare at the hundreds of shards of glass that made up the shattered lens. Refusing to believe what she was seeing, she numbly reached her trembling index finger forward and nearly screamed with horror as her finger confirmed her brain's assessment of the state of the lens.

"I'm sorry," Alex said solemnly as Caroline backed away, still staring motionlessly at the destroyed telescope. "I should have been more careful with it when I was bringing it out."

She shook her head. "You're a terrible liar, Alex. We both know what happened. Olivia always does things like this to me. She's the reason it was in the back corner of the shed to start with. I used it only two weeks ago. It should have been in the front. She ordered it sent to the back." Her voice cracked and she made herself stop talking and look away before the tears fell from her eyes.

"That doesn't mean..."

"Yes, it does." She swallowed convulsively. "She must have broken it herself, though. None of the servants would have ever done such a thing, even if she ordered them to."

Alex came up to stand in front of her and wrapped his surprisingly thick arms around her trembling body, pulling her against his chest. "Shhh, Caro," he crooned softly in her ear. "It'll be all right." He used the pad of his thumb to wipe away a tear that had slipped out the side of her eye.

Her body shook with sobs, and he held her close. She inwardly commanded herself to stop crying, but it was useless, her tears continued to pour, creating a large, warm stain on the front of Alex's shirt.

"I'm sorry she did that." His voice was soft and quiet. "And I know this won't fix anything, but I know of someone who has a telescope you can borrow tonight. You may not be as familiar with it as your own, but I assure you, you'll be able to see the stars all the same."

She shook her head the best she could against his hard chest. "I can't borrow someone's telescope on such short notice. It would be rude to even ask," she whispered. She drew in a ragged, shaky breath. "Besides, they may not even be willing to lend it to me."

"Yes, they would. They'd let you use it on a moment's notice, I promise." One of his big hands slowly caressed up and down her spine. "It's not portable like yours, I'm afraid, so you'll have to go somewhere else to use it. Will that be all right?"

She wiped the tears from her cheeks and bit her lip, embarrassed she'd shown such a display in front of him. She was accustomed to Olivia doing such things to her. This was nothing new. Years ago, she'd entertained thoughts of seeking revenge on Olivia for the dastardly things she'd done, but the two times she'd ever gone through with her plans it hadn't had the desired effect. Olivia just plain didn't care. Knowing Olivia would never stop doing these things hadn't eased the pain though. And now she was making a fool of herself by letting it show just how much Olivia could hurt her. "There's no need," she said, smiling weakly. "As you said earlier, I don't need a telescope to see the lunar eclipse."

"I know. But you wanted to look at the constellations, did you not?"

She nodded. "I did. But now it looks like I'll have to do that without a telescope, too." If there was one thing Caroline was, it was resilient. She'd had to develop resiliency to survive Olivia's maltreatment of her for so long.

He frowned down at her. "Are you saying you wouldn't like to use the finest telescope ever built to look at the stars tonight?"

She laughed. "It's not that. I would love to," she admitted. "But I don't think Marcus would like me to go off to some stranger's house and use his telescope."

"Ah, I see," Alex said slowly, nodding. He rolled his eyes upward toward the sky. "And what if this wasn't a stranger's house you were going to? Would that be all right?"

"I don't know." She used the tip of her right index finger to wipe beneath her eyes before returning her hand to Alex's broad shoulder.

He pulled her closer. "If I can get Marcus' approval, would you be willing to go?"

"Go where?" a shrill voice asked, making Caroline's body stiffen up like a fire poker.

"Lady Olivia," Alex said sharply.

"Mr. Banks, Caroline," Olivia said archly. "I strongly advise you to get your thrice-mended gloves off my betrothed, Caroline."

Caroline flushed. Alex still had his arms around her, and her head was resting on his chest with her hands braced on his wide shoulders. "I...uh..."

"Don't bother, Caroline," Olivia snapped, her green, squinty eyes full of fury. "Release him now, and do not even *think* of touching him again. I'll not be made a fool by having it spouted my husband is carrying on an affair with my whore of a cousin."

Stung, Caroline's mouth worked fruitlessly to form an answer.

"Have no fear, Lady Olivia," Alex began in a hard voice Caroline had never heard him use before. "Such rumors will never be spoken. I'll not be having an affair with my bride's cousin. My affections will be solely for my wife. Which, contrary to what you may believe, will not be you."

Olivia sucked in a hard breath and her hand slapped her bosom so hard the noise made Caroline wince. "I'll sue you for breach of contract!"

"Try it," he said with a simple shrug. "You'll lose."

Olivia gritted her teeth and pulled her lips back into a snarl. Her gaze dropped to Caroline's telescope and a smile so sweet it made Caroline's stomach clench spread across her face. "I see you found the surprise I left for you."

"I did." Caroline's body went numb all over again. "I'd say you should expect to find a similar surprise soon, but since I consider myself to be above such tasteless tactics, you won't."

Frowning, Olivia shook her head. "You're no fun."

Alex went rigid, his eyes hard. "You think it's fun to destroy other people's things?"

"Yes. It's a game we play." Olivia blinked her eyelashes at him in a way Caroline had once seen a woman of ill repute do to a gentleman she was talking to on the street.

"I see," Alex cut in smoothly. "And what of yours did you have in mind for Caroline to destroy?"

Olivia shrugged as if she didn't have a care in the world. "I honestly don't give a fig what she does," she answered airily.

He ground his teeth. "All right. I think I understand it all better now. Your dislike for Caroline is so fierce you wouldn't care what she did to you as long as you hurt her more."

"Something like that," Olivia said, nodding and smiling. "We understand each other very well, Mr. Banks."

"We don't understand each other at all," he spat. "The only reason I understood your true motive is because I know Caroline well enough to know she has a lot for you to be jealous of."

"Of her!" Olivia shrieked. "Never. She's not even a lady."

"She's more of a lady than you'll ever be." Alex's voice remained even and cool as he spoke. "You might outrank her with your courtesy title of Lady right now, but I'd be willing to bet every piece of science equipment I own that one day Caroline will have a real title—one that she'll gain from her husband."

A low whistle sounded from around the corner of the shed. "Now, that's quite a wager, ladies," Marcus said, limping over to them. "I've never known Alex to part with even the smallest, most insignificant piece of his equipment." He looked at each of the three. "And to be honest, I'd never bet against him."

Alex and Marcus exchanged a glance Caroline couldn't see. "No, I don't part easily with anything that's mine. Consequently, I'd like to depart company with your sister, post haste."

Marcus gave a curt nod in Alex's direction. "That can be arranged. Olivia, I need to speak to you in my study about the drawer full of purple cravats I was greeted by this morning when I went to dress."

Olivia cackled. "Oh, that was Emma."

"No, it wasn't." Marcus clamped his jaw tight and grasped hold of Olivia's elbow. "She'd never do such a thing. You, however, would. I've told you before what will happen if you keep..." His words continued to flow, but just not to Caroline's ears as the two of them walked away.

Caroline sighed. She truly pitied Marcus. What could a gentleman in his position do with a problem such as Olivia? Send her away, she supposed. But Marcus was too tenderhearted to subject all the poor, unsuspecting souls living at the asylum to Olivia and her dreadfulness.

"You never answered me," Alex said abruptly, squeezing her affectionately. All the tenderness from earlier filled his voice once again.

She blinked. "About what?"

"Using the finest telescope in England to stargaze with tonight," he said, grinning. "If I can talk Marcus into it, that is."

It took her less than two seconds to weigh her options of spending the night here with a very irate Olivia, or being anywhere else, looking at the stars through what Alex claimed to be the best telescope in the country. "I'd love to," she said.

"Excellent. How about if I come back by and pick you up at seven?"

She nodded. "Wait a second, Alex. I forgot to ask. Whose estate am I going to, and whose telescope am I borrowing?" It was nice he was arranging this for her, but she still needed to know where she was going and whose generosity she was imposing on.

He took her hand in his and led her toward the house. "You have to ask?"

"Yes," she said, knitting her brows.

He shook his head. "And here I thought my reputation preceded me," he mumbled under his breath. "Darling Caro, you will be spending the night at my family's estate, and we will be using my scope."

Chapter 10

With a stroke of luck, a bit of convincing, and perhaps a few evasive sentences that might be considered misleading, Alex gained Marcus' approval for Caroline to come stargazing at his estate. He had only a second's worth of guilt about purposefully withholding information from Marcus. While it was true his mother would be there, she just wouldn't be *there*. Instead of chaperoning Alex and Caroline, she'd be sleeping soundly in her bed, blissfully unaware the two were together.

After making a quick stop on his way, Alex rode home to get ready for Caroline's visit tonight. First, he wanted to go over his notes regarding his experiment. After that, he'd get the gazebo that housed the telescope ready.

He dropped his tall frame into a leather wingback chair behind his desk in the library. To his right was a drawer where he kept the notes to his unfinished experiments. He slid it open and reached to the bottom of the stack. Locating the paper he was looking for, he pulled it out and set it on his desk.

He grabbed a quill, inked it, and got poised to update his experiment notes wherever necessary as his eyes scanned the paper:

OBJECTIVE(S): Avoid marriage to Lady Olivia at all costs, including, but not limited to, finding a tart from Lady Bird's brothel at the last minute if necessary. Marry Caroline instead(?). If able to fulfill latter objective, marriage to Caroline, that will fulfill objective listed above without requiring a soiled dove.

HYPOTHESIS: Marriage to Caroline.

RESEARCH: Attached are three case studies of hasty

marriages. The basis of the studies was: remarkable admiration and affection were poured out upon the young ladies. Thus, close contact, praises, and affectionate touching are required for a hasty marriage.

EXPERIMENT: Ideas to win Caroline's hand:
Affectionate touching (continual).
Bring her to Watson Estate to meet family and become familiar with estate. Done.
~~Impress her with chess skills.~~
Shower her with compliments (continual).
Tell her something you wouldn't particularly want anyone else to know. Done. (Pall mall took care of that.)
Sneak her off alone whenever possible. Done—almost anyway, stargazing alone together will count.
One grand gesture to be followed by marriage proposal.

CONCLUSION (currently unresolved, this is a hopeful conclusion only): Marry Caroline.

He sighed and put down his quill. He hated having to do things this way. Caroline seemed to be such a nice young lady. Unfortunately, he couldn't read her any better than he could read Japanese. If she'd give him even a little hint she was interested in him for something other than his telescope or to discuss the damned membership of his *Society,* he'd be eternally grateful. But that wasn't the case. As it was, he didn't know where he stood with her. She used a lot of facial expressions when she spoke, he just didn't know exactly what they meant.

In desperation and for no other reason than his love for science and experiments, he'd gone through with Marcus' suggestion and had literally written out his courtship as if it were a common experiment. First, he'd written the objective. Then he'd racked his brain to think of anyone of his acquaintance he'd witnessed have a quick wedding and written down what he could remember of their courtship. From there, he had made a list of what he could do to win her and prayed it would be enough.

Today he'd set up the framework for his grand gesture, and by the end of the week, he hoped to have her agreement to marry him. He didn't have much time beyond that. His birthday was a little over three weeks away and he not only needed to gain her agreement to the marriage, but he also needed her to agree to a quick wedding. He ran his hand through his hair in aggravation. This had all the workings for another experiment. He scowled and pushed *that* thought from his head before it could take root. If she didn't agree to a quick wedding, he'd have to take drastic measures, which either involved another experiment or abducting her and dragging her to Gretna Green.

He snatched the paper off the desk, then yanked open the drawer to bury it again. There was no two ways about it, he'd have to talk her into a quick wedding. He wouldn't seriously consider abducting her and he absolutely wasn't doing another "experiment". One was bad enough.

He shot to his feet, grabbed a few of his favorite astronomy volumes, then went to his gazebo to get ready for her visit.

The day dragged by, and when he could finally wait no longer, he left to get Caroline.

"Mr. Banks," Marcus' butler, Chapman, intoned when he greeted Alex at the door. "Lord Sinclair would like a word with you, sir."

Alex frowned. "Very well. In his study, I presume."

"Yes, sir."

Alex walked down the hall impatiently, hoping Marcus hadn't changed his mind. "You wanted to see me?"

Marcus was sitting behind his desk. There was only one candlestick burning, giving off just enough light for Marcus to see his work. "Yes, I did, Alex. You're actually later than I expected."

"I had a lot to do this afternoon," Alex said inanely, glancing at the clock on the mantle to confirm he was only thirty minutes early for the time he'd told Caroline.

"Yes, well, you occupied yourself longer than I'd thought you might."

Alex stared unblinkingly at his friend. What was that supposed to mean? Was he supposed to be here earlier? Or did Marcus think Alex was a slobbering suitor who could do nothing but paw at Caroline's skirts all day?

"I meant no offense, Alex," Marcus said, putting his quill down. "I just wanted to talk to you before you left."

Alex sat in an empty chair. "Have you changed your mind?"

"No. She may go. I wanted to ask a favor of you." Marcus shifted in his seat. "We both know the events of this evening are highly unusual. Generally speaking, nobody in his right mind would allow such an outing. But I think I know you well enough to know you'd not do anything with her you shouldn't." He glanced away and the edges of his scarred face turned an unusual shade of pink. "The crux of it is, Alex, I know you have no plans to shame her, but anyone else who might learn of this might not. Caroline doesn't have a suitable chaperone to accompany her in her travels tonight. Normally her maid goes with her, but tonight she can't. She has to stay and help Olivia bathe or some other such nonsense." He exhaled and flicked a glance out the window. "Just promise me if someone finds the two of you, you'll take her immediately to Gretna Green."

Alex nodded. He had no problems with Marcus' request. "If she's not back by breakfast, assume that's where we've gone." He stood up to leave.

"Oh, wait a minute, if you will," Marcus called. "I've something else to ask you."

He turned back around. "Yes?"

"What do you know of E. S. Wilson?"

Alex twisted his lips and bit the inside of his cheek in contemplation. "Not a lot, I fear. He started anonymously writing articles for *Popular Plants* about four years ago or so. I didn't recognize the name and spent nearly two years trying to track him down, to no avail. The editors told me he sends in a batch of articles every few months. Other than that, they have no idea who he is, where he lives, or even his education."

"Seems to be a recluse," Marcus suggested.

Snorting, Alex nodded. "More of one than you, it would seem. You're at least possible to locate. He's not."

Marcus chuckled. "That seems to bother you."

"Damn straight it does," he said, falling back into the chair he'd vacated less than a moment earlier. "I wanted to compare notes and discuss with him an experiment I was doing, but the man seems to be as elusive as the rainbow."

"Besides your clear irritability at his elusiveness, it sounds as if you value his opinion." Marcus' mouth stretched into a smile that made Alex feel like they were fifteen and carefree again.

"I do value his opinion," Alex conceded. "At first I did all his experiments to find a flaw. But now, after more than a year and a half, I have to admit his work wasn't flawed at all."

"Do you still replicate his experiments regularly?"

"Of course!" He loosened his cravat then pressed his elbows into his knees and leaned forward as if he were about to entrust Marcus with some highly confidential state secret. "He researches things I'd never thought to pick apart before. For example, last month he suggested—"

Marcus held up his hand to halt Alex's longwinded speech. "I don't need to hear it."

"Right," Alex clipped, remembering who he was talking to. His eyes narrowed on Marcus. "You're not him, are you?"

"No. I'm afraid not," Marcus said with a slight shake of his head. "Caroline mentioned him the other night. She said I needed to get her a subscription to that horticulture circular you read because everyone at your organization reads the articles by this fellow." He shrugged carelessly. "I thought he might be a friend of yours."

"No, he's not. But, oh how I wish he were."

Marcus grinned. "All these years certainly haven't done much to change you. Caroline is upstairs. She's ready to go when you are. If you hurry, you can collect her without Olivia plaguing you."

"I'll be on my way, then." Alex stood and walked to the door. His feet barely across the threshold, and he turned back around. "Marcus," he said quietly, trying in vain to push away the gentleman inside him that was prompting him to say his next words. "Do you think I'm doing your sister wrong by jilting her for her cousin?"

"No," Marcus said firmly. "What you're doing is perfectly fine. There was that addendum, remember?"

"I remember. I just don't want everyone to hate me when this is all over."

"Nobody will. Not even Olivia," Marcus assured him. "Now,

go get Caroline."

With a nod, Alex left the room and followed Chapman to the private sitting room Caroline was occupying. He was pleasantly surprised to find Marcus had been right and he hadn't encountered Lady Olivia when he went into the sitting room. He made a quick greeting to Miss Green and escorted her outside along with Caroline.

Miss Green's carriage was waiting and, after she said a quick goodbye to Caroline, Alex helped her ascend.

"Are you ready?" he asked, turning back to Caroline.

"Yes." She nodded her head wildly. "Where's your carriage?" She craned her neck, looking for his invisible carriage.

Hell's afire, in all his excitement, he'd ridden his horse, completely forgetting he'd need the carriage. Good thing she didn't have a chaperone or that would make for one very uncomfortable ride. "I thought we'd share a horse. We'll get there faster."

"Oh, all right," she agreed, blushing furiously.

"Your skirts are going to be a problem," he said thoughtfully. "You'll have to sit sideways on top of my lap." He looked around for a large rock or something she could stand on to mount the horse, or him, as the case may be.

"There's a stump over there," she said, pointing.

"Excellent." Alex walked his horse to the stump and mounted. "Now, stand on the stump and I'll help pull you on."

She stepped up on the stump, and in one quick motion, he pulled her petite frame onto his lap. She immediately wiggled, presumably to get used to her seat.

He groaned and urged the horse to go. The sooner they left, the sooner his torture would end.

She wiggled again. "Alex, there's something prodding me," she said, inadvertently making the situation worse by shifting yet again.

"I know," he said hoarsely. "Just be still."

"But I can't," she protested. "Something hard is pressing into my underside." She moved one of her hands to her hip and tried to push her fingers between them.

"Stop," he barked.

Her big blue eyes met his and her fingers stilled. "I just wanted to move it," she explained. "I'll not be comfortable until it goes away."

"Neither will I," he muttered under his breath. "Be still and it will go away shortly."

"How do you know?"

He coughed. For a girl who claimed to have an interest in biological matters, she sure was naive. "I just do," he explained evasively.

She looked at him and he avoided eye contact. "Oh, Alex, I'm so sorry," she said suddenly, clapping a hand across her mouth. "I didn't mean to embarrass you. I didn't realize I was sitting on your erection."

He choked on his laughter. "I do believe that's the first time I've ever heard anyone of your sex use that word."

She shrugged. "That's what it's called, isn't it?"

"Yes. Yes, it is." He grinned. "Now, be still so it will go away."

"Right. Sorry." Less than a minute later, she looked back up at him. "Alex, how long does it normally last?"

"That all depends on you," he said silkily.

"Me?"

"Yes, you. I could be in this state for hours or a matter of minutes. It all depends on you," he murmured in her ear, then dropped a kiss on the spot where her shoulder met her neck.

She gasped. "Really?"

"Really," he whispered. "You have power over me you don't even know how to use. But one day you will. I promise."

Her body shivered. "I look forward to discovering it."

"I do, too. But for now, you need to be still so our guest will depart company."

Forty-five torturous minutes later, the gazebo came into view.

He slowed his horse. "This is it," he said, bringing his stallion to a stop by a big tree nearby. "Let me help you down." With an ease he didn't feel, he helped her get her feet on the ground.

"Thank you," she murmured, shaking out her skirt.

He jumped down. "Why don't you go over there and wait? I'll be right there." He tied the reins loosely around a low limb of the tree then walked to the gazebo. He opened the door and held it for her. "After you, my dear Caro."

She stepped into the moonlit room, Alex a step behind her.

"Pardon me," he said, stepping past her to light the three candles he'd put in there earlier. "I've brought out several of my newer books if you'd like to have a look." On a long plank of wood that was just part of the construction of the gazebo, he'd laid out four books, all open to pages about lunar eclipses. There wasn't a lot of room inside the gazebo, really only enough room for one person to be in here comfortably. With the two of them in such a cramped space, it was difficult to move without bumping into each other. He smiled. Perhaps the lack of space wasn't such a bad thing after all.

Caroline barely glanced at his books before she climbed the ladder to look through the telescope. "What's the story behind the ladder, Alex?" she asked from ten feet in the air.

He *tsk, tsked*. "As a good student of astronomy, you should know the history of the ladder."

She looked down at him and contorted her face in a way that made him chuckle. "I prefer to study the stars when I use my telescope, not the history of how a ladder was used."

He smiled at her frankness, then said, "Though my main academic of preference is science, and math naturally, history falls a short second. Nobody really knows that, though." He waved his hand dismissively. "Anyway, I like to keep things historically correct if I can. Including how I set up my telescope. Early astronomers didn't have tripods or stands like we do. Instead, they'd place ladders in front of their windows and if they wanted to see a different section of the sky, they'd move the telescope to a different rung."

"Fascinating." She looked through the eyepiece then moved a lever. The telescope tube moved up, down, and sideways. "Hmm, Mr. Banks, I do believe you've cheated."

"I have not," he said in mock indignation. "I merely said I set up my telescope to be historically correct. It wouldn't be functional if I'd made it truly correct. I'd spend most of my night moving the thing up and down the ladder. I'd miss everything of any importance. No, I just put the ladder there to raise the scope in the air and make it appear historically correct."

She grinned at him. "You sly devil, you."

He did a partial bow. "See anything up there yet?"

"Not really," she said. "I think it needs to get a little darker first."

"You're likely right. Shall we go outside and watch the sky from the ground?" He reached up to help her down the ladder. Alex blew out the candles, grabbed two blankets he'd left out there earlier, then followed her out the door.

"Where's your mother?" Caroline asked as soon as they were out of the gazebo.

He stopped walking and took her hand in his, then gently twisted her around to face him. "She's not coming. It's just the two of us tonight."

"Perhaps I should go home," she said, trying to tug her hand from his.

"No. Caro, nothing is going to happen except us stargazing together."

"I know," she admitted. "I know I can trust you. But if someone should see, it will cause scandal, and I cannot repay Marcus that way. Nor can I do that to Olivia. As awful as she is, I cannot embarrass her that way."

"What of you, Caro?" he asked, squeezing her hand. "Who is to think of you and what you want?"

She shook her head. "That doesn't matter. Marcus has suffered greatly since his accident. I cannot risk bringing a scandal to him. Nor Olivia's wrath."

"That won't be a problem," he assured her. "There will be no scandal. Everyone from the lowest scullery maid to the baron himself is tucked up nice and warm in their bed. Nobody knows you're here, and nobody is going to know. Now, stop worrying and get ready to enjoy the lunar eclipse."

"All right," she said with a swallow.

He led her to a clear patch of the lawn with just enough slope for them to be able to look at the moon without having to crane their necks.

"Here, help me spread this," he said, handing her one side of the folded blanket.

When they'd finished, Caroline went over to the folded

blanket he'd set off to the side and picked it up. "Is this one for me?"

"No." He took the blanket from her loose grasp and tossed it to the ground. "It's for us. We'll use it to cover up with when we get cold tonight. Now, lie down with me."

Chapter 11

Caroline stared down at Alex as he stretched out like a cat on the blanket. He patted the spot beside him. His smile couldn't be described as anything but wolfish. He may have said nothing was going to happen between them tonight, but she was not so sure. Something about Alex Banks sent a shiver down her spine and made her want to act in a most inappropriate manner.

She had no idea what spurred these reactions in her. She'd like to blame it on all her years of being overprotected. But that was false and she knew it. She could try to blame it on the fact she had compassion for Alex since Olivia was planning to cuckold him. That wasn't true, either. No, her responses to him were her own sheer wantonness. And sitting down next to him right now just might push her over the edge. Too bad he was too much of a gentleman to ever act dishonorably, she thought cheekily, then chastised herself for such a wicked, wicked thought.

"I'm waiting, Caro," he said, extending a hand up to her.

Against her better judgment, she put her hand in his open palm and let him pull her to the ground next to him. "Wait no more," she said with a smile.

"Are you cold?" He chafed her chilled hand between his two larger ones.

"A little," she admitted with a swallow.

He let go of her hand and grabbed the extra blanket. He shook it out and draped it over the front of her before going up on his knees and using them to walk behind her. He sat back down and placed one leg on either side of her, pulling her body back to rest flush against his.

She wiggled her shoulders a bit to get more settled against him, slightly surprised at the firmness of his chest. She didn't think an academic would have any muscles. Hmm, she was discovering there was more to Arid Alex at every turn.

"Do you like constellations?" His voice was smooth as butter.

"Of course. What kind of astronomer would I be if I didn't?"

He chuckled and brought one hand up to play with the loose curls on the right side of her head. "What's your favorite?"

"The Big Dipper," she said automatically.

"Good choice. Easy to find. And not easy to confuse." Alex twisted her hair around his finger.

"My mother loved the Little Dipper best," she said for no other reason than just to talk. "As a little girl who wanted to be just like her mother, I would always tell her my favorite was the Big Dipper. Ironic how things never change." She sighed. "The only difference is, back then I said it to be like my mother, and now, it truly is my favorite." Looking at the Big and Little Dippers had always made her feel closer to her mother in a way nothing else did. She started. She usually felt a pain—sometimes sharp, sometimes faint—in her chest when she thought of her mother. But for some reason, the pain wasn't there just now.

"Do you miss her a great deal?" Alex asked somberly, his fingers frozen.

She closed her eyes. His question was about to be his own reality. He was about to lose someone he was close to and her answer meant a lot to him. She couldn't lie. "Yes, I do. But, it was a long time ago now, and I've found others to love and care for in her stead. It's not the same, of course. But it's better to love others than to sit miserable without loving or being loved in return."

"You love Marcus and Miss Green, don't you?"

And you. She bit her tongue to keep that from slipping out. But not saying it aloud didn't make it untrue. Somewhere in the last few days, she'd begun to fall in love with the one gentleman she could never have. She'd never dreamt of marriage and children as a child; she'd not been allowed. Her aunt had informed her frequently she would not get to marry. But now that she was almost of an age to marry without consent if she so wished, she suddenly wished to and couldn't. She swallowed a lump of raw emotion that had formed in her throat. "And Olivia," she croaked.

"You cannot be serious."

"I am. She's my cousin, after all. To quote Marcus, 'I may not like her most—nay, all—the time, but I do love her.'"

Chuckling, Alex squeezed her a little tighter. "Loyal to a fault, aren't you?"

"When you have only a handful of people to love and accept love from, you can't be too particular," she jested with a smile.

"I guess not. One day, you'll have more people to love and accept love from, Caro. I promise it."

She nodded, not sure what to say. "What's yours?" she asked, her voice cracking.

"Pardon?"

"Your favorite constellation."

"Lynx."

"Lynx?"

"It's a smaller, dimmer constellation. It's said that you have to have catlike vision to see it. It's between Ursa Major and Auriga."

"I know what it is and where it is, I'm just surprised *you* do," she teased.

He rested his chin on the crown of her head and wrapped his arms around her. "You teasing minx. I just got that. It took me a second, but I got that."

She laughed. "I'm glad. I wasn't sure if you'd get my jest or if you'd shrug and tell me you can see it just fine with your telescope."

"I almost did," he admitted with a chuckle. "If it weren't for your shaking shoulders and the change in your tone, I wouldn't have realized you were jesting."

"Sorry, Alex." She covered his hands with hers. "I know you're a serious sort. I'll try not to tease you in the future."

"It's all right," he assured her. "You can tease me if you wish. I rather like it. "

She nodded, trying to force herself to think about their conversation and not wonder how it would feel if Alex moved his big hands a few inches higher. "I'm glad you like it," she said with calm she didn't feel.

"Is something wrong?"

Yes, I can't stop thinking about how you're too much of a gentleman, and I'll never know what it's like to have a man's hands on me. "No. Why?"

"You keep shifting around. I just wondered."

"Oh, sorry. I was just trying to get more comfortable."

His hands loosened their hold on her, but she held them in place. "Do what you need to do to get comfortable," he murmured in her ear.

She made a show of kicking her feet out in front of her and twisting her body around. When she finished, his hands rested just beneath her breasts.

"Better now?" he asked.

Nodding, she whispered, "Much."

"Good. I'm glad you found a position that makes us both more comfortable." He moved both his thumbs up to caress the bottoms of her breasts.

"Alex," she squeaked, surprised by his boldness.

"Hmm?" His thumbs made a second sweep of her breasts and came to settle on the outer sides of them, gently pushing into her swollen flesh.

Her fingers pressed into his and she bit her lip so as not to sigh as his thumbs and forefingers kneaded her breasts.

His probing fingers made her breasts swell to the point of straining against her bodice while her nipples hardened and jutted out like twin points beneath the fabric. "Do you like this, Caro?"

She didn't answer. She couldn't answer. She did enjoy it. Immensely. And that was the problem. She was enjoying her cousin's intended. Suddenly, Caroline felt like she was fifteen again and Olivia had just dumped a giant pot full of ice chips, snow, and cold water on her head while she read a book by the fire. Or in other words, cold reality was washing over her. "Alex, please stop." She grabbed his hands to pull them off.

His fingers immediately left her breasts. "I'm sorry," he said raggedly. He cleared his throat. "Excuse my behavior. I thought... Never mind what I thought, I was wrong. It won't happen again."

"It's all right, Alex. You didn't misinterpret anything." Shame washed over her. "I did."

He scoffed. "I doubt that. As Marcus so nicely reminded me last week, I am very obtuse. I know that. I always have. I have difficulty reading people's faces and knowing what their tone or actions really mean." He snorted. "Isn't it ironic? I can list off nearly every scientific fact or mathematical formula discovered, but I struggle to know what people are really saying if they don't just say it."

She squeezed his hands affectionately. "I promise this wasn't your fault. It was mine." She felt like the lightskirt Olivia had always claimed she would grow up to be if not for Uncle Joseph. "Wait. You realized I was jesting earlier."

"I know," he said with a sigh, then interlaced his fingers with hers. "As I said before, you were shaking with laughter, and your tone changed. It's difficult to explain. I don't always make sense of everything right away, which is why it took me a minute to put it together. But when I remembered that you'd made a comment yesterday that my mother laughed at, your tone was similar to the one you'd just used and your shoulders shook. That's why I knew to think about your words. After a few seconds, I realized you were just having fun." He dropped a kiss on the top of her head. "It really doesn't matter. The more time we're together, the better I'll get about it. Just give me time."

"It's all right, Alex," she murmured, leaning her head back against his chest. "We all struggle with something."

"What do you struggle with?" His voice as soft as velvet.

"Just about everything," she said dryly. Nothing had ever come easy for her. And right now it wasn't easy for her to feel Alex's hands wrapped around her midsection, knowing he'd never really be hers. Allowing him those brief minutes to touch her had done nothing to satisfy her hunger for him. But it would have to be enough. He belonged to someone else.

They both sat quiet and her eyes found the Big Dipper, the Little Dipper, and finally Lynx. She smiled. How like Alex to pick the one constellation that was so opposite him. He was a mystery.

"Alex?"

"Yes?"

She bit her lip and screwed up her courage to ask the one thing she had to know. "Are you really going to marry Olivia?"

"No."

She sighed. "I know you say that now, and you told her earlier today you weren't, but she told me—"

"Shhh." His soft lips pressed a kiss against her ear. "I'd rather not discuss all the details, but I've no plans to marry your cousin. If I did, I wouldn't be here with you." His voice was firm, decided, final.

She closed her eyes and let her head fall to the side a bit. Alex's body was big and warm. He smelled of sandalwood. So intoxicating. So masculine. She inhaled deeper, not able to get enough of his spicy scent.

Right next to her ear, the strong, steady beat of his heart held her captive—its rhythm as mesmerizing as his scent. She turned her face to rest her cheek against it.

Normally bigger, stronger men scared her. But not Alex. He wasn't a giant that towered over her and had muscles so big his clothes ripped at the seams every time he walked. But he wasn't weak or lanky like she'd originally thought him to be, either. A few days ago, he'd said he had an interest in swords and pistols. She imagined slinging swords around had a lot to do with why he was so firm and well-formed under his clothes.

In the past when she'd encountered gentlemen who were tall or strong, a numb feeling would take her as memories of her father would flood her mind. Thankfully, that was not the reaction she had when she was with Alex. With him, it was the opposite. She felt safe. Cared for. Protected.

She really should open her eyes and watch the sky. That's what he'd brought her out to do. She just couldn't. Not yet. For now, she just wanted to lie in his arms and pretend he was hers. In a minute she'd open her eyes. Just a minute longer to enjoy the moment.

"Caro, wake up," Alex whispered, giving her shoulder a gentle shake.

Caroline's eyes snapped open and she blushed. She was literally lying on top of Alex. Without a hint of grace, she rolled off and looked up at the sky. "Has it started yet?"

"Yes." He pushed himself to a sitting position. "It's ended, too."

"Oh."

"Don't worry, there'll be another one in a few months."

She did an exaggerated eye roll at his dry remark. "Thank you for the reassurance. And just why is it you let me sleep through it,

Mr. Banks?"

"I didn't," he said, catching her hand and pulling her toward him. "My fate was the same as yours, I'm afraid."

"Well, now I feel a little better. At least I'm not the only one who slept through it."

"I daresay most of the world did, darling Caro," he remarked. "But that's not important just now. I need to get you home before sunrise."

She nodded and her free hand flew to her hair.

"It's fine," he said, pulling her hand away. "Nothing you're able to do to it just now could possibly improve it."

"That bad?"

"Yes."

He let go of her hands and they stood up. She folded the blankets while he went to get his stallion. He came back and helped her onto his lap.

"Thank you for letting me use your telescope for three minutes," she said primly as they trotted down the lane.

"You're welcome, Caro."

She twisted the wrinkled fabric of her yellow skirt with her fingers. "Can I ask you something?"

"Of course."

"Do you promise not to laugh?"

"No."

She sighed. "Last night, when I fell asleep, did I do anything?"

"Yes. You slept."

She shook her head. "No. I meant did I snore or drool or talk in my sleep, or anything embarrassing like that?"

He pulled his horse to a stop and nearly doubled over with laughter. "Caro, my girl, you are something else."

Crossing her arms, she pursed her lips. "What is that to mean, Mr. Banks?"

Laughter continued to wrack his body. "Nothing," he said in between howls.

"Yes, it did. Now, tell me."

A minute later when his laughter stopped, his warm brown eyes met hers. "Most young, unmarried ladies would be more concerned about their reputation. They'd want to know if I'd touched them inappropriately or taken their virtue. But not you. You want to know if you made an unladylike noise or drooled."

"That's because I knew you wouldn't do any of those things." She smirked when his smile vanished.

"And what makes you so certain?" His voice was hard and his face rigid.

She laughed. "Alex, relax. I just meant you're too honorable to do something like that. No need to get defensive. I wasn't insulting you."

"You're rather trusting," he muttered, nudging his horse to go.

"And you're darling when you get angry."

"Don't say that, Caro," he warned through clenched teeth.

"What?" she asked innocently.

"Don't call me darling. No gentleman likes to be called darling. Ever."

"Even if he is?"

He shuddered. "Even then. It's unmanly."

She ran her finger along the ridge of his jaw. "Unmanly?"

"Yes, unmanly. Handsome and dashing are much better adjectives to describe a man."

"I'll try to remember that." She pushed a lock of his brown hair off his brow.

"See that you do," he said before turning his head and pressing a warm kiss into her palm.

She leaned her head against his chest and closed her eyes again. She liked being this close to him. Did all ladies feel this way when they were with the one they loved? Last night he'd given her a little glimmer of hope when he'd denounced his engagement to Olivia. But she knew better than to hope he'd fall in love and marry her. Such things were reserved for daydreaming girls and fairy tales.

"We're here," Alex said, nudging her lightly. He slowed his horse about a hundred yards in front of her house. "I had better let you off here so we don't wake everyone."

She nodded and allowed him to help her down. "Thank you again, Alex. Sorry I fell asleep."

He jumped down off his horse next to her. "It's fine," he said dismissively. He took her hands in his. "I was wondering what you're doing Sunday."

"Sunday?"

He nodded.

"I don't think I have any plans."

His thumbs moved back and forth across the points of her knuckles. "Would you be willing to spend part of the day with me?"

"Yes," she chirped excitedly, blushing. "I mean, of course."

"How about if I pick you up—in my carriage this time—at noon? We'll spend the afternoon together."

She willed herself not to do or say anything as embarrassing as before. "That would be lovely. I look forward to it," she said in as light of a tone as she could force.

"I'll see you then." He dropped a quick kiss on her cheek, let go of her hands, and mounted his horse.

For some reason she wasn't ready for him to leave yet. "Alex?"

"Yes, Caro?"

"What are we going to do?"

He smiled down at her. "You'll see."

"Will I like it?"

He nodded. "Yes. And I will, too."

"Ah, then we'll not be playing pall mall again, I gather," she teased, grinning.

He scowled. "Definitely not. I'd best go before someone sees me and your reputation suffers."

Hang her reputation. "Are you sure you don't wish to stay for breakfast?"

"No." He shook his head and pulled on the reins. "I must be off, Caro. I'll see you on Sunday." Without waiting for a response, he snapped the reins and galloped down the drive.

"Sunday can't come soon enough," she whispered to herself.

"Yes, it can," Marcus said from behind, scaring her half to death.

She turned to face him. "How long have you been there?"

"Long enough to know you planned an outing for Sunday without seeking the permission of your guardian first." His lips curved upwards and she rolled her eyes at him.

"I didn't realize you'd care."

"I don't," he said easily, putting an arm around her shoulder. "Cheer up. He'll come back on Sunday like he promised."

Caroline squinted to see Alex and his horse as he rode away. "Marcus, he says he's not going to marry Olivia." She didn't really know why she was telling him this. Probably because she wanted to hear the words again, even if she was the one who spoke them.

"He's not," Marcus agreed, startling her. "I would never allow it."

She stared at him. "What about me, Marcus? Would you allow me to marry him?"

"Yes," he said without hesitation.

She frowned. "Why?" Not that she really expected Alex to ask her. But if he did, she wanted to know why Marcus would approve of a marriage between her and Alex but not Olivia and Alex.

Marcus shrugged and squeezed her shoulder. "You're different."

In less than a second, all the happiness she'd had from thinking of her time with Alex was replaced with bitter sadness. In the past thirteen years, almost fourteen, Marcus had not so much as even alluded to the differences of their birth. But now she knew his true feelings. He did view her as lower. He'd just told her he'd let her marry someone who he considered unworthy of his sister. Tears stung the back of her eyes. She stiffly pulled away from Marcus' touch and walked straight up to her room.

If Alex asked her to marry him, she'd say yes, with or without Marcus' approval. As far as she was concerned, Marcus could go to the devil. Olivia might have treated her poorly for years, but at least she'd been forthcoming about her feelings. Marcus hadn't. He'd let her believe he cared for her only to find out he didn't, and that hurt worse than anything Olivia had ever done to her.

Chapter 12

Sunday could not get here fast enough for Alex's taste. Not only was he ready to be engaged to Caroline and have his future secure, he wanted to see her again. Several times he talked himself out of going to see her early. His fear of ruining everything with one little slip kept him safely tucked away at Watson Estate.

But today was the day—the day he'd make his grand gesture, win her heart, and ask her to marry him. He'd planned everything to a T and hadn't slept the night before in anticipation. The only part of his plan that wasn't in his control was the company they'd keep today. To make his plan work, he'd had to depend on one of his cousins to help him. Unfortunately, Brooke was one of those sorts who always wanted to be involved, and she'd withheld her help until he allowed her to be a part. Not surprisingly, once she was included in his plan, she'd invited her sisters to also join. Therefore, the end result was Caroline would meet all of his cousins and their spouses today. He sighed. Oh well, she'd have to meet them eventually.

His carriage came to a stop. He descended and told his coachman he'd be back in a few minutes.

"Afternoon, Marcus," he called, climbing the stairs to the house.

Marcus was seated in a lounge chair under the covered porch. "Alex," he said, rubbing his jaw and looking everywhere but in Alex's eyes. "I don't know how to say this, and I doubt you do, either, so I'm just going to say it. I don't think Caroline's going to be good company today."

Alex stiffened. "What do you mean? What's happened?"

"Not what you think. It's just that Caroline has been crying a lot these past few days." He paused long enough for Alex to take his meaning. "I know you have a sister and mother, so you'll know to be careful while she's having her..." He dropped his gaze to the ground and cleared his throat. "I just thought I'd warn you."

"Thank you," Alex said tightly. He really didn't think it was his business to point out to Marcus that it was neither of their business what was going on with Caroline's body at present. And yet, it was a good thing Marcus had said something. He'd just make sure to allow her plenty of time to sit and try not to say anything she might find upsetting.

"You're welcome," Marcus stared down at his boots. "By the bye, I'm sending along a chaperone today. She's as much for your protection as she is for Caroline's."

Alex snorted. "I suppose daylight demands a chaperone."

"Even darkness demands one; she just doesn't have one. More's the pity," Marcus said with what Alex interpreted as Marcus' best attempt at a snarl. "She's inside. Best of luck."

Alex walked up to the door. "Are you coming?"

"Hell no."

Chuckling, Alex walked inside and ignored the butler who was trying to attend him. He found Caroline in the blue salon. "Are you ready?"

"Yes!" She smiled at him in a way that sent a jolt of lightening straight to his groin.

He offered her his arm and escorted her to the carriage, throwing Marcus a triumphant smile as they walked by.

Marcus just shook his head.

Inside the carriage was a slim woman dressed as a maid. Alex stared at her.

"Alex, this is my maid, Nettie. She's acting as my chaperone today. Nettie, this is Mr. Banks."

Alex nodded once to her and she did the same. He was glad she hadn't attempted a curtsy in the carriage. That would have been awkward for all three of them.

"Where are we going?" Caroline asked as the carriage traveled down the drive.

He clucked her on the chin. "You'll see when we get there."

She scowled. "Oh, I brought my notes for our project."

"Pardon?"

Sighing, she grabbed her reticule and dug out a stack of

papers. "You know, our campaign."

"Of course." He'd nearly forgotten all about that confounded thing.

"I know you wanted to call it a campaign, but I think that's too boring. And I wanted to call it an experiment, but as you said, it's not. I thought we could both compromise and call it a project. What do you think?"

"Whatever you want." He waved his hand dismissively. They could call it the Magna Carta for all he cared. Hopefully after today his "experiment" would be over.

She kicked him with the toe of her slipper. "Would you please pay this some mind? The next meeting is a week from Thursday."

"All right," he agreed testily.

"Good. Now, why don't we go over my ideas?" she suggested.

He scrubbed his face with his hands. "I can't read in the carriage. It makes me sick."

"Really?"

"Really. How about we talk about it later? We're almost there anyway."

"But we just left," she protested.

He smiled. "I know. We're not going to Watson Estate today."

Caroline frantically shoved her papers back into her reticule. "Where are we?"

"In the carriage."

She rolled her beautiful blue eyes. "You're quite the jester today, aren't you?"

"I try." He stretched his legs out and put his arms along the back of the squabs.

Nettie smiled at him and he winked at her.

Ten minutes passed and a big, grey brick house came into view. The main part of the house used to be a castle. It even had the slim windows that archers used to stand in to fire their arrows at the intruders.

"Where are we?" Caroline breathed, staring out the window in awe.

"Rockhurst. This is where Andrew and Brooke, Lord and Lady Townson, live."

"We're going to see them today?" she squealed, her eyes as

big as tea saucers.

He nodded. "Sorry. It couldn't be helped. But not to fear, there will be others here, too."

Her fingers tightened on the strap of her reticule as the carriage came to a stop. "Could you take me home, please?" Her voice was barely more than a whisper.

Alex got out of his seat and held the door shut when the coachman tried to open it, telling him to wait a minute. Sinking to his haunches in front of Caroline, he took her hands in his. "What's wrong?"

"I can't meet them," she said, her eyes blinking rapidly and her hands as cold as ice.

"Why not?" he demanded softly. "They're not going to hurt you, I promise."

She didn't even crack a smile. "I know that."

"Then what's the problem?" he asked, flummoxed. His family could be a bit much at times, but they were nothing to be afraid of. Well, at one time, one or two of them might have been, but that was mainly rumor.

"I just can't meet them," she said, her voice uneven.

"But they want to meet you. Brooke insisted I bring you here today. And Uncle John, Aunt Carolina, Liberty, and Paul all came here right after church to see you. Madison and Benjamin have traveled since yesterday to meet you." When her eyes nearly popped out, Alex realized he'd said too much. "The point is, they're harmless and they came today because they wanted to meet you."

"Alex, you don't understand. I won't fit with them. They're titled and proper. I'm not. I'm a poor relation to an earl who's been packed off in the country for the past thirteen years. I can't even do a proper curtsy." Her lower lip quivered and she broke eye contact. "They'll know instantly I don't fit with them and the whole afternoon will be awkward. Please, take me home."

"You're not going home," he said firmly. "Not until you spend the afternoon with me. Caro, your fears are unwarranted. Those eight adults in there are the most socially unfit lot I've ever met. You included." He snorted. "Only one of them has ever given a hang about their reputation, and to the enormous relief of us all, that is no longer the case. Look at me. You'll fit in just fine. You won't be expected to do a curtsy or call anyone 'my lord' or 'Your Grace'. Nobody in that house cares about such things. You could break wind at the table and nobody would care."

She swatted at his shoulder. "Stop. You're exaggerating."

"No. I'm not." He brought her hands to his mouth and kissed each knuckle. "Just come in with me. If, after you meet them, you feel out of place, I'll take you home."

"All right," she agreed.

Before she could change her mind, he swung the door open and jumped down. She took his hand and descended from the carriage, then stood back while he helped Nettie down. "Rather glib, I'd say," Nettie whispered in his ear as she passed by him.

He smiled at her before offering Caroline his arm.

Stevens, the butler, met them at the door and directed them to the drawing room.

"Smile, Caro," he whispered as they walked in.

"Alex," Andrew called. "It's about time you got here. Brooke claims she's gutfounded."

Laughter rippled through the room, and Alex grinned.

"If your pocket watch is broken, I hear the duke knows someone who can fix it," Paul said, winking at his wife.

He waved them off. "My watch is in working order and if I know Brooke, she's not gutfounded. She's probably been snacking on biscuits." He flashed a smile at Brooke who had her hands spread open to show she hid no biscuits. "Anyway, Brooke will have to wait a moment longer. I'd like to introduce you all to Caroline." He turned to a rigid, overwhelmed Caroline. "Caro, you remember Andrew, Earl of Townson—" he pointed to Andrew— "next to him is his breeding wife, Brooke. Over by the pianoforte arguing over who gets to hold the baby is Paul, he's a vicar, and his wife Liberty. She teaches illiterate bastards to read in her spare time." He paused and waited until the snickers stopped. "Sitting over on the settee is Madison. She's also expecting a baby this summer. Next to her is her husband, Benjamin. You probably know him best by his ducal title, Gateway."

"It's nice to meet you all," Caroline said, glancing at all of them tentatively.

"It's nice to meet you, too," Benjamin said. "And just so you know, even though your family connection does not recommend you, we shall all look past that flaw and either love you or hate you for your own personality."

His wife smacked him in the chest. "Ignore him. What my notoriously tactless and extremely rude husband means to say is, we've all had our differences with your cousin, but none of us will hold that against you."

"Exactly," the duke agreed. "She said it much better."

"I always do." Madison flashed him a smile.

"Well, I for one think your relation to Lady Olivia is a point in your favor," Paul said, smiling grandly. "If not for her pulling Liberty and Alex through the ice while skating on the Thames last year, I'm fairly certain I wouldn't have married Liberty."

Liberty rolled her eyes and Caroline gasped. "You went in, too?" Caroline whispered.

Alex nodded. "It's not a day I like to recall, but yes. I went in, too. In all fairness to your cousin though, the reason I fell in was because the ice cracked further while I was trying to help Liberty out. Lady Olivia had already been escorted out of the vicinity."

"Good gracious," Caroline muttered. "How did the two of you get out?"

"Benjamin," Liberty and Alex said in unison.

"He graciously pulled us both out," Liberty continued. "He took me to my home, and since I was unconscious, I'm not really sure what happened to Alex."

Alex waved a hand. "It's not important." The duke had been kind enough to help Alex that day. The details were unimportant.

"Have you all had some sort of unpleasant encounter with Olivia?" Caroline's voice was nearly inaudible.

Nobody moved to answer. "Yes," Alex said at last. "Nobody has experienced her the way you have. But yes, they all know what she's like."

"I'm so sorry," Caroline rushed to say. "I hope nobody has been driven to nightmares."

Brooke snorted at her jest. "Nobody as much as Andrew," she said, nudging her husband with her elbow. "Tell her."

"No," her husband said, shaking his head. "I don't think she'd like to hear any more disparaging stories about her cousin."

This time Caroline snorted. "I assure you, the things I've experienced at her hands are far worse than anything you could possibly tell me." She forced a weak smile and took a nervous breath. "But that matters naught. I would like to apologize to all of you for anything she may have done or said that was offensive."

"Apology unaccepted," Brooke said. "Her sins are not for you to apologize or pay penance for."

"Thank you," Caroline said.

Just then the butler came into the room and announced luncheon.

Andrew and Brooke walked out first, leading the way. Following them were Paul and Liberty. Liberty stopped a moment and handed Michael, her two month old son, to Nurse.

"Caroline, may I have a minute with you?" Madison said before Alex could walk her out the door.

"Of course." Caroline glanced at Alex with an unreadable look.

He smiled, hoping to reassure her. "We'll wait in the hall," he said to no one in particular as he and Benjamin walked to the hall.

"Do you think you'll marry her?" Benjamin asked when it was clear the ladies weren't right behind them.

"I plan to," Alex admitted.

The duke nodded. "She seems nice. A bit shy, but nice."

"Wouldn't you be?" Alex countered in Caroline's defense. "She's never met anyone here before and she has that awful brand of her cousin to overcome."

"I know," Benjamin allowed.

A moment of silence passed. "What do you suppose they're talking about in there?" Alex asked.

The duke shrugged. "I have no idea. If there's one thing I've learned from having a wife, it's one can never truly know what to expect."

Alex eyed him quizzically. What on earth was the man talking about?

Benjamin shrugged again. "Just wait. You'll know what I'm talking about soon enough."

Alex shook his head. For as long as he'd known the duke, the man had always gone out of his way to speak cryptically, not to mention, he was almost always concocting some ridiculous scheme. Best to just nod in agreement and hope the ladies came out soon.

"They actually waited," Caroline said, emerging from the room a few minutes later.

"Of course we did," the duke said jovially. He offered his arm to his wife. "Duchess?"

Madison took his arm and they walked down the hall, Alex and Caroline tagging behind.

Walking into the dining room with Caroline perched on his arm, Alex had never been so close to bursting with pride.

"Did you four get lost?" Andrew asked, looking up from the paper he held in his hand.

"No," Alex countered, noting his aunt and uncle had joined them now. "We just prefer our own company to yours."

"And I can see why," Uncle John said, glancing at Caroline.

"Caroline, this is my Uncle John and his wife Carolina," he said, gesturing to his aunt and uncle.

"Did you both just arrive?" Caroline asked, smiling.

Uncle John smiled broadly. "No. We were visiting Nathan."

"Nathan?" she echoed.

"The grandson we don't have to fight to hold," Aunt Carolina explained, squinting her eyes in Paul and Liberty's direction.

"We let you hold him," Liberty countered.

Uncle John snorted. "Yes, you do. As soon as a foul odor starts emanating from the region of his waist."

Paul shrugged. "Are you complaining?"

"No," Aunt Carolina put in hastily.

"And here I thought Alex and Caroline were the most intelligent two in the room," the duke remarked.

Paul smiled. "Academically speaking, they probably are. Well, except for one academic." He glanced down to his wife. "There's one academic I'd say Liberty has them beat at."

"Paul, if you'd like to ride home *inside* the carriage this afternoon, I'd suggest you stop talking right now," his wife said, pretending to scowl at him.

Her husband laughed and ran his hand over her shoulders.

Taking their seats to eat, several conversations started at once. Alex, however, was not part of any of them. Instead, he was content to shamelessly stare at the beautiful lady who sat next to him.

"Alex, after we eat do you think we could discuss our project?" Caroline asked between bites of roasted chicken.

He wanted to groan. "No."

"But you promised," she protested. "The day I came to your estate, you said we'd talk for a half an hour about it. We never did."

"I know. I'm sorry," he said. "Another time."

She frowned. "Why not today? After we eat we'll just go find a private place for a half an hour."

"No." He shook his head. "If we disappear for half an hour someone will suspect something improper is happening."

She almost choked on her food. "No, they won't."

"Yes, they will. You do realize three of the four married couples in this room married due to some scandal related to an inappropriate situation."

Her brows drew together. "I have no idea what you're talking about. But we'll go find a quiet place after we eat."

"No," he repeated firmly. "I'll not have people thinking I'm debauching you in my closest friend's home."

She snorted. "Nobody will think that. Madison even said I could parade naked in front of you, and as long as I was talking about science you wouldn't even notice."

"Madison doesn't know everything," he muttered, glancing down the table at his cousin. "Is that what the two of you talked about in there?"

"Yes." She blushed. "Now are you satisfied nobody will think you're debauching me?"

He ignored her. "Would you care to test your newfound theory, Caro?" He brushed her upper arm with his knuckles.

Her eyes lit up at the same time something of his went up. "Absolutely."

He groaned. "You're going to be the death of me."

"What has you so tense over there, Alex?" Andrew called to him with a grin.

"Membership to the *Society of Biological Matters*," he said quickly.

"That would make me tense, too," Andrew remarked.

"Would you, or anyone else, like to join?" Caroline asked, oblivious to Andrew's cleverly worded jest. "We're campaigning to increase membership."

Andrew groaned. "Will a bank note do?"

"It would help. But your physical presence is what we're looking for." She flashed him her best smile.

"When is it? And what do I have to do?" Andrew asked through clenched teeth.

"Just come," Caroline said, tucking a lock of her dark hair behind her ear. "The meetings are held the third Thursday of the month."

Andrew ground his teeth. "For how long?"

"Membership depends on you," she said, glancing at everyone as if they were all champing at the bit to join. "You don't have to come to every meeting, and when you're no longer interested, you may completely stop."

Andrew nodded once. "How long do the meetings last?"

"Three to four hours, I believe," she said primly.

Alex bit down on the inside of his cheek to keep his smile in check. The grimace on Andrew's face was beyond price. "Don't worry, Andrew. A bank note will do nicely. I'd say a thousand pounds will go a long way to help us campaign for new members."

"Done."

"Tell me," the duke broke in from down the table. "At these lengthy meetings, would you say one is able to glean enough interesting scientific tidbits to entertain their friends for a while?"

"Of course," Caroline said, beaming. "I'd say—"

"Caro, stop," Alex said quietly. "He's scheming."

She frowned. "He wants to join."

"No, he doesn't. None of them do. Especially him. Look at his wife. She's elbowed him three times since he started talking."

"You're mighty perceptive today, Mr. Banks," she said smartly.

He shrugged. "I've known him since we were thirteen. He rarely doesn't have ulterior motives. He's got a reason for asking you those questions. Madison elbowing him only confirms it."

She sighed. "He's right, isn't he?" she asked loud enough for everyone to hear.

"If he told you nobody in this room has a true interest in joining your *Matters of Biology Society* or whatever it is, then yes, he's right," Uncle John informed her with a shudder.

A fetching pink stained her cheeks and she turned back to her food.

"Don't fret about it," Alex murmured to Caroline. He looked around to make sure everyone was done with their meal, then caught Aunt Carolina's eye and winked.

Aunt Carolina jumped out of her seat faster than a bullet leaving a gun. "Would anyone be interested in playing a game?"

Murmurs and groans soon followed.

Ignoring them, Aunt Carolina looked down at Andrew and winked. "Charades, perhaps?"

"No," Andrew said, scowling. "Charades has been banned from this house."

Madison and Liberty looked like they were about to burst with laughter while both trying to imitate Andrew's scowl.

"But I do have the equipment for bowls," Andrew added, freezing Liberty's mirth on the spot.

"Absolutely not," Paul said tersely, shaking his head.

Andrew grinned. "Are you sure? I believe I have enough *balls* that we'll not have to bowl in teams."

Several snickers followed his remark, most notably not from Liberty or Paul. "I hear hiding and waiting to be sought out is a personal favorite nursery game among a few in this family," Paul suggested helpfully, succeeding in deflecting the attention off of him and his wife.

"No," Aunt Carolina said, shaking her head. "This house is too big. Nobody will ever be found."

"Exactly," Benjamin muttered. "All right. What about snapdragon?"

His wife rolled her eyes. "Benjamin, if your idea of an afternoon of fun is to light a bowl of brandy on fire and try to pull out a little button with your bare fingers, then suit yourself. But you'll have no competition."

He shrugged. "I don't know why not. The person who retrieves that little button gets a boon. And—" he leaned his head closer to his wife— "I know exactly how I plan to claim mine."

She blushed.

"That's enough of that," Uncle John said, curling his upper lip. "How about five stone?"

"That's boring," Brooke said, waving her hand through the air. "What about twirl the trencher?"

Her father snorted. "Brooke, as amusing as it would be to see you and your sister try to sit on the floor and get back up, run across the room, and grab an object before it reaches the floor in your conditions, I am an old man now, and I would be struggling right along with you. No, thank you."

Madison shook her head and sighed. "Let's see, that eliminates charades, bowls, hide and seek, snapdragon, five stones, and twirl the trencher. What else is there?" She looked directly at Caroline. "Any ideas?"

Caroline shook her head. "The only other game I can think of Alex hates."

"Pall mall," Uncle John supplied, smirking.

Aunt Carolina sent her husband a warning glance before turning her attention to Alex. "What about you? Do you have any ideas?"

"Hmm, I don't know," he drawled slowly, glancing at Caroline. "By any chance would anybody care for a game of *lawn chess*?"

"You can't mean?" Caroline cried excitedly.

He shrugged. "Would you like to go outside and see for yourself?"

"Yes," she chirped.

Grinning, he stood up and held his hand out to her.

She took his hand and merely glanced at the table full of smiling faces before leaving the room.

Outside, he led her in the direction of the black and white painted wooden platform some of the footmen had set up after Benjamin and Madison arrived with the chess set.

When they rounded the corner and the set came into sight, Caroline's arms flew around Alex's neck and her lips landed squarely on his.

Chapter 13

Caroline froze. She was kissing Alex right in front of his entire family! Well, they weren't out there of course, but from what she'd gleaned from them in the past hour, she wouldn't be the least bit surprised to glance at the house and see all of them with their faces pressed up against the glass.

"Sorry," she breathed. "I just got excited."

His strong hands framed her face. "No need to be sorry," he murmured. "I wanted you to be excited."

"Oh, Alex, thank you."

A lopsided smile took his face. "I can't accept your gratitude, darling Caro. The set belongs to the duke and duchess."

A sultry smile took her lips. "Then perhaps I should have kissed them."

"Never," he growled. "Your kisses are for me alone."

"May I?"

He nodded.

She walked around and looked at all the pieces.

"Is it what you remembered?" he asked after a minute of watching her inspect the thirty-two gigantic pieces.

"Yes." She fingered the intricate carving of the queen. "Thank you for convincing me to get out of the carriage."

He smiled. "This was the real reason we came here today."

She walked up to him. "You mean it wasn't because your entire family wanted to meet me?"

"Oh, they did," he said with an affirmative nod. "I came to talk to Andrew about finding a lawn chess set, and Brooke knew right away who had one. From there, she invited Benjamin and Madison here with the set." He shrugged. "This family does nothing in half measures."

She grinned and was tempted to kiss him again.

"Shall we play?" Brooke waddled in their direction.

Caroline hid her smile. Just last night, she'd listened to Olivia wax for an hour about the Countess of Townson having *another* baby. Olivia had even gone so far as to use all ten of her fingers and one toe to discover the two children would be only eleven months apart.

"Absolutely," Alex said jovially. "How shall we divide?"

"Mama and Papa don't want to play," Liberty put in, coming to stand in front of her husband, allowing him to wrap his arm around her shoulder.

"How about those born Bankses versus the others?" Uncle John suggested, smiling at his three sons-in-law.

His sons-in-law groaned. "I don't think so," Andrew said, pulling his wife closer to him.

"Ladies versus gentlemen won't work, either," Madison put in. "Unless Caroline is some sort of a chess master..."

Caroline was good at chess, but wouldn't consider herself a master. "I'm fair, but certainly not a match for four men."

Benjamin laughed. "It's not the three of us you have to worry about—" he gestured to himself, Paul, and Andrew— "it's him."

All eyes went to a casual looking Alex. "Are you that good?" she asked sheepishly.

Alex shrugged.

Andrew snorted. "Yes. Now, let's divide up and get on with it."

"What about Lords and Ladies versus the untitled?" Alex suggested. He bent his head down to whisper in her ear. "Like Andrew, I want to play on the same team as the lady who's caught my fancy."

A shiver ran down her spine at his words. They were no declaration of some great love to come, but it gave her hope all the same. "And I want to be on yours, too."

"Good. It's settled then," Alex said loud enough for everyone to hear. "We'll join Paul and Liberty versus the duke, duchess, earl, and countess."

"You just couldn't resist, could you?" she asked as they took their spots by the white pieces.

"No. Looks like we're going first. Where shall we move?"

Without much input from Paul and Liberty, Caroline and Alex moved the pawn in front of their queen's knight forward two spaces.

Twenty minutes later, the lesser gentry had the nobility's king cornered.

"Can we just all acknowledge your team won, Alex?" Andrew asked as he hauled a captured piece off the game board.

"No." His tone was very serious. "We have not won yet."

"To death shall we play, then thee shall pay," Andrew muttered as he frowned at the two lonely black pieces that were still in play.

"Pardon?" Caroline asked Andrew. "What did you just say?"

"To death shall we play, then thee shall pay," the earl and duke answered in unison.

"It's what Alex used to say whenever his opponent would ask to end the game early," the duke explained.

Caroline smiled. "That's hard to imagine."

Andrew scoffed. "It's true. But that's not as far as it went. When he won, which he always did, he'd make the loser kneel at his feet and pay up his bet by saying, 'This shilling now belongs to the smartest boy at Eton. This shilling now belongs to the smartest boy at Eton'."

"You're having me on!"

"No, we're not," the duke said, shaking his head, a very serious, genuine look on his face. "Not only was he the 'smartest boy at Eton', he was also the richest. Everyone's allowance went to him at least once, accompanied by the words, 'This shilling now belongs to the smartest boy at Eton'."

"I can't believe it," she said in shock. "It's just hard to picture him doing such a thing. Alex?" She looked at him to confirm or deny their charges.

Alex only smiled at her.

"See, Caroline," Andrew began, "the Alex you think you know is shy. And he is, for the most part. But when it comes to science or chess, it's as if that clamshell of his ceases to exist and he talks and acts in ways you wouldn't recognize."

"Clearly," she remarked dryly.

"And do you plan to make us do that today?" Brooke asked hesitantly, clearly concerned about having to kneel in her condition.

"No, Brooke." Alex shook his head. "I won't expect you and Madison to do such a thing. Your husbands..."

Benjamin scowled. "We weren't foolish enough to place any bets."

"Not to worry," Alex said offhandedly. "You don't have to surrender any of your hard earned pounds to me. You can just kneel and say, 'Alex Banks is the smartest man in England'."

The duke rolled his eyes. "That will not be happening outside your slumber. Even if you are," he added under his breath. He cleared his throat. "My days of kneeling at your feet ended more than fifteen years ago."

"Fifteen years ago? I was of the mind he did this all through school," Caroline said, confused.

"He did." Andrew nodded. "But to a different group of boys each term."

"After we'd all been wiped clean of our allowances a few times, none of the boys our age wanted to play him anymore. We'd rather lose our money on games of luck, not skill. But with each term came a new group of boys who thought they'd beat him and ended up emptying their coffers to him."

"Did Marcus ever do that?" she couldn't stop herself from asking. The thought of Marcus doing that was beyond laughable.

"Of course. No one was immune. They all thought they could best me, but none could." Alex's tone was sure, confident, but not cocky or demeaning, making her all the more drawn to him.

"You never lost a game?"

"No," Alex answered. "Never. Not even the game they made me play after they tied me to a chair and covered my eyes with a stocking because they suspected Marcus and I had been conspiring together to cheat everyone out of their allowance."

She looked at Benjamin and Andrew. She'd already deduced Paul wasn't there. He was a bit younger than the others, and likely if he were there, he'd have already said something. "You really did that to your friend?"

"They weren't my friends back then. Furthest thing from it," Alex informed her easily.

"He's right." Andrew agreed, at least having the decency to

look shamefaced for his youthful actions. "We didn't become friends until Cambridge."

"Actually, I think I got off rather easily being tied to a chair and made to play chess with a blindfold," Alex mused. "They never bothered me again after that. And compared to what some of the other boys suffered, I was rather relieved to have paid my dues so early on."

The duke snorted. "And don't forget, after that game, we all had to give you all of our funds and you bought that fancy telescope."

A wistful look came over Alex's face. "If I remember correctly, Professor Chalk bet his barometer on that match. I won that, too."

Shaking his head in disbelief, Benjamin looked at Alex. "And what exactly did you do with that?"

"Used it."

Madison cleared her throat. "All right, children. How about if we come back to the present and finish playing out this game so Benjamin and Andrew can kiss Alex's feet then rub mine and Brooke's?"

"Sorry, ladies," Alex said. "This will be over in two moves, then you'll all be able to sit down for a spell." He cast a long glance at Caroline.

She had no idea what he meant by that look and ignored him and his glances as they finished out the game.

"Excellent game," Alex's uncle said, walking up to the group before anyone could leave. "While I must say I was not surprised to hear what a good player Alex is, I can't help but wonder how good Caroline is."

Caroline couldn't stop her eyes from widening. Chess was fun. And she wasn't terrible. But it had only taken her a few minutes to learn she was no match for Alex. "Not so good," she said airily.

"That does nothing for my curiosity," Alex's uncle said, matching her tone. "What if the two of you were to play a game?"

"Perhaps Caroline would like to sit for a while." Alex put his hand on the small of her back.

"I'm fine. I'm not in a delicate condition and require rest," she said a bit defensively.

"Excellent," the elder Mr. Banks said excitedly. "Gentlemen, set the game back up for Alex and Caroline, would you?"

Alex went to help put the pieces back on the board with the other gentlemen, and Caroline spotted Liberty standing off to the side, watching.

"I'm sorry if we excluded you," she said, walking up to Liberty. They'd been on a team but had hardly said more than three or four sentences to each other.

Liberty smiled at her. "I didn't feel excluded in the least. I'm the youngest of three daughters. I grew up being excluded. I recognize it when I see it, and for once I chose to sit back and watch rather than be an active part."

Caroline nodded. "Good." She didn't know what else to say. Of the three sisters, Liberty was closest to her age, making them most likely to have something in common. The problem was Caroline didn't know what Olivia may or may not have said about her or her past to Liberty and how Liberty might truly feel about her. Olivia had claimed to be close friends with Liberty—up to the time of the ice skating incident, that is. If they were that close, who knows what she might have told her.

"Thank you for coming today," Liberty said suddenly. "I know you came for Alex. But really you came for everyone."

Caroline's eyebrows rose. "Pardon?"

Sighing, Liberty looped her arm through Caroline's. "It's obvious you and Alex share feelings. And that's good and all. But it seems to me your presence here today has made everyone closer, not just you and Alex."

"I see," Caroline said slowly, not seeing anything at all.

"No, you don't. But you will," Liberty said, pushing a hank of her light brown hair behind her ear. "See, our family has had its share of, shall we say, trials. They've not all gotten along or only feigned politeness with each other because of the family connection. I speak mainly of Andrew and Benjamin, of course. However, I think your coming today allowed them a chance to put their walls down and truly get along. And as much as I hope things work out well for you and Alex, I'll never be grateful enough to you for loving lawn chess so much that Alex inadvertently created this opportunity."

"I suppose I've earned the family's approval, then," Caroline jested, trying to not let it be obvious that she craved it.

"That and more. It looks like they're ready for you. Good luck. And, thank you again. It will be good to spend time with both my sisters again without worrying their husbands are going to kill each other."

Caroline smiled at her and walked over to where Alex stood in the middle of the gigantic chess board.

***

Alex leaned against an oversized pawn and took in Caroline's form as she sauntered over to him. He tried to keep his expression bland as she approached. That was not an easy task for a man who'd often been told his facial expressions often said more than his mouth. He scowled at the notion, but didn't dispute it.

Before walking off to join their wives, both Andrew and Benjamin had clapped him on the back and winked. He hadn't understood what they were trying to communicate and just nodded to them like a simpleton. Paul, however, was a bit more observant than the others and whispered three words in Alex's ear that chilled him to the bone. *Lose on purpose.* Now how was he supposed to accomplish that after everyone had just spent the last half hour talking about what an excellent player he was?

Hell's afire.

Only once had he ever tried to lose on purpose, and even then he won because his opponent was such a dolt he couldn't see any of the four easy wins Alex had set up for him. He scowled. Even after fifteen years, Raymond Treymore was still as thick as a tree trunk.

Alex planned to use arranging for them to play lawn chess as his grand gesture, but letting her win would only help him gain her favor more, wouldn't it? He shook his head to clear his thoughts. "White goes first."

She directed Paul, who had graciously agreed to move her pieces, to move her pawn from B-2 to B-3, thus freeing her bishop. Smart girl.

He moved his knight from B-8 to C-6 and smiled at her as he waited for her next play.

She commanded Paul to move her next piece, her bishop from

C-1 to B-2 like he thought she might. "I do wonder what is so humorous over there," she murmured when a loud chorus of laughter erupted from where the other seven sat beneath the shade.

"I have no idea." Alex moved his other knight into play.

Twenty minutes later, the laughter was louder, Caroline and Alex had only captured one piece each, the rest of their pieces were all over the board, both with several easy captures, and Andrew walked up to take Paul's place.

"What is so blasted humorous over there?" Alex asked Andrew through clenched teeth after he moved his rook right into the path of Caroline's queen.

Andrew shrugged. "Why would you ask me? I never find anything humorous."

Snorting, Alex crossed his arms. "I would have believed that answer two years ago, but ever since you married Brooke, you've walked around grinning like a simpleton."

Caroline called Andrew over to move her knight, of all pieces.

Alex frowned. She was afraid to move her queen to take his rook because it would expose her queen to be taken by nothing more than a lowly pawn. He shook his head. She really was a decent player.

"Are you sure you don't know what's so comical?" Caroline frowned.

"I couldn't say," Andrew said evasively.

"No, you *won't* say," Caroline muttered.

"Exactly so. Your turn, Alex."

Alex moved his piece and shook his head at the sight of Brooke bouncing off her lounge chair and running inside. "Where's she going?"

"I have no idea." Andrew shrugged and drummed his fingers on the pointy edge of Caroline's queen. "But don't worry. I'll be sure to find out when I sit back down in a few minutes."

"I just bet you will," Alex retorted. "And I bet you'll not be sharing the information with us."

"You just might be the smartest man in England, after all," Andrew mused sarcastically, grinning at Caroline who was leaning against a giant knight.

Brooke came flying back out the door with a piece of

parchment, a large tome, and quill and a pot of ink.

"She has writing implements." Alex furrowed his brow. "What are they doing over there, penning a book?"

"No, not a book." Andrew looked to Caroline to give him her next directive.

A few minutes later, Benjamin came up to take Andrew's place.

"And are you going to tell us what's so comical under the eaves, Your Grace?" Caroline asked with an enormous smile.

He shook his head. "No. You'll find out soon enough." He kicked a stick off the side of the platform then looked to Caroline for his instructions.

Alex and Caroline played another forty minutes, interrogating both Benjamin and Paul in between moves. Finally, Andrew came back up for his second rotation after Paul's.

"Are you almost done?" Andrew whispered so Caroline didn't hear.

"Almost," he whispered back. "I was afraid if I let her win right off she'd grow suspicious. But then, I realized she was actually a decent player and losing without being obvious became harder than winning."

Andrew chuckled and went to move Caroline's piece for her. "Think you might best him, Caroline?"

She bit her lip. "I don't know."

Alex moved his piece and waited for Andrew to move Caroline's. "I think it will be over in two plays."

Andrew nodded and moved Caroline's piece.

"I wonder why all the laughing has stopped," Caroline said loud enough for those up by the house to hear.

"Because we don't want to miss the end," Brooke answered, kicking her foot in a way that the toe of her slipper kept peeking out from under her skirt.

Alex made quick work of moving his next piece. He wanted to make it look like a lapse of judgment so she wouldn't catch onto his plan.

Caught up in the excitement, Caroline pushed her own piece over a square. "Checkmate!"

"You win, Caro!" Alex picked her up and gave her a twirl.

It took less than ten seconds for his family to be off their chairs and surrounding them.

"Now, Alex, as loser of this game, it's only fitting you kneel at Caroline's feet and recite lines praising her and her win," Brook informed him. "And since nobody expects her to think up on the spot what you should say to her, we've taken it upon ourselves to think of the lines for her." She handed Alex a piece of paper.

He grabbed the paper and quickly scanned the lines they'd collectively penned for him to say. He scowled. "I'll not be saying this." He shoved the paper in his breast pocket before someone could grab it back and show it to Caroline. "I'll kneel at her feet and praise her. But the words will be my own, thank you." His own words may not be as poetic or romantic, but they would be genuine, which, he was certain, would mean a lot more to Caroline.

Swallowing his nervous pride, he took Caroline's hands and dropped to his knees on the hard, wooden platform. He cleared his throat and looked up into Caroline's blue eyes.

"Caro," he started, then paused to scowl at Brooke who was prematurely gasping. They all knew he was going to propose. Couldn't she at least wait to gasp until he'd gotten the words out? He raised his eyebrows at her, waiting for her to get the unspoken message to stuff it until the appropriate time.

Instead of a nod or some small gesture to communicate she understood, a rather bizarre noise erupted from Brooke's throat and her finger pointed beyond Alex's shoulder.

Slowly, Alex turned his head over his shoulder at the same time Caroline raised her eyes and simultaneously their eyes followed the invisible line extending from Brooke's outstretched finger.

Beneath his grasp, Caroline's hands turned cold and stiffened just as his eyes fell upon the worst thing his imagination could possibly think up at a time like this.

He sucked in a breath. Hell's afire. Walking straight toward them was Lady Olivia.

Chapter 14

Good gracious. Olivia was trotting at them faster than Caroline had seen her move in years, and she looked angrier than a terrier chasing a rat. Caroline glanced down. Olivia was not going to be happy about this. Alex was on his knees at her feet, holding her hands, with his entire family standing around. Olivia's first thought would probably be that Alex was about to propose to Caroline, which he wasn't, but to an outsider that's exactly how it looked.

She tried to jerk her lifeless hands from Alex's, but he wouldn't let go. He stood up and murmured something about everything turning out all right.

"I thought I told you to keep your hands off him," Olivia snapped bitterly, putting her hands on her hips.

"Olivia, stop. There is no need to make a scene." Caroline and Olivia could argue about this another time, preferably without an audience.

Ignoring her, Olivia shook her head and clucked her tongue. "I knew this would happen to you. Mama always said it would, but tender soul that I am, I held out hope you wouldn't turn into the whore your mother was. I suppose she was right after all."

Blood pounding in her ears, Caroline didn't hear what Alex said in response. She tried to force herself to pay attention to what was being said when suddenly an arm looped around hers. "Caroline, dear, why did you not say something sooner?" Brooke exclaimed. "I, myself, have heard several unsavory whispers behind my back—some of which included being called that same unflattering term you just were—after I got myself ruined at my uncle's house party two years ago, or some such nonsense. I daresay this revelation has created a bond between us as deep as the bond I share with my sisters."

Olivia's mouth fell open. Likely she'd never expected the countess to openly refer to herself as been called a whore. Quite honestly, Caroline was a bit surprised, too. But not enough to not accept the show of friendship Brooke had just extended to her.

Olivia snapped her mouth shut and waved her hand dismissively. "Yes, I knew that about you, Lady Townson. I recognized you as a tart the night we met. The two of you shall have a very close friendship."

"You mean the three of us," Liberty amended, stepping up to stand next to Brooke. "I think you forget I seduced a country vicar while my parents were out for the night. The story appeared in the *Daily Times* last year. If you require a reminder of the events, I'll be happy to loan you my copy."

Olivia gasped. "That was you?"

"Yes," Liberty said proudly.

Caroline nearly choked on a giggle as she glanced at the grinning face of Liberty's husband then back to the horrified look on Olivia's.

"And to think I called you my friend," Olivia said with a sniff. "You are just as despicable as your sister."

"Which one?" Madison asked, pushing forward to join the ranks. "The night my engagement was announced, I was openly accused of carrying on an affair with my sister's husband. Thankfully, Benjamin was there and decided instead to make me his duchess. But that pales in comparison to my other premarital transgressions." Her tone left no doubt in anyone's mind she was being brutally honest.

Caroline looked at the three sisters and hoped they could see in her eyes just how thankful she was to them for exposing themselves to ridicule for her. Nobody had ever stood up for her like this before and their willingness touched her deeply.

"It's amazing you three doxies were able to snag husbands," Olivia said bitterly. "And two of rank."

"That's because we're just as depraved," Andrew informed her jovially. "I once signed an agreement to accept payment to ruin an innocent girl without offering marriage."

"And I'm the one who was going to pay him," Benjamin remarked, coming to stand behind his wife.

Olivia's eyes nearly popped out of her head. Then she brought out her fan. After three tries, she successfully snapped it open and fanned herself so fast one would think a light breeze was blowing through.

"Don't leave me out," the vicar said. "As I like to remind my wife from time to time, I may be a man of God, but I'm still a man. And believe it or not, I've had more than one scandal that would curl your stockings attached to my name." He twisted his lips. "I'm not really sure which is the worst, so I'll let you decide—"

"There is no need, Mr. Grimes," Olivia snapped. "This whole family is depraved." She narrowed her eyes on John and Carolina. "I don't even want to know the story behind your marriage."

"That's good, because it's not up for discussion," John said tightly, garnering a little nudge from his wife as her face grew pink.

Olivia blew out a deep, foul-smelling breath and looked at each of them with a disgusted scowl before her gaze fell to Alex, who looked as proud as could be of his scandalous family. Suddenly, Olivia's face transformed and she carelessly flicked her hand in the air in front of her. "Alex, darling," she said in a voice so sweet it could give someone a toothache, "I forgive you."

"Pardon?" he asked, his face completely blank.

"I know you cannot help who your relations are—" she cast Caroline a look that told her just what she thought of *her* relation— "but I'll not count it as a point against you. They're only cousins, after all."

"Excuse me?"

She huffed. "Alex, I'm telling you I'm willing to overlook this nuisance." Her face scrunched as she said the word. "I know you're not like them. You're a good and decent gentleman who doesn't have a scandalous bone in his body. I know that. I will grow to turn a blind eye to your family in time. Now, let's plan this wedding of ours, shall we?"

Alex stared blankly at her for a minute before flickering a glance to Caroline. Caroline's throat went dry and the blood roared in her ears. He didn't know Olivia like she did. He didn't know how insincere she was being just now in order to get what she wanted. But Caroline knew, and all she could do was stand paralyzed while she waited for Alex's response.

"Lady Olivia, I'm sorry to hear that you dislike my family so much," he said solemnly.

"Yes, well, that can be overlooked," she said, batting her lashes at him.

"Is that so? Well, it's not really of any import, because you see, I'm just like them."

She slapped him on the shoulder flirtatiously. "Don't be silly. You've never done anything scandalous."

Alex's response to her accusation wasn't what Caroline expected. Quite frankly, it wasn't what *anyone* expected. He squared his shoulders and, without so much as a blink, blurted, "A few years ago, I went to a nitrous oxide party and stripped off my clothes in front of all the other guests." The grim smile he wore after he said those unbelievable words slipped when the entire group erupted in laughter.

"Of all the lies you could have told, that was the worst, my beloved," Olivia crooned after her laughter died. She brought her hands to his chest to smooth his lapels and fix his twisted cravat.

He encircled her wrists and pulled her hands away from his body. He looked over at Caroline. "I don't have to defend or explain myself to you. But if you do not believe my story, ask Marcus. He was there, too." Even though his words were for Olivia, his eyes had been locked with Caroline's and she saw the truth in his eyes. A truth that no words alone could expose.

Where? When? Why? She wanted to ask all those questions and more, but instead she just smiled at him. He'd chosen her. For as odd a confession as that had been, it proved he'd chosen her, and the knowledge made her heart soar.

Olivia's face twisted in disgust. "Apparently Caroline was correct when she said there was more to you than I originally thought. Unfortunately for you, it's not something I'd care to further explore. If you decide to come to your senses, I shall be waiting at Ridge Water to hear your words of apology, and *if* they're good enough, I might consider forgiving you and going through with the wedding." She turned to Caroline. "Come, Caroline, let's go home. I suppose I'll forgive you, even if you are the daughter of a whore and addict."

Caroline sucked in a breath, perhaps from the shock of Olivia's comment, but most likely due to the loud clap of thunder overhead.

"Come, girls, let's go in before the rain starts," Alex's aunt murmured, pulling on the elbows of her two pregnant daughters.

Reluctantly, the three sisters followed their mother inside, leaving Caroline, Olivia and all the gentlemen outside.

"I agree," Olivia said. "We need to go before the rain starts, Caroline."

"No," Caroline countered firmly. "You go. I'm an invited guest." She glanced up to Andrew and waited for him to nod his agreement. "As such, I intend to stay."

Olivia clamped her plump hand on Caroline's upper arm. "Let's go before my hair gets wet."

"Let go of me." Caroline tried to yank her arm from Olivia's grip. "You're hurting me."

"Let go of her. Now," Alex said sharply.

Olivia's fingers tightened their grip. "Make me."

Without breaking eye contact with Olivia, Alex asked, "Would someone please go ask her coachman to bring the carriage up to the house?"

"Not me," Andrew answered immediately. "There's not a chance I'm leaving now."

"Me neither," the duke inserted just as soon as Andrew's last word had escaped.

Alex's uncle shook his head. "I'm not going anywhere."

"Well, I'm not going to leave this fiasco-in-the-making, either," the vicar added, interest evident in his sparkling, green eyes.

"Then flip a coin," Alex bit off.

"Excellent idea," Andrew agreed. He dug into his pocket and pulled out a silver coin.

The four proceeded to act like schoolboys and have a series of coin tosses that resulted in the duke being pronounced the loser. "I'll be right back, nobody move or say anything while I'm gone," Benjamin warned before scampering away in search of the coachman.

The five minutes he was gone seemed to last forever as the six of them who remained stood silent.

Equal parts relief and nervous excitement coursed through Caroline as Olivia's carriage came into view, the duke grinning as he rode up on the coachman's bench. The coach stopped by the house where the drive ended, about two hundred yards away from where they were standing. Before the brake was set, the duke was down and practically running over to rejoin the group.

"Very good," Alex said, still holding Olivia's daring gaze.

With no word of warning, Alex reached over, grabbed Olivia's hand, and yanked it off Caroline's arm. Not letting go of her wrist, he raised it in the air and wrapped her arm around his neck. He put his free arm around her midsection, hoisted her into the air, and slung her over his shoulder. Without a hint of strain or discomfort, Alex walked in the direction of the carriage. Everyone stayed close at his heels, watching in keen interest as he carried a kicking and screaming Olivia atop his shoulder to the carriage.

Thankfully the coachman had had enough foresight to open the door to the carriage. Alex only had to pull her off his shoulder, toss her up inside, and swiftly close the door. With a quick flick of his wrist, he locked the door from the outside and called to the coachman to drive on, heedless to Olivia's banging on the glass and demanding he let her out.

The coach was only about ten yards down the drive when Alex turned around. "Is everyone ready to go inside?" he asked as if nothing had happened.

"Are you all right?" Andrew asked, concern filling his face and his voice.

"Why wouldn't I be?"

"Because you just hoisted something at least fifteen stones over your shoulder and carried it more than two hundred yards," the duke retorted, a newfound admiration for Alex shining in his eyes.

"Actually, the physician said she's seventeen stones," Caroline blurted before she realized what she'd said and to whom.

"When there's that much mass, it's hard to tell a difference," Alex said with a flick of the wrist.

She blushed and flashed him a grateful smile. He'd only said that to make her feel better about what she'd just publicly revealed about her cousin. She looked at the four other gentlemen standing by Alex. They all shared that same gleam of admiration for Alex. She nearly laughed at the absurdity of the situation.

"Are you sure you're not hurt?" Paul asked, his unblinking green eyes wide behind his spectacles.

"I'm sure. Now let's go inside before we get wet."

Caroline held her palm out and caught half a dozen raindrops almost instantly. She'd been so absorbed by the excitement of Alex's dispatching of Olivia she hadn't noticed it was raining.

Alex held his arm out for her and they followed the other four men, who, like little boys, insisted on telling each other the story from their point of view of the events.

"You can tell me if you're hurt," Caroline whispered to Alex.

"I'm not." He brushed a kiss on her temple.

She chose to believe him and let the matter drop.

"Caro?" Alex pulled her to a stop once they were inside the house. "If you need a few minutes of privacy, I'll wait."

She shook her head. Why would he think she required a moment of privacy?

"Very well." He tugged her into a little dark area hidden in the shadows. His arms snaked around her and pulled her up against his chest. "Caro," he said raggedly, tracing her shoulder blades with his fingertips. "I wanted to talk to you about something. Something important."

Caroline blinked at him. His brown eyes looked more intense than she'd ever seen them. Why did she get the impression he didn't merely want to talk about something as trivial as the membership to the *Society of Biological Matters*? "Yes?"

Alex swallowed hard, and for some reason, his nervousness caused a jolt of excitement to shoot through Caroline. Just what did he have to say? "Caro, will you—"

"Hurry up, you two," Andrew called down the hall. "Mother has taken it into her head we need to dance."

Andrew's footsteps were coming closer and Alex released her. "We're coming," he called to his friend.

The very brief moment had passed. Caroline followed Alex's lead down the hall to the drawing room.

As soon as she entered the room her eyes fell on a woman

with silver-streaked black hair who was enthusiastically playing the pianoforte. Even if Andrew had not referred to her as "Mother" in the hall, Caroline would have known instantly who she was. Their looks were not identical by any means, but what they did have in common made it obvious they were mother and son.

"Grab your gal, Alex," the dowager countess called from behind the pianoforte. "I'm about to play a waltz."

Caroline's eyes grew wide as Alex held her in a tight, close embrace. They were the only two in the middle of the floor. The others were on settees and chairs that had been pushed up against the walls to allow room in the middle for dancing.

The music started and Caroline nearly tripped over Alex's feet as he moved. Panic washed over her. She'd never been allowed to share in Olivia's dance lessons and she had no idea what to do.

"Alex?"

He looked down at her, trying to move her backward. "Something amiss?"

"Yes." She glanced at the others, hoping they didn't see how much she was struggling as she stepped backward to avoid being knocked down.

Alex stopped moving. "Caro, do you not wish to dance?"

"It's not that," she said quickly. "I just think I need to sit for now."

Alex blinked. "Oh, Caro, I'm sorry. Yes, let's sit." He ushered her off to the side of the room and moved the pillows off a settee to make room for both of them.

The music abruptly stopped and Andrew's mother jumped off her bench. "Everyone needs to get their derrieres onto the floor this minute. I am not playing for my benefit."

Four couples immediately took the floor.

"She sure knows how to get people to do what she wants," Caroline remarked.

"That she does."

Caroline mindlessly flicked the nail of her middle finger with her thumbnail, creating an annoying little *click, click, click* sound as she tried to make her eyes look anywhere except to where Alex was tapping his foot in time with the beat. He wanted to dance. She swallowed hard. "If you'd like to dance with one of your cousins or your aunt I won't mind."

His foot stopped. "No, thank you."

"Are you sure? I know you want to dance, Alex. Don't try to lie about it."

"I'm not lying. I just don't wish to dance with them."

"But you want to dance."

"Of course I do. With you."

She clenched her teeth. "I'm sorry to have ruined your fun."

He shrugged. "You didn't. If I can't dance with you, sitting and talking to you is second best. Besides, we'll have another chance to dance."

"Pardon?" When did he think they were going to have another impromptu dance?

"Next time," he said simply.

Her heart skipped a beat. The prospect of a next time filled her with both hope and dread. "Alex," she said, licking her lips. "I don't think there will be a next time."

His eyes snapped to hers. "What do you mean?" His voice sounded like it was ripped from his throat.

"I...the reason I—" She looked down at her slippers. "I can't dance."

"I know. I understand that."

"No," she said, still staring down at where her toe was drawing shapes on the floor. "I don't know how to dance."

"Wait." He encircled her wrist with his fingers. "The reason we're sitting here is because you don't know how to dance—not for any other reason?"

She nodded. "I never learned how."

"I don't pretend to know why not," he muttered, raking his fingers through his hair. "Will you come out there with me?" He looked out at the middle of the floor. "We don't have to do the steps, just come out there with me and let me hold you in my arms."

"All right," she said with a swallow.

Abruptly, he jumped to his feet and pulled her into his arms. His right arm held her around the shoulders while his left arm wrapped around her lower back, his fingers lightly resting on her ribs.

She leaned her head on his chest and let him sway her, only moving her feet every few beats.

"Caroline," he whispered, capturing her full attention. He hadn't called her by her full name since the day they'd discovered her broken telescope.

"Yes?"

"Look at me."

She obeyed.

"I'm not a romantic," he said, his voice silky. "And I know you deserve all the romance the world has to offer. Unfortunately, I cannot provide such, so I hope you'll accept what I do offer." He paused and Caroline read in his eyes the question his mouth had yet to speak. "Caroline, will you marry me?"

"Yes!" she exclaimed before her brain could remind her mouth they were surrounded by a room full of people.

Alex's lips didn't turn up into the grin she'd expected. Instead, they descended on hers in the sweetest kiss she'd never imagined.

Chapter 15

Alex paid no mind to all the noise going on in the room around him. He was too focused on tasting the sweetest lips a man could ever know. Under his, Caroline's lips moved and responded in a way that made him crave more. More kissing. More of her. More of everything.

He pulled back before his lusty thoughts gave him away.

"Congratulations," Andrew said with a cough. "However, that was only the proposal. Best keep something for the wedding night."

Caroline blushed and Alex squeezed her affectionately. "Don't listen to him. He ought to be ashamed of himself for the things he did in my house."

"Ought to be, but I'm not," his friend said, hugging his wife with one arm.

"Now that I'm your betrothed, I have a few questions for you," Caroline said after the rest of the group had offered their congratulations and had gone back to dance.

"And what would those be?" Alex bent his head to bring his mouth by her cheek so he could shower her with kisses when the rest weren't watching.

"It's about earlier. Your scandalous deed at the nitrous oxide party," she said quietly, digging her fingers into the back of his hair.

He groaned. "I'll tell you the story another day. It's not something I want a lot of people to know about."

"Because you took your clothes off?"

He swallowed the bile that had risen in his throat. "Partly. There's more to it than that. I'll tell you everything after we're married and it's just you and me. Will that do?"

She nodded against his chest. "Yes. Just don't forget."

"I won't," he promised. During his earlier confession to Lady Olivia about taking his clothes off at a nitrous oxide party, he might have left out several important details. Details he hated to remember, but details he owed to Caroline all the same. She was to be his wife, his future. She had a right to know his past. Even the parts he'd rather not remember.

"Nephew," Uncle John called from across the room. "Just out of curiosity, when do you think you'll have your wedding?"

"Soon, I expect," he answered, still swaying Caroline.

"Don't you think you need her guardian's approval?" Benjamin asked.

"He'll give it." Alex looked down at Caroline. She'd stopped swaying with him. "Do you not think he'll give it?" he asked quietly. Marcus had all but given it already. Surely she wasn't worried he'd refuse.

"He will," she said, not meeting his eyes. "I think we should go."

"You're right," he agreed. "You wait here. I'll send for the carriage and Nettie."

Quickly, Alex ran down the hall to the butler and asked him to ready the carriage. He walked back in the room and spotted Caroline sitting on the fringe of the room, staring down at her fingers that were twisting the fabric of her skirt. Something was off, he just didn't know what.

She looked up and gained her feet. They said their goodbyes and walked down the hall. He stopped. "Do you need to do anything before we leave?"

"No. I'm just ready to go home."

He sighed and walked her to the carriage. For having a female condition that normally led to frequent visits to the necessary, Caroline had not been once.

Once in the carriage, he wrapped his arm around her and pulled her up close to him. Nettie was in the seat across from them, but the low light of the moon made it hard to see her.

Thinking talk of a wedding was a safe subject for a young lady who suffered a condition that made her prone to vapors, he asked, "Would you like to talk about our wedding?"

She shrugged her response.

He resisted his strong urge to sigh. "Do you have anything in mind?"

"No. Not really."

He threaded his fingers into his hair and pulled. "Do you want a London wedding?" As soon as the words were out of his mouth, he was astonished they were not followed by a silent prayer she'd say no. He may not be able to afford to wait for her to plan a London wedding, but if she did say yes, he'd do anything in his power to make sure she got it, even if he had to get on his knees and beg Marcus to accidentally burn that betrothal agreement.

She snorted. "No. I have no one to invite."

His heart twisted. She was right. Besides his family, most of whom she'd met today, she only knew three other people to invite to the wedding—one of whom would not be a welcomed guest. He'd always known he was unusual and an outcast from Society for his unusual interests, but until now, he'd never realized just how much his family had always supported him by looking past what the world saw or thought and accepting him in spite of his strangeness.

"Do you think Miss Green will stand up with you?" he asked hoarsely.

"I think so." Caroline rested her head on his chest.

He moved his fingers to her head and idly played with the curls overflowing her coiffure. "What of Marcus? Will he walk you down the aisle?"

"I don't know. He might not want to go out in public. Then again, he might think it's a small price to pay to be done with me."

The bitterness in her voice was unmistakable, even for him. She wasn't on her courses; she was angry with Marcus. "Why did Marcus make you cry?" he asked, irritation for Marcus and whatever he did to upset Caroline chilling his tone.

"Who told you that?"

"He did."

"Then he should have told you why." She ran her fingers along the top edge of his waistcoat.

"He didn't know why. He just said you'd been having a rough couple days with—" He broke off and waited a moment for his unease to ebb. "I'm the one who came to the conclusion it wasn't a female complaint but something he did. Now, tell me what it was."

She jerked her head off his chest. "Excuse me? You cannot demand I tell you anything. Besides, you and Marcus have no business discussing me, especially something so personal, not to mention indecent. Do you always ask him about my moods before you come to greet me?"

"No. He was waiting for me outside today and said—"

"Said what?" she snapped.

Heat crept up his face. "He may have mentioned you were going through an emotional stretch just now." This awkward conversation would make him think twice in future before asking what was wrong.

"Oh, good gracious! It all makes sense now. All day, you thought I was having my monthly. No wonder you kept asking if I needed privacy and didn't question why I didn't wish to dance." Laughter overtook her, each peal taking a little more sting out of the argument they'd just had. "Oh, I can't wait to tell Emma! She's going to die!"

Alex stayed quiet. It was probably best to wait for her to speak first.

"Alex, not that it's your business, but I am not having my courses. And if I were, unlike Olivia, the whole house would not know about it. Black moods, tantrums, and screaming are not my way." She brought her head back to rest against his chest. "I'm sorry I snapped at you. It wasn't very well done of me. But yes, I am upset with Marcus. However, there's nothing you can do to fix it, and I'd rather not speak of it."

"All right, we won't speak of him any longer. But I do wish to ask you something about our wedding. You said you wouldn't like a London wedding, but what about a long engagement?"

Her fingers once again set out to explore his chest. "No. There's not really a reason to have a long engagement if there's to be hardly a wedding."

His thoughts exactly. "Would later this week be acceptable? I'll leave tomorrow to get the special license."

"I'd like that very much."

He dropped a kiss on the crown of her head. "We're here."

The carriage came to a stop and Alex helped her down. He

escorted her up the steps, inside, and to the bottom of the grand staircase.

"It'll take me a few days to get that license." He cupped her chin with his hands. "I should be back no later than week's end. Will that be enough time for you to be ready?"

She nodded and smiled a smile so bright he almost hated to extinguish it with a kiss. Almost.

He lowered his mouth to hers and covered her lips. Her arms wrapped around his neck, holding him closer, his fingers digging into the back of her thick hair. His impulse was to deepen their kiss, then, remembering where they were, he pulled away.

Flashing her a smile, he whispered, "I had better speak to your guardian about the wedding."

Walking away from her was the hardest thing he'd ever done. At some point in the past days, an imaginary string had developed that connected her body and his heart, and whenever he turned away from her, the pull on that string became nearly impossible to resist.

"Marcus," he called, entering the man's private sanctuary.

Marcus was sitting in his chair, head bent, hair wild, and looking absolutely defeated. He must have heard about what happened today. Alex didn't plan to bring up his actions from earlier. If Marcus asked him why he had treated Lady Olivia that way, he'd explain any of the details she might have left off. If not, he wasn't volunteering anything.

"I understand your day was better than mine." Marcus gave a weak smile. He put his quill down and propped his feet up on the desk.

"You understand correctly," Alex said. "We'd like to get married later this week if that's acceptable with you."

"Is it acceptable with Caroline?" Marcus scraped the edge of one boot across the other.

Alex nodded. "She said it was."

"You're not pushing her, are you?" Marcus plucked his quill off his desk and twirled it between his fingers. "I know you don't wish to marry Olivia, but I don't want Caroline cheated due to your haste."

"I've already offered her a long engagement and a London

wedding. She declined. She said she didn't have any guests to invite."

Marcus groaned and made a face. "I'll speak to her about it later. Just be prepared, if she does want a fancy wedding, she'll have it."

"Very well. I don't expect she'll change her mind though."

"You seem awfully certain," Marcus said with a snort, leaning back in his chair in a way that lifted the front two legs off the floor.

"That's because I am. I'm also certain that she'd like you to walk her down the aisle."

Marcus anxiously tapped his quill against the side of his scarred face. "I don't know, Alex. I'm not one for social events. You know that. I've only left Ridge Water maybe half a dozen times in the past twelve years."

"There won't be that many people there." Alex crossed his arms. "I'd say fourteen at most, including you."

Dropping his quill to his desk, Marcus grunted. "Do you honestly think she'd want me to come? I'll steal all her attention."

"Nonsense," Alex replied easily, flashing Marcus a grin. "I'll be doing that. Everyone will be in a state of shock because I'm actually getting married."

Marcus shook his head and took his feet off his desk, bringing all four chair legs safely back to the ground. "You know what I meant."

"I do." Only a complete fool couldn't have guessed what he was talking about. "I don't think that will happen." He uncrossed his arms and idly picked at his hangnail. "Even if that does happen, I think Caroline would consider it a small price to pay to have you there."

Marcus shut his eyes and swallowed so hard his Adam's apple could have been seen bobbing from across the room. "Are you sure she'd want that?"

"To have her only male relation walk her down the aisle? Absolutely. Whether you know it or not, she adores you, Marcus, and I think it would hurt her far worse if you don't come than if you do and 'steal her attention'."

"I'll be there," he said softly.

Alex gained his feet. He'd wanted to talk to Marcus about the events of the nitrous oxide party, but Marcus didn't look in the mood to rehash the past. However, there was something he would bring up. He owed it to Caroline to help make things right between her and Marcus before she left his house and started a life with Alex. Actually, both Caroline and Marcus deserved that.

Shifting from foot to foot, he tried to decide just how to word what he needed to say. Finally, he swallowed his pride and blurted, "I think you should know Caroline is not suffering the complaint you seem to think she is. She's been crying because you hurt her feelings." The words were out so fast he wasn't sure whether to feel relieved he'd gotten it over with, or to feel a complete idiot to have just said it like that.

Marcus blinked at him three or four times. "I'm not sure I want to know how you discovered the first statement you told me," he said carefully. "But I do appreciate your discovering the truth of the second and telling me." He rested his hand on his cheek and swiveled left and right in his chair. "I suppose I should go speak to her," he said at last, looking to Alex for what Alex assumed was confirmation.

"Probably," Alex agreed quietly, slipping out the door.

***

Marcus scrubbed his face with cold hands, running his fingertips over every repulsive groove and scar that marred his once handsome face. He brought his face out of his hands. Would his life have turned out this way if he'd not acted thoughtlessly and been hurt?

He laughed bitterly. He knew the answer to that. His life would have been no different (except perhaps worse) than it was now. Louise wouldn't have helped him with Olivia and Caroline. She'd have been too busy worrying about pleasing herself. Either way, he'd have had to go about it alone, and, as it was, he was making a horrible hash of things every step of the way.

Not that Caroline was difficult, of course. She'd always been extremely easy to get along with. They'd become quite close since she'd come to live with them. In fact, they got along better than he ever had with Olivia. Not to say he didn't love Olivia—he did. She was his sister, after all. And being his sister meant he'd love her unconditionally. Even if she drove him—and everyone else in

England—insane. But the same was true for Caroline. He loved her just as much.

The problem with Caroline was she was so opposite Olivia that instead of touting her connection and being unhappy when things didn't go to her satisfaction, Caroline accepted everything good and bad with a smile. At nearly one-and-twenty she had never discovered her own value. Who could blame her, though? Olivia and his mother had taken every opportunity they could to remind Caroline of what she'd come from and what she would have been without Father's intervention. He sighed. His father hadn't been much better, really. He may have saved her that night, but he'd never been able to stand up to his wife and make her treat Caroline as an equal to Olivia.

When Father died last year, Marcus vowed to do whatever it took to see that Caroline had a bright and happy future. Sadly, he hadn't known how to go about it. But then one day about three months ago he stumbled upon that nearly unbelievable betrothal contract his father and Lord Watson signed. After his shock faded, it had occurred to him how he should go about giving Caroline, and coincidentally Alex, a "happily-ever-after" as it were. He'd seen the sloppily signed addendum on the back and sent word to Barnes to remind Lord Watson. He doubted Alex had even heard of the agreement before. If he had, Marcus was sure Alex wouldn't have waited so long to begin his search for a wife.

His hope had been that Alex would come around and he and Caroline would see they were well matched. Marcus congratulated himself. With only a little shove in the right direction, that was exactly what happened.

Too bad Olivia had caught wind of the agreement. He didn't know who had told her, but someone had, and it seemed she was planning on marrying Alex more and more as each day passed. He scowled. What was he going to do about her?

In a way, she deserved to marry Alex. That was the agreement, after all. But the match would be disastrous. She'd drive the poor man to do himself in. He'd been tempted to do that very thing several times over the past decade due to Olivia's atrocious personality. Perhaps he'd try to secure her another match. Or, if luck were on his side, she'd agree to go to the convent in Ireland like he'd been urging her to do for the past five years.

No matter. He'd worry about that another day. For now, he needed to seek out Caroline and find out what he'd done. Since she'd come here all those years ago, they'd never had a row. He wasn't even aware she'd ever been upset with him before. This was all new to him.

Grimacing in pain as he climbed the stairs, he ran his hand along the smooth banister and tried in vain to think up what he'd say when he reached Caroline's room.

However, for all his thinking, he hadn't formed a single sentence by the time he reached her door and knocked.

Caroline called for him to come in, probably thinking he was a maid.

He cracked the door a sliver. "Caroline, it's Marcus. Are you decent?"

"Yes. Come in."

Shoving the door open all the way, Marcus took his time crossing the threshold. He left the door open and looked around her room, snarling. Nothing about Caroline had changed. She still insisted on lighting every candle at her disposal when she was in her room at night. Not that he cared about the expense. The cost of all those beeswax candles was immaterial. But the sensation of his heart sinking to his stomach was a direct result of knowing she was still living with her past nightmares.

"I spoke to Alex," he said, falling into the most uncomfortable chair he'd ever rested his arse upon.

Caroline put her book down beside her and readjusted her coverlet. "I don't require a large wedding, Marcus."

"I know that." He shifted in the chair to find a more comfortable position. He wasn't sure if the chair was really *that* uncomfortable or if it was because he was a cripple. Knowing Caroline though, he'd bet the chair was truly that awful. She never asked for anything and was usually reluctant in accepting anything he'd ever offered her. "Would you like one though?" He sucked in a deep breath and hoped she'd say no. A dozen or so people he could handle for an hour. A large group, on the other hand, he wasn't sure if he could manage. He sighed. If that's what Caroline wanted, he'd find a way to get past his discomfort and go.

"I don't need a London wedding or anything of the like. I've already told Alex we could marry as soon as he was ready. He said he would leave tomorrow to see the archbishop about a special license."

"If you want a long engagement and a London wedding, you can have it," he offered again, giving her another opportunity to have what he assumed all young girls dreamt of.

She blinked. "That's all right. I don't need one."

Idly rubbing his throbbing leg, he sighed. "What's wrong, Caroline? What have I done?"

"Nothing," she said quickly, not meeting his eyes.

He didn't believe her for a second. Tired of sitting in that awful, about-to-be-firewood chair, he stood up and walked to her open wardrobe. It may be rude to dig through other people's things, especially when they were in the room, but it had been a long time since he'd been confused for a gentleman.

Irritation turned to fury as he picked through her clothes. All but four of her gowns were dyed black from her year of mourning for his father. He quickly discovered the four dresses that *had* escaped the transformation were faded and had been mended several times. Which only meant they were in bad shape, indeed, if he were able to detect their flaws. He sighed. She had nothing. Nothing nice, nothing suitable for a wedding. Practically nothing at all.

"Why didn't you tell me you needed new gowns?" he demanded, not unkindly. "I would have commissioned new ones the day after our mourning period was over if I'd known you were in such dire need."

She shrugged. "I don't need anything, Marcus."

He snorted. "Yes, you do." He folded his arms across his chest. "You're to be married soon, and you have nothing to wear to your wedding. And while Alex might enjoy that particular costume, the rest of us will not be so thrilled to see it."

Her lips turned up into a smile and a small burble of laughter escaped them.

He smiled back at her and leaned against the side of her atrociously half-filled wardrobe. "Caroline, anything I have is at your disposal. I know I'm not the easiest person to approach at times. I just hoped you would have come to me if you needed something."

She looked down and studied the fringe on her counterpane. He'd never been the cause of her quietly staring intently at an inanimate object before, but he'd seen her do it enough times after Olivia had upset her to know she was truly upset.

"Caroline, I'm a man. I'm not good at emotional things. Please, just tell me what's wrong so I can fix it. I obviously did something, but I don't know what. Just tell me what it was." His fists clenched while he silently waited for her response.

"It doesn't matter," she said quickly, letting go of the fringe between her fingers and flashing him the falsest smile he'd ever seen.

"All right, I'll leave, then. Oh, before I go—" he paused at the doorway— "I think I'm going to deny Alex his request for your hand. As your guardian I still have that privilege until your twenty-first birthday, which is in what, six months?"

Her eyes went wide. "Why?" she asked, her voice cracked by a sob, causing his chest to ache and a pang of guilt to shoot through him.

He shrugged as nonchalantly as possible. "As you say, you don't need anything. Why should I allow you to marry Alex? At one-and-twenty, you can make that decision for yourself and marry him inside Astley's during a trick where a man stands on a horse and shoots out the flames on a five candle candelabra balanced on a lady's head, if you wish. But until then, I shan't give my permission."

She turned her head away from his view, but not before he caught sight of the tear that slipped from the corner of her eye. "I understand."

"Now, Caroline, I will take all that back, and let you marry him whenever you wish if you will just please tell me what's going on." He really didn't like playing female games, and oh, how he'd played them for years. First with Louise, then with Olivia, and now Caroline.

"It's hard to explain," she said at last.

"Try."

"It's just that I always thought you liked me. You never once brought my past up and flung it in my face like Olivia and your mother." She used the tip of her index finger to wipe the edges of her eyes where unshed tears had pooled, just waiting to fall. "But then the other day, you said you wouldn't allow a match between Olivia and Alex, but you would allow me to marry him." Her voice cracked and she stopped to swallow convulsively.

Twirling her fingers into the gold fringe on her counterpane again, she continued, "Olivia has always made clear to me that she is the daughter of an earl, therefore, she is entitled to marry a gentleman of equal or higher rank. My mother may have been the daughter of an earl, but that ceased to matter when she married a commoner." She shook her head and cleared her throat. "Olivia has time and again informed me Alex is not good enough for her, due to his lack of rank. I know he'll be a baron one day, but to her that seems to mean nothing. Until just a few days ago, that is. But then you practically told me the same thing the other day. She's too good to marry him, but I'm not."

Marcus blinked at her. He remembered having a conversation with her after Alex had returned her from "stargazing" about how he'd not allow a marriage between Olivia and Alex, but would allow Caroline to marry him. However, his acceptance of the match had nothing to do with rank, or lack thereof.

"Do you not wish to marry Alex?" He'd honestly thought they'd be a good match. But if she didn't care for him that way, he wouldn't force her.

"Yes," she said quietly.

"Does his rank bother you?" He had to ask. He had to know the truth. He'd never thought Caroline was so shallow as to care about titles and rank, but her earlier statement gave him pause.

She shook her head. "I don't care that he's a mere mister who is heir to a barony. But once again you've missed my point." She sighed. "Just forget I said anything."

"No. I want to know." He glanced around the room to find a suitable piece of furniture to sit on. Standing for extended periods was difficult, and he might be here a while. Only spotting that awful chair he'd vacated earlier, he resigned himself to standing.

"There's a chest at the end of the bed," Caroline murmured, pointing to where a fluffy quilt was resting. "Just pick up that coverlet and put it on the bed. I assure you, that cushioned chest is far better to sit on than that chair."

"A rock would be preferable to that chair," he muttered, picking up the coverlet and taking a seat on the cushioned chest.

"Better?"

"Yes. Now, tell me the error of my ways," he said with a quick grin.

She groaned. "Marcus, I like Alex, I really do. I'd probably wish to marry him if he were a chimney sweep. His lack of 'sufficient' rank is not the problem. It was—" she bit her lip and balled her hands up— "well, you said you wouldn't allow a match between them, but you would let me marry him because I was different. And though you've never so much as alluded to my past before, you did then and it hurt. It hurt that you wouldn't allow your sister to marry him because of his lower rank, but I was good enough because I was not born with the same rank and privilege."

"So the problem isn't Alex's rank, but because I'm allowing you to marry him, and said I wouldn't let Olivia—"

"Yes, beca—"

His hand shot up. "Let me finish. Because of that, you think I was implying Olivia was too good for Alex, but you were more suitable due to your past?"

Caroline nodded glumly.

He ran his hand up and down his face, contemplating how to word his defense. "Caroline, I didn't mean to hurt your feelings. You misunderstood me the other day. Alex and I were very close friends for most of our boyhood, and though you are my cousin and Olivia my sister, I still feel a sense of loyalty to him. When I made that mindless statement, it was more on his behalf than anything." He shifted on the seat, becoming more comfortable about what he was saying. "Olivia would make him miserable. The two have nothing in common. You, on the other hand, have a lot in common with him. That's why I'd allow a match between the two of you. Not because I think you're of a lower station."

"You don't think less of me because my father was—"

"Enough," he said abruptly. "I don't give a hang about any of that. I never liked to hear Mother or Olivia speak of it, and there is no reason for you to, either. The past is the past. Let it go,

Caroline. Look to the future. Alex will make you an excellent husband. You'll be happy with him."

"You'll agree to a quick wedding, then?" she asked, hopeful.

"Yes. If that's what you wish."

"It is. There's no use in waiting. His father's very ill," she said sadly. A second later a cheeky grin took her face. "And anyway, it's not like either of us have a lot of friends to invite."

A harsh bark of laughter escaped Marcus. "You were planning to invite Patrick, weren't you?"

Caroline's eyes went wide and Marcus bit back a smile. Patrick Ramsey, Viscount Drakely was nearly as much of a recluse as he was. That was part of the reason they'd gotten along so well all this time.

"He has three little girls, remember? They'd probably love to go to a wedding," Marcus explained carefully, not sure why he so strongly wanted Patrick to be at her wedding.

"Of course. But I don't think Drake would."

She had him there. Patrick, or Drake as he was more commonly known, would not love to go to a wedding. "That may be, but it wouldn't hurt to ask, would it?"

"I suppose not."

Chapter 16

The wedding was a small, somewhat hectic affair. Due to Father's illness, the wedding had to be held at Watson Estate, which put Brooke into a frenzy. Andrew didn't want her traveling so close to the end of her confinement. But Brooke had a mind of her own, and after a compromise that involved four hours in a carriage going at an extremely slow pace, the two with their baby arrived at Watson Estate with fifteen minutes to spare before the wedding.

And that was just the beginning.

Paul and Liberty rolled up a few minutes later. As soon as the carriage door swung open, Paul went about his task of trying to scrape up a change of clothes, saying his wife would kill him if he even *suggested* to perform the wedding wearing the clothes he had on. Apparently their little boy wasn't much of a traveler yet.

The duke and duchess arrived just as Paul's coachman cleared the drive. Benjamin carried his wife inside and deposited her on one of the settees in the drawing room. Standing outside, Alex could hear them exchanging words. Not bitter arguing, of course, just bantering in the way they normally did. When their words stopped, Alex peeked in the window in time to see Madison kick off her slippers and prop her feet up on the end of the settee with her arms crossed. Benjamin soon emerged from the side of the house, muttering something about as crazy as she made him, he'd always love that blasted female.

Benjamin then went out and started giving directives to the coachman who had driven the second coach to their caravan. Alex didn't even want to know what *that* was about. He was still waiting for Caroline and Marcus to arrive, becoming more nervous as the minutes stretched on.

He checked his pocket watch. There were less than ten

minutes before the ceremony was to start, and his bride was nowhere to be found.

He didn't want his guests to guess at his unease, so he went for a walk to calm his nerves. What if she didn't come? His heartbeat picked up pace. Had she changed her mind? After he'd procured the special license, he'd written to his family and made a trip to see her to secure the details. She wasn't available though. Marcus told him she was out and agreed on the wedding time in her stead.

He kicked a stray stone. "Damn," he muttered in agitation, kicking another stone. "I should have waited. I should have talked to her." He raked his hair with his fingers and sat on a rock. If she'd changed her mind at least he'd have known and could have avoided the embarrassment and unease of being jilted at the altar.

He swallowed hard and stood up. Turning to walk back down the path, he nearly collided with Marcus.

His unease immediately intensified to horrification when his eyes met Marcus'. "She's not coming, is she?" he asked unevenly.

Marcus shook his head. "She's coming. She's just...um...been detained."

"Where is she?" Alex asked tightly, pushing past Marcus. He started back down the path and froze. Marcus' traveling coach was parked nearly at the servants' door of his house. He opened his mouth to ask what was going on, but just then, a female clad in a horribly tattered nightrail slipped out of the carriage and ran the ten feet from the door of the coach to the open door in the back of his house.

"Don't ask," Marcus barked from behind him.

Alex ignored him. "What's that about?" he asked, spinning around to face his friend and jerking his thumb back to point behind him where Caroline had just entered the side of his house.

The sound of Marcus' teeth grinding filled the air. "Olivia. Between the two, I've had one horrifying week," Marcus muttered, leaning against a tree. "Alex, I'm going to tell you something about Caroline you should know. I can't tell you how to handle it since I've yet to learn, but you should know all the same."

Alex nodded, too anxious to speak.

"She won't say a damn thing when something's wrong."

Marcus shoved two fisted hands into his trouser pockets. "The night you proposed, I went to her room and found she had no suitable clothes. None at all. Not for everyday wear, and definitely nothing for a wedding. The next day I commissioned her an entire new wardrobe. Now, stop clenching your jaw. I meant no offense to you. I know you have the funds to dress her in the best money can buy. But as her cousin and her guardian, it had been my responsibility and I'd neglected it. Not intentionally, mind you. She just never said anything to me, and I just didn't notice the sorry state of her gowns the past few weeks."

"All right," Alex said, not sure what to do with this information. His brows knit together. "Does that have anything to do with why she's nearly late for her wedding and arrived in a tattered nightrail?"

"No," Marcus bit off. "I paid nearly thirty pounds to have a very flattering dress made ready for today. The dress was delivered yesterday afternoon. Caroline was thrilled. That woman was well-worth every shilling, having such a beautiful dress made up so quickly." He shook his head. "But that's not important. Last night Caroline didn't come down to dinner. I thought she was just nervous, so I went to see her before bed. When I went in the room, I found a needle and thread in her hand sloppily weaving in and out of that fabric at an alarming rate. At first it looked like she was making a minor alteration, but when I walked up closer, I noticed she was repairing it." He blew out a breath and turned his head to study a nearby tree. His jaw clamped so tightly Alex thought it would be a miracle if Marcus had any teeth left to eat with at the wedding luncheon. "As it turns out, Olivia took a pair of cutting shears to the dress and Caroline missed dinner because she'd spent the previous five hours trying to fix the dress."

The air left Alex's lungs in one big whoosh. He knew Lady Olivia was vile enough to stoop to just about anything—that didn't surprise him. The air absent from his lungs was brought on by the pain and hurt he felt on Caroline's behalf. He may not be a lady, and he sure as hell didn't pretend to understand them, but even he knew to have such a thing happen must have hurt her deeply.

"Now, calm down, Alex," Marcus said. "I can see the steam coming out of your ears. Olivia has been dealt with and my two best footmen are watching her to make sure she stays at Ridge Water today, where she belongs. The only reason I told you any of this was so you'd know two things. One, Caroline did want to be here today. She wanted to be here so badly she spent most of last night trying to mend her destroyed wedding dress. She even rode here today in a nightrail that should have been reduced to cleaning rags years ago. I'm not a seer, nor am I particularly good with the fairer sex, but I know that has to mean something. She wants to marry you, Alex. Which leads me to the second thing. Please treat her right. Between her family and mine, I fear that hasn't always happened. I tried, but I didn't know how to go about it, and it seems I've done too little too late. I'm trying to tell you what I didn't know so you can have a better chance of meeting her needs and desires." He scuffed the toe of his boot in the soft dirt and twisted his lips.

"Alex, Caroline hasn't had an easy life, but she's made a habit to make the best of things. She'll never come to you when something's not right. As her husband, I pity you this. But it's just the way of it. You'll have to ask and push Caroline to get her to allow you to take care of her. She'll never volunteer the information." He paused and tapped his finger along his jaw. "Curious, she did tell you she was angry with me..." What was left of his eyebrows moved closer together, and he looked in deep contemplation.

"That's only because I embarrassed her and suggested she was having an emotionally trying time of the month." He was torn between excitement that she'd been so eager to marry him and uncertainty of what to do next. He wanted to marry her today, but he didn't wish to embarrass her by making her walk down the aisle to him in a hideous nightrail. "Thank you for telling me all that, Marcus. I need to talk to Caroline before anyone else sees her. Would you like to come, too?"

"No, thank you. I'll wait here until I get the signal."

"The signal?"

"When I see Emma take her spot, I'll know to get Caroline." He shifted his weight off his injured leg.

Alex frowned. "You don't have to hide, Marcus. Nobody here would ever be rude enough to say anything to your face *or* behind your back. Besides, they've all had plenty of gossip fly about themselves."

Marcus swallowed. "You're right. It was most insulting for me to imply otherwise. Perhaps I'll sit over in the shade next to your father until Caroline is ready to be walked down the aisle."

"About that," Alex began uncomfortably, "there won't be a wedding today. I'll not have Caroline be embarrassed by walking down the aisle looking like a scullery maid. Not that my family would care, of course. They probably wouldn't even bat an eyelash, truth be told. However, today is about Caroline and she deserves better than that. Everyone can wait another day or two for her to be ready."

"No need," Marcus said with a nod in the direction of the drive where off in the distance a lone rider was riding at a breakneck speed to the front of the house, a large brown paper package in his hand. "A message sent at midnight accompanied with a shredded wedding dress and an additional fifty pounds, and Caroline's dress is ready just in time."

A grin split Alex's face. "Thank you." Sometime since the day he'd proposed to Caroline, he'd discovered he wasn't looking forward to marrying her because it was a means to escape marriage to Lady Olivia, but because he truly wanted to. But for as much as he wanted to insist he'd still marry her in that awful scrap of garment she called a nightrail, he couldn't have truly done that to her.

"Perhaps you should inform your guests the wedding might be delayed a few minutes," Marcus suggested, pushing off from the tree trunk.

"Right." Alex uprooted his feet from where they were planted in the ground.

He walked over and made a quick announcement about how Caroline's dress had suffered an unfortunate accident (he left off exactly *what* the accident was and *who* had caused it, but the guests weren't dimwits—they knew the who and what of it). He then told them the wedding would start as soon as she was done changing.

Before anyone could ask questions, he sat down, pulled his fisted hands from his pockets, and took a deep breath.

Sitting in a little row of chairs behind him, Andrew, Brooke, Madison, and Benjamin talked about names they'd picked out for their unborn children. He fought the urge to snort when the duke suggested Andrew and Brooke name their son Benjamin in honor of the gentleman who had helped them discover each other. Even more absurd was Andrew's suggestion to Madison and Benjamin to name their son Andrew since he had such a large role in their marriage and lasting happiness.

Alex shook his head at the foursome. He assumed Andrew and the duke only got along because they both loved their wives, who just happened to be sisters, but he'd often noticed they still couldn't help exchanging harmless barbs whenever possible.

"What of you, Alex?" Andrew asked. "If you and Caroline have a son, what do you plan to name him?"

Alex froze, stunned. His eyes grew wide. He'd never really thought past the wedding. Except perhaps the wedding night. What man *didn't* think of that? Children, however, had never entered his mind. He turned around to face the group. "Following the suggestions you two have been giving each other, I think my son's name will be Marcus," Alex said dryly.

"Marcus?" Andrew asked, one eyebrow arching. "And why not Andrew?"

Alex shrugged. "Like I said, if I had to name my son for the man who helped me the most in ensuring my marriage to Caroline, it would be Marcus."

"But what of *my* suggestions?" Andrew asked with a wink.

Staring blankly at him, Alex said, "*Your* suggestions were completely vague. All you said was take her to the orangery and let instinct take over."

A high-pitched strangled, choking noise came from Brooke's throat, her eyes growing round as a pall mall ball. Next to her Madison and Benjamin laughed, and Andrew merely shrugged. "Did you really want me to be specific?" Andrew asked, garnering him a nudge in the side from his wife. He rolled his eyes up and to the side. "Perhaps I should have suggested you take her to your little telescope hut."

"Andrew Black, stop it right now," Brooke squealed, her face flushing crimson.

"Andrew, is there a single place on this estate you didn't try to seduce my cousin?" Alex asked testily.

"Hmm—" Andrew looked to his blushing wife then back to Alex— "her room perhaps."

"Well, that's good to know. At least you stayed away from the one place with a soft, inviting surface," Alex retorted.

"Except the thick green carpet of grass during their picnic," Madison put in helpfully.

Alex ground his teeth. Brooke shot her sister a look Alex couldn't catch and muttered, "See if I ever tell you anything again," before scowling at her chuckling husband.

Madison responded, but Alex didn't hear her words. He'd lost interest in their conversation. Instead, Caroline's emergence from the back of the house had captured him completely.

She was wearing an elegant grey gown with shiny streaks of shiny silver fabric running down the skirts and wrapping around her wrists. The gown was so long and fluffy he couldn't even see her slippers peek out the bottom as she walked. The bodice was covered with thousands of sequins and beads that had been embroidered around the edges of her cuffs, neckline, and hem. She was a vision as she clutched onto Marcus, who was dressed in solid black and wearing a top hat no less than eighteen inches tall.

Alex took his place under the trellis along with Andrew, his attendant, and Paul. Miss Green wore a light blue dress and walked up and stood opposite them, a smile as big as the moon on her face.

Slowly, Marcus walked Caroline to Alex and winked at him when he placed her hand in his.

Alex nodded, and the next minutes blurred together as he recited vows and vaguely listened to her do the same. When at last Paul announced they were now husband and wife, Alex could wait no longer. His hands came up to cup her face and tip it up toward him. He leaned his face to hers and captured her lips, not giving her a chance to make this a quick, chaste kiss.

This was a wedding and he needed to keep that in the back of his mind, of course. But that didn't stop him from parting her lips with his. He sucked her lower lip into his mouth to run his tongue along it before releasing her mouth. Alex took a measure of pride in seeing her fingers move up to rest on her red, kiss-swollen lips.

He covered her hand with his and turned to face their applauding audience as Paul announced them Mister and Missus Alexander Banks.

A quick meal that could pass as either a late breakfast or a luncheon followed. Alex couldn't help but smile and inwardly congratulate himself once again for finding the perfect bride. Caroline didn't pick at her food as he'd seen many brides do. She was definitely different. No bridal nerves for her.

"Shall we have some dancing?" Mother asked, jumping from the chair she'd been occupying next to Father.

A pang of dread filled Alex's heart. This would likely be the last chance his parents would have to dance together. He couldn't deny them that. They may have had an arranged marriage, but Alex had never considered either of them miserable. If he had to guess, he wouldn't be so sure if love hadn't developed between them in all these years. He glanced at Caroline and hoped the same would be true for them.

"Would that be all right with you?" he asked Caroline quietly, taking into consideration she may not be comfortable with dancing since she didn't know how.

She smiled at him. "I've already danced with you once before, Mr. Banks. I believe we had very good results that time. I can only imagine what will happen this time." Her smile widened a touch and her eyes sparkled with an emotion he couldn't name.

"Dancing it is," Alex said to his mother. He watched in quiet amusement as his aunt jumped off her seat so fast one might think her skirt had caught fire.

Together his mother and Aunt Carolina left to locate a few musically inclined servants.

When the duo came back inside, they announced dancing would be held in the drawing room.

The small group stood, ready to walk down the hall. Caroline abruptly let go of his arm and said she'd be back in a minute. She came back on the arm of a gentleman Alex hadn't seen before today. The man looked to be close to Alex's age and height. His hair was solid black and his face appeared hard as stone.

Alex had spotted the man during his grand announcement about the slight delay due to Caroline's dress. He had to be the possible guest Marcus had spoken to him about. Three young girls were either sitting on his lap or climbing on him at all times. These must be his daughters. His wife however, was nowhere in sight.

"Alex, this is Lord Drakely. He's been Marcus' closest friend for as long as I can remember." She turned to look up at the other man. "You two met the day of his accident, did you not?"

Lord Drakely nodded. "Yes. I stopped his horse."

"Right," Caroline agreed. A crooked smile took her lips. "Marcus always jests that he and Drake here only became friends because no matter what Marcus did or said to drive him away, Drake clung to him like a bur."

Alex barely nodded and forced his lips to hold a brittle smile while inwardly guilt consumed him to the point of making his palms moist with sweat. Her last words hadn't been meant as anything but a lighthearted jibe at Lord Drakely, but Alex felt every word like a blow to the gut. At a time when his friend had needed him most, he'd not been there. He'd heeded Marcus' harsh commands to be left alone and though he didn't see it then, he realized now what his friend needed most was for someone to stay. He raked a clammy hand through his hair and pulled. Hard. He shouldn't have let Marcus put him off so easily. But he had and that was one of Alex's biggest mistakes, but that didn't mean he couldn't make an earnest attempt to rekindle their friendship. Perhaps he should plan to visit Marcus more often and—

"The three little girls you see running around are his," Caroline continued, pulling Alex from his deep contemplations.

Alex greeted the man and his little girls and was about to ask after his wife when Caroline's delicate cough halted his words.

"Lead us down, boy," Father hollered, prompting Alex to offer Caroline his arm and start walking down the hall.

"Where is his wife?" Alex whispered, unable to hold his question any longer.

"She passed away in childbirth about four years ago," Caroline explained without much emotion.

"Oh, I'm sorry. Did you know her well?"

Caroline misstepped a fraction. "No, not well at all."

In the drawing room, a group of servants holding instruments that varied from an ancient looking violin to two spoons bound back-to-back were assembled together.

"Shall we?" Alex asked, leading her close to where the musicians were assembled.

Caroline walked with him to the middle of the floor and let him take her into his arms the way he had a few nights before. "It's all right, Caro, just follow my lead."

She moved her feet to follow where his went.

After the first song, several couples joined them, his parents included.

Over Caroline's head, Alex's eyes fell on his father and mother who were standing still and swaying to the music, their arms wrapped around each other. The pair's eyes were each fixed solely on the other and nobody else.

Uncle John spun his wife, and she squealed as she almost bumped into Liberty and Paul, sending both ladies into peals of laughter.

The earl and countess along with the duke and duchess had each found a corner of the room to dance alone. He mindlessly pulled Caroline closer, marveling at the way her soft body felt against his.

"Alex," Caroline whispered, catching his attention.

"Yes?"

She glanced down at his snowy-white, emerald-pinned cravat before looking back to his face. "Could you please dance with Emma?"

He froze. "Am I making you uncomfortable?"

"No, not at all." She ran her hands along his shoulders in a comforting way, then bit her lip and glanced over his shoulder for a brief second. "She'll never get to dance if you don't ask her. Marcus can't dance well because of his leg. Drake won't dance at all. And as for your friend Andrew—" she shrugged— "I think he's forgotten it's the responsibility of the male attendant to dance with the female attendant at least once." She reached up and pushed a lock of fallen hair behind her ear. "Anyway, I wouldn't wish to remind him. He looks too content with his wife. So would you please dance with her?"

He glanced to where Miss Green sat next to Marcus and Lord Drakely. The three didn't look to be having a conversation. They appeared to be sitting quietly, watching the couples and Lord Drakely's three daughters dance. "Of course. As soon as this song is over I'll ask her. Will that do?"

"Yes. Thank you."

The dance ended and Alex walked up to where Miss Green was seated. "Miss Green, would you do me the honor of this dance?"

"But I couldn't. You're the groom!"

"Yes, and as the groom I'd like a dance with the second most beautiful lady in attendance." He shut his mouth and turned his eyes away. That was *not* the best thing he could have said to charm a lady. But really, he couldn't have said she was the most beautiful lady in attendance when she wasn't. Not to him, at least.

She laughed. "It's all right, Mr. Banks. I'm in no way offended, and I would love to dance with you."

Miss Green was an excellent dancer. She danced with far more grace and confidence than Caroline. He glanced at Caroline. She was currently engaged in a rather arresting conversation with Marcus and Lord Drakely, from the looks of it. One of Drakely's girls climbed onto her lap and ran her fingers over all the beadwork on Caroline's dress. She'd make a good mother. Her way with those little girls was so natural and easy.

"Your children will be very lucky," Miss Green said, startling him.

"Thank you," he said, nodding. "She has a way about her, doesn't she?"

"She sure does. She always has. The two of you are very lucky to have found each other."

"Thank you again. But I cannot take credit. Marcus is the one who pointed out to me how well suited we'd be," he admitted, not wanting to mention—or even *think* about—his father's role.

"Indeed?" she asked as she nearly tripped. "Pardon me. I was merely shocked to hear Marcus was involved."

Alex chuckled. "Surprising, isn't it? I was rather shocked when he first suggested it to me, and my shock did not stem from who he was suggesting I should court, but that he was suggesting someone in the first place."

"Who knew he was a romantic?" she murmured.

"You'd never guess by looking at him, would you?"

"No," she agreed, turning her head to look at the man in question. "Not by looking at him anyway."

The music ended and Alex led her back to her chair. She might have more talent for dancing than Caroline, but Caroline was his wife, and she was the one he wanted to spin around the floor with.

That was not meant to be, however. "Dance with me! Dance with me!" three little girls squealed, tugging at his clothes.

Still sitting in her chair, Caroline made a gesture he took to mean he should give each of the three girls a turn of the floor.

A chuckle from Marcus caught his attention. The man winked at him. Next to Marcus, the viscount looked at his three daughters, but didn't say anything.

Each of the two older girls grabbed onto Alex's hands while the youngest wrapped her arms around his leg.

"All right," he said, resigned. "But one at a time. I'm not as talented as your father or Caro. I don't think I can manage all three of you at once."

One by one, he took each of the three girls into his arms and danced them around the floor, refusing to meet the curious eyes of his amused family.

"Caro, are you ready to dance again?" he asked, reaching his hand out to Caroline.

"Yes." She stood and glanced back to Marcus, Lord Drakely and Miss Green. "The three of you are welcome to join us."

Lord Drakely declined.

Marcus started to decline, but Caroline cleared her throat. He frowned, and Caroline cocked her head.

With a sigh, Marcus gained his feet. "Emma, could I interest you in a dance?" His voice gave nothing away.

Miss Green briefly looked at Caroline before declining Marcus' reluctantly spoken request.

Caroline frowned and sighed. "I wish he'd at least try to dance with her. She cannot possibly be having any fun."

"I am," Alex countered with a grin. "Well, now that you're in my arms again I am. I like dancing with you, Caro."

She allowed him to pull her closer. "Thank you."

"Alex, we need to go," Andrew said after a short time.

"Right," Alex said with a slow smile. "If you don't leave soon, you'll not be home before nightfall."

"Exactly. Unless you'd like us to stay the night?" Andrew asked with a slanted grin.

"No. I'm afraid I'll not be available to entertain you tonight if you stay," he added cheekily, admiring the way his words made Caroline's face flush.

Andrew closed his eyes and shook his head. "Brooke would like to say goodbye, then we'll be on our way. Congratulations to both of you." Andrew kissed Caroline's cheek and turned to his wife.

Brooke hugged him. "Congratulations, Alex." Releasing him, she wrapped Caroline in a hug and whispered something in her ear.

"Are we all saying our goodbyes?" Marcus asked, slowly walking up to their group.

The music stopped just then, and everyone gathered around them to say their goodbyes. Alex couldn't pretend to be disappointed they were leaving. Once they were all gone, he'd get to spend the rest of the day alone with Caroline. That suited him just fine.

"Oh, we've a wedding gift to give you," Madison said. "Actually, we can't exactly give it to you here, seeing as it's outside."

Everyone followed Alex and Caroline outside to where Benjamin had directed them to go. Alex knit his brows. Why the duke led them to stand on a wooden platform that was draped with white sheets was most bizarre.

"Benjamin, are you planning to move the cloth?" Madison murmured, patting her stomach to indicate her inability to lean over easily.

Her husband made a comical facial expression. "Anything to please the duchess." He kissed his wife's cheek then dutifully leaned over, grabbed a handful of fabric, and pulled it to the side, revealing two black and two white squares.

"It's a lawn chess set," Madison exclaimed.

"The pieces are in that shed," Benjamin explained, pointing vaguely in the direction of a shed some hundred yards to the east.

Marcus chuckled. "Poor, Alex. I think you're about to spend

your wedding night playing chess. Caroline *loves* lawn chess." He flashed Alex a grin then turned to Caroline. "I should warn you, Caroline. Alex is the best I've ever seen. He can have the best players beat in less than fifteen minutes. Thirty, if he's just trying to make sport of them. I've only seen him play one game that took longer than thirty, and after about an hour I realized—"

"Say, Sinclair, I believe I owe you an apology," the duke broke in, rendering the entire group silent. The duke never made apologies. "I seem to remember Andrew and I once accused the two of you of cheating, and we may have acted, shall we say, irrationally?"

"Thank you, Gateway," Marcus said offhandedly. "But it's of no consequence now. We all suffered something unpleasant or embarrassing at school. Some of us were tied to a bed so we could clear our names of being accused of cheating, and others had to sink to their knees and render all of their allowance to Alex, declaring him the smartest boy at Eton in the process." He shrugged. "It's the past. What I was going to tell Caroline was—"

"He let me win," she finished for him flatly, making all the blood rush from Alex's head.

"You've already played?" Marcus shifted his weight from one foot to the other and mouthed something in Alex's direction that looked oddly like the word: sorry.

"Yes," Caroline clipped. Her earlier smile was a mere memory now. "On Sunday. We played for more than an hour."

"Sorry, Alex," Marcus said aloud this time. "I didn't know you'd played, or I wouldn't have said anything."

"It's quite all right," Alex said tightly, wishing everyone would just disappear. He turned to face Caroline. "Yes, I let you win. Which proved to be more difficult than winning. You're a good player."

"Why did you do that?" Her eyes bored into his.

"I was looking for an excuse to get on my knees in front of you." It was partially the truth. He *had* planned to propose to her that day. His losing chess—and consequently getting that ridiculous slip of paper from Brooke—created the perfect opportunity. But she didn't need to know that insignificant detail.

"I see," she said slowly. "Well then, now that you've no

ulterior motive, I demand a rematch."

His jaw clenched and his mind spun. This was not how he pictured the ending of his wedding. His bride was upset he'd let her win a chess game, and now he was facing a rematch that, no matter what the outcome, could render his wedding night a disaster.

An idea popped into his head.

"All right. I'll give you a rematch." He leaned close so he could whisper in her ear. "I'll bring a chess set with me when I come to your bed tonight."

Chapter 17

Caroline's skin grew warm from the roots of her hair to tips of her toes. Had he really said that? The wolfish smile on his face cleared up any doubt. Yes, he'd really said it. She could scarcely believe it. Alex never did or said *anything* scandalous.

Wait. That wasn't true. Less than a week ago, he'd admitted to stripping at a nitrous oxide party, and only a few days before that, they'd shared a horse while she rode to spend the night alone with him. And, if that wasn't enough, he'd even touched her breasts. Granted it was nighttime and only a light caressing of the sides and a few brushes past her nipple, but he'd done it all the same.

She cleared her throat and tried to force herself to say something, but nothing could come out. She couldn't form a single word, let alone a coherent thought. His three cousins and their husbands appeared to be quite amused at the current situation. One of the men even muttered something under his breath that was definitely *not* meant for mixed company. She flushed. They all knew what Alex said. They may not have been close enough to hear his exact words, but they'd all understood his message. Likely, Alex had stunned them once again and probably moved up a little more in their regard. She couldn't help but smile at the knowledge. Always being thought weak or unmanly or too cautious for one's own good had to be hard on Alex. It was good his friends were seeing him for who he really was.

As if to emphasize Alex's remark had been understood by the entire group, she caught sight of Marcus' scowl, and a slightly sad, shuttered look on Drake's face. Alex's aunt, uncle and mother were the only ones not openly showing any understanding of his words. Instead, they'd all taken to either studying their nails or gazing at the clouds in the sky.

Her new father-in-law, on the other hand, was the only one

who openly acknowledged what had just happened. "I'm not sure I've ever been prouder," Edward said. "Not only have I gained a daughter, but I think I was just given the assurance that I just might be a grandpapa nine months from today." When his wife gave him a sharp look, he shrugged. "It gives me something to live for," he said unapologetically, quieting everybody's laughter from his earlier remark.

"Sorry, Caro," Alex said softly. "I didn't think anybody would hear." His face looked so sweet and apologetic, she dared not deny him forgiveness.

"I don't think they heard you. I think I gave it away when I turned as red as a beet."

"Exactly so," Andrew agreed. "I was standing the closest and I didn't hear your words."

Alex relaxed remarkably. "Good. They weren't meant for you. Only Caro."

"Enjoy your night, you two," Andrew said. "We really must be off."

"Can I see you a minute in my room, son?" the baron said as Alex escorted Caroline inside once all the guests had gone.

Alex went off with his father and Regina invited Caroline to the drawing room. "Mrs. Crofter sent a note this morning saying she wasn't quite finished with some of the personal things you'd ordered and it would be a day or two before they arrived. If you'd like, I have some things you may wear until then." She poured them each a cup of tea.

Caroline took the tea, trying in vain to ignore the blush she knew had to be staining her cheeks. "Thank you, but I don't wish to impose on your generosity."

"No imposition." Regina waved her hand. "You're my daughter now. I look forward to becoming further acquainted with you. Even allowing you to borrow my things if need be." Her smile was so soft and warm, it left no doubt in Caroline's mind she was being sincere.

"Thank you but I shan't need anything, I don't think." Caroline selected a biscuit.

"Yes, I suppose you won't require a nightrail." Regina held her teacup in a way that would have hid her smile if it wasn't as big as Scotland.

"No. Remember, I came wearing one," Caroline said with a lopsided smile.

Regina's eyes went wide. "I do remember. But you're not planning to wear that, are you?"

Caroline's face flushed yet again. "Yes," she said quietly, tamping down her anger for what Olivia had done and the embarrassment of having to arrive today in her best—but still awful—nightrail. With any luck, this was the last thing Olivia could ever do to her. How unfortunate the seamstress hadn't been able to deliver her dress an hour earlier to Ridge Water. Then nobody would have ever known.

"Oh, but you can't wear that one," Regina protested, bringing Caroline back to present.

Caroline ducked her head in embarrassment. She had known Alex's parents would be there tonight. It was custom that families all shared the family estate. With how large the estate was there was no reason not to. However, it still did nothing to ease the embarrassment that his parents would know what they were doing tonight.

"Caroline, I don't know how to say this." Regina put her teacup on its saucer with a soft clink. "About tonight...um...that nightrail..." She bit her lip and smoothed her skirts with her fingers. "Caroline, dear, you will not be able to wear that nightrail tonight."

Caroline froze. Her mother-in-law of less than four hours was about to have the wedding night talk with her. Not that she needed it. She didn't. She'd practically grown up on a farm and had seen almost every species of animals procreate. She had no questions about what would happen tonight in that regard. Unfortunately, she couldn't think of a tactful way to tell Regina this.

"I'm so sorry," Regina said quietly, twisting her wedding ring nervously. "I didn't realize you had an attachment to that particular nightrail, and I had it thrown out."

A burble of laughter built up inside Caroline. "That's all?"

Regina nodded. "As I said, I'm sorry. If I'd known it was a favorite, I would have just ordered it washed."

"It's not a problem, Regina." She tried not to laugh at the look of worry on her mother-in-law's face. "I've no great fondness for that dirty, old thing."

"Good. Let's go upstairs so you can pick out what you might need before Alex returns."

"Truly, I don't need anything. I can wear what I have until the things arrive tomorrow."

Regina eyed her skeptically. "If you say so, but you're still coming up to my room. I have something to give you up there that you will not refuse."

Caroline nodded.

Regina brought her to a room that looked a bit small and too disheveled to be a baroness' room. Caroline sat on an empty chair as she was instructed while her mother-in-law went to her wardrobe. Regina turned around holding a pair of soft sided cream slippers that would not only be comfortable, but would also match Caroline's current gown. She nearly groaned with relief. She'd forgotten to bring an extra pair of slippers from Ridge Water under the assumption that the modiste would send her new ones today. Which, of course, she hadn't.

"Take those stiff slippers off and put these on, Caroline. No protests. You may deny borrowing my chemises and stockings, but you *will* wear my slippers. Those things you're wearing are going to blister your feet in the worst way. Come now, Caroline, take them off."

Caroline obeyed. She had no desire to refuse this request. "Can I borrow something else?" she asked quietly, causing Regina to pause.

"Yes. Anything. What do you need?"

"A nightrail," she said uncomfortably. "Now that the other one is gone..."

Regina opened a drawer in her bureau and pulled out a brown package tied with a strand of white twine. "This one is new. I've never even worn it."

Holding the package to her chest, she smiled at Regina. "Thank you again for all your generosity."

"Think nothing of it. I'm more than happy to share my things with you. My son is very lucky to have married you."

Caroline blushed with embarrassment. She wasn't used to this much attention and praise.

Caroline reached down to pick up her discarded slippers when Regina's hand fell to her wrist. "Do you know what to expect tonight?" No discomfort or embarrassment sneaked into her voice.

"I think so, yes." Caroline tried not to sound like a lightskirt, but still did what she could to avoid having an uncomfortable discussion with her mother-in-law.

"I thought you might, growing up in the country and all," Regina said with an assuring smile. "However, I'll say this and nothing more. If something makes you uncomfortable, you have to tell him. Gentlemen aren't very perceptive at times."

Flushing, Caroline murmured an agreement.

"Shall I show you to your room?" Regina offered.

"No need. I'll take her," came the familiar voice of her new husband.

"Very well," Alex's mother agreed, taking the slippers and package from Caroline's hands and giving them to Alex as fast as she could. "If she needs anything else, just come and get it. She's being bashful."

"Come along, Caro. I'll show you to your room."

"Where are we going?" she asked after a few minutes of navigating the halls.

"As far away from them as possible."

"I believe it. I feel as if we've traveled to another shire."

He chuckled. "No. Just the opposite end of the house. We'll have the entire wing to ourselves." He stopped in front of a large oak door and swung it open. "We'll put your things in here for now."

Caroline walked into the room and nearly jumped up and down with excitement. All along the window sills, little plants of different sizes and variety were lined up in rows. A small desk was covered in papers and instruments. She walked over and picked one up. "Is this the barometer you won in a chess game?"

"The very one," he said with a nostalgic grin. He put her things down on the bed before going to a small table in the back corner that was covered with little items she couldn't distinguish from where she stood.

"Am I right to assume this is your room?" She fingered a

mercury thermometer.

"No. It's *our* room."

Her heart squeezed and she looked away.

Watson Estate was huge. By her guess, there had to be at least sixty bedchambers. She couldn't help but wonder why they were sharing one. Not that it mattered overmuch. She was rather excited at the prospect of spending all night with Alex. It just seemed odd. The house was so big and yet his mother, the baroness, was in a room smaller than this one, and the two of them were sharing one.

"Will that be all right, Caro?" He walked up behind her and wrapped his arms around her waist. He pulled her flush against his hard body and nuzzled the sensitive spot where her neck met her shoulder.

"Yes," she breathed. A wicked thought crept into her head. "I just hope we have enough time tonight for that chess rematch."

He groaned and parted his lips against her skin.

Loving that she had him just as lust-fogged for her as she was for him, she wanted to push him a bit further. She pressed her bottom against his erection. "Yes, with all this science equipment for me to explore, we may not even make it to bed."

He froze. "We're leaving. We'll go find another room," he said raggedly, picking her up.

She squirmed in his hold. "Put me down! Put me down!"

He put her feet down on the ground, not releasing her. "You weren't serious, were you?"

She turned in his hold to face him. "About which part? Putting me down? Yes. Spending the night exploring your science equipment?" She rolled her eyes up to look at the ceiling and tapped her fingernail against her teeth.

"I've got some science equipment you can spend the night exploring," he muttered, pressing said equipment into her soft stomach.

She nearly lost her calm, reserved, mock-contemplative composure at his gesture. "My, my, Mr. Banks, and here I was under the impression you always had science on the brain."

"I do," he conceded. "Tonight we'll study some. The main topics I have in mind include some physical science and biology. Perhaps, after we get more comfortable with each other, we can test a few laws of physics."

"You're incorrigible."

He smiled. "I do believe you're jesting again."

She shook her head. "I'd hope you understood that. I was rather obvious about it."

His look was hard to interpret. He wasn't angry or offended, but he wasn't smiling, either. His right hand left her back and came around to rest on her side, the heel of his hand pushing against her breast. "I can't wait to get you alone tonight," he said before his lips descended on hers.

Why wait? She wanted to say the words aloud, but didn't want to seem too forward. She knew what would happen tonight. She was looking forward to sharing her body with Alex—knowing him and letting him know her in every way possible.

The pressure of his lips spurred hers into action, and she pressed hers to his the same way, allowing his to move over and between hers. He licked the seam of her lips the same way he'd licked her lower lip at their wedding. When his tongue flicked the corner of her mouth, she gasped. Taking advantage of her parted lips, Alex's tongue sought entry into her mouth and swept the inside of her cheeks before withdrawing.

She sighed at the absence of his tongue, and his hand moved to cover her breast, leading her nipple to harden in response. "Alex," she murmured, arching into his hand like the wanton she always seemed to transform into while in Alex's presence.

He pulled his lips from hers. "Later. I promise."

She swallowed and chastised herself for the flicker of disappointment that had shot through her when he'd pulled away. "A—all right," she stammered, pulling out of his arms.

Barely a second later, two maids came in carrying a few simple morning gowns. Caroline blinked and sighed. There was no use fighting it. Regina had probably insisted they bring her those gowns to wear until her things arrived. Caroline shook her head and shot Alex a grateful look. He must have heard them coming and stopped touching her so as not to embarrass her in front of the staff. What a thoughtful gentleman he was. She reached for his hand and gave it a light squeeze. She couldn't have asked for a better husband.

"Annie," Alex called. "Would you please hang the gowns on the dressing screen and put this..." He picked up the package the nightrail was in and looked at Caroline to finish for him.

"Just leave it there." There really wasn't another place to put it, and she certainly didn't want the maid to unwrap it in front of Alex.

Annie looked at Caroline uncertainly. "Do what the lady said," Alex said for her. "Shall we go down and wait for dinner?"

"That would be wonderful."

Caroline blinked when her eyes landed on the baron sitting in the drawing room. He was far sicker than she had originally surmised. Of course she'd seen him lying abed last week, and earlier she'd seen him weakly sway his wife at her wedding, but just now he looked so tired and worn out she could hardly believe he was joining them. She swallowed the lump in her throat. Death couldn't be too much longer away for him. She rubbed Alex's arm, trying to convey her sympathy at having to watch his father die in such a cruel way. She'd been fortunate not to witness such a thing with her mother or her aunt and uncle, so she didn't know what she could do or say to make it better. She did know, though, he needed support now and he'd need it later. That was something she could give him in abundance.

"Good to see you, gel," Edward said, nodding to her as she came in. His eyes still held their mischievous spark, despite his illness.

Caroline felt a slight tug on her heart. She'd forever admire this man. He was dying, but he wasn't going to let it keep him away from the things and people he loved. He'd attended their wedding—he'd even made what would be considered a vulgar joke at the end—with nary a complaint or a pessimistic word. He'd come to dinner and even dressed for the occasion. All the while, he looked like he should be in bed with his blankets up to his chin and his eyes closed while being read Bible verses.

"It's good to see you, too," she replied with a sweet smile.

"Is it? Well then, I suppose you'd like to eat dinner next to me instead of my son?" he asked with a cheeky grin. "But, I had better decline. For as much as I'd love that arrangement, I doubt my wife would approve."

"Neither would Caroline's husband." Alex put a possessive hand on the small of her back.

She looked up at Alex and smiled. He may only be playing his father's game, but she still liked that he was pretending to be possessive of her.

The butler came in then and announced dinner was ready. The meal was as excellent as the company. It may seem odd to some—all right, to most—to eat their evening meal on their first married night with their family members, but Caroline wouldn't have preferred it any other way.

The circumstances couldn't have been changed unless they'd either ridden to London to stay at Alex's bachelor's quarters or gone to Bath and stayed at Dog and Fox, which was rumored to be the worst inn in England. The truth was, neither of those were options with how sick Edward was, nor was ignoring the other inhabitants of the house. This was still Edward and Regina's home, too, and avoiding them or asking them to go elsewhere was not going to happen as long as Caroline had breath in her body.

After dinner, Alex's father dismissed the servants from the dining room after Regina asked a footman to retrieve the post, saying now was a good time to read it since the whole family was here. Apparently a letter had arrived from Alex's brothers earlier that day, along with some sort of package.

Caroline sat quietly and listened intently as Regina read the letter from Henry and Elijah aloud.

It would seem Henry and Elijah had recently received their mother's missive and would be coming home shortly. Caroline would never admit it aloud, but she was actually excited to meet them, despite the circumstances that would bring them here. What would they be like? One, or both, of them obviously had to have a sense of humor or else they wouldn't have carved Alex's name into the pink pall mall mallet.

"May I ask something?" she interrupted, trying to think of something—anything—to get her mind off the pink mallet story. "Why didn't Edwina come today?"

"She wanted to," Regina said quietly. "We wouldn't allow her to."

Caroline went still. She didn't understand why her parents

would keep her from coming to her brother's wedding. Then suddenly she knew. Regina and her mother had gone to school together, the same school Edwina attended currently. Likely Edwina had heard rumors about the promiscuous girl who had once attended and was forced to leave because she got with child. Alex's parents probably didn't wish to expose Edwina to censure from the other girls due to her newly formed connection.

Caroline's face burned with shame and embarrassment like she'd never known before. "I see."

"No, you don't," Regina countered, not unkindly.

Edward placed his hand on his wife's then glanced from Alex to Caroline. He coughed and wiped his mouth. "I know what you're thinking, gel. But that's not the reason." His eyes bored into her, sending her an unspoken message declaring he did, indeed, know what she was thinking. "I'm the one who denied Edwina the choice to come today. She's particularly sensitive and I was afraid if she came, she wouldn't go back."

Caroline understood his words and another round of embarrassment passed through her. She'd been selfish thinking she was the reason Edwina wasn't allowed to attend, when in reality it had been because they were trying to protect Edwina by keeping her from seeing her father in such a state. "I'm sorry," she said softly.

"No need," Edward told her with a smile. "You'll get to meet her soon enough, I expect."

She nodded sadly.

"Well, enough of that talk," Regina chirped. "Edwina may not have been able to come, but she did send a wedding present." She turned to her side and picked up a small package with a little note attached to the twine and held it out to Caroline.

Caroline's fingers reached out took the package from her mother-in-law.

"Open it," Alex encouraged.

"I can't." Caroline stared at the little card attached to the twine.

"Sure you can," Alex said, reaching for it. "Here, I'll show you how."

She moved her hands—and the package—just in time to

escape his grasp. "Here, read this." She handed him the notecard attached to the top. "She addressed it to me specifically and told me to open it in private. I intend to do that very thing."

"Oh, Edward, what have you done?" Regina put her face in her hands, her shoulders shaking.

Caroline's eyebrows snapped together. "What's going on?" she asked of no one in particular.

Nobody answered her. They were all too busy avoiding eye contact and if she wasn't mistaken she'd swear both Alex and his mother appeared to be on the verge of laughter.

Caroline pursed her lips. Truly, what could they possibly find so funny?

Alex shook his head and tried his best to wipe the grin off his face and replace it with a serious look. He wasn't very successful, however. "That book," he said, pointing to the package she'd already deduced was a book, "is not something any gently bred young lady should ever lay eyes on."

Caroline's eyes went wide and she couldn't decide whether to drop the offending package or grip it all the tighter. "How do you know?"

Alex shrugged. "It's just a guess."

"A good one, I'd wager," his mother added, wiping her watering eyes.

"Open it," Edward prompted. He chuckled when Caroline shook her head violently.

"Oh stop, Edward. You're embarrassing her. She probably had no idea what she was getting herself into by marrying Alex," Regina said in her defense.

"Exactly," Alex agreed. "But it's too late now. You've already vowed to love, honor, and cherish me—and coincidentally my unscrupulous family—until death do we part."

She smiled at his words. That was a task she'd gladly do. However, she still had one concern. Well, not a concern really, because it might explain why the family seemed so accepting of her and her mother's scandalous past. "How exactly did Edwina get this book to send to me in the first place?" she asked carefully. Or as carefully as one could when they were practically accusing someone's daughter of being a trollop.

No offense seemed to be taken though.

"Actually, I highly doubt *she* ever even came in contact with it," Edward said proudly. "No, though she's got her papa's unusual humor, she probably paid a servant handsomely to buy it for her and attach her note before sending it here."

Everyone seemed to accept his suggestion either because they believed it or didn't wish to entertain the notion of Edwina not being the proper young lady they thought she was. Caroline didn't know which, and she wasn't going to press.

Suddenly, Alex and his mother started chuckling again. She stared at them both. "What's so amusing?" she demanded, perturbed.

"You," Alex said as if that explained everything.

"What he means to say," his mother intoned, holding her napkin in such a way her grin was mostly hidden, "is that the dubious look on your face is absolutely hysterical."

Caroline looked to a shrugging, innocent-looking Edward. "What are they talking about?"

"I have no idea," Edward said.

Their laughter started again, louder this time. "Tell her, Alex," Regina said between bursts of laughter.

He shook his head. "I can't."

"Good," Edward murmured, then turned to Caroline with a wink. "Now, are you going to open that book or am I?"

"Not now." She brought it to her chest so he couldn't grab it from her and open it in front of everyone. She would open it later. Preferably while she was hidden behind the dressing screen so nobody could see her face. She flushed. The book was extremely heavy and thick, presumably due to the many delicious pages that were bound between the covers, begging an innocent and curious girl to devour them like the wanton she couldn't deny she was swiftly becoming.

"Open it," Alex encouraged again.

She looked at him and resisted the urge to whack him upside the head with the book. She'd open it when she was ready to.

Regina's amusement died and she adopted a more serious look. "Caroline dear, that book is *not* what you think it is," she said, a smile cracking her lips. "And, it's not from who you think it is."

"All right," Edward spoke up, throwing his hands up in the air. "I sent it. There, are you satisfied? Edwina is a good girl who would not bribe a servant to buy a naughty book."

Caroline didn't know if she was relieved to hear that about Edwina or embarrassed that her new father-in-law had bought her a dirty book. Actually, the last prospect was just plain uncomfortable. She looked at Alex. He was *still* laughing. Not loudly. Actually, not at all, physically. It was just his eyes really. They were full of laughter.

"Alex." Caroline glanced at his parents with unease. "What's going on?"

His face suddenly transformed and he looked uncertain. "My father gave you a wedding present. And disguised it as being from Weenie," he added a moment later.

"Go on, open it, gel," Edward said yet again.

Now she was certain she didn't want to. A naughty book from Edwina, a young girl who knew probably as much, if not less, than Caroline did about marital matters was one thing. A book from her father-in-law on the subject was quite another. "I can't." She handed it to him. He could have it back and do with it what he wanted.

"I'll do the honors then," Edward agreed, turning the package so the knot of twine faced him.

Caroline's eyes nearly bulged from their sockets. "Surely you don't mean to—" She leapt from her seat as he broke the twine and tossed it on the floor.

He grabbed hold of the edge of the paper and gave a mighty rip. Caroline clapped one hand over her eyes and the other over her mouth in horror as he continued to unwrap the package.

Trying to be nonchalant, Caroline moved her fingers apart just a fraction. All right, she'd admit it, but only to herself—she was still curious as to what that book contained.

"Here, gel," Edward said, holding it out to her in a way that she couldn't see the title. "I've marked the good parts for you."

She gasped.

He chuckled and waved the book at her. "I see you peeking."

She grunted and lowered her hands, exposing her heated face

to them. She quickly snatched the book and brought it to her chest, wrapping both arms around it to keep everyone else from seeing even a corner of it.

"What's the title?" Alex murmured, moving his hands to try and pull it from her grasp.

She swayed away and shot him a crippling look that seemed to have no effect on him. "Please don't, Alex," she said quietly. Where had the sweet man who hadn't wished to shame or embarrass her in front of their families or servants gone?

All the humor in the room died and Regina came to her side. "We're sorry, Caroline. We didn't mean to embarrass you. You may not know this, but the Bankses are notorious for..." She trailed off. "Just look at the title."

Embarrassed she'd just ruined their fun by acting like a ninny, Caroline shot them all an apologetic look then relaxed her arms and let the book naturally fall with her arms until the title was in front of her. She blinked. "Good gracious," she said, exacerbated. "You gave me the Bible?" A giggle passed her lips. They probably all thought she was a goose. She fingered a little slip of paper that poked out of the middle of the book. "I suppose this is where I'll find the beginning of Song of Solomon," she mused, flashing Edward a wry smile in hopes of recovering his joke.

The man's eyes went wide and he brought his hands to his chest as if he were having a sudden pain in his heart. "Absolutely not. That mark is in the book of Ruth, young lady." He turned to Alex. "Son, I do believe your new bride has her mind in the mud."

"What a shame," Alex murmured, not a bit apologetically. "I shall do my best to reform her."

Caroline flipped to where the slip of paper hung out the end. It was indeed placed at the first chapter of Ruth. She flashed them a quick smile then read the words that were written on the parchment.

Dearest Caroline,

We are very happy to welcome you into our family, dear girl. We wish you many years of happiness with our son.

Much love,
Edward and Regina

"Thank you," she said, her voice uneven. Their gift had not been the Bible. Well, it had, but it wasn't the main part. The real gift was in that simple, two line note. They were welcoming her into their family with open arms. She'd never felt as safe and welcomed as she did just then. They'd even gone so far as to initiate her into their fold with one of their ridiculous jests, and nothing could have brought her more joy.

Alex came to stand next to her. "Is everything all right?" he asked quietly.

She nodded, unable to speak through the emotion clogging her throat. She replaced the note into the book of Ruth and shut the Bible before meeting the warm, loving gazes of Regina and Edward. She took a deep, calming breath. "That was most kind."

Edward coughed. "Are you disappointed?"

"Disappointed?" she echoed.

"Yes. That you didn't truly get a naughty book," he teased.

"No, not really." She returned his smile.

"Good. Welcome to the family, gel. I've played that trick on all my brothers and their wives," he explained with a grin that spoke of all kinds of mischief.

"Even John and Carolina?" she asked in disbelief. John was a minister, after all. Surely his wife would not have found that joke any more amusing while it was happening than she had.

"Yes, even them," Regina said, tittering. "Except Edward didn't claim it was from Edwina since she wasn't even born yet. Instead, he said it was from me. He even had me write the note on the outside and give it to her at their wedding breakfast." She stopped talking and tried her best to purse her lips. Her shoulders shook and she held up a single finger while she recomposed herself. A second later, she took a deep breath. "The look of embarrassment on Carolina's face when I handed it to her and she read the note paled in comparison to the look of sheer horror that took its place when four-year-old Alex yanked it from her hands and started running around the room unwrapping it and yelling, 'A present! A present!'"

Caroline could hold her composure no longer and joined his parents in dissolving into laughter at the mental picture Regina's story created.

Her amusement, however, died on the spot when Alex leaned over to whisper in her ear. "I'll meet you in our room in thirty minutes."

Chapter 18

Alex watched the second hand on his watch tick by with all the speed of a tortoise in a race. He frowned and tapped the glass with his finger. Perhaps he should wind it. That was the second time the thing had stopped ticking. Oh hell's afire, the watch had *not* actually stopped. He was just being so impatient he'd imagined it had. He leaned back and closed his eyes. He needed to think of something—anything—else.

Finally, twenty-nine minutes had concluded and Alex shoved to his feet. From where he was, it would take him exactly one minute to get to his room. If he walked at a leisurely pace, that is. Which he would. He wasn't going to enter that room one second before thirty minutes had passed. He didn't wish to appear impatient.

A minute and three seconds later, he took a final breath and knocked on the door to the room he'd slept in for as long as he could remember.

"Come in."

Needing no more encouragement, he swung open the door, walked inside, and blinked in surprise. Every candle in the room was lit. He'd always thought virgins were skittish and would prefer it to be completely dark. He shrugged off the notion along with his coat, waistcoat, and cravat. Placing them on the back of the chair, he sought Caroline with his eyes.

She was sitting in his bed, leaning against the pillows she'd propped up against the headboard. The covers pooled around her waist, and she wore a white, virginal nightrail buttoned all the way to her throat. He swallowed. That nightrail would be gone post haste. Turning his attention to his boots, he quickly untied them and kicked them off, not giving any thought to where they landed.

He walked to the bed and sat down on the edge. Scratching his temple, he smiled uneasily at her. "Caro, do you...um...do I need..." He trailed off and broke eye contact with her. Perhaps he should have asked his mother to talk to her about what to expect tonight. Surely Marcus hadn't, and she'd had no other relations who would even know what to tell her.

She laughed and leaned forward, resting a hand on his shoulder. "Nobody needs to explain anything to me," she said softly. "I'm a member of the *Society of Biological Matters*, remember?"

"That's right. And I promised you a lesson in physical science and biology tonight, didn't I? Well, Mrs. Banks, I am a man of my word and I am about to deliver."

She smiled at him, and he pressed a kiss to her sweet lips. "Will this be the topic of the next *Society* meeting?" she asked, grinning.

"No. And I'd strongly recommend you don't suggest it become the topic, either." He silenced her next remark by pressing his lips back to hers and sliding his hand to the back of her head.

"Alex?" she asked, breaking their kiss.

"Yes?"

She glanced at the open button at his throat then back to his eyes. "Never mind," she murmured.

"No, ask." He stroked her cheek with his thumb. If she had any questions or misgivings, now was the time to address them.

"Are you a virgin?" she blurted.

His jaw almost dropped to the floor. Hell's afire. Where had *that* come from? Why did everyone assume he'd never been with a woman? Was his awkwardness around ladies so obvious everyone believed he'd never been able to get one between the sheets before? And how was he to answer her? It was one of those questions which only led to trouble, no matter the answer. This must be one of those conversations the duke had warned him about. Opting for honesty, he met her eyes and said, "No. Why?"

She shrugged and played with the red fringe on the edge of the counterpane. "I just wondered, that's all."

"That's not all," he countered. His thumb stilled, but he couldn't make himself take his hand from her face. Not yet anyway.

She glanced at the buttons on his shirt. "Yes, it is. I had just wondered if I'd be your first," she said at last, her face turning pink.

"Oh, I see. You would have liked that?" He wasn't sure whether he should laugh at the situation or not. Nobody expected he'd ever been with a woman and many had openly jested about it, but then he got married and his wife was disappointed she wasn't the first.

"I suppose so." She lowered her lashes. "You're my first..."

"I know," he said softly, feeling like the biggest cad in England. He quickly dismissed the feeling. He'd bet no other gentlemen were asked such a question on their wedding nights. He'd also bet they'd all had more bed sport than he had. Still, he wanted to offer her something of himself. "How about this?" he said, looking into her eyes and tracing the line of her cheekbone with his thumb again. "I'll tell you a secret about me that nobody else knows."

She put her fingers on his lips. "You don't have to, Alex. I shouldn't have asked. No man is a virgin on his wedding night. I had no business asking."

He used his free hand to move her hand away. "Caro, you may not be my first, but you'll be my last. And—"

"That's your secret?" she burst out. "I'd hope that wouldn't have been a secret. This morning you took vows in front of your entire family that said you'd be faithful." She frowned. "Unless you mean to tell me gentlemen make those vows, but they never really mean to honor them."

He sighed and used his index finger to smooth the furrow between her eyes. "Some don't, but I plan to. That wasn't the secret I was going to tell you, though. Now, are you ready to keep quiet long enough to hear it?"

"Yes," she said, blushing.

"Good. As for my secret, you're not my first, but you're not my hundredth, either." He smiled at her, hoping she'd take the bait.

And like the good girl she was, she took it. "Oh how wonderful," she retorted sarcastically. "I'm only the ninety-ninth."

"Close," he agreed. "But perhaps still a bit high."

She shook her head. "It doesn't matter, Alex."

"It does to you." He shifted to get more comfortable. "Since it matters so much to you, I shall admit to you something no man ever wishes to impart on his new bride. As we've already addressed, you're not my first, but you will be my second. Is that good enough?"

She grinned and tugged the sleeve of his shirt toward her. "Yes. I can accept that. I could have accepted being ninety-ninth if it meant I was to be your last."

He groaned and rolled over onto his stomach. He pulled her fingers from his shirt and gently pushed her backward to lie down on the bed. Coming up on his hands and knees, he crawled up the bed and covered her body with his.

He brought his hand to the back of her head and he massaged her scalp, tangling his fingers in her hair then bringing his mouth to hers. Her arms circled his neck and her fingers sank into the thick hair that covered the back of his head.

"Alex," she sighed as his lips left hers to kiss her cheeks and jaw. He kissed until he reached her ear and placed a warm kiss just behind the lobe.

Alex's hands cupped her succulent breasts. He shaped them through the thin fabric of her nightrail. All thoughts of removing it were gone as her breasts swelled and her nipples hardened under his touch.

He reached his right hand up and with three quick flicks of his fingers, he undid the top three buttons on her nightrail and spread the fabric open. His lips dropped kisses on the skin he'd just exposed, his hands continuing to knead her breasts.

"Caro," he murmured. He slid his left hand away from her breast and grabbed onto the side of her nightrail, pulling handfuls of the white fabric up. He groaned in aggravation of not being able to touch her skin because of the blasted counterpane that still lie between them. He let go of her nightrail and with a savage growl, yanked the offending counterpane out from between them, throwing it to the other side of the bed.

Running his hand up the bare calf he'd just revealed, need like never before simmered through him. It set him on fire. Made him possessed.

Supporting his upper body on one forearm, he reached down

and dragged the hem of her nightrail further up her legs, uncovering more of her creamy, shapely legs as he went. "Your body is beautiful," he rasped, hardly holding onto sanity as his gaze took her in.

"Touch me, Alex." She ran her hands along his shoulders and upper arms.

Alex obeyed her request. He glided his hands over the pliant flesh of her legs, taking time to feel every curve and contour as he went before disappearing under the hem of her nightrail. Glancing at her sweet, relaxed face, he trailed a single finger from the middle of her thigh to the sloping dip by her hip, then just a little further over to rest in her springy curls.

A shiver passed through her body, making Alex swallow his urgency. He leaned closer to bury his face in the crook of her neck, letting his finger make a slow trail from her curls to the swollen, silky flesh that made her a woman.

Caroline's body bucked under his daring fingers when they passed over her tender flesh. Alex kissed her neck and slipped his finger into her waiting, ready body. He was rewarded as her inner muscles clenched around him.

With gentle ease, he moved his hand, sliding his finger in and out. Not too fast or hard, just enough to let her get used to him touching her thus and learn to enjoy it. A minute or so later he found a steady rhythm and slipped in a second finger. She sighed and her body arched into his hand.

"Alex," she gasped, lightly rocking her hips to match his movements.

"Shut your eyes and reach for it, Caro," he whispered against her warm neck. He lowered his head and sought her hardened nipple with his mouth. Caroline's body rose off the bed again and she sucked in a sharp breath.

Breathing loudly, Caroline's hands clasped onto Alex's shoulders. Her fingernails bit into his skin as her entire body tensed, followed by her inner muscles convulsing around his fingers. A staccato note passed through her lips.

Alex kept his pace until the contractions of her muscles ceased. Then, he removed his hand and leveled himself on top of her, bringing his face right in front of hers. "Open your eyes now,

Caro," he commanded gently.

A second later her wide, dilated eyes opened and met his. "That wasn't what I expected," she said suddenly, her lips curved upwards.

He smiled at her. "And what *did* you expect?" Even with need coursing through him he still wanted to know.

"I don't know." She blinked her eyes rapidly and looked over his shoulder. "I've only seen animals—"

He nearly choked and held up a finger to halt her words. "Say no more. I know what you were expecting."

"You do?"

"Yes. You're surprised you're still on your back, aren't you?"

"A little," she said, her face turning pink.

"You know we're not done, don't you?" he asked with a swallow. She'd better not think that was it. He'd go mad if she was ready to roll over and go to sleep.

"We're not?" she asked, rapidly blinking her eyes at him. "What did we forget?"

He couldn't tell if she was teasing him or not. He wasn't good at knowing the difference anyway, but just now, with lust fogging his brain, it was even harder to know.

"Good gracious, Alex." She playfully swatted his shoulder. "How could you possibly think I'd forgotten with your erection pressing into my leg?"

"Oh, sorry about that." He shifted, pressing it more firmly into her thigh.

Her arms looped around his neck and pulled him down toward her. "You're forgiven," she murmured before their lips met again.

Alex took his lips away and groaned. There was only so much he could take, and he was nearly there. Rolling to support himself on one forearm, he undid the fall of his pants and groaned in relief as his erection was freed from the strain of his trousers.

Alex settled back on top of Caroline and positioned himself at her entrance. "Are you ready?" he asked raggedly.

"Yes. Always." She dug her fingers into his hair.

Alex clenched his jaw and, with a slight grunt, pushed in as gently as he possibly could to allow her time to get accustomed to him being inside her again. He stopped when he reached what he was certain had to be her maidenhood.

He closed his eyes and willed himself to move forward as fast and smoothly as he could, then thrust forward and froze a split-second after Caroline's cry pierced his ears.

"I'm sorry," he rasped, stilling his body and bringing his fingers to idly comb through her soft hair. "I didn't mean to hurt you so."

She didn't speak. Her eyes were closed, and around the edge a tear was trying to push its way out. "It's all right," she said in a small voice.

"No, it's not. I didn't mean to. I mean, I certainly meant to put my—" He cleared his throat. "What I mean to say is I knew it would hurt. I just thought if I did it quickly, the pain for you wouldn't last as long."

Caroline's eyes opened and her body trembled with what he assumed might have been pain or discomfort.

For as much ardor as he had only a minute ago, this had certainly been as effective in cooling it as a cold bath. He started to move away.

"Where are you going?" Caroline asked, her voice even and her body completely still, normal.

"We don't have to do this." He kissed her on her cheek.

"What?" Her voice was slightly high-pitched. "Why not?"

"Because I've ruined it," he said, easing out a little further.

Her hands were suddenly on his backside, and she used all her strength to keep him from moving out. "Oh, no you don't. You started this, you're going to finish it."

"But I hurt you." He stilled inside her.

"But it doesn't hurt now," she countered.

He glanced down at her. Was she telling the truth? She must be. Her wide eyes implored him and her hands were still on him, encouraging him to continue. He swallowed and returned her kiss when she brought her lips back to his, simultaneously pressing her luscious breasts against him in a way that made his erection grow yet again. With more care and ease this time, he slid back inside her and stilled, waiting for her to readjust to his intrusion.

Need fired his blood again and he could wait no longer. Gritting his teeth, he moved his hips in a steady and sure in-and-out rhythm.

Caroline's hands grabbed onto his shoulders, not tight, not loose, just there. He closed his eyes and scattered kisses across Caroline's forehead as he continued to move over her steadily, building up to what he thought might be the greatest climax he'd ever experienced. He bent his head down, his lips intent on capturing hers—but they couldn't. His eyes sprang open and his body came to an abrupt stop. He swallowed. Then again. Her face was flushed from the exertion, but she was biting her lip. Hard.

"Caro?" he rasped.

"Yes?" she whispered, not opening her eyes.

He clamped his mouth shut so he wouldn't curse out loud. What kind of monster was he? He'd been treating his wife as if she were a common whore, completely oblivious to her pain and discomfort. He pulled out. "We're done," he said raggedly.

Her teeth released the brutal hold they'd had on her bottom lip before her tongue soothed it. "Oh," she said, opening her eyes and turning her face toward him.

He rolled onto his back and threw his arm over his face.

"Thank you, Alex." She rested her head on his chest.

He ground his teeth. "For what?"

"For everything. For being gentle with me. For giving me pleasure. For just being you."

Rage and shame washed over him. He'd not been gentle. He'd ruined everything by being a brute and treating her no better than a prostitute. He couldn't lie next to her while she continued to praise him. He needed to get up and leave. He buttoned the fall of his pants. Hell's afire. He was still wearing his pants. And his shirt. And his stockings. And she was still wearing her nightrail. In his big hurry, he hadn't even allowed time for them to get undressed.

He rolled her off his chest and onto her back before standing up.

"Are you leaving?" She blinked up at him.

His heart clenched and a lump formed in his throat. "I'll be back," he said uncomfortably, unable to look at her a moment longer.

"You're not going to get chess, are you?" she asked, her voice barely a whisper.

Excellent idea. He had a set in his room, but he could go down to the library and grab the bigger set. It would take him at least twenty minutes. Thirty if he walked at a snail's pace. That should be enough time to clear his thoughts and allow her time to fall asleep. "Yes. I promised we'd play tonight."

She smiled. "Forget chess. Come back to bed. We'll play tomorrow."

"I'll just be a minute," he said, ignoring her. Before she could object again, he opened the door, stepped into the hall, closed the door, and nearly gave in to the urge to beat his head on it. How could he have been so thoughtless as to treat her that way? He raked his fingers through his hair and went down to the library.

He deliberately took longer than necessary to get the chess set and breathed a sigh of relief when he reentered the room they shared, only to find all the candles still burning and Caroline fast asleep.

He set the chess set down and blew out the candles. Then he shrugged off his clothes and slipped into bed next to her.

A small sliver of moonlight peeked in from the break in the curtains. It allowed just enough light for Alex to see his relaxed and sleeping bride. His heart ached as he looked down at her. She was beautiful, fragile, and all his. Kissing her forehead for a final time that night, he silently vowed he'd treat her better in the future. If she didn't enjoy a certain aspect of marriage, he'd never force her—his brother could inherit.

Alex closed his eyes and rested his head on the pillow. What felt like only a moment later, a spell of intense fidgeting accompanied by a strangled cry of alarm rent the air. Startled, he snapped his eyes open and his body tensed.

He blinked a couple times to make sure it wasn't *his* dream that woke him, but a look at his wife told him otherwise. "Caro?"

She was sitting straight up in the bed, hand on her heart, breathing heavily. She didn't look in his direction, just stared straight ahead, unable to make a coherent noise with her mouth.

"What's wrong?" He wrapped his arm around her and pulled her close to him.

Her body tensed and she pushed at his chest.

His hands held her tighter. "Shhh, Caro, it's me, Alex. You're all right."

The tension slowly left her body and she rested her head against his chest, her breathing still ragged.

"Shhh," he crooned, running his hands soothingly up and down her arms and back. "It's just a bad dream. People have them all the time. I'm here to hold you. You're perfectly safe with me."

Tears wet his chest and he gently rocked her. "Do you want to talk about it?"

She shook her head. "The candles," she croaked.

He looked around the room. Not a single candle was lit. He didn't think it unusual they were sleeping without any light in the room. Most did. "You like to sleep with them lit?" he ventured, remembering both times he'd entered the room tonight she'd had more candles than would fit in the king's grand chandelier lit.

"I know it's silly," she said with a sniffle. "I just don't like the dark."

"Do you require all of them lit?"

She sniffled again. "At least a few."

"All right." How he would be able to sleep in a lighted room was a mystery to him, but if Caroline wanted it, it was hers. "I'll be right back," he murmured, leaning her back against the pillows.

He slipped out of bed and put on his spectacles so he could at least see what he was about to light. A minute later, he found a couple lanterns he'd had since he was a boy. At least this way the flame would be contained behind the glass. With so many papers and plants lying about in this room, it was by far better to have the flames contained, he reasoned.

He lit the lanterns, stoked the fire and replaced the screen, removed his spectacles again, then slipped back into bed. "Better?" he asked, pulling her to him.

"Yes. Thank you." Her face was still damp but at least the tears had stopped.

"Would you like to talk about it?"

"No," she said, bringing her hand up to rest against his heart. "Just hold me. Please."

He kissed the top of her head. "Always."

"Thank you, Alex."

"That's what husbands are for."

Chapter 19

Caroline woke up in Alex's arms the next morning. She looked up at his face and ran her fingers over the stubble that had covered his handsome face in the night before letting her finger trace the blade of a nose and his eyebrows. When he'd joined her in bed last night, that was the first time she'd seen him without his spectacles, however, she hadn't really been too concerned with that at the time. She'd been too busy enjoying the way he touched her.

"Good morning, Caro," he said, opening one brown eye.

She blushed. She'd just been caught staring at him. Good thing she wasn't looking *down there* when he'd woken up. That would have been mortifying. Mortifying, but at least she'd have an answer to her curiosity. She'd been slightly disappointed the opportunity to see him naked hadn't presented itself last night. Well, it had eventually. But only because he was climbing out of bed to light a lantern for his ninny of a wife. She sighed. Would she ever feel safe sleeping without the candles?

"Do you have any plans for today?" he asked, trailing his fingers along the top edge of her nightrail.

She shrugged. "My clothes and things are to be delivered today."

"Good. Are you hungry? We can ring for breakfast to be brought or go downstairs. I'm sure it's been laid out already."

As much as she'd love to lie in bed with Alex all day, she couldn't. Too many other people lived in the house, and they'd all be speculating on what they were doing if they didn't make an appearance. She blushed again. "Downstairs. Let's eat downstairs."

"Downstairs it is."

She sat up, freeing Alex to get out of bed. In a quick, fluid motion, he did. Too quick, too fluid for her taste. He'd been so fast to stand, all she'd glimpsed were his tight buttocks.

Keeping his back to her, he pulled on his dressing robe before selecting a pair of trousers and a shirt. "I'll send for Annie to help you dress." He brushed a kiss on her forehead then picked up the rest of his clothes. "I'll meet you downstairs."

Alex was already in the breakfast room by the time Annie showed her to it. His hair and clothes were in perfect order, a complete contrast to the way they'd be in less than an hour. He stood up when she entered the room, then escorted her to the sidebar to help her fill her plate, and carried it to the table.

It was just the two of them for breakfast, and for the life of her she couldn't think of a single thing to say to the gentleman with whom she'd shared the greatest intimacy not ten hours earlier. But it didn't matter. There was no awkward silence that filled the room; instead, it was comfortable, companionable. When she'd accepted his offer of marriage, she knew he didn't love her. She might feel that way for him, but he didn't for her and she knew that. She'd never asked for nor expected love. He'd treat her right. That was all that mattered.

She caught his eye and smiled at him. "Awfully silent today." She lowered her cup of chocolate to the table.

"You didn't marry a man of many words, I'm afraid," he said, returning her smile.

She let her eyes go wide and dropped her mouth open. "But you always seemed so chatty before."

A self-deprecating smile bent his lips. "About that...I...uh...I'm really not a good conversationalist."

"Unless the conversation is about science," she interrupted, smiling.

He nodded. "Unless the conversation is about science." He drummed his fingers on the table. "What I meant to say is that I can keep a conversation going for a while, but if you're expecting me to chat your ear off, you're going to be disappointed."

"That's all right. I've not had a lot of companionship in the past. I shan't require so much attention."

He looked relieved. "Just to clarify," he said a moment later. "I'm not a good conversationalist, but that doesn't mean I intend to ignore you."

"I know that. And if I do require conversation, your chatty

cousin Brooke lives close by," she retorted, making him smile.

"Pardon me, Mr. Banks, Mrs. Banks," Johnson, the butler, intoned from the doorway. "I was asked to determine if Mrs. Banks would be available to meet with Lord Watson following breakfast."

Panic welled up inside Caroline. Why did the baron want to see her?

"We'll be up shortly. If it's agreeable with Mrs. Banks, that is."

"Pardon me, Mr. Banks, but Lord Watson has requested Mrs. Banks attend him alone."

"Alone?" she squeaked. She never knew what to expect when she was around the baron, but at least with Alex there, he could shield her if the baron started to make her uncomfortable.

"He says he would like to speak to you alone for a few minutes, madam," the butler replied.

She swallowed uncomfortably. "A—all right."

The meal ended soon after, and Alex walked her through the maze of hallways leading to his father's room. He kissed her lips, whispered a few soothing words of comfort in her ear, then opened the door for her.

She glanced at Alex one last time before going to stand before his father's bed.

"You wanted to see me?"

Edward coughed and rolled over to face her. He looked worse this morning than he had last night at dinner. "Yes, gel. Sit down a minute."

She sat in the empty chair and waited for him to speak again.

"I see by the flush in your cheeks, my gift last night was useful," he teased.

"Indeed," she agreed primly. "I slept at Alex's feet just as Ruth slept at Boaz's."

His nose wrinkled up. "Perhaps I won't be holding a grandchild in nine months, after all," he remarked dryly.

"Perhaps. Perhaps not." A telling blush warmed her cheeks.

He grinned. "Now that we have that settled, let's discuss what I called you away from my randy son for. First, you should know I never make sincere apologies, so if I've said or done anything to offend you, I'm not sorry and you'll not be hearing a word of a true apology from me." He frowned and fluffed his pillow before shoving it back under his head.

She smiled. In his own way the baron *had* just apologized for anything she may have found offensive about him. The other day when Alex had pressed him to apologize, it had been insincere, but this one was real. Of this, she was certain.

"The second thing I wanted to talk to you about—" he punched his pillow two times— "I'd get around to if this blasted pillow would do its job and support my dying head." He sat up, flung that pillow to the end of the bed, then grabbed another. "Much better," he muttered, squeezing the feather pillow to keep the part under his head firm. "The second thing I wanted to say is about Alex. You should know he cares for you far more than you may realize."

"Yes?" she prompted when he stopped talking, her heart soaring. She wanted to hear more. To know just how much Alex cared for her.

"That's all. My son cares for you and he does a two-bit job of showing it."

"No, he doesn't," she said, jumping to her husband's defense.

His blue eyes traveled her face. "Think what you wish," he said at last. "What I'm trying to tell you is I want you to know he does care a great deal for you, no matter what he says or does to the contrary."

Caroline stared blankly at him. Why was he insulting his son in such a way? Furthermore, why did he think he needed to be the one to tell her Alex's feelings? She sighed. Perhaps it was a medication he was taking, or maybe he was becoming delusional so close to death. Yes, that must be it. "Thank you. I'll make sure to keep that in mind." She used a handkerchief to dab the sweat from his forehead.

"Thank you, gel," he said softly, closing his eyes. "I'm glad Alex married you."

She smiled. She was, too.

A low, ragged chuckle sounded in his chest. "I knew the moment I saw you, you'd make a good match for Alex. That's why I pressed Joseph to have that contract amended." He snorted. "You might have only been seven at the time, but the way you clung to that telescope and insisted it went or you stayed, I knew instantly you and my son were kindred spirits."

She froze, her skin turning stone-cold. The only gentlemen who had ever seen her with a telescope at that age had been her father, her uncle, and some stranger who had come to her house to carry her away in the dead of night. The latter, she only remembered by the conversation they had as he came into her room and told her to grab whatever it was she valued above all else, because she was leaving and not coming back. Immediately, she'd gone to what she'd believed to be her mother's telescope (she later found out it wasn't because her uncle had already taken the real one to his house following her mother's death so her father couldn't sell it). The big man half covered in shadows shook his head and told her to pick something else, something smaller. She'd refused. She'd put her hands on her hips and informed him the telescope went or she stayed. The strong man then scooped her up in one arm, and the telescope, stand and all, in the other and carried her out the back of the house.

"That was you?" she whispered at last, tears pricking the back of her eyes.

His eyes fluttered open and his brows snapped together as if he was confused, perturbed even. "Yes, gel. I came with your uncle that night. I thought you knew that."

She shook her head. "No. Uncle Joseph never so much as breathed one word about that night again, and neither did I."

"Probably for the best." Edward reached out to take her hand. "I admit I was the one who came that night. Joseph asked me to help him. Do you know why?"

She swallowed. "Because my father was an addict," she said weakly, not able to meet his eyes.

His hand squeezed hers. "That's a large part of it. But there is something else. Do you remember anything else? Anything happening around that time?"

She shook her head. She'd been only seven, barely seven at that. All she remembered from the time she'd either chosen to forget about, had recurring nightmares about, or only remembered snatches of—usually with an incorrect timeline.

"That's probably for the best, too," he said, squeezing her

hand again. "Try to forget it, dear girl."

"I'll try," she muttered, sitting back down and closing her eyes tight.

"Alex doesn't know," Edward said suddenly.

Her eyes snapped open. "Pardon?" She cleared her throat and forced a smile to cover up her rude outburst.

Edward waved her off. "Unlike my son, I suffer no difficulty deciphering facial expressions. Yours clearly indicates you're worried about what he does or doesn't know. Am I right?"

"Yes," she admitted. "He seemed to know exactly how awful Rupert Griffin was the other day."

"That he does. But Alex doesn't know Griffin is your father or the details of your past before you went to stay with your uncle. He only knows what you've told him. I promised your uncle I'd take it to my grave. Regina knows only because she was able to deduce where I went that night—the clues were very obvious, all things considered. But I never told Alex. And I meant what I said the other day. Your secrets will go to my grave." He flashed a rueful smile at her. "Whenever that might be."

She smiled weakly at his jest. "I thank you for all you've done," she said, wiping away a tear that had slipped from her eye.

"You're more than welcome, my girl," he murmured, patting her hand. "Now, go see that rapscallion I call a son and let an old man rest."

She got up to kiss his cheek before she left, then turned to the door when his voice called her to halt. "I didn't know your mother well. She was a bit too young to be my playmate. But Regina knew her. They were roommates at a school for young ladies. Perhaps you should speak to her." He coughed a couple times, and when he spoke again his voice was low and scratchy. "Though we all love our mothers unconditionally, and often choose to ignore the unsavory information we learn about them, you might be forgiving her for a sin she didn't commit."

Caroline looked back at him to elaborate, but his eyes were shut and the blankets were high around his chin.

Numbly, she turned back around and left the room, closing the door behind her as quietly as she could on the way out.

"Is he sleeping?" a feminine voice asked from across the hall.

Caroline's eyes fell on Regina, who was sitting in the chair across the hall. "I think so."

Regina stood up. "Just as well. I'll let him rest for now. That dress looks lovely on you, dear. Green is your color."

"Thank you," Caroline murmured, flashing her a shy smile. Compliments were not something she was used to receiving so often.

"Would you care to join me in the drawing room?"

Caroline blinked. Like an act of fate, Regina had been unoccupied and waiting outside Edward's room just after Edward had told her to ask his wife the truth about her mother. "I'd love to," she said, feigning excitement. "Though I feel I must warn you, I'm terrible at embroidery, and sewing isn't my specialty, either."

Grinning, Regina shook her head. "You're as bad a liar as my son."

"I really am bad at—"

"I believe *that*," Regina interrupted. "I do not believe, however, that you'd like to join me in the drawing room. I know all about you, Caroline Banks. Alex is in the conservatory mucking around with some flowers or something. Why don't you go join him?"

Caroline walked to the conservatory as fast as her slippers would carry her, slowed only by the doddering old butler who had agreed to show her the way.

She swung open the door and her eyes fell right on Alex. He was kneeling in the dirt. His coat, waistcoat, and cravat had been discarded in a pile on a bench ten feet away. His shirt sleeves were rolled up to his elbows, and the top three buttons of his shirt were open, treating her to an unobstructed view of the column of his throat and a triangle of his tan chest.

"Caro." His eyebrows lifted in surprise. In his palm, he held a delicate flowering plant, the roots dangling in between his splayed fingers.

"I've come to join you. Is that all right?" She walked to where he was kneeling. "No conversation required," she teased.

He grinned. "In that case, take your gown off and you can help me replant these."

She gaped at him. Was he teasing or did he really expect her to undress out here where anyone could come walking through the door?

He must have read her thoughts. "Nobody's going to come in and see you in your chemise. But you'll get your gown dirty if you leave it on."

"I don't think I can take it off," she said, glancing at the door skeptically.

He put the flowers down next to the others and stood up, not bothering to dust off his knees before he walked over to a large bowl that was on another bench. He picked up a little brush and dunked it in the water. He scrubbed his fingers for a few minutes before setting the brush back down and drying his hands on a nearby towel. "Turn around."

Hesitantly, she turned her back to him and sucked in her breath as his hands made quick work of the row of buttons on the back of her dress. With all the tenderness of a lover, Alex slipped his hands inside her gown and pushed it off her shoulders, letting it fall to the ground, forgotten.

"Put it on the bench," he instructed hoarsely.

Clad in only her chemise, she put her gown, slippers, and stockings by his clothes and willed herself to stop being embarrassed. He'd seen just as much, if not more, last night. She walked back to him and knelt down. He was still digging up the same row of plants and there were at least thirty to go.

Side by side, the two of them dug up the rest of the plants, the silence only broken by the sounds of dirt clumps falling from the roots back to the ground.

"I want to replant these along the south wall," Alex said after he'd dug up the last one. "I dug the holes day before yesterday." He picked up the little box they'd been putting the flowers in and stood.

She followed suit and walked with him down the length of the conservatory until they reached the holes he'd dug a few days ago.

Once again, the pair worked in companionable silence to replant the row.

"You have quite the collection," she remarked, allowing him to help her to her feet. She glanced around at all the plants, trees, flowers, and other greenery.

"Would you like to look around?" He took her hand.

"Of course." She allowed him to interlace their fingers.

He took her around and showed her all his prized trees and flowers, answering any of her questions as they went. When they'd finished, his eyes swept her from her horribly disheveled coiffure to her dirty bare feet. "You, my darling Caro, are a mess. And while it's a good thing you took that gown off, we now have another problem."

A nervous burble of laughter escaped her lips. "I hope you're not going to suggest I run to the house like this and try to sneak in the servants' door."

"Never," he said, bringing her arms up around his neck. "There's a little creek just outside. It's behind the conservatory so no one will see us."

"Sounds scandalous." She grinned up at him and brushed some dirt from his shoulders. "But I'm not really surprised by your suggestion. You seem to be known for taking your clothes off as your claim to scandalility."

A lopsided smile took his lips. "I may have taken a first in both science and mathematics, and possibly a second to last in English at Cambridge, but I'm fairly certain that is not a word." He wiped a smudge from her cheek.

"We can argue about it later. For now, let's go to that creek you mentioned."

Before she knew what was happening, Alex's arms came around her, picked her up, and carried her out the back of the conservatory and down to the creek. He lowered her feet to the ground. "Your bath, Mrs. Banks."

"That was much more graceful than the way you carried Olivia."

He scowled. "If I had carried her that way and not thrown her over my shoulder, I *would* have hurt myself. Now, let's not talk about her and ruin this. Go on and get in. I'll be there in a minute."

Caroline nodded and walked to the water. Bravely, she dipped her toe in then immediately brought it back out. That water was like ice. She glanced over her shoulder. Alex was still unlacing his boots. Would he leave his drawers on? She shivered, and not because her toes were frozen.

Tearing her eyes from him, she blew out a deep breath and took a step forward. Then another, and another. Refusing to act a ninny and run out of the cool water and back to the conservatory, she kept walking until she was waist deep.

She grinned and forgot about her discomfort when Alex swore under his breath just as his bare feet made a light splash as he stepped into the freezing water.

"A bit chilly, eh?" she teased, turning around to face him.

He wore only his drawers and she couldn't stop herself from shamelessly staring at him. She'd leaned against him and had run her hands over him before—with and without clothes—but she'd never had such a good view of the front of his body. Contrary to what she'd pictured, his upper body was firm and muscled. The muscles along his stomach were flat, with pronounced dips and indentations separating them. Higher up, the muscles in his chest and shoulders were more rounded, less rigid. Her fingers itched to skim them and tangle in the small mat of curling hair in the middle of his chest that formed a trail down his stomach then disappeared beneath his drawers.

"Chilly, doesn't even begin to describe it." He then muttered something else she didn't quite catch. Something about shriveling and an effective way to kill something.

She bent her knees to sink lower into the frigid water then moved closer to him. "Join me."

He humored her and came just as much into the water as she was. He dipped his hands into the water then used his wet fingers to wash the mud and dirt from her face. She copied his action. She ran her hands along his shoulders and down his arms, then back up again. She buried her face in his chest and reveled in the moment when his hands came up behind her to hold her there. Alex's embrace was undeniably her favorite place in the world.

His lips found her ear and whispered sweet and tender words while his hands roamed along her back and sides. He brought his hand up and squeezed her breast, sending sparks of hot fire shooting through her cold body, warming it instantly.

His other hand moved up to cup and shape her other breast, making them both swell beneath his strong fingers. His lips tenderly kissed her below her ear then down to her neck where he used his tongue to trace her collarbone and taste the hollow of her throat.

Alex's knee pushed between her legs, parting them. She willingly complied and was sweetly rewarded when his hand left her breast and touched her where she ached for him most. "Lean against me," he whispered before covering her lips with his.

She returned his kiss and parted her lips for him when he ran his tongue along the seam of her mouth. She sighed against his mouth, and his tongue crossed her lips the same time as one—or perhaps two—of his fingers slid inside her.

Trying not to repulse him and give in to her wanton instincts too much, she clenched her eyes shut and willed herself to stay still as his thick fingers worked. With each stroke, the intense pressure inside her built, serving only to make her yearn to match his movements. And then she did. Twice. She bit down on her lower lip and tightened the muscles in her thighs and abdomen to keep her willful body still as his pace increased once again, putting delicious pressure so deep inside her she couldn't stop her body from writhing in his hold. Each of his thrusts stoked the inner fire burning within her. A second later, his thumb entered the fray, massaging her aching flesh. She could stop herself no longer and rocked her hips in response to the movements of his fingers and thumb. Then, as if a dam broke, a heated release washed over her.

Alex's mouth left hers and she spiraled back to reality. She opened her eyes to find his dark, desire-filled, brown eyes looking straight at her. He moved his hands to her waist. Which was a good thing, otherwise she would have melted right here in the creek.

"Ready to get out?' he asked, his voice so rough she hardly recognized it.

She licked her lips. "What about you?"

"I don't think that will be happening just now. It's too cold," he further explained when she stared blankly at him. He helped her from the water and offered her a lopsided grin. "It looks like we'll have to let the air dry us in the conservatory."

She nodded. The sun may be out, but there was no doubting the inside of the conservatory was at least ten degrees warmer, providing a much nicer place to dry off than standing by the creek.

Inside, Alex grabbed her hand and together they explored the conservatory again, each trying to catch the other unaware and stealing a kiss.

And so it was for the next two weeks. Nighttime brought about steamy nights of one-sided passion where Alex took Caroline to heights she'd never imagined, and during the day, they'd act like children together, digging in the dirt, playing tag in their bare feet, stealing kisses, and swimming in the creek.

But something was missing. And for the life of her, Caroline didn't know precisely what it was or how to get it.

Chapter 20

Alex was nearly mad with want for his own wife. He'd thought there was an imaginary string attached from her body to his heart before they'd married; now the damned thing had grown into a cord. Forget that. The thing was a bloody rope now. There was no refuting it. He was in love with his wife. What had started out as a ploy not to marry the worst creature in England had turned into him marrying the best woman in the world, and had cost him his heart in return. Not that he was complaining he'd lost it. Better in her possession than beating empty in his chest. No, the problem was for as much as he loved her, he couldn't share the greatest joy life had to offer with her.

She seemed to enjoy his caressing just fine, and he'd even been tempted to try to make love to her again, but the memory of her shriek and the image of her turned face, complete with closed eyes and lip clenched between her teeth, had kept his pants buttoned with his privates safely tucked away.

Most gentlemen kept a mistress because they didn't enjoy intimate relations with their wives, presumably because either their wives didn't enjoy such attention or the gentleman in question didn't enjoy his wife. But Alex wasn't most men. He didn't want a mistress. Not only did the idea of paying a woman for the use of her body repulse him, he'd never be unfaithful to Caroline. That's what love was about, wasn't it? Accepting the good with the bad.

He sighed and ran his fingers through his hair. He opened his eyes and looked down at the missive on his desk, needing to distract himself somehow. Marcus had sent him several notes in the past fortnight, asking him to come to see him about Caroline's dowry and whatnot. He'd been so busy having fun with Caroline during the day that he'd put it off until today. Last night while he was trying once again to sleep with three lanterns glowing in his room, he'd made up his mind that today he'd go see Marcus. A glance out the window ended that plan. It was raining too hard to ride on horseback, and he wouldn't risk the health of his horses or coachman to take the carriage over something as paltry as Caroline's dowry. He had enough money as it was; hers didn't really matter. Not that he expected it to be very high anyway. He'd actually been surprised to hear she had one. He'd always assumed she was a poor relation, literally.

"Mr. Banks," Johnson said, cracking the door to the library.

"Yes, Johnson?"

"Masters Henry and Elijah have just arrived from London and have inquired as to your whereabouts, sir."

"Send them in," he said excitedly. It had been months since he'd seen the pair and couldn't wait to hear all about their trip to America. He'd only been there once when he was four, and except for Aunt Carolina's hysterics about him grabbing the Bible from her hand and running around the room, he didn't remember the place.

"Congratulations, brother," Henry said, sauntering into the room like the carefree lad he was. He was clad in only his shirtsleeves and his blonde hair was windblown and wet from the rain.

Elijah followed right behind, also offering his congratulations.

He thanked them both and asked for details of their most recent travels, which they were all too excited to give.

An hour later the door opened and Caroline walked in, freezing in place just past the threshold. "Oh, I'm so sorry, Alex. I didn't realize you had company."

"No need to be sorry." Henry winked at Caroline. "You're welcome to join us anytime you'd like, just as long as you sit right here." He patted a space on the settee between him and Elijah.

Elijah scooted over to give her more room, and Caroline's eyes nearly popped out.

"Go on," Alex encouraged. He and his brothers might share the same parents, but that was where the similarities, physically and personality-wise, ended. His brothers were so charming it bordered on disreputable, but he trusted them with Caroline. Their flirting with her was all in good fun, nothing more.

She didn't move. "I can't stay," she protested. "I just came to —"

"To see if your attentive husband was going to pay you any attention today," Elijah finished for her.

She blushed. "And how would you know how attentive he is?" she countered. Alex couldn't tell if her words were spoken in fun or defense.

"Because he's a Banks," Henry answered matter-of-factly. "And Banks gentlemen are always attentive to their ladies."

"Is that so? And do they always fight over their brother's lady?"

Alex chuckled.

"Only if she's as pretty as you," Elijah said smoothly.

A throaty, sultry, groin-hardening laugh filled the air. "Well, if I'm to be fought over, I suppose I should at least be comfortable." She took a seat between the two. "I do feel honor-bound—if such a thing applies to ladies—to inform you both that you'll both have to present a very good case to persuade me away from your brother. I've grown quite attached."

Alex didn't hear their responses over the excitement raging through his body at her words. She didn't say she loved him, but it was close. Close enough for now, anyway.

He watched the three of them talk and laugh over on the settee. "What's so entertaining over there?" he asked when Caroline wiped a tear from her eye.

"You don't worry about us, Alex," Henry said, flicking his wrist. "Just think about one of your science experiments and ignore us like you normally do."

Alex scowled. "Caro?"

She looked at him with eyes that positively sparkled with joy.

"Oh, all right. Tell her. Tell her every embarrassing story you remember about me." Alex shook his head in resignation.

"How did you know?" Caroline burst out.

"You told me. Or should I say, your squeal and burst of giggles did," he clarified. "They told you about the bees, didn't they?"

She nodded, her shoulders shaking with mirth, his brothers merely grinned like jackals, confirming his suspicions.

"We told her to check you for scars tonight, too," Henry said helpfully.

"Perhaps you can give her a quill and she can connect the dots to see if there was some sort of picture the bees thought to leave," Elijah added.

He rolled his eyes. "I hate to disappoint you two numbskulls, but bee stings do not leave lasting marks. And if they did, I doubt Caroline would be interested in using my arse as a drawing canvas."

"Stop, Alex!" Caroline buried her head in her hands. Her body shook with waves of laughter and in that split-second it made all the discomfort he'd suffered at fourteen after he'd accidentally sat over an active beehive worth it.

"Alex," Elijah said suddenly. "I have a question."

"What?" Alex asked testily. He might love to see Caroline so delighted, but back only an hour and his brothers were already trying his nerves.

"How exactly did that happen anyway? We all know you'd just gone for a dip in the creek and sat on a log to dry off, but how did you not know there was an active beehive in the hole in the log? I mean, you're the scientist and all, but weren't the swarming bees a clue?" he asked, snickering.

"Actually," Caroline said calmly. "It's more of a common mistake than you think. During certain times of the year, the bees are inside the hive and it's possible for the hive to look completely abandoned."

Alex smiled smugly at his dumbfounded brothers.

"Beauty and brains," Henry marveled. "She's perfect."

"Especially for Alex," Elijah agreed.

Alex grinned at them again then whistled as he pulled out the drawer where he kept his ongoing experiments. "Don't mind me," he said casually, making a big show of leafing through the pages. "I plan to take your earlier advice and read through my experiments while you three chat it up about me."

"Very well," Caroline said sweetly before she turned to look at each of his brothers. "I've been wondering something, fellows."

"Yes?"

"Which of you carved Alex's name in the pink pall mall

mallet?"

Laughter filled the room and Alex couldn't hide his grin. They'd never tell her. They'd never told him, and he'd been asking since it happened more than ten years ago.

The three started whispering and laughing again, warming Alex's heart anew. To have his wife be so well-liked by his family was a boon in and of itself. But to give his wife the family she'd never had was beyond worth.

He leafed through the pages and froze when his eyes landed on the front page of the bundle of notes he'd used for his "experiment" in wooing Caroline. Nausea swept over him and his stomach clenched. How could he have been so careless as to treat her as nothing more than an experiment?

His fingers itched to ball it up and throw it in the rubbish bin on the spot. But he couldn't do that. If he did, he'd likely draw their attention, and Caroline would want to know what he was throwing away. He glanced at the fire. He could casually drop it in and hope she had enough sense not to try and pull it out. No, that wouldn't work. She was smart enough not to pull a burning piece of paper out of the fire, but the fire was across the room. There was no way to casually put it in there. Walking across the room to drop something in the fire when there was a perfectly good rubbish bin at his feet would definitely rouse curiosity.

Quietly, he folded the papers and shoved them in his breast pocket. He could dispose of them later.

He grabbed a random sheet from the remaining stack and pretended to read it while he leaned back in his chair and watched the three on the settee.

"Mr. Banks," Johnson said from the door. "Your mother has requested your presence downstairs." The grim look on Johnson's face did not bode well for what was about to happen downstairs.

Alex hastily excused himself from the room. Caroline was safe with his brothers. They may be shameless flirts, but they were harmless, shameless flirts.

He didn't have to follow Johnson to know where his mother was requesting his presence. He knew. He walked down the stairs and to the little room his father had taken up residence in. Uncle John was just coming through the door when he arrived and patted

Alex on the shoulder as he went inside.

His father lay deathly still on the bed. Standing to either side of him was Alex's mother and the physician.

Father's chest raised and lowered very slowly as he labored to breathe. "Alex," he wheezed.

"I'm here, Father." Alex walked up to the other side of the bed.

His mother looked up at him with tears in her eyes before leaving the room, murmuring something about giving them a moment alone as she went. Behind her was the physician. He paused a minute to whisper to Alex that Father's condition was worsening and he didn't expect Father would make it through the night.

Alex went numb and slightly nodded his understanding of the news.

"Alex, my boy," Father said weakly after the door closed again.

"Yes?"

Father coughed and Alex helped to wipe his mouth. "I wanted to talk to you about Caroline."

"What about her?" Alex asked, shocked. His father was dying and he wanted to talk about Alex's wife?

"Be good to her, son. Treat her right or you'll lose her," he said, his voice gravelly and broken.

"I will," he vowed, though the papers burning the inside of his breast pocket demonstrated the exact opposite. The taste in his mouth went sour with disgust for his past actions toward her.

"Good. See to it that you do. She deserves the best life has to offer."

"I know."

"Take care of them all, son. They all depend on you far more than you know."

He nodded as emotion clogged his throat, making words impossible to speak.

"I've a letter for you to give your sister. It's on the table."

He nodded again.

"I'd like to see your brothers."

Alex got up and walked to the door, ready to send for them.

Father's time was too short for him to wait to send for them.

"Wait, Alex. Don't call them yet."

Alex sat back down and looked at his father, willing the overwhelming pain settling in his chest to go away. He'd never survive the night if it didn't.

Father's thin, bony hand grabbed the edge of his blanket and lowered it enough to see Alex better. "I want you to know, Alex, I've always been proud of you. There's never been a second when I've doubted your decisions." He grinned in a way that momentarily transformed his face to resemble the man Alex had grown up watching smile and laugh. A man without illness or pain. Just a man full of pure joy and happiness. "I know you've taken a hassling, even from me, for being as proper and dependable as a straight pin, with an identical personality, but it was all said good-naturedly and you know that. It's what makes you *you* and what I admire most about you, son. I never worried in all your years of schooling that you'd embarrass me or bring shame on my name. And I thank you for that."

"But I did embarrass your name. Once."

"No. Not even then," Father said, seeming to know exactly when that once had referred to. "You did the right thing. Even if it turned out badly, your intentions were good, and that night, more than all others, I was proud to claim you as my son. And I still am, Alex."

Tears stung the back of his eyes and he blinked them away before his father made a jest about it being unmanly to cry. "Thank you, Father."

"No, Alex. Thank you. I may be the older man, the one who is supposed to be admired, but it was you I've always admired." His throat worked to swallow and his breathing grew louder. "Even when you were a boy, I admired you. Partly because you shared my love for science, but mostly because you always managed to do the right thing."

Alex closed his eyes, paralyzed. He had no idea his father had thought so much of him all this time. Of course he'd never intentionally brought shame or embarrassment to his father's door. That was part of being a good son, wasn't it?

"I won't get the chance to meet the children you have with

Caroline, but I'll go to my grave—according to the physician, that will occur sometime tonight," he paused to smile at Alex and wait for him to acknowledge his weak attempt of a joke with a slight smile. "Anyway, I'll go knowing I would have loved them and been as proud of them as I am of you. With parents like you and Caroline, I've no doubt my title will one day pass into hands of yet another capable, judicious man."

"Thank you again, Father," Alex said solemnly, forcing himself to stand up before his father could praise his black soul any further. "I'll send Mother in while Henry and Elijah are being located." He silently pocketed the letter for Edwina and left the room to do his tasks.

He sent his mother in and waited with Uncle John while the butler went to find his brothers. It seemed those two had bloody good timing to show up today, rain and all.

"I'm sorry for your loss, Alex," Uncle John said softly. "I remember it hurt your father far more than the rest of us when my father passed."

Alex nodded numbly. His uncle had been a minister for decades, but just now his condolence speech wasn't doing the trick for Alex. He longed to be alone more than anything. "Would you come get me when everyone else has finished?" He pointed to a door just down the hall. "I'll be right in there."

His uncle agreed and Alex walked down the hall and into the room he'd always known as his father's study.

He quietly shut the door and walked to the big desk that sat in the middle of the room. So many times he'd been in this room in the past almost thirty years. When he was a little boy, he'd follow Father in here and marvel at all his books and science equipment. Sometimes Father would help him take apart his automata toys and show him the gears and pulleys inside.

His favorite thing they'd done together in here was when he was six. They built an automata of four couples waltzing that his father had designed for his mother. When Father asked Alex if he'd like to help him put it together, he'd nearly burst with excitement and pride. When they were done, he watched the couples in fascination as they danced all over the box every time he spun the dial. His fascination and attachment were so strong, when it was time to give it to Mother, he cried, not wanting to depart with it. His mother let him keep it. A hint of a smile touched his lips. He still had that old automata. Caroline would probably like it.

He walked around the desk, not daring to sit in the large chair like he had so many times before. After Cambridge, he'd treated this room as his own on many occasions. Father hadn't minded. Actually, he'd been the one to invite Alex to use it. They'd work on science experiments together or have lengthy philosophical discussions in here, neither of them giving a second thought to which of them was sitting in the coveted chair behind the desk and which had to sit in one of the less comfortable chairs on the other side. He snorted. That wasn't always the case. No, he'd spent many afternoons as a boy seated in one of those uncomfortable chairs, receiving a lecture on being a gentlemen or being interrogated when he'd been caught doing something he shouldn't have been. His father may have been right about him not publicly getting into trouble and embarrassing the family, but he must have forgotten all the scrapes Alex had gotten into around the estate over the years.

Alex found another empty chair and took a seat after removing his coat and laying it across the back. This room had always been Father's. And right now it seemed as if it always would be. Alex had always opted to use the library when alone, his use of this room contingent on his father's presence. He swallowed. Soon, too soon, this room would rightfully be his.

He bent his head and threaded his fingers though his hair, waiting to be summoned.

***

Caroline knew something wasn't right even before Alex left the library. Everything seemed to change the moment Johnson walked in. Alex's face turned serious and his posture was stiff as he left the room. Elijah and Henry must have taken note of Alex's change as well because neither of them had any further interest in discussing Alex's embarrassing secrets any more than she did.

She excused herself, murmuring something about seeing them again later as she went. Though she liked them both well enough and felt comfortable around them, she'd rather not be with them just now.

She had an idea where he'd gone. But that was his father. Her presence would be unwanted just now. Instead, she'd wait alone in a quiet parlor until Alex was ready to see her.

An hour or so later, Regina came in with her hair slipping from its pins, and tears streaking down her face. Caroline wound her arms around Regina and offered her the only thing she could: the support of another woman. She'd never lost a husband, so she couldn't fully empathize. But she had known the hurt of losing others she was close to and tried to offer what support she could.

"I think it's time for you to say goodbye," Regina said, wiping her tears.

"Me?" Caroline asked weakly. She wasn't sure Edward would really consider her important enough to him to spend his final moments in her company.

Regina sniffled and dragged her fingertip along the bottom of her red-rimmed eyes to dry her tears. "Yes, you." She smiled weakly. "Edward's had a tender spot for you since you were seven. Oh, don't worry. I don't know exactly what you did to make him so fond of you, but I could tell he liked you quite a bit when he'd ask your uncle to brag about his uncommonly intelligent niece."

Caroline couldn't stop the watery smile that took her lips. "All right. I'll say goodbye."

"Good. It will mean a lot to him. To both of them."

Caroline understood her meaning perfectly. She also understood it would mean a lot to Regina, too, she was just too stubborn to say so. And, more than any of them, it would be meaningful for Caroline, too. She'd grown quite attached to the cheeky old fellow and was glad his family was allowing her the chance to go see him.

She nearly collided with Alex outside his father's door and inwardly grinned at his appearance. He was clad only in his shirtsleeves and trousers, and of course, his hair resembled a porcupine.

"Are you going in?" he asked, his voice rough with emotion.

"Yes. I'll just be a minute."

He opened the door for her. "Do you mind if I join you, or would you like to be alone?"

She glanced at his father. There wasn't anything he could say to her now that couldn't be said in front of Alex. She grabbed

Alex's hand. "Come with me."

Together they walked into the room, potentially for the last time as merely Mr. and Mrs. Alex Banks.

"Caroline, my gel," Edward said, his breathing loud and labored. "Joined by none other than her doting groom."

She smiled and kissed his sunken-in cheek. While she was close, she whispered her goodbyes as evenly as she could, considering it a success her voice only cracked twice and only four tears slipped out.

"Remember what I told you, gel." Edward wiped away her tears with one long, thin finger. "You're a special girl. Always were. But remember what I told you about my son."

"I remember," she said, choking on a sob. "I'd better leave so you can talk to Alex."

"Now, why would I want to do that?" Edward asked loud enough for Alex to hear. "You're so much better company than he is. Prettier, too."

She smiled at him. "Goodbye, Edward."

She dared not to look at Alex with the unshed tears in her eyes as she left him to be alone by his father's side.

The hallway was full with the family sitting and standing about. Regina gave her a watery smile as John went into his brother's room.

She didn't want to stand in the hall with them, but she still wanted to be close in case she was needed. Spotting an open door just a few steps down the hall, she slipped inside. The room was large, massive even. It had bookshelves that lined the walls and reached to the ceiling. There was a large fireplace on the back wall and about half a dozen chairs and a giant desk in the middle of the room. This had to be the baron's study.

This was not the room she wished to be waiting in. Caroline turned to leave and glimpsed Alex's coat on one of the chairs. Likely he'd come from in here when they'd passed each other in the hall. She picked up his coat off the chair then hugged it close to her chest and closed her eyes. She inhaled deeply, letting her nose fill with his heady scent. She sighed. For a reason she couldn't explain, that simple action had given her the greatest comfort. She opened her eyes and shook her head. His cravat was lying on the floor. She bent to pick it up and flung it over her shoulder. "Silly man," she muttered, scooping up his waistcoat while she was down there.

Arms full of his clothes, she walked out the door.

"It appears Alex has once again lost his clothes," Henry remarked when Caroline came into the hall carrying Alex's clothes.

She shook her head sadly. At least, like their father, he could attempt a joke at such a low moment.

"You could have left those, dear," Regina said. "The staff has been picking up Alex's discarded clothes for almost thirty years. They won't know what to do with themselves if they don't find any tomorrow."

She smiled weakly. "I didn't realize it was a daily ritual for the staff to comb the house in search of the clothes Alex wore the previous day. Should I just drop these here in the hall, then? I wouldn't wish to cause them any distress at not finding their daily treasure."

The small group chuckled, and it seemed for a brief second, spirits and hearts lifted.

"You can stand with us," Elijah offered.

She accepted his offer and went to stand by the identical brothers. A few minutes ticked by and one of the brothers left for a minute, coming back with two chairs. "Here, ladies. Have a seat."

Regina sat down first and Caroline offered her thanks and took a seat, still holding Alex's clothes, not wanting to let them go. The chair wasn't overly comfortable, and she shifted to find a better position. It wasn't working. She seemed to be sitting on her skirt in an awkward way. She carefully laid Alex's things in her lap and pulled on the side of her skirt to free it from where it was bunched up underneath her. It didn't come right away. Perhaps she should just stand and try sitting again. She looked down at Alex's clothes on her lap. No, if she stood she'd have to hold his clothes in both hands again and she'd end up sitting on her skirt like this again. She'd just pull a little harder this time. "Oops," she said, her skirt pulling free and Alex's clothes spilling onto the floor.

"Here, allow me," Henry offered, reaching down to pick up the fallen clothes. He handed her the silk cravat and waistcoat first.

She took them and folded them across her lap before holding

her hand out for his coat. He handed her the coat and she put it with the other things across her lap.

"Dropped something." Elijah leaned down to pick up what appeared to be several pieces of paper. He wordlessly handed her a sealed piece of vellum that had Edwina's name on it. "This must have been one hell of an experiment," he muttered, unfolding a small stack of bundled papers. "Oh, pardon my language." He flickered a glance to his mother, who'd just coughed delicately.

"Why do you say that?" Henry asked, his blue eyes alight with mischief.

Elijah shrugged. "First, it's thick enough to be a treatise. Second, I saw him scowling like the devil as he shoved it into his pocket while we were in the library earlier."

"Are you planning to read us the objective or what?" Henry asked. He turned to Caroline while Elijah continued to unfold the papers. "Alex and his experiments never cease to amaze us. Besides to see our lovely mother—" he glanced at his mother, presumably to make sure she heard him— "reading Alex's experiments is a large part of the reason we come home every so often. We've read details on everything from the mating habits of hedgehogs to which type of grass works best for using as a whistle. The things his brain thinks up to study are astounding."

"Or atrocious," Elijah muttered. "There have been a few clankers. Just be prepared, this might be one of them."

"All right, Elijah, enough chatting. Read that objective," Henry said.

Caroline had an impulse to grab the paper from Elijah. She didn't though. They were just having innocent, brotherly fun. They weren't hurting anyone, least of all Alex. Not everyone understood Alex the way she did. She smiled. No, she'd wager nobody understood Alex with his bizarre tendencies and unusual love for science like she did.

Elijah cleared his throat and held the paper out flat in front of him, ready to read. "'Objectives, avoid marriage to Lady Olivia at all costs, including, but not limited to, finding a tart from Lady Bird's brothel at the last minute if necessary.'"

He barely got through the sentence before joining his brother who was bent over, howling with laughter. Caroline sat stock-still.

The blood roaring in her ears only becoming louder with each passing second. She glanced at Regina, she looked positively pale.

"That's not all. There's more," Elijah said, still doubled over, his body convulsing with laughter. "Just a moment and I'll read the rest."

"I don't know who this Lady Olivia is—unless, wait. Is she that awful creature the late Lord Sinclair sired? If she is, I believe I understand his desire to marry a tart in her stead," Henry mused aloud, his eyes red and glistening with tears.

Caroline pursed her lips. She may not like Olivia overmuch, but that was her cousin and they had no business talking of her that way, nor did Alex have any right to pen such a statement. Rage and anger settled in her chest and she stood up to take the paper from Elijah. This was enough foolishness.

Elijah regained his composure and pulled the paper out of her reach. "Sit back down, dear sister. This is proving to be his most interesting experiment yet, and I have every intention of being the one who gets to read it first."

She sat. What could Alex have possibly written that could be worse than what Elijah had already read? And anyway, how in the world could avoiding marriage to Olivia be an experiment? Her anger ebbed slightly and curiosity took its place. His brothers were right. There was no telling what his mind could conjure up for an experiment.

"Ah, here we are, 'Marry Caroline instead—question mark. If able to fulfill latter objective, marriage to Caroline, that will fulfill objective listed above without requiring a soiled dove.'"

This time nobody laughed at the end of Elijah's words. Nobody moved or spoke or even blinked for what felt like an eternity. Anger and rage coursed through her all over again, this time accompanied by their close companion: hurt. She stood up, letting all of Alex's neatly folded clothes fall from her lap. She reached out and numbly took the stack of papers from Elijah's loose grasp.

"I'm sorry," he whispered. "If I'd known, I wouldn't have read it aloud."

"You couldn't have known," she said without much thought. None of them could have known. She looked down at the papers and read over his research and experiment ideas. Nearly every single thing he'd done before their wedding had been planned. Choking back tears, she carelessly dropped the bundle of papers to the floor and willed herself to keep her chin high as she walked away.

Chapter 21

By midnight it was over. Caroline wiped her eyes for the last time and froze. There was a slight commotion in the hall, followed by the front door just closing, signaling the doctor's departure. Her heart ached and her eyes watered again, this time for a different reason. Edward was gone. She brought her knees up to her chest and rested her head against them, waiting for the house to grow quiet again.

Hours ago, she'd determined her anger at Alex was misdirected—in a sense. Yes, what he'd done was wrong. Very wrong. But she couldn't blame him. Not completely anyway. Facing marriage to Olivia had to have been a scary prospect for any man. To handle their courtship the way he did wasn't the most respectable or preferable, but there was nothing to be done for it now. The past was done and being angry about how he'd conducted his courtship was of no use. Unfortunately, acknowledging this did nothing to relieve her current state of humiliation.

She'd learned from all her years of dealing with Olivia that returning an unkind gesture with one of her own rarely ended the way it was intended to. Therefore, she wouldn't try to humiliate him in any way but do to him exactly what he'd done to her. If she was nothing more than just an experiment to him, she'd make an experiment out of him. But her goal wouldn't be one he'd want to give up as easily as she'd given him her hand in marriage. No, she wanted his heart. And come what may, she would get it.

The faint ticking of the second hand on the clock behind her was the only noise she heard now. She gained her feet and tiptoed down the hall. Only a few candles were lit, giving her an eerie feeling as she made her way down the corridor.

"Caroline," Regina said, coming around the corner and

wrapping her in a hug. "I've been so worried about you. The servants have been looking everywhere for you."

Not everywhere. Not once had anyone peeked into the lighted parlor she'd been sitting in. "I apologize for not being there," she said solemnly.

"It's quite all right. I've been in an awkward situation a time or two myself and feel your actions were quite appropriate. Besides, I didn't stay out in the hall but another minute or two after you'd left."

Caroline didn't know what to say. She didn't know what would bring her mother-in-law the most comfort nor what would ease the tension that had seemed to settle on them all after Elijah read aloud from Alex's latest experiment.

"Caroline," Regina began softly, "while I'm Alex's mother and I love him dearly, I do think he was wrong, but his apologies are his alone to make. I sought you out because I wanted to let you know I didn't feel it my place to tell him what you've discovered. It's your business and you should have the right to do that in your own way." She blotted her eyes and wiped her nose with the wrinkled handkerchief in her hand.

Caroline hugged her mother-in-law tightly and didn't let her go until Regina's sobs stopped and her body relaxed a fraction.

Regina squeezed her hand then let go so Caroline could go back down the hall.

"He's in the library," Regina called out to her.

Caroline's steps halted. He was in the library. Alone most likely. Her heart constricted. His father had just died and he was alone at a time when he might need someone the most. Words she'd once spoken to Olivia rang through her mind, *It's going to mean a lot to Alex when his father dies, and as his wife, you're going to be the one he turns to for comfort.* "Thank you."

She walked forward again, this time her destination certain. She was going to the library. She might be hurt and humiliated, but right now he needed her.

"Alex," she said softly as she opened the door to the library.

Silence answered her.

She stepped inside and let her eyes adjust to the dimly lit room. She scanned the room until her eyes connected with a man's form sitting in a chair with his elbows resting on his knees and his head in his hands. She padded over to him, stopping when she was at his side. She reached her fingers out to push back the hair that had fallen in his face. "Alex," she whispered, hurting to see him in such a state.

He didn't respond.

She moved her fingers from his hair to where his hands rested on his cheeks. "Alex," she said again, coming to kneel in front of him. She covered both his hands with hers and used her fingers to pry his rigid fingers from his face with as much care and tenderness as she possessed. "Alex," she murmured, bringing her lips to kiss his tear-stained cheeks.

His hands loosened their hold on his face as she continued to kiss his cheeks and forehead. She brought her mouth to his lips and tenderly kissed his lips. His fingers let go of his face only to slip around and engulf her hands, pressing her palms against his damp cheeks.

He sought to deepen their kiss and she allowed him entry, marveling at how different his kiss was tonight. Normally his kisses were gentle and tender, but this one was demanding and hungry. Without breaking their kiss, she slipped her hands out from under his and gently pushed his shoulders back, putting him more squarely in the middle of the chair instead of on the front edge.

She broke their kiss and stood in front of him, her fingers undoing the buttons of his shirt.

"Stop," he said harshly, closing his hand around her wrist.

Her fingers stilled. "What's wrong?"

His breathing was heavy and ragged. "Don't, Caro."

"Don't what?"

"Don't start something you can't finish. I can't offer you any pleasure tonight."

"I'm not asking you to," she murmured, pulling her wrist from his grasp and putting her fingers back to work unbuttoning his shirt. "Tonight is about you." She meant those words. Every one of them. She loved him enough to put aside her hurt feelings and wounded pride for tonight. He needed her tonight and she wouldn't let anything stop her from being there for him. Tomorrow was a different day. Tomorrow she'd use her wiles to beguile him and steal his unsuspecting heart. But not tonight. Tonight she'd offer him all the love and comfort she had to give.

He made a noise that could pass as a groan or a growl and wrapped his arms around her before savagely plundering her mouth with his tongue once again. She pulled back for a mere second to push his shirt off his shoulders, then settled on his lap, her hands kneading the sinewy flesh of his muscles.

His lips left her mouth and pressed hot, open mouthed kisses down the column of her neck to the exposed plane of her chest. "Caro," he groaned against her skin as his hands found her swollen breasts.

"Alex," she whispered against his hair, her fingers frozen, unable to move from where they held his shoulders. Against her knee, his erection grew, reminding her of what she wanted. What she'd wanted since their wedding night. With strength she didn't know she possessed, she moved her hands from his shoulders and boldly pressed her hand against the top of his erection.

He groaned and she moved her hand lower, to slide down the long shaft of his arousal. "You're killing me, darling," he rasped, releasing her breasts and reaching for the back of her gown. A second later his fingers grabbed tightly onto the fabric and he gave the sides of her gown a hard jerk that sent the row of buttons flying from her dress to make *clink, clink, clinking* noises as they hit the floor.

Alex pulled her loosened bodice down enough for her breasts to spill out, and his mouth immediately sought one hardened nipple while his hand explored her other breast, squeezing and shaping it as if he'd never done so before.

Caroline shifted her body to straddle him and undid the fall of his pants, wrapping her fingers around his hard length as it sprang free from his trousers. Instinctively, she tightened her grip and glided her hand up and down with slow, even strokes. He groaned and his hand came down around hers, stilling her. "Take me inside you," he panted.

She froze. Only once had he been inside her that way: their wedding night. At first it had hurt, but then it felt good. Very good. So good, she'd had to bite her lip to keep silent. That was something she still hadn't perfected after all the times they'd been together. But tonight, with how achy her body was for him already, she was sure if she took him inside her she'd not be able to control herself.

"Please, Caro," he rasped, reaching under her skirt. "Just this once."

Why he only wanted her just this once she'd never know, but that didn't matter. She wanted him inside her, too. Even if it was just this once, Caroline wanted it. She shifted, allowing him greater access under her skirt.

"You're ready for me," he murmured, running his fingers over her entrance. He grabbed her thighs and pulled her closer to him.

"Alex, shouldn't we go to the settee?"

He shook his head. "No. Just take me inside you like this." He ran his erection back and forth along her sensitive skin. "Rise up on your knees, then come down on me," he whispered, grabbing her hips to help her move.

Timidly, she allowed him to ease her up onto her knees.

"Now, come back down," he murmured in her ear, positioning himself at her entrance.

His tip slid into her as she lowered her body on him, excitement building within her at the way he groaned in torment at her deliberately slow movements.

"I mean it this time. You're going to kill me, Caro." His voice was hoarse and terribly uneven, as was his breathing.

She smiled and moved back up, taking her time to revel in the feel of him so deep inside her. Alex's hands clamped tightly on her hips, urging her to move faster. "Release me, Alex, or I shan't move an inch."

He groaned again, louder.

She sank back down, taking his full length inside her. She moved up and down twice more, deliberately taking her time to torment him and drive him to distraction.

"Caro," he rasped. "This is torture." He bucked his hips under her, sending sparks of desire shooting through her every vein.

In response, Caroline lost her last shred of control, placed her hands on his shoulders and rose up and down on her knees like a woman in need. Then again. And again. And again. The friction of him being inside her only intensified her excitement, driving her to move faster and cry out his name.

"That's it, my Lady Godiva. Ride me." He buried his head in the valley of her bare breasts.

Any thought of being embarrassed or shy was abandoned as this need and aching pressure inside her continued to build. She'd experienced this before, but never so intensely.

His hands slipped under her skirt and caressed her thighs as his mouth tasted and explored her breasts, sending her over the peak. She dropped her head and pressed her mouth to his shoulder to muffle her shriek.

"Wrap your legs around me," he commanded gently, putting his hands under her bottom for support. He stood up and walked them a few feet away to a settee, then helped her to lie back before moving in her again. His thrusts were deliberate and with purpose, arousing her all over again.

His pace stayed fast as he buried his face in the crook of her neck and kissed and nipped the sensitive spot by her pulse. His hands roamed, touching, squeezing, caressing, and massaging any bare part of her he could find.

Once again, a rush of fire covered her body and sent her mind reeling out of the reality of the moment, only to be brought back by hearing Alex's hoarse cry of release as his body tensed and he spent himself inside her.

"Give me a moment," he murmured against her neck.

She pushed a hank of hair off his sweaty face. "There's no rush," she assured him. She actually enjoyed the weight of his body resting on hers. She smoothed his hair once again before moving her hands to his back, where a thin layer of sweat covered his skin. She'd seen his back many, many times during their swims or when he'd take his shirt off to go to bed. He had several long, skinny scars across his back that intrigued her. She'd never had the nerve to ask him about them. Likely he'd tell her if she asked, only she wasn't sure she wanted to be a hypocrite and expect him to tell her something he might not want her to know when she still kept hidden from him the reasons for her insistence on keeping the lanterns on at night.

Her fingers skimmed his back, up and down, down and up, side to side, feeling every muscle, rise, dip, scar, and vertebrae.

She loved him. Loved touching him. Loved holding him. Loved kissing him. Just plain loved him.

"Caro?" he whispered, propping himself up on his forearms.

"Hmm?" She opened her sleepy eyes to look up at him. She already missed the feeling of his body on top of hers.

He scratched his head and cleared his throat. "I'm glad you came to me tonight," he said at last, his voice husky.

She kissed his lips. "I am, too." And she truly was. No matter what happened for the rest of her life, she'd be glad she'd come to him tonight.

"Let me help you up to bed." He withdrew and quickly redid the fall of his pants before helping her gain her feet. "I believe I've ruined your gown. And unfortunately I've left my coat in another room." He raked his hand through his hair and glanced around the room. "Caro, how scared of the dark are you?'

Startled, she stopped trying to stuff her breasts back into her bodice and stared at him. "Why?"

"There's another way to go. One that I know for certain nobody would see us. But it's completely dark and the most light we'd have would be the two candles we'd carry."

She sucked in a breath. The library was dimly lit by the fire and the moon pouring in from the open windows. It wasn't as bright as she normally liked, but it wasn't too dark, either. "I can try," she said bravely. She really didn't have a choice unless she wanted the whole house to know what they'd been doing in the library.

Alex pulled on his shirt and spectacles then went to the door and grabbed two candles from the wall sconce. He didn't say a word as he lit them and handed one to her. "We'll take the old servants' hall." He led her to an exterior wall. His hand reached behind a giant portrait and suddenly the wall panel creaked open a fraction. He pulled it open and stepped inside, pulling her with him. "Just hold onto my hand. We'll be there in a few minutes."

That "few minutes" was actually ten, and those ten minutes felt like ten years. She'd not been locked up in a dark, cramped space like that since she was seven; and after tonight, she'd never willingly enter one again. Even if it meant she and Alex were caught completely naked walking back to their room, the hidden servants' hallway was not a consideration for future use.

"Could you light the lanterns, please?" she asked as soon as they were securely back in the room they'd been sharing.

"Of course." He lit the lanterns and she continued to disrobe. With all the fastenings gone there was no need for assistance. "Go ahead and go to sleep. I'll see you in the morning," he told her after she'd changed and climbed in bed to wait for him to join her.

Hurt pierced her heart. He would see her in the morning? Why? Why not now? Why was she good enough for him an hour ago, but now she wasn't? "Did I do something wrong?"

"Not at all. I just want some time alone."

She nodded. Very well. He could be alone for a spell. He needed to grieve. She understood that. And while he sat in an empty library, she'd lie in their bed and dream about how to capture him, heart and soul.

"Good night, sweet Caro," he whispered, kissing her forehead before leaving the room.

Chapter 22

The next three weeks seemed the equivalent of one long continuous day for Alex. The morning following his father's death, Edwina arrived. After a bit of searching, he located the letter for her he'd misplaced, then held her while she cried.

Mother had also been in need of consoling. He hadn't realized how true his father's words were about everyone depending on him until, one by one, the family and staff turned to him looking for advice, directives, or just a beam of support. Everyone but Caroline. With her, it had been the other way around.

She gave him time alone to adjust to life without his father, but when he sought her out, she always accepted him with open arms and a warm heart. She held him in her arms and made no demands. She listened to his past stories and his current struggles. Never pointing out the mistakes he'd made or condemning him for his choices.

At night, he enjoyed the solitude of the library before going upstairs where she had a warm bath waiting. Even for as tired as she had to be, she sat by his tub and talked to him or rubbed his shoulders, many times going so far as to surprise him by grabbing the soap and bringing him to completion, never expecting anything in return. Not that he could have given anything. Stress and exhaustion had taken everything from him. He felt like a shadow of the man he'd been before, just passing through the day without much emotion, only with the knowledge that when the day was done and the sun set, he'd be in the safest haven imaginable: Caroline's arms.

Not only had Caroline become the rock he leaned on at night, she'd stepped up to help the rest of his family, too. She'd spent hours crying with Edwina over the loss of a close parent, something Caroline had experienced personally. She'd taken his mother's place giving directions to the housekeeper and staff, which actually was now her responsibility as Lady Watson.

Caroline had also volunteered to represent the family on another front when nobody else could handle the task. She'd gone to Rockhurst to help Brooke deliver another baby boy (which, he had it on best authority, was *not* named Benjamin). She hadn't so much as uttered a word of complaint for having to do any of these new duties that had suddenly befallen her.

When she wasn't doing her duty to him or his family, she occupied her time doing little things that she may not think were even noticeable. But he'd noticed. He noticed that she'd been keeping up with the documentation of his four current experiments. He noticed she'd taken his giant stack of science notes and organized them by putting a larger sheet of paper between the bundles to separate the different experiments. On the larger sheet she wrote what he'd studied and the dates. She also ordered a maid to bring him a tray of fresh tea and biscuits every hour. There were other things, too. Things that to most would seem insignificant, and yet, not to him. To him, everything she did had only made him love her more.

He sighed and folded his hands across his stomach. Today was the first day he'd been in this room without feeling his father was about to walk through the door. For the first two weeks, he wouldn't so much as glance at the door to his father's study. But then he had to go in. There was correspondence to attend. Tenants with problems to be solved. Accounts to be balanced. Now he was Lord Watson, and it was his responsibility to take care of it all. His father had survived the loss of his own father and still managed to run the barony, and so could Alex.

Just as he stood up to leave and find Caroline, a knock came at the door, followed by his two brothers barging in.

"Alex, we need to talk," Henry blurted, unable to meet his eye. His face was bright red, his clothes were disheveled, and his hair was windblown; in short, he looked like he'd just run here from London. Right behind him, his twin was a mirror image, right down to the clenched fists hanging by his sides.

"What's going on?" Alex fell down into his chair.

Neither spoke. They just stared at each other, communicating in "twin speak" as he'd always referred to it when they did this.

"Tell him, Elijah," Henry prompted.

Elijah shook his head. "No. You."

Henry crossed his arms. "I don't think so. You're the one who said he needed to know."

"But you're the one who said we were the ones who needed to tell him," Elijah countered.

"I don't give a damn whose idea it was," Alex burst out, mentally preparing himself for the worst. "Would one of you numskulls just tell me what the blazes is going on?"

"Well, Alex, it's like this..." Henry started, shifting from foot to foot.

Elijah dropped his gaze to the floor. "We wanted to go see the conservatory and—"

"You? The conservatory?" Alex asked in awe. He'd always doubted if they even knew what was in a conservatory. Unease settled in his chest. What had they done in his conservatory? Was it still standing? Were his plants still alive? So many horrible possibilities passed through his head, he was unaware his brothers were still talking until the quill he was holding snapped followed immediately by Elijah blurting, "We left as soon as we saw her."

Alex shook his head to clear his thoughts. "What?" he asked, staring at his red-faced brothers.

"Have you even been listening?" Henry countered.

"Of course I have," he snapped. "You said you were in my conservatory. Then you said something about leaving."

"Did you happen to hear anything else?" Elijah asked, crossing his arms.

Alex dropped the two pieces of his broken quill to his desk. "I don't have to answer to you two. Now, just start from the top. You were in my conservatory..." He made a rolling gesture with his hand.

"We walked in and saw Caroline," Henry answered quickly.

He blinked at them. "Well, she does live here. She has my permission to visit the conservatory."

His brothers rolled their eyes at the same time. "Thank you for clarifying that, Alex," Henry said sarcastically. "That wasn't the point. I had stopped talking in hopes Elijah would deliver the next sentence."

"Oh, sorry." Elijah winked at Alex. "Our brains must be running independently today."

Alex glared at the pair of them. "Remind me to send up a prayer of thanksgiving tonight that we were not triplets."

"Just think," Henry said excitedly, "if we were, then you'd already know what we wanted to tell you."

Alex dropped his head into his hands and mumbled an incoherent sentence about being related to a bunch of bumbling idiots. He raised his head back up and looked up at the witling he called a brother. "Well, since I don't know, half-wit, why don't you tell me?" What was wrong with these two today?

Henry exchanged a look with Elijah that Alex didn't even try to understand. "All right," Henry said, gulping. "When we walked into the conservatory we saw Caroline. She was digging in some flowers, wearing only her chemise." His face flushed dark red, causing Alex to chuckle.

"What in tarnation is humorous about that?" Elijah snapped. "Aren't you concerned someone might see her? Aren't you concerned *we* saw her?"

Alex's grin faded. "I'll speak to her about it."

"Good," Elijah said, sitting in one of the chairs across form Alex's desk. "I spent many long, arse-numbing hours in this chair."

"Didn't we all?" Alex remarked, thinking of a way to get rid of his brothers so he could go catch Caroline before she finished rinsing off in the creek. He missed spending time with her getting dirty in the conservatory followed by being dirty in the creek. A smile pulled on his lips.

"Look, Henry, there he goes again," Elijah commented. "He's probably picturing her digging up those plants in her chemise."

Henry snorted and fell into the chair next to Elijah's. "That must be a fantasy come true for Alex. A half naked lady alone in his conservatory."

Alex scowled at them. "Put the image out of your minds before I put it out for you."

"We meant nothing by it. We were merely surprised she was out there mucking around in her chemise like that and thought you might like to know before someone else finds out," Elijah explained.

"Thank you. However, I already knew," Alex told them.

"So then it *is* your fantasy," Henry mused, propping his feet up on the edge of Alex's desk.

The measuring stick Father used to bang on the corner of his desk during a lecture to make sure his sons were still paying attention rested against the side of the desk. Alex grabbed it and used the end to push his brother's feet off his desk. "That's enough. I'm the one who told her she could do that. At the time I saw nothing wrong with it. It was just the two of us replanting some flowers, and I didn't want her to ruin her gown. Now that you two have taken up residence for the foreseeable future, I'll advise her to keep her gown on from now on."

"It must be nice to have someone who loves you so much," Elijah marveled, not a hint of sarcasm in his voice.

Alex's heart squeezed. "Do you really think she loves me?" He tried to keep his face neutral so they wouldn't know just how much their answer meant to him.

"She must." Elijah propped his right ankle on his left knee. "If she didn't, she wouldn't be out there digging around your conservatory in her chemise right now."

Alex was too pleased with the overall meaning of their words to care Elijah had just mentioned Caroline's current state of undress again. "I suppose my unusual personality must put a lot of people off," he conceded.

Two snorts rang out. "That's the least of it, brother," Henry said, shifting in his chair.

"What's that to mean?" Alex's personality and fascination with scientific interests might be a bit discouraging, but there was nothing wrong with his looks, or family connections, or manners, or anything else for that matter.

"You're an ass," Elijah said simply.

"A big one, at that," Henry put in helpfully. "She already knew you were a bore before she married you."

"Excuse me?" Alex asked.

Henry sighed. "See, we knew she liked you well enough because she married you. Which at the time, she only knew you were a bore—"

"She said that?" Alex interrupted.

"No." Henry shook his head. "She never said it. But with a nickname like Arid Alex, she had to have known." He snorted. "Anyway, even if you planned your courtship to the letter, there still had to be a few moments where you had to carry your end of the conversation—which is likely when she realized you really are a bore. None of that really matters so much because she married you despite your being a dullard. But she *stayed* after she'd discovered you were an ass."

Unease took hold of Alex's stomach and crept over the rest of his body. He didn't care they thought him a bore. Everyone did. That didn't bother him one whit. He was more interested in how they knew he'd planned his entire courtship out and how they knew she thought him an ass. "Go on," he encouraged, his voice rough.

"There's nothing more to say," Elijah said with a shrug. "She must love you if she stayed here and didn't run back to her family after being so thoroughly humiliated."

Panic settled in his chest and his hands clenched into two tight fists. She knew. She'd seen that stupid bundle of papers. He'd thought it odd Mother had been the one with Edwina's letter and none of the servants had given him the things from his pockets like they normally did when they took his clothes to be laundered.

"How do you know?" he asked, swallowing convulsively. Had she been so hurt and he so distant that she'd had to confide in someone else and seek solace from another when it should have been him? He should have been the one to offer her comfort and beg forgiveness for his stupidity. But he'd been so caught up in his own pain, he hadn't taken time to notice hers. And he'd have had to notice. She wouldn't have come out and told him. Before their wedding, Marcus had told him as much. Caroline never confided her problems in anyone. That gave him pause. "How do you know?" he barked again, pinning both of them with his gaze.

Less than a minute later the tale was out.

"That's why you two were out in the hall disrespecting Father by laughing like jackals while he was dying?"

"Pardon me, brother," Elijah shot back angrily. "But if there was any disrespecting going on that night, it was done by you. And the wronged party was not Father, but Caroline. If I know Father, and I think I do, he probably asked you to open the door so he could find out what was so damned amusing. He always did hate to be left out of a joke."

Alex swallowed the bile in his throat. Elijah was right. Father had asked him to do that very thing. He'd wanted to know what was so amusing, and Alex had refused. And now more than ever, he was glad he had. She'd suffered enough humiliation by having his brothers and mother present. Anger built up inside him. "Why did you two have to do that? Why didn't you stop after the first line? Or just after it, where I'd suggested Caroline as a potential bride? Why did you have to read it all?"

"Why did you write it?" Henry countered quietly.

"Out," he roared.

Offering no further unsolicited advice, his brothers left the room, leaving him alone with his self-loathing thoughts.

He covered his eyes with his fingers and gave a sharp bark of laughter. He was no better than his fool of a friend Andrew. He may not have done the exact same things, but in essence the result was the same: he'd ruined Caroline.

The soft steps of a servant broke into Alex's thoughts. "Go away," he barked. He needed to be alone so he could think of what to do next, not drink more tea and eat biscuits.

"Will you be attending dinner, my lord?" Johnson called through the door.

Hell's afire. It was dinnertime. He couldn't face Caroline at dinner knowing he'd hurt her and couldn't make it right. "No."

He waited for the butler's footsteps to fade down the hall before standing up. He should go up to their room and wait for her. She wasn't one for lingering in a drawing room any longer than necessary after dinner. She'd be up in an hour, two at most. He'd use that time thinking of what to say and how to make things right.

"Pardon me, milord," Annie said, passing him in the hall just outside his room.

He didn't think he'd ever get used to being called that. He gave her a curt nod in return before stepping inside the room. He let his eyes travel over the furniture. Everything was covered. There wasn't two inches of surface space that didn't have a book, instrument, or half-finished science project on it. Even the vanity was covered with clutter. Brushes, combs, shaving supplies, hand mirrors, all sorts of things. He sighed. The room was too small. She deserved bigger. Better.

The night of his wedding, his father had requested Alex and Caroline take the master suites and make them their own. He'd refused, of course. He wasn't comfortable moving into his parents' chambers while they were both clearly still alive. Now he was the baron, and she the baroness. Those rooms were rightfully theirs now, and Caroline deserved it. Her sitting room alone would be twice the size of this bedchamber.

He'd put it off long enough. Tonight would be the last night they'd sleep in here. By noon tomorrow, this room would just be a passing memory of where they'd slept the first five weeks of their marriage.

He walked to the wardrobe and swung open the door. It was a shame she'd never really gotten a chance to wear all those beautiful gowns Marcus had commissioned for her. She wore black now and would for a year. His eyes scanned the wardrobe. Several brown paper packages rested at the bottom, calling his attention. She was his wife; she had nothing to hide. They'd seen each other naked—and with any luck they'd get to again tonight—there wasn't anything she'd have in there he couldn't see. He grabbed the package and pulled off the twine. He turned the bundle over and pushed back the paper, exposing a little black square of neatly folded material.

He walked back to the bed, put the paper down, and unfolded the square. His excitement grew each time he undid another fold. When he was done, he held up the two straps that were about as wide as a quill tip. He did a slow perusal of the transparent garment, taking in the low bodice that formed a perfect V with red trim around the edges and the slits in the side that had to go up nearly to her waist. Desire fired through him. He may have seen her naked, and he might like to again later tonight, but first she could put this on. This he liked.

Tearing his eyes away, he looked to the wardrobe. She had another, one, two, three, no wait, four, identically wrapped packages. His mouth watered. He'd been too preoccupied lately to enjoy Caroline the way he ought. No more. Tonight he'd make love to her until the sun came up. He wouldn't hold anything back and wouldn't let her, either. She'd enjoyed it last time. He was certain she had. She might be insecure about letting her inhibitions go and vocalizing her enjoyment, but he'd have to be completely daft not to have realized she was enjoying it. A fool he may be, but daft he was not.

He folded the garment back up and tried to put it back in the package as neatly as he could. Before he could even suggest she put that on, he needed to think of what to say to her. She didn't strike him as the type who could be seduced into giving forgiveness. She was too smart for that. Nor was his sin small and trivial; it was enormous and had caused her great pain.

Collapsing into the only chair in the room, he sat alone with nothing but his thoughts as the clock ticked, the candles melted, and his mind raced.

Chapter 23

Caroline sank down into the plush red settee in the drawing room, exhausted. She'd spent the early afternoon observing some of Alex's new blooms then came inside to record her findings. Just as she'd finished that, Regina invited her to tea then Edwina asked her to help reorganize part of the library. Then it was time for dinner, which, though she didn't feel inclined to eat, she still attended. And now it was time for her to find a quiet corner of an often unused drawing room and sit in peace for a few minutes. She loved Alex and his family, and would do anything for them, of course, but just now she needed a little time alone.

She closed her eyes to block out any and all distractions when suddenly one in the form of a light scratching came from the direction of the door.

"Yes?" she greeted, peeking her head out the door.

"A letter arrived for you today, my lady." Johnson held out a piece of tattered and wrinkled parchment.

Caroline plucked it from his fingers and closed the door before turning the folded paper over in her hands. Her brow knit. The writing looked familiar... Almost like...

Her left hand squeezed the paper tighter as the trembling fingers of her right hand worked to break the sloppy wax seal that held the missive closed. On her fourth attempt, she was able to break the seal and willed her trembling hands to unfold the paper. They obeyed. She didn't know how or why, but somehow she managed to unfold the letter.

Her skin grew warm and her heart raced as her eyes skimmed over the carelessly penned words.

You owe me! I should think ten thousand is a fair amount. I'll be by to collect on the morrow.

Caroline's hands tightened around the unaddressed and unsigned note, anger bubbling inside her. Though the sender hadn't been polite enough to properly style the letter, Caroline knew exactly who it was from and who its intended recipient was.

"Caroline?"

Caroline jumped nearly a foot in the air. She turned her head to meet the warm, concerned gaze of her mother-in-law. When had she come in?

"Is something wrong?"

Unable to so much as think of anything to say, Caroline dropped her eyes down to the paper that was now rattling in her shaky grasp.

Regina placed a tender, yet firm, hold on Caroline's right wrist and pulled the paper free from her tight grip. Regina's lips curled into a sneer as her eyes passed over the words. "Don't you mind this," she said, refolding the missive. She threw it on the floor, forgotten.

Caroline nearly fell over trying to bend down to pick up the paper. Don't mind this? Was Regina mad? She had to mind this. This was too important not to mind.

"Caroline." Regina's soft voice gave her pause. "He's not coming. Stop worrying. He's just trying to scare you."

"It's working," Caroline whispered, her fingers closing around the edge of the paper.

"It shouldn't."

Caroline shook her head. Regina didn't understand.

Regina's gentle hand descended onto Caroline's shoulders, gently squeezing. "Look at me. I know you're distraught right now, but you must realize you're worrying for nothing. No self-respecting man would show up and demand a bride price for a woman he didn't even have the power to give into marriage."

Her words shocked Caroline to the core. "You're right," she breathed. Biologically, he was her father, but legally speaking, he wasn't. He'd given that claim up years ago when Uncle Joseph had somehow gotten her father to relinquish his legal claim and adopted Caroline.

"He's just trying to scare you," Regina repeated.

Caroline shivered. That vile man had somehow managed to scare her her whole life, why should now be any different? "What should I do, then?"

"What do you want to do?" Regina countered, giving Caroline's shoulders another affectionate squeeze.

"Burn that blasted letter," she answered with a shaky laugh.

Regina marched across the room and came back with a three candle candelabra. She set it down on the table then moved the teapot and cups off the silver tea tray that rested in the middle of the table. "Burn it."

Caroline hadn't been serious, but now... She looked down at that dratted piece of paper that only served to taunt her. To remind her who she'd once been; what she came from; where she'd once been destined to go. Logic gave way to emotions and she extended the paper forward, letting the hot flame lick at the edge of the paper until a flame consumed the bottom half inch. She dropped it to the tea tray and stood motionlessly beside her mother-in-law as the paper became consumed by flames and shriveled to a little black mess.

"Do you feel better now?"

"A little."

Regina pulled on Caroline's hand. "Sit with me."

Caroline sat.

Regina wet her lips, her eyes held a serious gleam. "Caroline, I think it's time we had a long overdue talk."

"I think so, too," Caroline agreed, remembering what Alex's father had said to her the day after she married Alex. It was time to know the truth about her mother. And Regina was the only one who would know.

"How about this, you tell me what you know, then I'll tell you what I know, then we'll see if together we can fill in the missing details?" Regina flashed her a mischievous smile. "That's how scientists would approach this, isn't it?"

A watery smile tugged on Caroline's lips. It was very apparent Regina had spent the last thirty or more years in the company of a lover of science. She took a deep breath and rubbed her sweaty hands on her black bombazine skirt. "I don't know much," she admitted. "My aunt told me my mother was carrying on an affair with my—my—" she waved a hand in the air, unable to say the word— "and when she found out she was expecting she was forced to quit school and marry him." She lowered her eyes to study the wooden floor.

"Is that all you know?" Regina's soothing voice did nothing to calm Caroline's sudden onslaught of nerves.

She nodded. What else was there to tell?

Regina fidgeted beside her. "I'm not sure how to word this, so I'm just going to blurt it. I don't think affair is the correct term in this circumstance," she said with a gulp. "I may have only been her roommate for two months, but it was just long enough to—" She broke off and exhaled. "Caroline, your mother did nothing either she or you should be ashamed of."

Caroline lost interest in the floor and searched her mother-in-law's eyes, looking for some sort of clue. What the clue would reveal she didn't know, but curiosity pressed her to discover it. "What happened?"

"Not long before your mother came to Sloan's, she'd gone with her family to a house party held by some close friends of your uncle's. She was only fifteen at the time, far too young to be there, but for some reason she'd attended. While there, she'd met Rupert Griffin. She told me he'd tried to pursue her, but she wasn't interested."

A sense of unease settled over Caroline. Call it an inkling, suspicion, premonition, or whatever you'd like, but for some reason Caroline had a feeling she wouldn't like where this story was about to go.

"He was relentless in his pursuit of her, so her brother decided it was in her best interest to send her to a school in London where she'd be away from him." Regina twisted her lips. "But he wasn't put off so easily. He plagued her with an endless stream of letters and even tried to pay a call on her under the guise of being sent by her brother and even once claimed to be her betrothed.

"She agreed to see him once and told him she wasn't interested in his suit, but he kept coming back. A few weeks later we had a small social to which our families were invited to come." A wistful expression crossed her face for a moment. She cleared her throat and her face grew serious again. "During the social, your mother disappeared for a while. When we found her, she was sobbing so hard we couldn't understand what she was saying. She went home with your uncle that day and never came back."

Silence filled the air. Both women knew why she never went back.

"Did he give her no choice?" Caroline didn't really know why she'd asked Regina that, likely Regina didn't know the workings of her uncle's mind any better than Caroline did.

"I assume you're asking if Joseph forced the match. Truthfully, I don't know. I never asked. But my heart tells me no. I've spent a lot of time at Ridge Water during my marriage to Edward and know that your uncle would have declared war on anyone brave enough to cut your mother." She sighed. "But I also knew your mother. She was a kind soul who was always thinking about others. I know it's just speculation, but I think she married him by her own will because she was afraid of the shame it would bring on your uncle and his family, not to mention her unborn child."

Caroline closed her eyes. She could understand that. She couldn't imagine Uncle Joseph forcing a match under such conditions. And though her mother had been gone so long, what Caroline remembered of her mirrored what Regina had just suggested. It wasn't for any great love for the man she'd married him, but to protect her family from scorn and scandal.

But why did her father want to marry her mother if he'd already—

Caroline's blood boiled in her veins. Money. Of course. Caroline's mother was from a wealthy, well-connected family who had money. He wasn't a fool. He must have known if he married Caroline's mother and started a family, her brother would give them money. And the more children they had, the more money he'd give them. Bile burned in the back of Caroline's throat. *That's* why her mother was always increasing, even after being told she shouldn't try for more children.

Her mother had been expecting more than nine times as far as Caroline knew, including the miscarriage she'd suffered not long after marrying Caroline's father. Eight of those nine pregnancies ended in either a miscarriage or stillborn. The last had resulted in death of mother and child.

Numbly, Caroline tried to stand. She had to leave the room. She needed to be alone. She needed to sort this out. She'd learned so much about both her mother and father in such a short time. Nothing was what she'd expected.

Regina's warm fingers clasped Caroline's wrist. Caroline shook her off, thankful for the gesture, but too consumed with her thoughts to welcome it. Her head spun with the facts—both said and implied—she'd learned in the past fifteen minutes. It was too much. All too much at a time like this.

She swiped at the steady tears coursing down her cheeks and wearily climbed the stairs. Her feet took her to the room she shared with Alex. He hadn't come down for dinner tonight, but he'd join her in their room later. She couldn't burden him with everything she'd learned about her mother and father right now with his own father's death so fresh. She'd wait a while longer to let him grieve for his father before telling him what she'd discovered about her mother and the fact that her father was not only an addict, but in turn a murderer, too.

Caroline's unsteady hand fumbled with the doorknob. She would have breathed a sigh of relief when it turned if sobs hadn't decided to start wracking her body at that very moment.

***

Alex sat alone with his thoughts in that chair until the last candle melted. Then the door finally opened and just as quickly closed with a noise louder than a clap of thunder.

"Caroline, dear," came Mother's muffled voice through the door no more than two minutes later. "I know you're upset. Would you like to talk about it?"

"No," Caroline answered, sniffling.

There was a long pause before Mother spoke again. "Caroline, my intent was not to upset you more."

"You didn't," Caroline said tersely. "*He* did. I wish I'd never set eyes on that blasted piece of paper. I *hate* him!" She'd put so much emphasis on her words "he" and "hate," Alex winced. She may never forgive him. The knowledge he'd broken her heart broke his.

"Would you like me to go get Alex?"

"No," Caroline replied, choking on a sob. "He'll be up soon enough."

Mother didn't respond, not that he would have heard her if she had. Caroline's sobs continued to pour out as she shakily lit the lanterns he left out for her each night.

A low light lit the room and he sat frozen in his chair, which was blessedly cloaked in the shadows. He sat quietly and watched her kick off her slippers and peel off her stockings before climbing into bed, gown and all. Crying females had never been his forte. He'd have better luck approaching her in the conservatory tomorrow. All he had to do was slip out and wait elsewhere until after breakfast tomorrow.

He waited until her crying stopped and he was sure she was asleep before attempting to leave his chair. As light-footed as he could, he walked across the room and to the door. He stopped a moment to gaze down at the woman he loved above all others. His heart thudded in his chest. He had to do something to make this right. What, he didn't know. But he'd think of something.

Not daring to kiss her goodnight like he longed to do, he reached his hand out to the door and turned the handle. The second the lock clicked, her eyes snapped open. He paused. Her eyes shut again and he slowly pulled the door open, praying it wouldn't creak.

"Alex," she said when he was halfway across the threshold.

His first thought was to run. He couldn't face her with nothing to say. No words of apology. No words of explanation that would be anywhere near satisfactory. "Yes?"

She sat up and smoothed back her hair. "Go on and sit down. I'll be right back as soon as I order your bath."

"Pardon?" he asked, bewildered.

Her voice was normal as always. She didn't sound at all as if only an hour earlier she'd cried herself to sleep.

She stood up and looked for her slippers. "I...uh...I fell asleep and forgot to send for your bath. It won't be but just a few minutes. Go on and sit down."

He closed the door and did as instructed. "You don't have to order me a bath, Caro."

"Of course I do. I always do. It will just take a few minutes."

She pulled her slippers on and tugged the bell pull.

He watched her move around and ready things for his bath. Besides the red rims around her eyes, it was nearly impossible to tell she'd been crying. "You fell asleep in your gown," he pointed out inanely.

She looked down. "Yes. Yes, I did." She went to the wardrobe and grabbed one of her white virginal nightrails before going behind the screen to change.

His bath arrived, and as usual, she sat by the tub and helped him wash his hair and back. She even kissed his cheeks and made a jest while she scrubbed the soap in his hair. To an outsider, nothing appeared out of place. To Alex, everything seemed out of place. Why was she pretending not to be angry with him when not two hours ago she'd claimed to hate him? Something wasn't right.

She helped dry him off and walked with him to the bed. She climbed in first, and just like every other night, he followed.

He got settled and she rested her head on his chest, their hands meeting under the covers. He bent his head and kissed the top of her head. "I'm sorry, Caro," he whispered.

"Did your mother tell you I was upset?" she asked, not looking up at him.

"No. She didn't have to. I can tell you've been crying."

She let go of his hand and brushed a tear away from her eye. "I don't wish to talk about it, Alex. Please, let's just leave it alone."

"All right." He rubbed her back soothingly. One hot tear fell on his chest and his heart crumbled all over again. "Caro, how can I fix this?"

"You can't. I just want to forget all about it and move forward. Can we do that, please?"

He swallowed. "If that's what you really want." He didn't know why she was letting everything go so easily, nor was he going to question it. He may have been granted a reprieve this time, but that didn't mean he'd count on it in the future. From today on, he'd treat her right. He'd show her how much he loved her every single day, never leaving a doubt in her mind how dearly she was loved. He'd never be a fool again.

Emotion overtook him and he rolled her over onto her back. "I want you, Caro," he said raggedly, kissing her cheeks, her neck, her chest. He reached his hands down to the bottom of her nightrail and grabbed a big handful, lifting the hem high above her waist. "Sit up, Caro. Let me get this off."

"No, Alex," she said, bracing her hands on his arms. "I'm sorry. But I just can't tonight."

He blinked at her. She couldn't be on her courses; she wasn't wearing drawers. "Do you have a headache from crying?" he asked, understanding her disinterest a little better. "I can think of a perfect remedy. The best remedy," he added huskily, reaching for her nightrail again.

"No. It's not a headache. I just don't feel like it tonight."

"Hmm." He dropped his head to the crook of her neck and kissed the spot where she'd always been most responsive to him. He sucked the skin into his mouth and nipped it with his teeth, then soothed it with his tongue in the way that typically got her excited. "How about now?" he murmured against her neck. He skimmed his hands up and down her sides. She was as responsive to him as a log. He pulled back. "What's wrong?"

She shrugged. "I don't feel well."

He muttered a curse and rolled away. "Was I mistaken thinking you enjoyed our time together in the library a few weeks ago?"

"No." She placed her hand on his forearm. "You were not mistaken. I did enjoy it then, I just don't think I'll enjoy it right now."

"Why?"

She said something, but he didn't hear her. He didn't need to. He already knew her answer. The one she'd never voice aloud. She was punishing him. She'd come to him that night, just hours after finding out what he'd done, and made love to him. His stomach clenched. He'd honestly believed she'd enjoyed their lovemaking in the library, but now to know she'd been feigning her enjoyment made him sick. And there was no denying she'd feigned her enjoyment that night. He remembered the look on her face during their wedding night. And now she was going to deny him. That was how she'd planned to punish him for what he'd done. She'd not forgiven and forgotten like she said earlier. She was getting her revenge and this was how she was doing it. All the nice things she'd done for him these past three weeks were only a decoy. A way to get him to believe she wasn't angry—or let him go on believing she didn't even know—a way to get him right where she wanted him: wanting her. Only so she could deny him in the end.

Fury burned in his gut and, without another word, he jumped from the bed, tied on his dressing robe, and left. Tomorrow she could move into the baroness' bedchamber and bolt the connecting door to him every night for the rest of her life if she wished. Tonight he was moving into the baron's bedchamber and throwing away his key to hers.

Chapter 24

By the time morning came, Caroline vowed never to eat again. Things that are delicious going down are *not* delicious coming back up. Yuck. She wiped her mouth once more and stood up slowly. Ever since breakfast yesterday she'd felt nauseated, dizzy even. Cook made her a foul tonic that tasted worse than it smelled and didn't produce any results, unless one counted making her sicker a result, albeit not a favorable one.

She grabbed a fresh gown and clutched it to her chest, wincing as she did. Her breasts even seemed different today. Tender, almost painful. She looked in the mirror. They didn't look different.

She'd taken to wearing gowns that didn't require help getting them on and off. It was just easier to put something on that had buttons on the side or in the front than it was to ring for help.

Finishing her *toilette,* she pinched her extremely pale cheeks and headed down for breakfast. Not that she was hungry. The mere mention of food made her queasy. Just like yesterday. No the real reason she was going downstairs was she wanted to see Alex. She needed to speak to him. Last night when he'd left, he'd been upset with her. He hadn't given her the chance to explain that she wasn't feeling well before his face hardened and he left. She'd talk to him today. He wasn't one who normally made rash decisions or acted instinctively; likely he'd had a rough day yesterday and wasn't quite himself. Either way, she needed to clear the air with him.

Besides, she had a feeling he'd want to talk to her, too. Yesterday his brothers had walked in on her in the conservatory, and when they both just stared at her dumbfounded, she'd jokingly asked them if they wished to undress and help her with the rosebushes. Neither of them so much as cracked a smile, and she wasn't sure if Alex would see the humor in it or not.

"Feeling better this morning, dear?" Regina asked as she came down the stairs.

"Much," Caroline lied. Her stomach was still uneasy and she could feel a fit of the vapors coming on. Earlier, when she had her head in a chamber pot for the tenth time in as many hours, she ran through the possibilities of what could be causing her illness, and the only one that made sense was she was with child. The thought of having Alex's child made her so excited she almost forgot about her nausea. Almost. The only trouble was she couldn't tell anyone. Not until she told Alex anyway. Which was soon to happen, because she spotted him coming down the stairs from the corner of her eye.

"Good," Regina said with a slight smile. "Won't you come join Edwina and me for breakfast?"

"I've something to do just now. I'll join you in a bit." She stood in the hall and waited for her mother-in-law to go into the breakfast room. "Alex," she called, feigning the normalcy she didn't feel. She hated feeling ill.

"Caroline," he said tightly, taking his hat and riding crop from the butler.

She frowned. Why was she back to Caroline? "Are you angry with me?"

"No." He put his hat on his head.

She blinked at him. "Can we speak privately?" she asked, looking pointedly at Johnson.

Alex shrugged. "Do we have something private to discuss?"

"Yes," she said, clenching her teeth. This was not a conversation she wanted to have in front of Johnson, who, for as old as he was, loved to gossip.

Alex pulled a card out of his breast pocket. "This is the direction of my secretary. He'll be glad to make you an appointment."

Her face burned with anger. "I am your wife! I will not be made to schedule an appointment to speak to you in your study for fifteen minutes while you look condescendingly down your nose at me and I am made to fidget in one of those terribly uncomfortable chairs."

He smiled thinly. "I'm sorry, but I have a meeting just now. I must be off."

"It can wait. Nobody takes precedence over your wife and child."

"Child?" he echoed hollowly, glancing at her midsection. "Impossible."

"Possible."

He shook his head. "I'll acknowledge it's *possible*, but it is not likely."

"And why is that?" she countered, hands on her hips.

"Johnson, leave." Alex stared at her until Johnson was out of sight. "That was three weeks ago. You might be merely late."

"No, it was five weeks ago," she snapped. "And I am three weeks late."

He scoffed. "Now, *that's* not possible."

"Yes, it is." She grabbed her skirt and clutched the fabric as tightly as she could. For years she'd been undermined, pushed aside, and trampled on by most of her family members. She'd never imagined Alex would ever treat her thus.

"No, it's not." He crossed his arms. "I have a little confession for you about that night. While you may have enjoyed everything I had to offer, I didn't—"

"Finish," she finished for him. "Yes, Alex, I realized that that night in the library. And though I don't know why you didn't finish on our wedding night—a little problem, perhaps—I do know that a man is not required to ejaculate for a woman to conceive."

His mouth fell open, presumably due to her word selection. "I concede your point," he said flatly. "Though how *you'd* know such a thing is rather hard to comprehend."

She smiled wryly. "And here you thought I needed to read a bunch of books and be questioned before joining the *Society of Biological Matters*." His face didn't soften a bit and she sighed. "All right, a year ago I overheard a footman and a maid arguing about something relating to his lack of using sheaths, whatever those are, and her current condition which would have been avoided if he'd used a sheath instead of..." She trailed off. She didn't relish the idea of using the exact term the maid used. He was a man. He knew. She cleared her throat and fanned herself, not sure if she was hot because of her condition or embarrassment. Not to mention the way Alex was staring at her. "Anyway," she continued, forcing a smile. "Thinking as a scientist, I filled in the details."

"Why are you even approaching me about this?" Alex asked frankly, his mouth forming a line so tight the edges grew white.

"Because I wanted you to know. You're the father. I thought you should know before anyone else."

"Well, thank you," he said, breaking eye contact. "Let's hope it's a boy since you seem to think I suffer a condition that might prevent me from siring another."

Caroline flushed with shame. "I'm sorry, Alex. I meant nothing by it. I was hurt by the way you'd been speaking to me and said the first cruel thing I could think of."

He shrugged. "It matters naught anyway. You have no interest in letting me share your bed as it is. If this baby is a boy, it will supply you a viable reason to refuse me."

"I'd never dream of refusing you." Her voice was barely a whisper. She'd not meant to let on to how much she enjoyed being intimate with him; it just slipped out.

He snorted. "Not only have you dreamt it, you've done it."

"Only once. And it was because I felt nauseated."

"Try again, Caroline," he said, his voice held a bitter edge. "We both know that's not the truth. You denied me last night because you're trying to punish me. That's right, Caroline. I know everything. You're angry with me because I was foolish enough to plan our courtship like an experiment, and you've decided to punish me by tempting and teasing me until I'm mad with want for you, then suddenly you're not interested."

"You're wrong," she said sharply, clenching her fists again. "I might have been excessively nice to you as a way to capture your attention, but I had no intention of using intimacy as a weapon."

"Oh, really? I find it rather curious that it wasn't until after you found that damn piece of paper that you suddenly became interested in fulfilling my needs. Until then, you seemed fully content to have all the attention for yourself."

Nothing he could have said could have hurt her more than those words. "Is it like that, then?" she asked bitterly. "Do you keep an observation notebook nearby that you use to record all the times we've been intimate and exactly who got what pleasure?"

"No." His voice was hard and his face red with anger.

"Are you sure? It wouldn't surprise me. You seem to think everything is a scientific study of some sort." She glared at him, daring him to object.

"I don't have time for this," he said, shaking his head. "I've someone to meet."

"My replacement?" she asked sharply, baiting him. She wasn't satisfied their argument had solved anything. She wasn't near satisfied.

"What the devil is that to mean?"

She lifted her chin. "Your mistress, of course."

He sneered. "I'm not going out to look for a mistress, thank you. I'm not so desperately in need of intimacy that I'd pay someone to use their body."

"You have before," she retorted.

His face turned redder than she'd ever seen it, his jaw clenched, and the muscle in his cheek ticked. "You're right, I have. And it disgusted me as much then as it does now."

"I find that hard to believe. You seem to like to keep score where we're concerned. I'd think you'd prefer to receive your favors in such a manner where both parties give and receive equally." She was pushing a matter that was insignificant to the whole, but she just couldn't stop herself.

He shook his head. "You don't understand, Caroline. I hate brothels. The whole premise behind them disgusts me. Those women are daughters, sisters, friends, mothers, people, and they get treated like little more than animals by the men who come in there looking for a quick, carefree release. Kept mistresses are no better. They may live in a nice home, have a staff, entertain fewer partners, and are undeniably classier and easier to present in public, but the facts are still the same. They still taking a man's money in exchange to let him freely use their bodies while they pretend to enjoy it."

He exhaled sharply and raked his hand through his hair. "When I was two-and-twenty, I met a widow who I formed an attachment to, if you will. It wasn't your normal situation, or so I didn't think." He swallowed and glanced away. "There was no formal contract. I wasn't offering her money or paying any of her accounts for her. The only exchange was companionship. The idea of companionship for companionship seemed ideal to me. And it was, for a time. Then one day she asked what I brought for her. She asked because I'd given her a small brooch the week before when we'd gone to the opera. As it turned out, she expected me to bring her things every time I came to visit her. Foolish boy that I was, it took me three months to find myself standing over a string of pearls before realizing I was paying her to pretend to enjoy something she'd not engage in otherwise."

Caroline blinked back tears. Alex was a gentleman through and through. Even in an area of a man's life where most took advantage and didn't act gentlemanly, Alex did. "You don't know that," she countered softly. "She might have enjoyed your attentions with or without the gifts."

He shook his head and looked at her coldly. "No. I was paying her. Just in an indirect way. She wouldn't have shared her bed with me otherwise."

"You don't know that," she protested again.

He shrugged. "Maybe you're right," he agreed, bitterness still filling his voice and marring his features. "Maybe she thought I was a good lover. But then again, maybe not. Nobody ever knows the truth when they're paying someone." He twisted his lips into a sneer. "What's ironic, I don't know if you ever enjoyed it, either."

"Alex, I did. I've enjoyed everything we've done together," she said, moving to be closer to him.

He snorted and pulled back. "I don't believe a word you just said. It was all a game to you," he replied icily, ruining her good image of him. "The first time you looked to be in complete pain and discomfort. And now that I know you were only trying to punish me, I believe you forced yourself to pretend to enjoy things the second time."

"Don't be hateful, Alex," she said in a low tone. "I did not pretend to enjoy myself with you. I did. I was merely unsure how a lady is expected to express herself in the bedroom. My mother isn't around to inform me. And anyone I know who would know, I didn't feel comfortable asking."

He closed his eyes for a few seconds before he looked at her again. "I'm sorry, Caroline. As your husband I should have told you. In the bedchamber—or any other place you might find yourself in such a situation—you are allowed to respond however you want. There are no rules or pretenses. You're not being judged and there's no need to be embarrassed. There's an unspoken understanding that what happens is private and stays private."

"So it didn't repulse you when I...um...responded?" she whispered, blushing with embarrassment.

"No. I wanted you to do that. But it's inconsequential now," he added, his voice hard as steel once again. "I'll not be seeking entrance to your bed any longer."

"Why?" she asked, on the verge of tears again. "Why are you doing this?"

"Because I'll not be led around by my genitals." He flashed her a cruel smile. "There are other ways a man can find satisfaction."

"But you said—"

"You didn't let me finish. A man doesn't require a woman's presence to find satisfaction. The idea may be frowned upon in polite society, but it works all the same."

She blinked at him. If he wasn't talking about getting a mistress, what did he intend to do? A rather unusual thought popped into her mind. Her eyes widened and heat crept up her face.

"I believe you take my meaning," he said, not a hint of emotion in his voice.

Tears streamed out of her eyes in two steady torrents. "What happened to the sweet gentleman named Alex Banks I married? Was that all an act for the purposes of our courtship?"

"No," he said, grinding his teeth. "That was not an act. He still exists, but he decided to vacate the premises when he discovered his wife was trying to lead him around by his prick."

She winced at the cruel intent of his words. "You, Alexander Christopher Banks, are the worst scientist I've ever met. You have no factual basis for your claims, and yet you believe them as if they're the very same gospel your uncle preaches every week." She wiped her eyes and took a deep sniff through her nose. "I've given you no reason to believe I intended to use my body against you. It's you who thinks I'm punishing you, and you have no basis for it." A sob cracked her voice and wracked her body.

"Yes, I do," he countered, matching her steely tone. "I was in the room when you told my mother you hated me and wished you'd never read that paper. I remember how angry you were and how you cried yourself to sleep. I foolishly chose to believe your acts of gentle politeness, complete with you wanting to just put it all behind us."

"You were there?" she asked, her knees buckling. Had he heard anything else?

He nodded.

"Then you know about the—"

"Stop. I don't have time for this just now. I am more than five weeks late for a meeting with Marcus. He sent a note yesterday that I must come today at the latest. Something about a dowry I didn't even know you had."

She wasn't sure if Alex's last words were spoken out of cruelty or disbelief, nor did she really care. She might have a past history of being too forgiving, but not anymore. His words cut her to the core and anything less than groveling wouldn't so much as grant him an audience with her, much less access to her bedchamber.

***

Alex rode his stallion as fast as he could go to Ridge Water. His words to Caroline might have been crueler than she deserved, but the meaning was not. He'd made a mistake and he'd gladly admit to it and pay penance for it. But for her to be so underhanded as to not say anything and punish him without knowing what he'd done to deserve the punishment was going too far. Fortunately, his brothers had let it slip so he knew *why* he was being punished, even if he hadn't even detected that *something* was afoot to begin with.

Looking at everything logically, he really hadn't done anything so terribly wrong. Many gentlemen planned out their courtships. Just not in such a detailed and intricate way.

He sighed, banged the brass knocker, then stood motionless and waited for the butler to show him in. Marcus wanted to talk about a dowry and he wanted to talk to Marcus about something, too. He had little doubt this conversation would prove to be more entertaining and enlightening than his last.

Chapman came to the door and led him down the hall to Marcus' study. Along the way, he couldn't help wanting to ask how Marcus felt sitting in the same chair his father used to sit in. He shook off the thought. That was another conversation for another day. Today they needed to take care of business. Besides, waiting to talk to him about filling his father's position gave him a reason to come back another day to see his friend.

"Alex," Marcus said, standing up. "I feared you'd not come and then I'd have a real mess on my hands."

Alex smiled. "I came."

"I see that," he remarked, sitting back down. "I know you have a lot demanding your attention what with your recent loss and Caroline and all, but this needs to be taken care of, and now that I'm no longer her legal guardian..." He shrugged.

Alex reached his hand out. "All right, just give it to me."

"Here." Marcus handed him an unusually tall stack of paper.

Alex frowned. The last time he'd just been handed a stack of papers with no explanation, he'd just been informed he was betrothed to Lady Olivia. "What's this?"

"The first sheet is the bank account information for the London bank where her money is," he said easily, giving Alex time to read over the page.

Alex blinked at the page. "Your father was mighty generous," he mused, scanning the numbers on the page.

Marcus snorted. "Not hardly. It was commonly thought Caroline wouldn't require a dowry so my father never saw fit to give her one. I, on the other hand, disagreed with that notion and took care of Caroline's dowry, to a point."

"To a point?"

"When I started the account for her four years ago my intent was just to raise enough money to give her a Season. My father couldn't afford to give her one. Not for lack of money, of course." He pursed his lips and shook his head. "He was more afraid of her being torn to shreds by the social piranhas due to some old family gossip about her mother and father. But I thought she deserved one anyway and I asked a friend of mine, the late Lady Drakely, to bring her out if I'd pay. She agreed, but I hadn't enough funds at the time. Since my father was still earl, and I wouldn't be able to touch the trust I inherited from my mother until his death or my thirtieth year, I had to find another way to scrape up the money. That's why I started the account. But she's the reason it kept growing, therefore, I can only take partial credit." He flashed a rare smile at Alex.

Alex stared at him. Despite everything Caroline had been through, she'd always had at least one person who'd loved her and would do anything for her. "Thank you, Marcus."

"Don't thank me," he said, twisting a quill between his fingers. "She did all the work."

"I'm not talking about that," Alex said softly. "I was thanking you for taking such good care of her. For loving her."

Marcus' gaze was unblinking. "I accept your thanks, and my hope is that you'll treat her the same."

Alex lowered his eyes. He surely hadn't been very caring or loving this morning. He'd treated her nastier than he'd ever treated anyone. Shame washed over him. The look on her face this morning flashed in his mind. Even for as socially inept as he was, he knew hurt and pain when he saw it. And he'd definitely seen it. And caused it. He swallowed.

"Look through the rest." Marcus propped his feet up on the desk and brought his hand up to rest against his left cheek. "You've kept me waiting for five weeks. I can wait no longer."

Alex picked up the first page and pulled it away to look at the second. It was a sales slip of some sort. He scanned the lines, confused. Had she paid money to someone or had they paid her? Her name was nowhere on the page.

"Flip the page again," Marcus murmured. "That might help you make sense of it."

Alex glanced at Marcus, then pulled back the next page and caught his breath. "Marcus, tell me what I'm looking at."

Marcus chuckled. "Why don't you tell me what you think it is?"

"That's what I'm not sure of," he began, turning his eyes up to Marcus. "I recognize the handwriting as yours. However, the name at the top reads E. S. Wilson, which, not only have you told me you are not him, but I also remember you having a severe lack of knowledge concerning biology."

"Just so. And now, Lord Logical, what can you deduce from those previously stated—and a few unmentioned, but not unknown —facts?" Marcus drawled, clearly enjoying the situation.

"Caroline is E. S. Wilson," Alex said, dumbfounded.

"Brilliant, Alex! You truly were the smartest boy at Eton."

Alex leafed through the stack. Every single article that had anonymously appeared by E. S. Wilson in *Popular Plants* from the past four years was right here in his lap. He'd read them all before. He'd even duplicated almost all of the experiments. But knowing Caroline had written them made them more than just interesting articles that had inspired him to search for another great mind to converse with. They were invaluable.

She was truly brilliant and sadly, he'd demeaned her all along. They'd sat in the room right across the hall not two months ago and he'd belittled her understanding of biology. He'd even gone so far as to suggest she read her own articles. And he'd done it again just this morning by quickly dismissing her claim to be carrying his child.

His heart clenched. His child. His child with Caroline. Their child. After the things he'd said to her this morning, this would likely be their only child. Would it be a little bespectacled boy who wore his clothes haphazardly and followed his papa around holding a magnifying glass in one hand and notebook in the other? Or would it be a beautiful, dark-haired, blue-eyed girl who was always getting into trouble for dragging the hem of her skirt through the mud while she dug around in the flowerbeds? He smiled at the mental image. Most men wished for a boy, but he'd gladly take a little girl who was just like Caroline.

"Alex," Marcus said loudly, unmistakable pride shining in his face. "I know you're in awe over this revelation, and probably can't wait to go home and kiss the person you had no idea was secretly your hero, but we need to discuss business."

Alex blinked at Marcus and his astonishing level of excitement. He doubted his friend had ever been this excited in the past twelve years, and he wasn't going to ruin it by telling him Caroline would deny his request for a kiss because she was angry with him and had every reason to be. "What business?" he asked quietly, placing the stack of papers on the edge of Marcus' desk.

Marcus scratched his jaw. "Well, there is one little, tiny snag."

Alex rolled his eyes. Of course there was. "What do I not know?"

"Actually, *you* know everything. It's Caroline who doesn't. When I put the first two hundred pounds in the account and sold her first article, I'd planned everything to be a surprise. But right before I had enough money, Lady Drakley passed, and with her my plans for Caroline's Season. By then, I'd heard my father casually mention something about the success of the article—he never knew what I'd done. So I continued to send her experiments in and planned to either give her the money when she reached her majority in a few months or use it as a dowry if she married.

"The problem is, all the experiments I'd sent were old ones I'd found in a little box she kept in her room. I'd just sneak in while she was out, copy down a handful of experiments, then send them off before she could find me with them and ask why I had them." He shuddered and curled up as much of his top lip as his scarred skin would allow. "Anyway, I've run out. Not that I find that to be a problem for which I am to find a solution. You are."

Alex stared at his friend and raked his fingers through his hair. "Let me get this right. You've taken it upon yourself to copy Caroline's scientific observations and sell them to a widely circulated publication for the past four years, garnering her all sorts of acclaim for being one of the brightest minds in the field of biological science, and she doesn't even know it?"

Marcus nodded.

"You do know she has a right to know her work has been published, don't you?"

Marcus nodded again.

"And you also know before the sun sets tonight, she'll know."

"I'd be disappointed if she didn't," Marcus said with a shrug. "She deserves to know. I only kept it from her at first because I didn't want to crush her feelings if the editor didn't accept her work. After that I didn't tell her because I didn't know how she'd feel about what I'd done."

"Wait, you just said you did it to make money for her to have a Season," Alex countered.

"I did. But if this hadn't worked out, I had other ways to make the money. It would have taken longer, but I would have done anything to scrape up the funds." He sighed. "The truth is she'd worked hard on all that. And while I personally may not care to read about it, others do. And you know as well as I do she would have never had the opportunity to get published or take the credit under her own name like she deserved. So I did what I could."

"You were afraid she'd be angry with you for doing this?"

"Yes. Wouldn't you be?"

Alex nodded. He'd have been furious. But Marcus had a point. If he hadn't done it anonymously, her work would have been dismissed as soon as the editor got to the by-line, no matter how good the content. "All right. Enough on that. I'll tell her and let her decide if she wants to continue to publish her work or not."

"Good," Marcus said. "As much as I love my cousin, copying her notes was pure torture."

Alex grinned for the first time all day. "I bet for you it was."

"Almost as torturous as it would have been for you to live with my sister, I imagine," Marcus parried.

"I doubt that." Things may not be going well for him and Caroline just now, but fighting with her was better than just being in the room with Lady Olivia. He glanced at Marcus and met the man's steely, grey gaze. "Marcus, I've wanted to talk to you about something for a while."

Marcus nodded. "I have a feeling I know what you're going to ask." His voice was serious, and all the excitement that had earlier lit his face vanished.

"The nitrous oxide party," Alex said flatly. "I remember most of the details, but there's one thing that's been bothering me."

"Which is?"

"Do you know what happened to her?"

Marcus blinked at him. "I suppose you're talking about the little girl we were caught sneaking out?"

Alex nodded. His throat was too tight with emotion to speak.

Marcus' eyes turned to look out the window. "I don't know what happened to her that night," he admitted softly. Slowly, he met Alex's gaze again. "But I know what happened to her later."

Alex just stared at him, waiting for him to continue. He didn't trust his voice to speak the words, to ask the questions he feared he didn't want to know the answers to. That little girl had haunted his dreams for nearly the past fourteen years. She'd been merely six or seven living alone with a man so addicted to nitrous oxide he'd have sold his own daughter into prostitution to feed his habit.

"She married," Marcus said a minute later. "Happily, I believe. One of those, what's the term I'm looking for—" he waved his hand in the air— "love match. That's it. She had a love match."

Alex nodded. "Good for her," he said at last, hoping his friend wouldn't comment on the roughness of his voice or the relief he was sure covered his face.

"Good for him, too." Marcus turned back to his work. "I trust you can find your way out."

Alex gathered the stack of papers from Marcus' desk and left the room. The ride home was much slower, almost leisurely even. He had no reason to rush home. His wife wouldn't be waiting with open arms to greet him. They'd both said and done hurtful things, but the cruelest of it all was he still wanted her. He might have tried to convince both her and himself to the contrary only hours ago, but with the cloud of anger gone, he could see the truth; and that truth was he still burned for her, but would likely never have her again. There was no reason for her to take him back. He'd let his emotions get the better of him this morning and he'd as good as lost her because of it. There'd be no more bright smiles to greet him or scientific banter in the conservatory. She'd not tease him about his clothes being in disarray when he came to their room at night. They wouldn't even share a room at night. All in one fit of hurt and anger, he'd somehow managed to lose it all.

Sadness in his heart and papers in his hand, he mounted the front steps to his house. Grabbing hold of the doorknob, the hairs on the back of his neck stood on end as the one voice in the world he never wanted to hear again floated to his ears.

Chapter 25

"What the blazes is going on in here?" Alex roared, bursting through the entryway of the front parlor where Caroline, Mother, and Rupert Griffin were engaged in a rather heated discussion.

Caroline wiped tears away with the back of her hand. "Nothing that concerns you."

He pushed further into the room. "Like hell it doesn't. This is my house and anything that goes on in here concerns me." He crossed his arms and turned to Griffin. "What are you doing here bothering my wife and mother? If you wish to speak to me, that can be arranged. But leave them out of it."

"I did make arrangements," Griffin spat, scowling. "It seems your *wife* was a little late to deliver the message."

Alex stared at the man's haggard and coarse face. In the past fourteen years he'd only seen the older man one other time, the same day he'd first met Caroline at the *Society* meeting. Even between then and now, there was a drastic difference. Time and addiction had been cruel to him. But not nearly as cruel as the man himself had been.

"Seems she has the good sense to know I'd not have allowed filth like you past the front door," Alex responded coldly.

Griffin snorted. "You always were a bit conceited, young Alex. Oh, excuse me, Lord Watson. How unfortunate that beating you received didn't humble your gentlemanly pride any."

"No, I suppose it wasn't nearly as effective as locking a little girl into a dark closet," he said bitterly, ignoring the sounds of distress coming from across the room.

"It's none of your business how I chose to deal with her," Griffin blustered.

"You no good, filthy bastard." Alex grabbed Griffin by the lapels and slammed him into the wall with such strong force the breath was knocked out of him and he crumpled to the floor. Alex bent down, grabbed hold of the front of Griffin's shirt, and yanked him back to standing position before moving his hand to hold Griffin about the throat.

"Unhand me," Griffin rasped against Alex's strong hold.

"Not on your life. What are you doing here?"

"I explained it in my note," Griffin replied, grabbing Alex's wrists.

Alex tightened his grip. "What the devil are you talking about? You never sent me a note. Believe me, if you had, I'd remember it."

"I didn't send it to you, I sent it to my daughter." Griffin tried to pry Alex's fingers off his throat.

"You sent it to your daughter?" Alex bellowed, applying more pressure with his fingertips. "What good does that do me?"

The disgusting smile that pulled on Griffin's lips made Alex hope Marcus had been right, and that poor girl had grown up and married a man who truly loved her. She deserved it after growing up with this man for a father. "A whole lot of good, I should think. You seem to have formed quite an attachment to her."

"Right, because I saw her once for less than an hour when I was sixteen, and since I'm thirty now, that makes a lot of sense," Alex said sarcastically. "Don't worry, I know you struggle with any kind of math that's not directly connected with measuring out the perfect amount of nitrous oxide for your nightly habit, so I'll tell you that means it's been nearly fourteen years since I've seen her last."

"I believe for once my math is better than yours, young Alex. You saw her less than fourteen minutes ago. Less than two even." Griffin cackled. "Caroline, dear, won't you be a good girl now and tell your husband to get his hands off your papa?"

"Caroline?" Alex repeated hollowly, turning his head to look at his pale, unsteady wife. He blinked at her and suddenly everything fell into place. Caroline hated total darkness. She'd become nearly sick and positively withdrawn the day he'd mentioned Griffin's name when Father had pressed him as to why he'd tossed Lady Olivia and Caroline out of the *Society*. Even that made sense now. Lord Sinclair hadn't been trying to protect Lady

Olivia from Griffin by having them thrown out of the *Society*; he'd been trying to protect Caroline.

Trying to protect her in a way two sixteen-year-old boys couldn't.

For that moment, the world stood still for Alex and he was once again transported back in time to when he was sixteen and Marcus approached him for a favor. One so enormous he claimed he'd never ask for a favor again. Alex had agreed instantly. With a promise of never asking for anything again, Alex knew this was important.

An hour later, Marcus took him to a nitrous oxide party in London hosted by Rupert Griffin. They'd paid their admittance fees and mingled for a few hours. At midnight most of the guests were intoxicated too much to notice—or care—what was going on around them. "Let's go," Marcus said, pushing Alex through the doorway of the drawing room.

Alex nodded and followed Marcus through a maze of darkened staircases and hallways until they reached a dead end with a door. Very slowly, Marcus eased the door open to reveal a little girl in a tattered nightshirt balled up in the corner. She sat trembling with her knees drawn up to her chest, her forehead resting against her knees.

"Come on," Marcus called to the little girl.

The little girl looked up at Marcus and moved to wrap him in a hug. Marcus squeezed her back, whispering something in her ear.

Over Marcus' shoulder, the young girl looked at Alex hesitantly, and the sadness in her eyes ate at his heart. Marcus murmured a few things to her before lifting her in his arms and carrying her down a different hall. They went to a room with a balcony that was three stories above where they'd tied their horses to a tree when they'd arrived.

Marcus handed Alex the little girl, then went to the railing of the balcony and threw his leg over. Alex hadn't asked too many questions until then, but as it was becoming more apparent they were about to kidnap this little girl, he'd questioned his friend's decision. Marcus paused only for a second to tell him earlier that day he'd overheard her father talking with a brothel owner about selling her into the trade when she was twelve and asked for an advance on the funds. Alex's stomach tightened at the thought, strengthening his resolve. He would help Marcus get this girl out of there at any cost.

Marcus scaled down the brick wall, leaving Alex to hold the trembling girl. Having a three-year-old sister at the time, he didn't feel too terribly awkward holding her, but couldn't think of a single thing to say to calm her trembles or stop her silent tears. He just held her close and ran his hand along her back, trying to comfort her any way he could.

At last Marcus reached the bottom and tossed up a rope to Alex. Alex set the little girl down, telling her it'd just be a minute while he tied his end of the rope securely around the handrail of the balcony.

Lifting her up, he wrapped her arms around his neck and told her to hold on tightly as he grabbed the rope in one hand and maneuvered them over the railing.

Using his feet against the wall to support their bodies, he scaled down the rope. Less than two feet from the bottom, a sharp click broke the eerie silence. Alex looked over to see a man with a pistol standing about three feet away. The man demanded Alex put his daughter down. Risking a glance at a frozen Marcus, Alex complied. The little girl immediately ran and hid behind Marcus. That was the last he saw her.

In the minutes that followed, Griffin and a few of his friends hauled Alex and Marcus inside, stripped them to their drawers, and, using a horsewhip, lashed them each at least a dozen times before hiring a hack. He then shoved their almost naked, blood soaked, and nearly unconscious bodies into the hack and sent them to Alex's parents at Watson Townhouse.

Alex had no doubt he'd gained the maturity of a man that night. He'd seen the ugly side of the world. A man who cared so little for his daughter that he'd locked her in a dark closet and made arrangements to sell her into a life of prostitution—only to be free of her and get the funds to further his addiction. That was the night Alex had made the unconscious decision to never visit a brothel. He couldn't even pass one without the image of a scared little girl popping into his head. He'd also learned the harsh reality that sometimes doing what was right could make things worse.

Until earlier today when Marcus told him that the little girl had grown up and married for love, he'd always believed his and Marcus' misguided intervention that night had made her life worse. And maybe it had, for a time. But never again. Never again would he let a day pass where she was forced to cower in the shadow of her past.

"Yes, he's my father," Caroline said weakly, pulling him back to the present.

Fury like he'd never known took over, and when he turned back to see Griffin's devious grin, he couldn't keep himself from wiping it off his face. Pulling his free hand back, he made a fist, and before Griffin could react, Alex hit the man straight in the nose. A sharp, cracking noise rent the air and blood sprayed from Griffin's nose, accompanied by a strangled gurgling noise.

Alex released his hold on the man's throat and let him fall to a heap on the floor. "Where's the letter?"

"It's gone," Mother said evenly.

"Gone?"

Mother raised her chin a notch. "It suffered an untimely meeting with a flame."

"I burned it." Caroline's eyes shone with tears she hadn't cried while tears she'd already shed coursed down her cheeks, making his heart ache for her all over again. She cleared her throat. "He wanted money. I—I—I'm sorry, Alex. I know I should have told you after we married who my father was, but I was ashamed." She swiped at the tears on her cheeks. "Then his letter came yesterday and I was too upset to tell you at first, but then I thought you knew this morning when you said—"

Alex nodded. Though her voice broke off, he took her meaning. That's what she'd been upset about last night when she'd gone to bed, not his "experiment." A crushing weight settled in his chest. He tore his eyes from her. Now wasn't the time to try to set things right between them. It wasn't the time to assure her there was not a single reason for her to be ashamed for having this good-for-nothing addict as her father.

"Always money with you, isn't it?" he asked Griffin, kicking his body with the toe of his boot.

"You owe it to me," Griffin cried, holding his bleeding nose with both hands. "If it weren't for you, she'd have fetched me a fortune when—"

Alex stomped down on his chest, halting his words. "Not another word." He applied more pressure with his foot. "I'll not even hear the rest of that sentence spoken in my presence. Nor will you ever again contact anyone of any relation to me. Understood?"

Griffin grabbed Alex's boot and tried to push it from his chest. "I should have killed you when I had the chance," he ground out, grunting as he struggled to move Alex's foot.

"And I should kill you now." Alex rocked back on his heel to give an extra amount of pain just below Griffin's sternum.

Griffin grunted in pain again, then relaxed his hands and rested his head on the floor. "But we both know you won't. Not only are you Arid Alex, but you wouldn't dream of going into exile and having to leave your breeding wife behind."

"How did you know?" he breathed, stunned.

Twisting his lips, Griffin said, "Caroline might be my only living child. But being married to her ever-spawning mother for almost twenty years, I learned to recognize the early stages of when a woman is increasing. Especially when they appear ready to cast up their accounts."

Alex glanced at Caroline. She didn't look so different to him. A bit paler than normal perhaps, nothing else though. Next to Caroline, stood his mother, a small smile slowly forming on her lips. She'd just learned Caroline's news.

"I predict five weeks," Griffin continued. "Though I've no doubt in my mind, like that whore she called a mother, she'd have anticipated her wedding vows, you wouldn't have."

Without taking his eyes from Caroline, Alex picked up his foot and brought it back down as hard as he could on Griffin's groin, grinding his heel against him a few times before having mercy and putting his foot back on the floor.

Griffin's hands flew between his legs, and he pulled his knees up as he rolled around on the floor, wailing in pain.

"I've heard enough from you." Alex nudged him in the ribs with the side of his boot. "Your comments and presence aren't needed here. Quit pretending your nonexistent ballocks hurt and get your arse the hell out of my house. And don't even think of coming back, or this will look like child's play compared to what I'll do to you then."

Griffin made no move to get up. Alex bent down, grabbed two fistfuls of his clothes, and dragged him from the room, passing a frantic-looking Marcus just outside the door.

"Open the front door, would you?" Alex asked gruffly.

Marcus opened the door and stood back as Alex deposited Griffin outside. Alex turned to Johnson and asked him to see to it that Griffin was removed, post haste.

"Alex," Marcus said softly. "I didn't know he was coming here. I only found out he was in the area about an hour or so after you left. I came because I didn't realize until earlier this morning that you didn't know..." He trailed off and shrugged.

The corner of Alex's mouth tipped up ever-so-slightly. "I should have known. The clues were all there. But as you said, I'm a bit obtuse."

Marcus chuckled. "Is she all right?"

"I honestly don't know," Alex said, crossing his arms and leaning his shoulder against the doorframe. "I don't know what was said before I got here. Nor do I know to what extent she's been hurt." And not just by Griffin, but by him, too.

Marcus ran a hand along his scarred jaw. "All she needs is love, Alex. Just love her."

Alex nodded. "I do."

Marcus smiled and put his hat back on. "Good."

Alex stood on the porch and waited until Marcus mounted his horse and rode off before going back into the parlor only to discover it empty.

Chapter 26

Caroline's nerves were much calmer after a nice warm bath and nearly an entire day of rest.

Unfortunately, Regina had been wrong in her ascertainment of Caroline's father's intentions. Not that Caroline blamed Regina for the events of yesterday morning. She didn't. Caroline was just as much at fault for nobody being properly prepared for their unwanted guest. She'd chosen to believe he was only trying to scare her and was caught unawares when only two hours after her terrible fight with Alex, her father showed up. With both of Alex's brothers gone and her father refusing to leave until he was allowed to see Caroline and Alex both, Caroline went down to talk to him. Regina went with her and asked a footman to be ready to see their guest out if things got nasty.

An argument soon broke out, causing Caroline to become more upset by the minute. She was beginning to fear Rupert was about to physically hurt one of them when, out of nowhere, Alex stormed in. The following argument between her husband and father brought up old sparks of a memory, but it wasn't until after Alex had left to throw Rupert out and Regina followed Caroline up to her room that she learned the whole truth.

She remembered vague snatches of the night when Marcus and his friend had taken her from the closet and tried to carry her away. In truth, she'd have never remembered Alex or his part in it, had Regina not told her the story. Like every other night since her mother had died, she'd been too scared to notice anything about anyone except those she knew. It was the following night, however, that Edward had come for her while her uncle was distracting her father in the drawing room—arguing about money, if she had to guess. That, or bribing him to give up legal claim to Caroline.

She wiped her eyes. She was done crying about it. For as upset as she was at receiving that letter from her father and the painful details that soon followed, she was also relieved. She finally had the information she'd always wanted. She knew the truth about her mother's decision to marry such a man, and how it had nothing to do with the reasons she'd always been told. Further, she now knew who'd saved her and why they'd stepped in. It was now time to truly put the past behind her and move forward with her life. Sadly, there was nothing to move forward to. Alex had told her in not so many words that he'd never love her. She shut her eyes to stop the onslaught of tears that once again filled her eyes. She loved him and he didn't want anything to do with her ever again.

She shook her head and opened her eyes. It shouldn't matter. She wasn't ready to forgive him yet anyway. She'd eventually forgive him, of course. It was her nature; she forgave everyone. But she wasn't ready just yet.

She rolled out of bed and pulled on her dressing gown. It was nearly noon already. It was well past time to start the day. She'd stayed in her room in complete solitude since shortly after her conversation with Regina yesterday. She needed to do something else and stop wallowing in misery. Misery had never suited her before, and it wasn't going to start now.

An hour later, she was bathed and dressed in one of her nicest mourning dresses. She dismissed Annie and went down to eat luncheon.

After lunch, she locked herself in her private sitting room with a book from the library she'd paid a servant to go get for her. The library was Alex's favorite room in the house; she didn't want to chance running into him there.

"Caroline?" Edwina's unusually loud voice drifted through the door, startling her.

She opened her door. "Yes?"

"Are you all right? I've been out here knocking for nearly ten minutes." Edwina pushed her way inside the room.

"Sorry," Caroline murmured, holding up a book to show her sister-in-law her reason for not hearing her knock.

"Must be one excellent book," Edwina muttered, plopping down on Caroline's settee. "You sure have a lot of candles."

Caroline smiled at the girl's complete lack of decorum. That was one of Caroline's favorite things about Edwina. They both struggled terribly with remembering how to act in polite society.

"I sure do," she agreed, looking at the dozens of candles that had been set up in her private sitting room. Her bedchamber, however, didn't have an overabundance of candles. In there, the staff had set up half a dozen lanterns for her to use at night. "I have a feeling you didn't come here to discuss my candles. Is there something I can help you with, Edwina?"

Edwina bit her lip. "I need to ask you a favor."

"Anything." Caroline sat down next to her, crossed her legs, and rested her folded hands on her knees.

Edwina glanced to the floor for a second then back up to Caroline. "Do you promise not to tell anyone? Especially my brother?"

Caroline sucked in her breath. This was not good. Edwina's face had trouble stamped all over it. "I can't promise that," she said quietly. "If you're in trouble, he may need to know." She prayed that wasn't the case.

"I'm not," Edwina assured her, shaking her head.

"Then why do you not want him to know?"

Edwina stared down at her fingernails. "I love Alex to death. He's actually my favorite brother, but..." She shrugged.

"But?" Caroline prompted.

"Don't tell him I said this, but sometimes he lives up to his nickname, Arid Alex," Edwina said quickly, a forced smile on her face.

Caroline had to catch herself from laughing. "All right. What's going on, Edwina?"

"I've taken an interest in astronomy, and I'm afraid if I ask Alex for help, he'll ruin it."

This time Caroline did laugh. She couldn't help it. "And you think I can help you?"

Edwina nodded. "Alex told me you know a lot about astronomy."

"I don't know that much," Caroline admitted.

"But you do know something about telescopes, don't you?"

Caroline nodded sadly. "I know some."

"Good," Edwina said cheerfully. "One of my friends at school loves astronomy and she got me interested in looking at the different constellations and reading *England Astronomy*. This morning I was reading this month's addition, and it said tonight, Uranus will be visible in the southern sky. I'd so dearly like to see it, but my study of astronomy is fairly new and I'm not positive I'll be able to find the planet. I know Alex would help me, but I just want to see it, not hear all about its rotation patterns, size, and who knows what else he might think my astronomical education would not be complete without knowing."

Caroline smiled at her. Edwina was correct in her ascertainment about Alex. He'd not only love to show her the planet, he'd also want to give her as many details as her brain could hold. He'd probably insist on giving her an examination afterward, too. "I think I can find it for you. Why don't you meet me here about eleven, and we'll walk out to the gazebo together?"

"Thank you, Caroline," Edwina said, giving her a hug.

Like Caroline expected, at precisely eleven, Edwina showed up at the door to her sitting room, lantern in one hand, *England Astronomy* in the other. "I thought I'd bring this just in case."

Caroline grabbed one of her lanterns and closed the door. "Let's be off."

The two talked of Edwina's recent interest in astronomy and what her favorite constellation was as they walked to the gazebo.

"Oh dear," Edwina said when they reached the gazebo. "I've got all sorts of mud on my slipper. Go on in and look for it. I'd better scrape this off or Alex will know I've been in here and he'll want to talk me to death about astronomy."

Caroline chuckled. Most people would have been concerned he'd be upset she'd tracked mud inside, not worry he'd want to talk about astronomy.

She went in and hung her lantern on a nail that was poking out of the wall. She remembered Alex's telescope was directly to the right of the entrance because she'd nearly tripped over the bottom of the ladder when he'd first brought her here. She frowned. The ladder wasn't there. She looked around and her eyes caught on the sight of the ladder across the gazebo. How odd.

Her eyes followed the ladder up to the top and collided with the eyepiece-end of the telescope. She blinked. Surely he had not moved and remounted his telescope. She walked forward and climbed the ladder.

At the top, she froze in shock. This wasn't his telescope at all. This was hers. How had he gotten it? And why had he bothered to mount it? Besides it being broken, he seemed to have no feelings whatsoever for her.

For reasons she couldn't identify, she put her eye to the eyepiece. It was broken, of course. She just wanted to pretend for one minute it wasn't. She moved the lever on the bottom and aimed it at the sky, then took her face away and blinked. Was it just her or had the images appeared clear and close? She looked through it again and moved the telescope around. "Well, I'll be," she muttered. He'd fixed it. How or when, she'd never know, but he'd fixed it and mounted it for her. Her traitorous heart swelled. His father had been right. He cared for her. He just did an awful job of showing it.

She looked around the sky for Uranus, thinking about Alex as she looked. He had to have fixed it in the past three weeks. If he'd done it before then, he'd have told her. And he certainly hadn't done it today or yesterday. That only left sometime in those three weeks after his father had passed.

She moved the telescope up and down, searching the sky for Uranus. Edwina had been gone much longer than she ought to be for wiping mud off her shoes. Caroline frowned. As soon as she found the planet, she'd go drag Edwina in here. If Alex asked who tracked mud inside, she'd just lie and say it was her.

A minute later, she'd found the planet and the door swung open. "I've got it," she announced, twisting the dial to sharpen the focus.

"And who has you?" a male voice murmured from behind her as its owner stepped on the ladder and closed his hands around her waist.

She stilled. "Lord Watson, I wasn't expecting you," she said tightly.

"Lord Watson?"

"That's who's in here with me, isn't it?"

He chuckled. "I suppose he is."

"Well then, what's the problem?"

He climbed another rung on the ladder, pushing his body against hers. "No problem. I was merely surprised to hear you call me by my title. You don't have to, you know."

She shrugged. "I know, but it seems the nice man I married named Alex packed his things and left, shortly after being falsely informed I'd planned to lead him about by a particular body part of his. A cruel man who has no interest in me named Lord Watson has since then taken his place."

He sucked in his breath as if he'd just been punched in the gut. "That's not true. He has plenty of interest in you. He even made an overnight trip to London to purchase the right lens and spent most of the day fixing your scope for you."

"Your sister is due back here any minute. She would like to use the telescope without your interference."

He snorted. "No, she wouldn't. She just said she would. Weenie can be a very persuasive actress. Particularly when being promised new gowns when she returns to school in a week."

Caroline closed her eyes. She'd been tricked. "In that case, I'd like to retire for the evening."

His hands climbed to her ribs and settled below her breasts. "You don't want to use your newly repaired telescope?"

"No. Not tonight."

"Hmm," he said, drumming his fingers against her ribs. "That's not the response I was hoping for."

"And what response were you hoping for, my lord? Did you think you could trick me into coming out here and we could stargaze together and act as if nothing is wrong?"

"That would be nice. But not exactly what I'd intended." He leaned his head down to rest his forehead on her shoulder. "I don't know what to do to make this right, Caroline," he whispered solemnly, as something hot that felt oddly like a tear hit her skin. "I didn't mean any of those things I said. I was angry with you and I thought I had all the facts, but you were right, I didn't. I didn't know you'd gotten an upsetting letter from your father. I thought you were telling my mother you hated me for finding what I'd written. That's why I assumed you were trying to use your body against me. I didn't realize you truly didn't feel well or that you'd been crying about your father. I thought it was about me."

"You give yourself far too much credit, my lord," she said crisply. "I'd forgiven what you'd done only hours after I'd read it. Most gentlemen plan their courtships out. Fortune hunters, mainly. You'd just taken it a step further by writing it down, checking the steps off as you'd accomplished them, and even jotted down some rather uncomplimentary comments—that's the only difference."

"I'm sorry about that," he whispered. "I shouldn't have written any of it down in the first place."

She pursed her lips. "But you did. Which, as I already said, isn't the part that hurt. It was the humiliation of being compared to a soiled dove." She clamped her eyelids down tight to keep her tears in check. "Alex, though I never truly understood Olivia's implications until recently, very recently, in fact, she always used to—" She bit her lip for a minute and blinked again. "Olivia used to imply *I'd* be a lady of ill-repute if not for her father rescuing me. That's why it hurt so badly that you'd think of me that way, too."

He swallowed hard. "I wasn't thinking of you that way," he said hoarsely. "When I wrote the part about finding a soiled dove, it was only to make light of a bad situation. Before my pen even scratched out the first letter on that sheet, I knew I wanted to marry you."

"I just don't understand why you had to write any of it," she replied, her voice cracking from hurt and frustration.

"Caroline, as you found out a few weeks ago, your cousin and I share a birthday. While my father and your uncle were celebrating her birth, they got carried away and decided to draw up a betrothal contract for their children. Eight years later, it was amended to say if I married someone else before the thirtieth anniversary of my birth, there would be no repercussions. I didn't know of any of this until the day I came to Ridge Water to talk to Marcus. That's what was in the papers he looked over, and his suggestion about treating something like a science experiment had been about my search for a bride in such a short time."

She nodded. She'd thought it odd Olivia had suddenly claimed she was to marry Alex when she'd never spoken kindly of him before. "So then you took Marcus' sage advice and applied it straight to me?"

"No," he said, rubbing his thumbs on her back. "When he left us in the library together, I was trying to make a list of potential brides. Unfortunately, I couldn't really think of any. I was too distracted by you, but never put you on my list because I didn't think you even liked me, what with the *Society* rejection and all. Then you left and Marcus took my list, crossed every name off and put yours at the bottom. That's why I decided to pursue you. Marcus seemed to think I had a chance, and I liked you. A lot. So I placed all my bets on one horse and pursued you relentlessly."

She rolled her eyes at his poorly chosen phrase, but let it pass. "What do you really want? It seems you wanted nothing to do with me before you learned of my alter-ego, E. S. Wilson. But now you're going to all lengths to fix my broken telescope and bribing people to help you create a situation where I'm trapped into listening to you."

"That's not why. I was actually rather angry with Marcus for what he'd done. He had no—wait, how did you know? You were locked up in your room so I didn't get the chance to tell you yesterday."

She shook her head. "You didn't have to. I've known for years what he was doing. Marcus just thought he was being sneaky. He wasn't. I found out six months after he started. My uncle borrowed a copy of the circular from your father and brought it to Ridge Water to let me read it. I recognized the article as mine right away. When I checked the box I stored my work in, I discovered it was out of order a bit. After that, I paid Emma to subscribe so she could bring me the circular to read because I was afraid if it was delivered to Ridge Water, Marcus would stop sending in my work. I didn't realize until yesterday what he'd been doing with the money though. I'm assuming that was what comprised my dowry that neither of us knew I had?"

"You're very smart," Alex mused, applying slight pressure to her midsection with his fingers. "You have excellent deductive reasoning skills."

Caroline cracked a slight smile. "I'd thank you for the compliment, but there were enough clues present even Olivia could have solved that mystery."

He chuckled, his light breath hitting the bare skin exposed at the top of her back, sending a shiver skidding down her spine. "Why didn't you say something to him?"

"I knew it was the only way to ever get my work read. I don't care that it was under another name. But that's not up for discussion. Your rotten behavior is."

"Do you want it under your name? I'm sure I can get something worked out for it to be under Caroline Banks, Lady Watson, in the future."

"I don't really care," she said offhandedly. If they'd have been having this conversation earlier this week she would have jumped at the chance of having her articles styled that way, or even Mrs. Alexander Banks, Lady Watson, or Alexander and Caroline Banks, Lord and Lady Watson. But not now. E. S. Wilson would suffice.

He sighed. "Yes, you do. Every scientist does. That's why I wasn't overjoyed about the news like Marcus thought I'd be. You're smart enough to have your work published. You should get credit for it under your name."

She shrugged again. "Moot point, Lord Watson. By now nobody will care. They're all used to E. S. Wilson." She shook her head. This was of no account. There was no reason to even discuss it. "I'd like to go to bed. Please let go of me so I can leave."

"No," he said, tightening his grip on her. "We still have things to discuss."

"You don't seem interested in discussing them. As usual, you want to discuss science."

"Can you blame me? Discussing science is enjoyable, whereas discussing what an ass I've been isn't."

"Then you shouldn't have behaved as one," she responded tartly. "You should have treated me better. All my life I've—Never mind," she finished dully, pushing away the hurt.

"No, it's not never mind. You've been treated poorly before, and you've learned to accept it. You shouldn't have to. The day I became your husband, I vowed to treat you well and I haven't done so. I'm sorry for that. I'm sorry I treated our courtship as an experiment. I'm sorry I treated you poorly yesterday. But most of all, I'm sorry for not listening to you when you were trying to tell me the truth. I should have listened. And not just about the misunderstanding regarding the letter you'd received, but about your other news, too." He moved his hands around to rest on her abdomen and the life that was inside. "I should never have been so heartless as to point out what did or didn't happen on our wedding night and the weeks that followed. I got pleasure all of those times, too, Caro. My pleasure came from yours. Every time you found fulfillment, so did I."

"Then why did you say those things?" She choked back a sob.

"Caro, you must realize you drive me to distraction, and all logic that has been engrained in my brain leaps out the nearest window when you're around and emotion comes in to take its place. When I said those vile things to you, I was hurting from what I thought you were trying to do and I wanted to hurt you back," he admitted, his voice terribly uneven. "I know that's not a good reason. There isn't a reason good enough for what I said. But it's the truth. You know I'm not good with words and flattery, so the truth is all I have to offer you."

"Then can I ask you something, and you'll only give me the truth?"

"Anything."

Steeling herself for an answer she may not like, she swallowed her unease. "Was anything you did during our courtship not planned?"

"Nearly all of it."

She smiled. She'd never admit it to him or anyone, but more than the humiliation she'd faced having everything displayed for the family and being compared to a soiled dove, she'd been slightly hurt thinking everything had been staged.

"Turn around, Caro," he said softly.

"I can't. There isn't enough room on the step."

His hands went to her waist. "Yes, there is. Just lift one foot up, and I'll spin you around. Trust me, Caro. I'll not drop you."

Nervously, she let go of the telescope and took one foot off the rung. Then, just like he'd said, he spun her on the one foot that was still on the step until she was facing him and put her other foot down. "What are you wearing?" Her eyes narrowed on the sight of his bare shoulders bathed in the moonlight that was streaming in from the little window at the top of the gazebo where Alex's telescope was attached.

"Nothing. I humiliated you. It's only right to allow you the same opportunity."

She blinked at him. "How is you standing naked in the stargazing gazebo a way for me to humiliate you?"

"You could refuse my apology," he said earnestly. "Then I'd have to walk all the way back and through the house wearing absolutely nothing. And while I suffer no insecurity about being undressed, it would still be extremely humiliating for my whole household to see me thus."

"And you think I should force you to do that?"

He shrugged. "I hope you don't. But it's nothing less than I deserve."

She couldn't keep from laughing at him and the workings of his curious mind. "I admit I was humiliated at first, but I never intended to humiliate you back."

"Were you planning to do anything in retaliation?"

"Yes," she admitted weakly. "And, as usual, it didn't work the way I'd intended."

"And what had you intended to do?"

She bit her lip. "It's not so important."

"Yes, it is," he said vehemently. "Tell me how you'd planned to seek your revenge and I'll do it. I'll do whatever you think I ought to do to make this right. Just tell me what it is."

"It doesn't work that way. What I wanted...well, it's not something that can be given easily or done without thought. Because if it is, then it's not real."

"Then how were you planning to get it?"

"An experiment."

He shook his head ruefully. "I hope you foolishly wrote it down like I did so I can go search for it."

"I didn't."

He leaned forward and pressed his lips against hers. "Then I'll just have to kiss you until you tell me." His lips moved against hers, first sweet and gentle, then turning passionate and intense. "Will you tell me now?"

"Your love, Alex," she whispered softly, turning her cheek to him. "That's all I ever wanted."

"Oh, Caro my love, you've had that all along." He cupped her face and turned it toward him. "I fell in love with you the moment you almost dumped all those heavy biology tomes on my feet and called me president-extraordinaire. You may not see this, but you've never had a problem standing up to me. Never. And I love that about you. You've never been afraid to fling in my face that I had you thrown out of the *Society*." He snorted. "You even had enough gumption to tell my father what I'd done. You may have trouble standing up to others, mainly that wretched cousin of yours, but not with me. When you nearly flattened my toes with those books, you instantly captured my attention, it wasn't until later that I realized that in that very same minute you'd captured my heart as well."

"Truly?"

"Truly."

"I love you, too, Alex," she cried, wrapping her arms around his neck and letting him lift her from the ladder.

He set her on the ground and tilted her face up to look at him. "Caro, I want you to know something. No matter what, I'll always love you. You may have had a shortage of people who loved you in the past, but not anymore." He swallowed. "I understand why you were afraid to tell me your sordid past. But you have nothing to be ashamed of. Nothing. Those were his choices, not yours. I don't want you to be afraid to tell me anything. Ever."

"I'm sorry, Alex, I—"

He cut her off with a soft kiss on her lips. "Don't, Caro. This isn't your apology to make. It's mine. Let me make it, please. Nothing about your past matters to me. All that matters to me is you, and I love you more than I can possibly express."

"I love you, too," she repeated. "I promise I'll never keep anything from you again."

"I know you won't." He pulled her closer to him. "Am I forgiven?" he whispered hoarsely, his dark eyes unblinking and a solemn expression covering his face.

She tapped her index finger against her cheek. "That depends."

"On?"

"If you're planning to put your clothes back on or not."

A slow smile spread across his lips. "And if I'm not?"

Her eyes went wide. She'd not been seriously considering

making him walk back to the house naked. "I was teasing."

"I'm not." He dropped a line of kisses from her forehead down her nose and to her mouth. "We've those blankets, remember?"

"You cannot be serious," she squeaked.

He nodded. "I am. They're already spread out behind the gazebo."

"What if someone sees?"

"They're not going to. I told Edwina as soon as she got you in the gazebo she'd better run back to the house as fast as her legs could carry her and stay there or she wasn't getting those gowns. As for the servants—" he shrugged— "I gave them each a coin, told them they could have tomorrow morning off and unless there was a death or a fire, if any of them ventured out here, they'd be sacked."

She laughed. "Always the cautious one," she mused.

"They don't call me Arid Alex for nothing."

"I don't think you're arid in the least." Caroline pressed her breasts up against him. "I actually find this rather adventurous of you. In fact, they should change your name to Adventurous Alex."

He grinned at her. "I wouldn't suggest that to anyone unless you want to explain why you think they ought to change the name."

"Just so. Now, take me on an adventure."

"My pleasure." Alex picked her up and took her from the gazebo to make unabashed and tender love to her on a blanket under the moon and stars.

(And Uranus.)

Epilogue

The Next Morning

"Good morning, love," Alex said as Caroline raised her sleepy head from his chest.

Caroline looked down at the face of her loving husband. How had she not taken notice before of just how much he loved her? She knew his family loved and accepted her long ago, but why had it taken her so long to realize he did, too? She shook her head. It didn't matter. She knew now just how much he loved her and would never doubt it.

"We should probably go back in before the sun rises too high and you get burned," she teased, letting her eyes do a thorough sweep of her husband's naked body.

"We will. But first, I believe we should make good use of my current state." He bucked his hips, drawing Caroline's attention exactly where he—and she—wanted it.

And they did—first, they made good use of his state, then, after helping her dress, they went back inside where Alex had to make his grand (naked) entrance.

Luckily for Alex, his previous precautions worked to his favor and not a servant was in sight to sneak a peek. Even better for Alex, they were able to take a route that allowed them to bypass his mother and sister, who were already racking up his bill with the modiste. His brothers, however...

Though they were polite enough not to say anything in front of Caroline to cause her any embarrassment, Alex later informed her they had come up with an entire list of new nicknames for him.

Caroline's personal favorite was Amorous Alex.

***

Nearly Eight Months Later

"Caro, you're doing brilliantly. Just a little longer and you'll be a mother," Alex whispered in her ear while he crouched down by the head of her bed.

Caroline glanced at her loving husband and a bit of sadness touched her heart. "What if—" she broke off, unable to finish.

He kissed her cheek. "It's not going to happen," he said firmly.

She looked at him and an unspoken message passed between husband and wife. "Are you sure?"

He nodded. "I believe your mother's difficulties with delivering babies was due to her environment, not her inability."

She closed her eyes. She'd been the only one who wasn't either miscarried or stillborn. "Really?"

Alex sat on her bed and put his arm around her. "I honestly believe what I said. But, if I'm wrong and this baby is stillborn, I'll still love you. And when you're ready to try again, we will. And if you don't wish to, we won't." He pressed a kiss to the top of her head.

Caroline's heart swelled once again. She wiggled closer to him, content to rest in Alex's embrace until the doctor came back in.

"I think it's time," the doctor announced after putting the sheet back down.

"Time to go, Alex." Caroline readjusted herself on the bed.

He snorted. "I'm not leaving, and there isn't a thing you or old sawbones down there can do about it."

Caroline glanced at him uncertainly then sighed. "Just as long as you don't make an experiment out of this, you may stay."

"And how would I do that?" he retorted, rubbing the part of her back that hurt the worst during her contractions.

"I honestly have no idea, but I wouldn't put it past you to find a way," she returned.

An hour later a healthy little boy entered the world screaming loud enough to alert all the family waiting in the hall of his presence.

Alex beamed as his mother cleaned the baby and handed him to Caroline.

"What shall we name him?" Alex ran his finger along his son's cheek.

"Were you set on having a namesake?" Caroline asked, smiling down at the beautiful baby in her arms.

"No. Did you have something in mind?"

"Remember our wedding?"

He nodded. "How could I forget?"

She shook her head. "Do you remember the conversation you overheard? The one where Andrew and Benjamin were acting childish," she clarified.

"Yes. I told them if I were to follow their suggestions, I'd be using the name Marcus. Do you like the name Marcus?"

She nodded. "Marcus is good. My cousin did play a large role in bringing us together. But I was thinking of someone else."

His eyes left the little boy in Caroline's arms and landed on Caroline's face. "Who else could there be?"

She lifted her face and smiled at him. "Edward."

"My father?"

She nodded again. "He played an even larger role."

"I suppose," Alex allowed, looking somewhat dismayed. "Without his private conversation with you, you might never have forgiven me for being such an ass."

She smiled and shook her head. "There's that. But that's not what I was thinking."

"Is it because he's the one who told me to do more thinking with the organ responsible for bringing us this miracle?" The earlier shadow on his face gone, replaced by a wide grin.

"There's that, too," she said thoughtfully. "But there's something else."

He rolled his eyes. "Please do not tell me you're thankful to him for making that blasted betrothal agreement with your uncle."

She grinned and nodded. "Particularly the amendment."

He returned her grin. "Edward Marcus Banks it is."

After the doctor and Regina got Caroline and the room cleaned up enough, a long parade of family bearing gifts that ranged from a magnifying glass, to a barometer, to a rattle shaped like a king from a chess set, came into the room to argue with Caroline and Alex for the privilege of holding their son.

***

Later That Week

"Are you sure?"

"I'm sure," Caroline told her husband, putting down the latest edition of *Popular Plants* which was opened to the showcase piece written by Lord and Lady Watson about the habits of harvester ants.

"You don't have to do this," Alex protested, watching his wife blow out the candle next to her side of the bed. "I've become conditioned to sleeping with the lanterns lit."

"Now who's scared of the dark," Caroline teased, leaning her tired head on her husband's chest.

Alex ran his hand through his wife's silky hair. "Does this new development have anything to do with that article you read earlier this evening?"

"You mean the one where my father learned the hard way—quite literally—that just because he was intoxicated to the point where he felt like he was flying did not mean he actually could and fell with amazing speed from the top of the Tower of London?"

He nodded. "That's the one. Do you feel safer now that he's gone, Caro?"

Caroline grinned up at him and slowly shook her head. "No, it has nothing to do with his passing. It's because I know I'm safe when I'm with you."

If you enjoyed *Her Sudden Groom*, I would appreciate it if you would help others enjoy this book, too.

Lend it. This e-book is lending-enabled, so please, share it with a friend.

Recommend it. Please help other readers find this book by recommending it to friends, readers' groups and discussion boards.

Review it. Please tell other readers why you liked this book by reviewing it at one of the following websites: <u>Amazon</u> or <u>Goodreads</u>.

Other Books by Rose Gordon

BANKS BROTHERS' BRIDES

His Contract Bride—Lord Watson has always known that one day he'd marry Regina Harris. Unfortunately nobody thought to inform her of this; and when she finds that her "love match" was actually arranged by her father long ago in an effort to further his social standing, it falls to a science-loving, blunt-speaking baron to win her trust.

His Yankee Bride—John Banks has no idea what—or who—waits for him on the other side of the ocean... Carolina Ellis has longed to meet a man whom she can love, so when she glimpses such a man, she's determined to do whatever it takes to have him—Southern aristocracy be damned.

His Jilted Bride—Elijah Banks *cannot* sit still a moment longer as the gossip continues to fly about one of his childhood playmates, who just so happens to still be in her bridal chamber, waiting for her groom to arrive. Thinking to save her the public humiliation of being jilted at the altar, Elijah convinces her to run away with him, replacing one scandal with one far more forgiving. But when a secret she keeps is threatened to be exposed, it falls to Elijah to save her again by revealing a few of his own...

His Brother's Bride —Henry Banks had no idea his brother agreed to marry a fetching young lady until the day she shows up on his doorstep and presents the proof. To protect the Banks name and his new sister-in-law's feelings, Henry agrees to marry her only to discover this young lady's intentions were not so honorable and it wasn't really marriage she sought, but revenge on a member of the Banks family...

Coming July 2013
Celebrate America's independence with the:
OFFICER SERIES
(American Historicals based in Indian Territory mid-1800s)

The Officer and the Bostoner—A well-to-do lady traveling by stagecoach from her home in Boston to meet her fiance in Santa Fe finds herself stranded in a military fort when her stagecoach leaves without her. Given the choice to either temporarily marry an officer until her fiance can come rescue her or take her chances with the Indians, she marries the glib Captain Wes Tucker, who, unbeknownst to her, grew up in a wealthy Charleston family and despises everything she represents. But when it's time for her fiance to reclaim her and annul their marriage, will she still want to go with him, and more importantly, will Wes let her?

The Officer and the Southerner—Second Lt. Jack Walker doesn't always think ahead and when he decides to defy logic and send off for a mail-order bride, he might have left out only a few details about his life. When she arrives and realizes she's been fooled (again), this woman who's never really belonged, sees no other choice but to marry him anyway—however, she makes it perfectly clear: she'll be his lawfully wed, but she will *not* share his bed. Now Jack has to find a way to show his always skeptical bride that he is indeed trustworthy and that she does belong somewhere in the world: right here, with him.

The Officer and the Traveler—Captain Grayson Montgomery's mouth has landed him in trouble again! And this time it's not something a cleverly worded sentence and a handsome smile can fix. Having been informed he'll either have to marry or be demoted and sentenced to hard labor for the remainder of his tour, he proposes, only to discover those years of hard labor may have been the easier choice for his heart.

If you never want to miss a new release visit Rose's website at www.rosegordon.net to subscribe to her mailing list and you'll be notified each time a new book becomes available.

plaguing him at every chance possible, he must find clever ways to avoid them and simultaneously steal the attention—and affections—of the the one lady he's sure is a perfect match for him and his imperfections.

Already Available--SCANDALOUS SISTERS SERIES

Intentions of the Earl—A penniless earl makes a pact to ruin an American hoyden, never suspecting for a moment he'll lose his heart along the way.

Liberty for Paul—A vicar's daughter who loves propriety almost as much as she hates the man her father is mentoring will go to any length she sees fit to see that improper man out the door and out of her life. But when she's forced to marry him, she'll learn there's a lot more to life, love and this man than she originally thought.

To Win His Wayward Wife —A gentleman who's spent the last five years pining for the love of his life will get his second chance. The only problem? She has no interest in him.

About the Author

USA Today Bestselling and Award Winning Author Rose Gordon writes unusually unusual historical romances that have been known to include scarred heroes, feisty heroines, marriage-producing scandals, far too much scheming, naughty literature and always a sweet happily-ever-after. When not escaping to another world via reading or writing a book, she spends her time chasing two young boys around the house, being hunted by wild animals, or sitting on the swing in the backyard where she has to use her arms as shields to deflect projectiles AKA: balls, water balloons, sticks, pinecones, and anything else one of her boys picks up to hurl at his brother who just happens to be hiding behind her.

She can be found on somewhere in cyberspace at:

http://www.rosegordon.net

or blogging about *something* inappropriate at:

http://rosesromanceramblings.wordpress.com

Rose would love to hear from her readers and you can e-mail her at rose.gordon@hotmail.com

You can also find her on Facebook, Goodreads, and Twitter.

If you never want to miss a new release please visit her website to subscribe to her mailing list and you'll be notified each time a new book becomes available.

TELL THE WORLD
THIS BOOK WAS

| Good | Bad | So-so |

Made in the USA
Middletown, DE
27 February 2016